Chanakya's Chant

By Ashwin Sanghi

Westland Ltd

westland ltd

61, Silverline Building, Alapakkam Main Road, Maduravoyal, Chennai 600 095
No.38/10 (New No.5), Raghava Nagar, New Timber Yard Layout, Bangalore 560 026
23/181, Anand Nagar, Nehru Road, Santacruz East, Mumbai 400 055
93, 1st Floor, Sham Lal Road, Daryaganj, New Delhi 110 002

First published by westland ltd 2010

This is a work of fiction. Names, characters, places and incidents either are the product of the author's imagination or are used fictitiously, and any resemblance to any actual persons, living or dead, events or locales, is entirely coincidental.

16 15 14 13 12

ISBN: 978-93-81626-81-8

Typeset by Art Works, Chennai

Printed at Thomson Press (I) Ltd.

Chanakya's Chant
The Shakti chant from Ashwin Sanghi's novel

At the heart of this novel lies a chant—a Shakti mantra that appears several times within this story. The young and incredibly talented music composer Ameya Naik has set this chant to hypnotic and reverberating music reminiscent of ancient times. Surprisingly, it dramatically transitions into rock fusion towards the end.

The chant has been recited in Vedic tradition by the enthusiastic Kushal Gopalka and choir. The four-minute track is divided into two segments, ancient and modern, in keeping with the theme of this novel, which also alternates between the past and the present.

The track is available as a free mp3 download for everyone to hear. You may download it at:

www.chanakyaschant.com

The YouTube video trailer of this novel is also available for viewing at the above web link.

We hope that you enjoy listening to this mantra as much as all of us enjoyed composing and performing it. It brought to mind the truth in the view that the journey *is* the destination.

westland ltd

Chanakya's Chant

Ashwin Sanghi's first novel, *The Rozabal Line*, was self-published in 2007 under his pseudonym, Shawn Haigins. The theological thriller based upon the theory that Jesus died in Kashmir was subsequently published by Westland in 2008 in India under his own name and went on to become a bestseller, remaining on national bestseller lists for several months.

Ashwin Sanghi's second novel, *Chanakya's Chant*, a political thriller with roots in ancient Mauryan history, shot to the top of almost every bestseller list in India within a few weeks of its launch. The novel went on to win the Crossword-Vodafone Popular Choice Award 2010, and film producer UTV acquired the movie rights to the book. The novel continues to dominate the fiction charts.

The Krishna Key, Ashwin's third novel, is a furiously paced and riveting thriller that explores the ancient secrets of the Vedic age and the *Mahabharata*.

Ashwin is an entrepreneur by profession but writing historical fiction in the thriller genre is his passion and hobby. Ashwin was educated at the Cathedral & John Connon School, Mumbai, and St Xavier's College, Mumbai. He holds a masters degree from Yale and is working towards a Ph.D. in Creative Writing. Ashwin lives in Mumbai with his wife, Anushika, and his son, Raghuvir.

To connect with Ashwin on email or social media please visit his website at www.sanghi.in.

AUTHOR'S NOTE

I am indebted to Aparna Gupta who first suggested a novel on Chanakya to me. The embryo of the idea planted by her eventually evolved into this novel.

I am obliged to my wife and son who ungrudgingly tolerated my persistent absence from their lives while I was writing this book and juggling the rest of my life.

I am beholden to my family, which supported me in my endeavours—including my writing.

I am thankful to various authors and producers of original or derived works. A separate acknowledgements section at the end of the narrative lists these in detail.

I am grateful to my editor, Prita Maitra, and my publisher, Gautam Padmanabhan, without whom none of my novels—including this one—would have seen the light of day.

I am delighted to have worked along with two very talented individuals, Kushal Gopalka and Ameya Naik. We could not have created the incredibly haunting audio track of *Chanakya's Chant* without their labour and inspiration.

Finally, I am fortunate to be the grandson of the late Shri Ram Prasad Gupta and grandnephew of his brother, the late Shri Ram Gopal Gupta. Their blessings move the fingers that hold my pen.

Prologue

The old man sat propped up in his hospital bed. Monitors beeped numbers and flashed graphs, measuring his vital signs. His frail arms had been punctured with an endless number of needles and a tube ran through his mouth into his lungs. He knew that life was ebbing from his body but had prayed to Shakti to allow him to live long enough to savour the moment he had been waiting for.

The room was dark, blackout curtains having been drawn to block out the sunlight, except for the psychedelic illumination produced by the moving images on television. The duty nurse sat on a chair beside his steel bed, dozing off intermittently. Light from the television sparkled in the octogenarian's eyes as he watched the eighteenth prime minister of India take the oath of office.

The incessant buzzing of his three mobile phones brought his personal assistant, Menon, scurrying in. The patient in the adjoining room was complaining that the relentless ringing was disturbing him. The fifty-something secretary peeped into the room to see his employer lying on the utilitarian bed, his gaze transfixed on the images flashed from New Delhi. He was oblivious to the cacophony of phones. He had waited thirty long years for this moment and was not about to let it be obstructed by phone calls. In any case, he couldn't talk with the damn tube in his mouth. Menon had suggested that the phones be turned off but he had refused. I'm not ready to allow anything—including my own life—to be switched off before I've relished this moment, he thought to himself.

The hospital in Kanpur was not equipped to deal with his condition. Pandit Gangasagar Mishra couldn't care less. He refused to bloody die in a hospital bed in New Delhi or Mumbai. Kanpur was home and he would go meet his maker from his own abode and on his own terms.

He watched the scene unfolding at Rashtrapati Bhavan. The President was administering the oath of office to the charismatic woman. She was dressed in her usual off-white cotton saree, trimmed with a pale gold border, and wore no jewellery except for a pair of simple solitaire diamond earrings. She quite obviously had the text of the oath before her on a single sheet of paper but did not seem to need it. It was almost as if she had spent her entire life preparing for the occasion. With a crisp Oxonian accent she was saying, 'I, Chandini Gupta, do swear in the name of God that I will bear true faith and allegiance to the Constitution of India as by law established, that I will uphold the sovereignty and integrity of India, that I will faithfully and conscientiously discharge my duties as prime minister and that I will do right to all manner of people in accordance with the Constitution and the law without fear or favour, affection or ill will.' The doyen smiled. Without fear, favour, affection or ill will! Bollocks! It was not possible to be prime minister without any of these, and she bloody knew it. It was only his opinion, though. But then, the wily Machiavelli had always believed that any clod could have the facts—having an opinion was an art.

He chuckled and the result was a rasping cough, a reminder of his mortality, and the cancer that plagued his lungs. The secret service detail standing outside his room heard him cough. They wondered whom they were protecting him from. Indeed there were many who wanted the bastard dead but it seemed that God had other plans. It was almost like Gangasagar was cocking a snook at his enemies and telling them 'Come and fucking get me, but I won't be around!'

A thin film of perspiration coated his head, the baldness of which was accentuated by two tufts of shocking white hair on either side. The nurse dabbed at it with a towel. He followed her movements with his deep, penetrating, all-seeing eyes—little video cameras that had seen and stored away the very worst of human behaviour in the gigabytes of his brain's hard disk. His thin lips quivered as he gasped for breath, his hooked nose struggling to suck in life-giving oxygen in spite of the tube. His skin had a pale translucent hue, like a rare parchment in a museum, and his thin frame occupied very little of the bed. How could this diminutive little man be so powerful?

In the lobby outside his room stood a posse of political associates. Pandit Gangasagar Mishra had no friends. In his world of politics there were only enemies. A clutch of newspaper hounds hobnobbed with the politicians outside hoping to get the inside scoop on Mishra's death before his death.

The old man seemed to be mumbling something, a laboured effort to get the words out. It was his daily prayer in Sanskrit. It said, '*Primal Shakti, I bow to thee; all-encompassing Shakti, I bow to thee; that through which God creates, I bow to thee; creative power of the Kundalini; mother of all, to thee I bow.*' He looked at his protégé— now sworn in as PM—fold her hands together in a humble gesture of acknowledgement to the television cameras... and then stumble backwards. The red stain that spread on her left shoulder—almost in slow motion —had been fired from a Stinger .22 Magnum.

The august Ashoka Hall of Rashtrapati Bhavan descended into pandemonium. Mishra, watching the scene unfold on television, continued chanting in Sanskrit, '*Adi Shakti, Namo Namah; Sarab Shakti, Namo Namah; Prithum Bhagvati, Namo Namah; Kundalini Mata Shakti; Mata Shakti, Namo Namah.*'

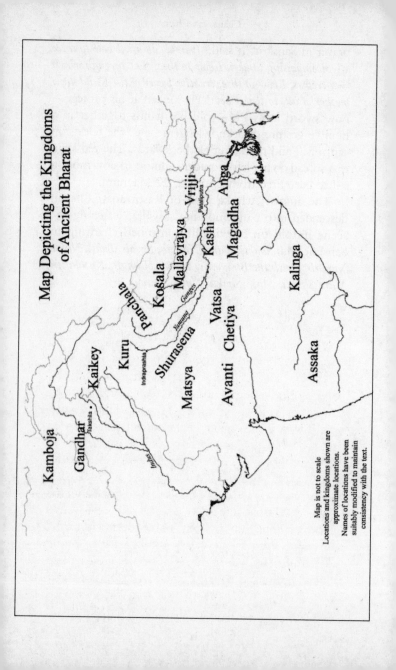

Map Depicting the Kingdoms of Ancient Bharat

Map is not to scale
Locations and kingdoms shown are
approximate locations.
Names of locations have been
suitably modified to maintain
consistency with the text.

CHAPTER ONE

About 2300 years ago

The kiss was a lingering one. She seemed to lightly graze her lips over his, causing little sparks of static that travelled down his spine as he craved for the impassioned ritual to move towards its gratifying conclusion. Her name was Vishaka—it meant *heavenly star*—and she was undoubtedly a celestial creature. Her translucent ivory complexion with just a hint of aqua, her sensuous mouth, and mischievous emerald eyes were partially covered by her cascading, silken, auburn hair as she bent over his face, planting little pecks of exquisite joy upon his eyes, nose and lips.

Paurus lay back on the silken bedspread in the chamber of the pleasure palace. Sounds of a veena wafted in from the antechamber as one of the courtesans played with chords from Raga Hindol—the raga of love. Along the north-eastern wall of the room stood a golden basin that had been filled with pure rose water, and opposite stood a large golden lamp that had been lit with sandalwood oil. Paurus was in a state of tender bliss.

Allowing himself to submit to Vishaka's ministrations, he sighed contentedly. He tried to recall which great guru had suggested that the path to nirvana was complete and utter submission to the divine. Was this delectable creature anything less? He reached out his arms to pull her face downwards towards his own while his lips sought to quench their thirst from her moist clove-and-cardamom scented breath. He was on fire.

His throat was on fire! Paurus let go of her hair in panic while clutching at his own throat as he felt the compound of arsenic and mercury scald his lips, tongue and throat. He tried to scream but no sound emerged from his larynx—it had already been destroyed by the Sankhiya poison on her lips. The ambrosial Vishaka continued to cradle his head in the warmth of her shapely bosom as she felt the living breath silently escape from him. The peacocks in the royal garden outside continued to dance, quite oblivious to the agony of the king inside. Paurus, mighty emperor of Kaikey and Magadha was dead. Long live the king!

Pataliputra, the capital of Magadha, the great Brahmanic empire in the cradle of the beautiful Ganges valley in eastern *Bharat* lay quiet at this hour. The crocodiles in the moat surrounding the city fort were in deep slumber and the guards had shut the city gates for the night. Within the town, the only activity was towards Yama Gate, the southern quarter that housed the *madiralays*—the drinking taverns—and the houses of the *ganikas*—the prostitutes. At the northern end of the capital, towards the Brahma Gate, which housed the palace and the Brahmin community, the streets were deathly quiet.

Inside a nondescript home, Chanakya listened to Vishaka intently as the glow of the two oil lamps on either side of his study desk threw ominous streaks of alternating shadow and light on his grimy complexion. He was a hideous-looking man. His skin was pockmarked and his features were slightly crooked. His clean-shaven head was tough, black and leathery and he boasted a sandalwood-paste trident on his forehead. Towards the back of his head started a long *shikha*—a lock of hair maintained by most Brahmins in the kingdom. The only garment on his body was a coarse cotton sheet and his only accessory a *yagyopavita*—the sacred Vedic thread. He rarely smiled because smiling exposed his crooked teeth. He had been born with a full set of teeth—the mark of a ruler, but a clairvoyant yogi had predicted that the boy would be even more powerful than a mere king— he would be the most powerful kingmaker of his time. To many he was known as Kautilya—the crooked one; to his childhood acquaintances he was Vishnugupta; but to most he was Chanakya—illustrious son of the great and learned Chanak, the most renowned teacher in all of Magadha.

He did not show the slightest emotion or exuberance as he received her detailed report of the assassination. The wily old Brahmin knew that it never paid to let others perceive what one's true feelings were. 'Three may keep a secret if two of them are dead,' he would often say.

But he couldn't help laughing inwardly. The fool Paurus had allowed himself to believe that the celestial creature in his bed was Vishaka—twinkle, twinkle, little star, indeed. Hah! Little had the imbecile realised that Vishaka was his trained *vishakanya*—a poison maiden. In fact, Chanakya had personally supervised the creation of an entire army of such maidens. His secret service would identify young and nubile girls whose horoscopes foretold of widowhood. These beautiful damsels would be sequestered at an early age and fed a variety of poisons in graduated doses, making them immune to their ruinous effects. By the time each of Chanakya's vishakanyas reached puberty, they were utterly toxic. A simple kiss with an infinitesimal exchange of saliva was lethal enough to kill the strongest bull of a man.

'Go tell Chandragupta that he's now emperor of Magadha,' the cunning Brahmin matter-of-factly instructed his venomous pupil as his mind wandered back to how and when the saga had started.

King Dhanananda of Magadha was in a foul mood. His Brahmin prime minister, the wise Shaktar, appeared to be lecturing him—God's representative on earth! Shaktar wanted the king to spend less time absorbed in wine-drenched carnal pursuits, and more time improving the lives of Magadha's citizens. Dhanananda found scholars such as Shaktar boring and insufferable. He tolerated them nonetheless. Patronage of Brahmins in his council made him appear wise.

The roof of Magadha's great audience hall was supported by eighty massive pillars. Rich furnishings and tapestries embellished the court of the world's richest king. Some distance away from the palace stood a gilded Durakhi Devi temple, a Buddhist monastery as well as an ayurvedic hospital—signs of Magadha's religious, material and spiritual progress.

Dhanananda looked to his right and observed the first chair. It was reserved for the most important Brahmin in the land—the prime minister, Shaktar. The chair was empty because Shaktar had stood up to deliver his sermon to the king. *The pompous bastard*, thought Dhanananda. They were all a bunch of self-serving rascals, recommending the most arrogant amongst themselves as ministers, and then using Dhanananda's money to award themselves honours, grants and titles, while attempting to tutor him—the mighty Dhanananda—on the duties of kingship! Their hypocrisy revolted him.

Dhanananda's eyes wandered towards his female attendants. Women always surrounded Magadha's monarchs. They performed various functions including guarding the king's person, controlling access to his chambers, tasting his food to ensure that it was not poisoned, delivering messages, polishing his armour, entertaining him with music, bathing and dressing him, gratifying his sexual needs, and tucking him into bed at night.

Dhanananda had over a thousand female attendants and courtesans serving him. Catlike, they were vicious and protective of their master. Dhanananda slyly winked at a delicious feline whose curvaceous figure belied her strength and capacity to kill and she returned the favour, smiling coyly at him.

The wink was the final straw. The usually coolheaded Shaktar lost his temper, allowing many years of pent-up anger to burst open like stinking pus from a festering wound. 'O King! No woman in your kingdom is safe anymore due to the lecherous ways of the court. Girls are routinely found on the banks of the Ganges—raped, murdered, or both. Usually their trail leads back to the royal palace!' he thundered.

Dhanananda, master of the largest standing army in the world, was furious. 'Hold your tongue, Shaktar, or I shall have it removed for you! You live off my grants and think that you have the right to come here and tell me—the most powerful emperor of the known world—how to do my job?' he shouted, white spittle bursting forth from his lips along with each word. 'Rakshas! Have this rascal thrown into Nanda's Hell. Let him experience first-hand what a pain in the ass feels like,' he ordered Rakshas, his minister for internal security.

Nanda's Hell was the infamous torture chamber in Dhanananda's prison complex. The overseer, Girika, was a monster. Even as a child Girika had enjoyed catching and torturing ants, flies, mice and fish. He had later graduated to torturing cats and dogs, using hooks, nets, hot wax, boiling water and copper rods. Bloodcurdling screams could be heard at all hours from the dungeons in which Girika worked, wrenching out helpless prisoners' teeth with metal pliers, pouring molten copper on their genitalia and thrusting red-hot embers into their rectums.

Rakshas shifted uncomfortably in his chair. It was his haemorrhoids acting up at the thought of the red-hot embers. He knew that he was wedged between a rock and hard place. Obey the monarch's orders and have the entire population brand him as the king's pimp—which he was—or disobey the diktat and be sent to the dungeon himself.

Fond of dance, drama, music, literature and painting, Rakshas was a cultured and refined artiste. Being surrounded by resplendent feminine beauty in his artistic world offered him the ability to supply Dhanananda with the most ravishing women of the kingdom. This was the key to his success with the king. The master politician in Rakshas hated open confrontation. Why did Shaktar, the foolish tightass, have to go around stirring things up? Rakshas rose from his chair and reluctantly commanded his guards to arrest the prime minister.

Outside the gates of the royal palace, a solitary figure was standing on a stone ledge spewing venom at Dhanananda. 'Citizens of Magadha, this tyranny has continued far too long. The imperial thug, Dhanananda, has imprisoned the only minister capable of standing up to him. Are we going to stand here helplessly while we see a guardian of the kingdom—the wise and illustrious prime minister Shaktar—be treated in this shameful manner? How many more farmers have to commit suicide because the tax inspectors of Dhanananda loot their grain? How many more soldiers must die in battle because their armour has been compromised to make wine goblets for the king's pleasure? How many more mothers must cry over the corpses of their violated young daughters? How much longer are we going to tolerate this evil sovereign?' he cried.

A crowd had gathered. After all, the orator was no ordinary individual. He was Chanak—the most respected teacher in the kingdom—father of the wise Chanakya and a close friend and confidant of prime minister Shaktar. Kings vied with one another to send their sons and future princes to be trained in and educated for princely duties by Chanak.

Inside the palace, guards had seized Prime Minister Shaktar and had whisked him off through a series of secret passages to the dungeons. Rakshas had quietly instructed the lieutenant that Shaktar was to be treated decently and that Girika was to keep his hands off. 'Tell Girika that I will personally rip off his balls, roast them like chestnuts, and make him eat them for breakfast if he so much as touches a hair of the prime minister!' he had hissed to the lieutenant.

Rakshas had been contemplating his next move when the commander of the royal guards rushed in and sought a word with the king. The visibly shaken commander nervously revealed the news that a large crowd was gathered outside the palace and was being incited to revolt by Chanak.

Dhanananda flew into a fit of rage. His face contorted and the veins in his neck throbbed to the drumbeat of the guards marching outside. 'Kill the son of a whore! I want Chanak's head chopped off and displayed along the banks of the Ganges. Now!' he shrieked. The hapless commander scurried off to obey his whimsical leader's royal edict for fear of his own head being served up on a plate at the dinner table and being sampled by one of Dhanananda's courtesan tasters.

❊

'He's dead, Vishnugupta. I am sorry for your loss, my son. The king's spies are everywhere. You must flee. They'll be looking for you,' explained Katyayan, a minister in Dhanananda's cabinet and a loyal friend of Chanak. While in court, he had heard the news of Chanak's slaying and had quickly hurried over to warn Chanak's son, Vishnugupta.

'But if I flee, who shall take care of my mother? She's too old to go anywhere,' began the boy.

'I shall look after her, don't worry,' said the gentle and assuring Katyayan.

'And Suvasini?' asked Vishnugupta. Suvasini was the daughter of the imprisoned prime minister Shaktar and had been Vishnugupta's childhood crush.

'I shall take care of everyone else if you will simply take care of yourself, Vishnugupta,' said Katyayan impatiently.

The blank expression on Vishnugupta's face startled Katyayan. There was no sign of either dejection or anguish. 'Do not call me Vishnugupta,' said the proud and angry boy to Katyayan. 'From today onwards the only identity I have is that of Chanakya—son of the noble Chanak!'

━━

It was *amavasya*—the darkest night of the fortnight—and Chanakya had waited patiently for two whole days to carry out the plan suggested by Katyayan. He had rubbed a mixture of charcoal and oil all over his body until he was jet black. The complete absence of moonlight and his shadowy appearance meant that he could move about stealthily along the unlit banks of the Ganges without being observed.

He followed Katyayan's precise instructions on how to locate the banyan tree along the riverbank. It was a sacred tree that would be worshipped on festivals and—aware of this—Dhanananda's guards had hung Chanak's head on the branches of this particular one, knowing that ordinary people would not touch it. Having reached the banyan, Chanakya ignored the oil lamp at its base and started climbing the massive trunk. A foul stench soon guided him to the point where he could see his beloved father's head hanging like a ghoul from a branch to which his single lock of hair had been tied.

Chanakya felt tears well up in his eyes as he saw his father's severed head swinging to the eerie whistling winds. His father's eyes were wide open and there were gaping holes in both cheeks where insects had already started feasting. His mouth was firmly clenched shut, a silent reminder of one of his favourite—and now unfortunately ironic—maxims: 'A man who opens his mouth too often may end up meeting a tragic end, either from indigestion or execution!'

Chanakya steadied himself, clambered up the branch and swiftly untied the shikha. As gently as possible, he lifted the head, cradled it in his arms and reverentially kissed the crown. His tears were in full flood and rained upon his father's skull. He had not wept until this moment but he silently promised himself that this would be the only occasion on which he would allow himself to cry; Chanakya would make others cry. They would pay for what they had done. His tears would be paid for in blood.

He quickly scampered down the tree and wrapped his father's head in fresh muslin that he had brought with him. He then tied the muslin to his upper torso and jumped into the dark and ominous river. The shock of the freezing cold water took a few minutes to subside and he was soon making his way with firm strokes across the Ganges to the little Durga temple that lay across on the opposite bank.

Katyayan had bribed the royal guards to part with Chanak's body and had secretly arranged for the remains to be transported to the temple grounds. According to Hindu custom, a corpse had to be cremated before sundown, but the circumstances of Chanak's death meant that tradition would have to be given the go-by. If Dhanananda ever caught a whiff of the fact that Chanakya was cremating Chanak, he would not hesitate to send his cronies after the boy.

Emerging drenched from the strong current, he found the priest, a fearsome hunchback clad in a blood-red sheet, waiting for him on the riverbank. He was holding a flaming torch and silently gestured to Chanakya to follow him to the funeral pyre that had been prepared. Wordlessly, he took the muslin containing Chanak's head and placed it along with the rest of the body enclosed in the pyre. He handed over a bundle of burning grass to Chanakya and asked him to circumambulate the body once and to light the pyre thereafter. As flames enveloped Chanak's body, the priest handed him a bamboo and asked him to smash the corpse's head—supposedly an act that would free Chanak's soul trapped inside.

As the flames ebbed, the priest instructed Chanakya to take another dip in the Ganges and gave him a dry set of ochre robes to wear. Bathed and dressed, Chanakya took the small bundle that the priest offered him. It was a parting gift left for him by Katyayan. It contained a small dagger for his protection, fifty gold *panas* for his sustenance, and a letter to the dean of Takshila University.

Located over nine hundred miles away in the distant northwest, Takshila was the world's first university. It had been established almost three hundred years previously and graduated over ten thousand students each year in more than sixty subjects.

Chanakya began the long and arduous trek that would take over a year.

CHAPTER TWO
Present Day

The dusty Birhana Road of Kanpur was a foodie's delight at most times of the day. Little roadside shops served mouth-watering snacks—golgappas, aloo tikki, dahi kachori—sweet-and-sour savouries made from the unhealthiest ingredients that one could imagine: deep-fried potatoes, refined flour, sugar, and salt. The full-frontal cholesterol attack did not usually deter gourmands from further exploring the sweet shops that sold laddoos, barfis, kulfi, jalebis, malai-makkhan, gulab jamuns and a hundred other syrupy, sticky and sinful desserts. Traffic clogged the street at all times of the day— autorickshaws spewing thick black fumes, cars, scooters, handcarts, buffaloes, cows, and humans. The air was dirty but exciting nonetheless. Smells of sweat and urine mingled with carbon monoxide, fried food, and incense from the temples that surrounded the area.

In one of the bylanes of Birhana Road was a building that had seen better days and was struggling to remain standing. Inside it, a rickety staircase led to a second-floor flat occupied by Pandit Gangasagar Mishra, Kanpur's foremost professor of history. Freshly bathed and dressed in a simple white cotton kurta-pyjama, Panditji was busy with his morning prayers. He sat on his prayer mat facing east—the direction of the rising sun—and offered flowers, incense and sandalwood paste to the little silver deities that stood inside his mini-temple. Having said good morning to his gods, he walked down the shaky staircase and out into the street.

It was obvious that Panditji had been a handsome man in his youth. He had aristocratic features, a broad forehead, and an aquiline nose. He was extremely fair-skinned but rather short. His short stature, however, was misleading—like Napoleon's. The hair on his head had fallen off almost entirely, and Panditji preserved the few remaining strands lovingly by combing them across his head from left to right.

The next thirty minutes would be occupied in a brisk walk down to Motijheel Chauraha, where a tea vendor with the rather unexciting name—Banarsi Tea House—would keep Panditji's tea ready and waiting. Panditji's manservant had often complained that he could make better tea at home but Panditji liked the morning walk as well as the bonhomie of the tea stall where he was part of the regular morning crowd. He would then stroll over to his newspaper vendor two shops away, and buy his day's information fix. Another thirty minutes later he would be back home, retiring to his living room where he would spend the next two hours poring over newspapers from all over the country. His newspaper vendor had developed a network through which newspapers from Mumbai, New Delhi, Kolkata and Chennai could be supplied to Panditji each morning, in addition to the local Kanpur and Lucknow ones.

'But Panditji, why do you read so many papers?' the lad had asked curiously one day. Panditji had answered, 'Because I need to know everything that happens in the country. How else can I rule it?' The boy had not replied, shaking his head in disbelief.

By ten in the morning, Panditji was ready to receive his first visitors of the day. His secretary, a sharp Keralite —Menon—had arrived and was sorting out Panditji's mail. The professor of history had another, even more important, facet to his life. He was the president of the Akhil Bharat Navnirman Samiti—abbreviated to ABNS by journos who could never quite remember the entire name. Panditji had launched the political outfit several years earlier and it had grown from a fledgling struggling non-entity into a mainstream political party that few could ignore.

'Good morning, sir,' said Menon, efficiently handing a one-inch-thick dossier containing the day's relevant papers to Pandit Gangasagar Mishra. 'Morning, Menon,' said Panditji, 'at what time have you asked Chandini to meet me?'

'She'll be here by eleven, sir. She's bringing the Opposition MLAs who wish to defect,' said Menon, smiling. He knew that the day was a momentous one. It was the day that the ABNS would topple the existing state government of Uttar Pradesh, India's most populous state—and the key to holding power in New Delhi—and instal its own chief minister. The man behind it all was an unassuming Pandit who drank tea at Banarsi Tea House every morning and liked to call himself a history teacher.

His close acquaintances knew that Pandit Gangasagar Mishra was not interested in teaching history. He was interested in creating it.

Gangasagar was born in 1929 in Cawnpore—the anglicised name for Kanpur—a sleepy town nestled on the banks of the river Ganges. Kanpur had originally been *Kanhapur*, named after *Kanhaiya*—another name for Krishna, the hero of the Hindu epic, the *Mahabharata*. The British came along and decided that Cawnpore sounded better after they turned the town into a garrison with barracks for seven thousand sepoys. The sepoys mutinied in 1857. Quite possibly they didn't like the new name.

Gangasagar's father—Mishraji—was a poor Brahmin who eked out a living from teaching at the local government-subsidised school on the banks of the river. When his son was born, his third child after two daughters, he decided to name him Gangasagar—*as vast as the Ganges*. Gangasagar's mother was a simple woman, perpetually struggling to meet the most basic daily needs of the family. Ganga, however, was her pet. In a society that treated sons as assets and daughters as liabilities, Ganga was the single item on her balance sheet that squared off the dowry that she would have to pay for her daughters' weddings. She would smilingly forego her own meals just to ensure that Gangasagar was well fed.

As per Hindu custom, Brahmins were usually in demand during the fortnight of *shraadh*, when wealthy families would feed them and clothe them in memory of their ancestors. One of Mishraji's wealthy patrons was a trader—Agrawalji. Little Ganga always looked forward to eating at his house during shraadh. There would always be unlimited quantities of sweet rice pudding along with the meal. One day, as they were eating at Agrawalji's house, Gangasagar asked his father, 'Father, shraadh is all about remembering one's ancestors, right?'

'Yes, son. By feeding Brahmins, one symbolically feeds the spirits of the departed.'

'So you too shall die one day?' asked Gangasagar sadly.

Mishraji smiled. All parents desperately wanted their children to love them and Mishraji was no exception. His heart swelled with pride to see his son's concern for him.

'Yes, Ganga. Everyone has to die someday, including me.'

Gangasagar looked crestfallen. Tears welled up in his eyes as he took another gulp of the wonderfully sweet rice pudding seasoned with almonds and raisins. Mishraji's heart melted. He tried to alleviate the obvious grief that he seemed to have caused his son. 'Why do you want to know about such things, Ganga?'

'I was just wondering, when you die, will we still be able to come over to Agrawalji's for rice pudding?'

Mishraji managed to scrape together enough money to send Gangasagar to a slightly better school than the government-funded one at which he taught. He asked Gangasagar to be always on his very best behaviour. He couldn't afford any other school in Kanpur.

On his very first day at the new school, Gangasagar's teacher asked him to stand up and answer some questions. The supremely confident Gangasagar was happy to oblige. The older students winked at each other, expecting a furious interrogation.

'Who was the first president of America?' asked the headmaster.

'George Washington,' replied Gangasagar.

'Very good. History tells us that he did something naughty in his childhood. What was it?'

'He chopped down his father's cherry tree.'

'Excellent, Gangasagar. History also tells us that his father did not punish him. Any idea why?'

'Because George Washington still had the axe in his hand?' asked Gangasagar as he sat down.

=■=

Within a few months he was grading papers for the headmaster and was his favourite pupil. School was about to break for Diwali vacations. Exams had just concluded and Gangasagar was helping his headmaster mark examination papers in history—his favourite subject. He laughed at the ridiculous answers proffered by some of his classmates.

'Ancient India was full of myths which have been handed down from son to father. A collection of myths is called mythology.'

'The greatest rulers were the Mowglis. The greatest Mowgli was Akbar.'

'Then came the British. They brought with them many inventions such as cricket, tram tarts and steamed railways.'

'Eventually, the British came to overrule India because there was too much diversity in our unity. They were great expotents and impotents. They started by expoting salt from India and then impoting cloth.'

One of the more difficult questions related to Chanakya, the wise guru of Chandragupta Maurya. The question was 'Explain whether Chanakya's treatise on political economy—the *Arthashastra*—was his own work or whether it was simply an aggregation of previously-held views.' One of the bright but lazy students had written, 'Only God could know the answer to this particular question given that Chanakya is dead. Happy Diwali.'

Gangasagar wrote in the margin, 'God gets an A-plus, you get an F. Happy Diwali to you too!'

It was to be Mishraji's last Diwali. Life had dealt him exceptionally harsh blows and the stress had eventually taken its toll. At the age of fifteen, Gangasagar was left fatherless with an ageing mother and two sisters, both of marriageable age. He knew that he would need to drop out of school, forget about college, and find work. His first port of call was Agrawalji, his father's patron who had always treated Gangasagar kindly.

The mansion of Agrawalji was located in a wooded and secluded corner of Kanpur, along the bank of the river Ganges. The ten-bedroom house stood on a ten-acre plot with a private riverbank where ten Brahmins performed sacred rituals each day to make sure that the Agrawal family remained constantly blessed with good fortune for the next ten generations.

Agrawalji's father had made the family fortune during the cotton boom of 1864 and had become one of the most famous figures in the Kanpur Cotton Exchange, the nerve centre of cotton trading. During the American Civil War, Britain had become disconnected from its usual cotton supplies and had turned to India to meet its cotton requirements. Cotton speculation became hectic and frenzied, and trading would continue till late hours of the night while merchants would await information on international cotton prices prior to closing their trading positions. Senior Agrawal loved the speculation. Unknown to most people of that time, however, he was no speculator. He owed his wealth to a simple technology known as the Morse Code. The wily market operator had employed two gentlemen, one in New York and the other in Tokyo. The employee in New York would relay cotton prices using Morse Code to the employee in Tokyo who, in turn, would relay the prices to senior Agrawal in Kanpur, also in code. The result was that the senior Agrawal knew the prices almost an hour before the others. Sixty minutes of pure arbitrage each day was the secret to the immense Agrawal fortune, not mindless speculation.

Senior Agrawal was succeeded by his son who inherited his father's cunning and raw intelligence. While the father had used the American Civil War to further his business interests, Junior used the Second World War to do precisely the same. The British colony of India would provide over two-and-a-half million men and spend an astounding eighty per cent of its national income on the British war effort, and the man who would provide most of these supplies at hefty margins would be Agrawal junior. But Agrawalji was by no means on the British side. He was a shrewd man who had foreseen the future. He knew that it was only a matter of time before the British would have to quit India, and in anticipation of that event he made sure he doled out large donations to the freedom struggle too.

When Gangasagar was a little boy, Mahatma Gandhi had visited Kanpur and stayed with Agrawalji. Gandhiji had come from Allahabad to attend the fortieth annual session of the Indian National Congress. A crowd of twenty-five thousand people had gathered at Kanpur Railway Station to receive him. Agrawalji had escorted Gandhiji home. Mishraji had volunteered that little Gangasagar remain by Gandhiji's side to take care of him during his visit. Agrawalji had readily agreed.

Gandhiji then delivered a speech at the famous Parade Ground of the city and appealed to the throngs of people gathered to support the non-cooperation movement and make it a huge success. During a private moment after the event, Agrawalji asked the great leader, 'Bapu, what gives you the conviction that you'll be able to fight the British?'

Mahatma Gandhi smiled. He said, 'We shall win because we're in the third stage of our four-stage struggle.'

'The four-stage struggle?' wondered aloud Agrawalji.

'First, they ignore you, second, they laugh at you, third, they fight you, and fourth—you win. That's the fourth stage, my friend, Agrawal,' said the Mahatma simply. The little boy pressing Gandhiji's feet listened to the wise leader very carefully. He hesitantly asked, 'Bapu, the British have guns and policemen. I'm but a little boy. How can I fight them? They are so much stronger!'

Mahatma Gandhi fondly placed his hand on little Ganga's head and said, 'Strength does not come from physical capacity. It comes from an indomitable will. I can see that you have it, son.'

From that day on, Gangasagar knew that one day he would also possess the power to make or break empires.

⊐⊏

Gangasagar sat before Agrawalji uneasily. He was dressed in Western clothes but they sat uncomfortably on him. His sideburns were long and wide at the bottom, Elvis-style. His prominent nose provided ample parking space for a pair of very thick-framed spectacles. His hair was oiled back with a very visible parting towards his left. He wore a dull full-sleeved shirt that hung out of bell-bottomed trousers that had seen better days. He was clean-shaven and had fair skin but was rather short, just a little over five feet in height and was wearing shoes that were at least two sizes too big for him. 'I didn't know who else to turn to,' said the young Gangasagar hesitantly. 'Sir, I was hoping that you could give me a job. I'll do whatever you ask of me, I promise I'll work hard. Please help me,' he pleaded.

Agrawalji took a puff of his saffron-and-cardamom-flavoured tobacco hookah and smiled at the youth. 'I don't have sons of my own, Gangasagar. I'll hire you but I'll drive you like a slave. Your salary shall be twenty-five rupees per month. Agreed?'

'You shall not regret this, sir. I am indeed blessed with good luck.'

'Yes, I do believe in good luck, son. And I find that the harder I work, the more I have of it,' Agrawalji joked.

━━

The very first lessons were in bookkeeping and accountancy. Agrawalji's books were maintained by his trusted Marwari *munim*—his treasurer—who was given the task of explaining the intricacies of double-entry bookkeeping to the young man.

'Gangasagar, what's two plus two?' asked the munim on the first day.

'Four,' answered Gangasagar.

'Wrong answer. I'll give you another try later.'

Several days later they had progressed to maintenance of primary books, ledger posting, and trial balance preparation. The munim once again asked him, 'Gangasagar, what's two plus two?'

'Four,' answered Gangasagar.

'Incorrect. You'll have another chance to answer it correctly.'

A few weeks later they had covered income recognition, expense estimation, and finalisation of the profit-and-loss statement.

'Your final chance. What's two plus two?' asked the munim.

The frustrated lad snapped, 'It's whatever you want it to be!'

'Correct answer,' laughed the munim. 'You've finally understood the beauty of accounting!'

Profit was in the Agrawal blood. Anything that could possibly be bought and sold for a profit was of interest to Agrawalji. Gangasagar soon realised that he was in the hands of a master teacher. One day, he sat in on a conference between Agrawalji and his munim.

'Munimji, why aren't we trading in jute?'

'The margins are terribly low, sir. Not worth the effort.'

'But why not export it?'

'Export prices are even lower than our domestic purchase prices. We'll end up buying the stuff and export-ing it at lower prices. It's a loss-making proposition, sir.'

'But what if we exported jute waste instead, and labelled it as jute? It *is* jute after all.'

'But sir, who'll buy rubbish from us?'

'I will.'

'What exactly do you suggest, sir?'

'What if we get Agrawal Hong Kong to buy your rubbish? You could buy jute waste here in India—which costs virtually nothing—and sell it to our own foreign subsidiary as jute.'

'But the profit will be fictitious. Our Indian arm would show a profit while the foreign arm would show a loss. It would still be a zero-sum game.'

'Not really, munimji. The government is offering import licences of equal value as incentives if we export the stuff. We may not necessarily make money on the transaction but we'll rake it in with the premium on the import licences!'

'You're wrong, it does affect us. The industry will go into a slump.'

'So?'

'The price of cotton will fall.'

'And how does this concern us?'

'Short-sell cotton.'

'Huh?'

'Sell cotton today and buy it later at a lower price.'

'But if nationalisation happens immediately, there won't be enough time to handle both sides of the transaction efficiently, sir.'

'We must make sure the minister enacts his drama of nationalisation a little later.'

'How?'

'We show him how he can partner us in this profitable scheme.'

Gangasagar began to understand the incestuous relationship between business and politics.

It was late in the evening. Gangasagar was on his way out of the office when Agrawalji called him in to his cabin. 'The planning commission has announced that over the next five years the country shall invest heavily in dams, roads and bridges,' he announced.

'But we're not in the construction business,' Gangasagar gently reminded his mentor.

'Then let's get in.'

'But it's a very specialised industry. We're traders, sir. We don't know the first thing about construction.'

'Just incorporate the company. Allot ten per cent of the shares to Lakshmi & Co. Register the company's name with suppliers of steel and cement.'

'Why?'

'You can start placing orders for construction materials.'

'But we do not have any projects! Why would we buy materials without projects in hand?'

'Because we plan to sell the construction outfit a year later.'

'But who will buy a construction firm with no projects?'

'Any of the other construction firms, because ours will be one of the very few that has huge stockpiles of cement and steel, both of which will be in very short-supply!'

'And what if the finance minister accuses us of hoarding?'

'How can he do that? His son-in-law owns Lakshmi & Co.'

<hr>

'I need you to go to Patna,' said Agrawalji to Gangasagar.

'I'm at your command, sir,' said Gangasagar.

'Don't you want to know why?' asked his mentor.

'If it's important, you'll tell me,' replied the young man.

'As you know, Patna is the state capital of Bihar. Bihar is rich in mineral deposits, particularly iron ore.'

'And?'

'The government is handing out mining concessions. We need to own a piece of the action.'

'And what is it that you want me to do, sir?'

'The government doesn't seem to know where the deposits are. I need to know what lies beneath *before* I bid, not *after*.'

'You want me to take a shovel and dig for iron ore?'

'No. I need you to go meet a friend of mine who used to be employed as a fighter pilot with the RAF. He lives in Patna.'

'We plan to drop bombs to open up the earth?'

'Enough with the sarcasm, Ganga. You'll see why you need him. It's a wonderfully simple and elegant solution.'

Squadron Leader Mohanlal was a typical scotch-and-soda gentleman. Whisky was his elixir of life, his thick white bushy moustache providing the perfect filter for whatever he drank. He had learned to fly at the Delhi Flying School and had been employed as a pilot for the Indian Post when he was requisitioned by the British Royal Air Force as part of a twenty-four-member Indian squad that would fly Hurricanes into Germany.

On his last sortie he had suddenly found his entire dashboard missing. He hadn't noticed because of the ruckus made by the engine. Black smoke and oil had started emanating from his Hurricane's engine at eighteen thousand feet over the English Channel. At seven thousand feet he was advised by ground control to bale out over the channel. A boat would pick him up. 'Don't send the boat,' he had replied over the crackling radio. 'Why?' asked the operator. 'Because I can't fucking swim, that's why!' he shouted. Mohanlal had soon glided towards the white cliffs of Dover but as soon as he opened up his airplane's landing gear, the Hurricane burst into flames. He managed to crash-land and had to be dragged from the burning wreckage. He hated the hospital food but loved his nurse and the scotch. He soon realised that scotch never changed its mind the way the nurse did.

After the war ended, Mohanlal returned to India with a rather generous pension from the RAF that enabled him to start up a limited-route air charter service using an old Hawker Hart. It was to lead to the wonderfully simple and elegant solution that Agrawalji spoke of.

'See? That's Patna city below you,' bellowed Mohanlal as the sputtering Hawker Hart lurched once more. Gangasagar was ready to throw up his breakfast, and cursed both Agrawalji and Mad Mohanlal for placing him there at five on a bitterly cold morning. The plane seated the two men one behind the other.

'Can you see those ruins, south of the railway lines? That's Kumhrar—the ruins of the ancient city of Pataliputra from which Patna derives its name,' yelled Mohanlal, oblivious to the discomfort of his first-time air traveller. Both men were wearing B-8 goggles with RAF helmets, A-2 bomber jackets and 1941 RAF Mae West parachute backpacks. Gangasagar peered nervously over the side of the aircraft to see what Mohanlal was pointing out.

'Pataliputra was the capital of Chandragupta Maurya's massive empire two thousand three hundred years ago. Difficult to imagine, given the pathetic state of Patna, eh?' he barked as he turned the noisy machine northwards to follow the river.

'The city is located along the south bank of the Ganges but the entire region is rich in iron ore. The trick lies in figuring out what the government hasn't yet done— identify exact locations!'

Gangasagar muttered some obscenities under his breath, thankful that the din of the engine would prevent the pilot from picking up on his utterances.

'Around the world, there's been a phenomenal increase in the use of geophysical techniques in mineral exploration. What I've got here with me up front is a piece of technology called a magnetometer. There are only a few of them in the world. Your boss managed to get one through his American contacts. It's bloody incredible!' exclaimed Mohanlal.

'So how does this thing work?' shouted Gangasagar, ignoring the sensation of his breakfast sloshing around inside his belly.

'What this *thing* does is measure the relative magnetic attraction of different parts of the earth's surface. Iron oxide gives the strongest magnetic pull of any mineral. So when we fly over mineral deposits we should see a definite variation in the magnetic pull,' explained Mohanlal, his voice partly drowned by the roar of the propellers and the ominous wobbling of the engine.

≡C≡

'We're going down!' screamed Mohanlal as the Hawker Hart lost altitude rapidly. Gangasagar cursed Mohanlal, then Agrawalji and then his own luck—in that order. For a moment he had thought that the crazy pilot was playing a vicious joke on him but within a few seconds he realised that it was no joke. The airborne junk heap was collapsing fast.

'We must bale out!' cried Mohanlal. Below them lay the ruins of Pataliputra, seemingly devoid of gawking tourists at this early hour of the morning. 'Just my luck,' thought Gangasagar, 'I'm going to die surrounded by two-thousand-three-hundred-year-old bones. Even if they discover my body later they'll think I'm just another relic of an ancient civilisation! Why did my greedy boss send me up in the air to fucking search for iron ore that is hundreds of feet underground? Instead of digging for iron ore they'll be digging for my body, entombed in this rusting iron bird. Look, Agrawalji, here's the iron you wanted!'

Gangasagar felt dizzy as the plane shuddered and went into a tailspin. 'Jump! Now!' shrieked Mohanlal as he ejected himself and pulled the ripcord of his parachute. Gangasagar blindly followed. He was now beyond caring.

He knew that he was about to die and didn't care if the damn parachute opened or not. Considering the state of Mohanlal's plane, it was very possible that there would be no parachute in the backpack at all!

He was in heaven. He was quite certain that he had died and was now floating above the clouds in Indra's heavenly abode. It was only when he looked over and found Mohanlal floating alongside him that he realised that they couldn't possibly be in heaven if Mohanlal was around. Both their parachutes had successfully deployed and Gangasagar felt the wind in his face as they gently floated towards mother earth.

Thud! The impact was anything but gentle. Weren't parachutes supposed to soften the impact? There was no time to ponder over the harshness of their collision with the ground. Less than a hundred yards away, the groaning mass of Mohanlal's Hawker plunged, shrieking a pierce, chilling scream, as it crashed into terra firma and exploded into a fireball. Both Mohanlal and Gangasagar braced themselves and hit the ground for protection from the heat blast that emanated from the wreck.

It was several minutes before either man raised his head. Their faces were covered in black soot and their clothes torn. Gangasagar's hair was standing straight up, almost as though an electric current had been passed through it. Cuts and bruises covered his arms, legs and face. Despite his weakened condition he had an overwhelming urge to strangle Mohanlal and fervently prayed that he would restrain himself from attacking the pilot.

He looked around him. The ruins of Pataliputra were like a ghost town at 5.30 in the morning. It was almost as if on a given day, Chandragupta's bustling empire had simply ground itself to a halt. At the centre of the Kumhrar site stood eighty massive pillars, probably once part of Magadha's great audience hall. Of course, there was no roof, no polished floor, no tapestry, no rich furnishings, which would once have embellished the court of the world's richest king. Some distance away stood the ruins of a Durakhi Devi temple, a Buddhist monastery as well as an ayurvedic hospital. 'This must have been one hell of a kingdom,' thought Gangasagar to himself, allowing his passion for history to take over.

'Hello? Which world are you in?' asked Mad Mohanlal, waving a hand in front of Gangasagar. 'We need to get near the crash site and ensure that there was no one in the vicinity. There could be casualties,' said Mohanlal as they started waking towards the fuel vapours and flames.

The ground had caved in at the crash site. Black acrid smoke puffed from the infernal machine, which had landed nose down. The ruins of the great assembly hall of Pataliputra lay a hundred yards to the west. 'Shall we walk towards Patna?' asked Gangasagar.

'No point making the effort. We're bang in the middle of the tourist circuit. Sit here for an hour or two and we'll have all the buses rolling in. We'll simply hitch a ride back into town,' suggested Mohanlal.

They sat down away from the circle of wreckage and watched the flames die down. Gangasagar dusted off the soot from his clothes, spat in his hand and used the saliva to clean his eyes. Mohanlal offered him a swig from his hip flask. Gangasagar ignored the pilot and continued to poke a twig he had found into the soil before him. It was soft red alluvial soil—rich in iron ore. *Agrawalji, look sir, I found your fucking ferrous fields,* thought Gangasagar.

The twig encountered an obstruction that prevented it from sinking deeper into the soft soil. Curiosity piqued, Gangasagar stabbed at it unrelentingly. Mohanlal drank some more in an effort to make Gangasagar bearable. Gangasagar got down on his knees and started digging with the twig. He needed to know what was obstructing it. A few minutes of digging by Gangasagar and a few pegs of whisky downed by Mohanlal, and the source of the blockage was discovered.

It was a small squarish block of black granite. Although it had remained buried in a few feet of soft soil for some time, it seemed polished and smooth. As Gangasagar used his palms to clear the soil that covered the face of the slab, he felt indentations along the smooth fascia—this was no ordinary rock formation, it was a rock inscription!

'Come on! Get up and help me!' shouted Gangasagar at the pilot. A visibly irritated Mohanlal got up, screwed back the cap on his hip flask and tucked it away inside his baggy flying pants. 'We need some metallic pieces of the wreckage that we can use as shovels,' Gangasagar told him. The intimidated pilot did not want to face the wrath of Elvis-sideburns. He found a metallic shaft, probably one of the wing supports, and touched it gingerly—it wasn't flaming hot. He picked it up and brought it over to Gangasagar who snatched it and began shovelling frantically.

'What's the big deal?' asked Mohanlal. 'Why're we getting horny looking at a block of fucking granite? It doesn't even have tits!'

Gangasagar ignored him and kept digging. Within fifteen minutes he had cleared away most of the soil and exposed the face of a block of stone, around the size of a tombstone lying flat on its back. It was perfectly polished granite and bore inscriptions in a script that Gangasagar could not understand. He knew that it was probably *Brahmi*—the calligraphy used in Mauryan times—but could not be certain.

'*Adi Shakti, Namo Namah; Sarab Shakti, Namo Namah; Prithum Bhagvati, Namo Namah; Kundalini Mata Shakti; Mata Shakti, Namo Namah,*' said the old teacher as he washed the stone with water and a *ghiya-tori*, a loofah. 'It's an ancient Sanskrit mantra extolling the virtues of feminine energy,' said Gangasagar's old headmaster.

Gangasagar and Mohanlal had taken the help of a couple of tourist guides to pry the block out of the ground, lift it into one of the buses that seemed even more dangerous than the aircraft that had just crashed, and take it into Patna city. From there Gangasagar had taken the train—no more flying—back into Kanpur.

Agrawalji had been happy about his safe return but had been even happier about the magnetometer readings that would allow him to bid with greater confidence for the mining concessions. Gangasagar's mother had been hysterical with worry and fear. She hugged and kissed him a hundred times, running her hands over his head and face, wanting to reassure herself that her son was indeed alive. His sisters had cooked kheer to celebrate his safe return. Ganga's mother was also celebrating the engagements of her daughters, dowry having been helpfully provided by Agrawalji.

Gangasagar, after a few days of rest, had taken the granite block—loaded on a bullock cart—to his old schoolmaster, who was the only person who would know how to interpret the rock inscription. 'You know, Ganga, it was always assumed that all rock inscriptions in Pataliputra were commissioned by Ashoka—the greatest of the Mauryan kings—the grandson of Chandragupta Maurya. But this cannot be an Ashoka inscription!' exclaimed his old headmaster.

'Why?' asked Gangasagar, curious as usual.

'Because the use of Sanskrit had almost entirely disappeared by Ashoka's reign. Ashoka became an avowed Buddhist after he massacred one hundred thousand people in Magadha's war with Kalinga. Buddhists shunned Sanskrit. They saw it as a language of the elite Brahmins and wanted their prayers to be understood by the common man. Ashoka's inscriptions were thus written in Prakrit, the language of the masses, not Sanskrit. But this is Sanskrit!' said the excited teacher.

'I thought this was Brahmi?' asked the confused Gangasagar.

'Brahmi is the script, not the language. Irrespective of whether you were writing Sanskrit or Prakrit, the script would have been the same—Brahmi.'

'So what does this chant mean?' asked Gangasagar.

'*Primal shakti, I bow to thee; all-encompassing shakti, I bow to thee; that through which God creates, I bow to thee; creative power of the kundalini; mother of all, to thee I bow,*' he said smiling. 'It's the ultimate recognition of female power.'

'But there seems to be an inscription on the other face of the block too. Is it a repetition of the same chant?' asked Gangasagar.

'Ah! No, I took a look at it. It contains instructions on the manner in which this mantra should be recited and its effects.

Gangasagar was wide-eyed in amazement. 'Tell me what it says,' he asked eagerly.

His old schoolmaster smiled. 'I've done better than that. I've translated and written down what it says on a sheet of paper for you.'

Four thousand days you shall pray
Four hundred chants every day.
Chanakya's power is yours to take
Chandragupta, to make or break.
If there's a lull, start once more.
King must be queen, to be sure.
Suvasini's curse shall forever halt
If you can cure Chanakya's fault.

CHAPTER THREE

About 2300 years ago

Takshila lay at the crossroads of two great trade routes, the royal Uttarapatha highway between Magadha and Gandhar, and the Indus route between Kashmir and the fabled Silk Road. Takshila was nestled in the valley kingdom of Gandhar—the Sanskrit word for *fragrance*. Surrounded by hills, orchards and wild flowers, Gandhar was a cornucopia of nature's abundance.

Shivering from the biting winter winds blowing in from the Himalayas and the Hindukush mountains and with nothing more than his worn-out robes for protection, Chanakya found himself standing before the *dwaar pandit*—the gate principal—of Takshila University. Dawn had just about broken and the air was filled with the smells of temple incense and the sounds of morning recitations of the Vedas. The well-planned streets were being swept and watered and the breakfast taverns had started preparing for their first customers.

'Whom do you wish to meet, boy?' asked the dwaar pandit. Chanakya replied that he needed to meet Acharya

Pundarikaksha, the dean of the university. Following the gate principal's directions, Chanakya reached a small cottage surrounded by fruit trees. The dean was in his garden, sitting bare-chested in the biting cold for his morning contemplation and prayers. Chanakya knew better than to disturb him and simply sat down in a corner of the nursery, trembling from the chill. A few moments later Pundarikaksha opened his eyes to find a rather dark, gangly-limbed, ugly and awkward-looking boy sitting in his garden, shaking in the cold.

'Who are you, my son?' he enquired. 'Sir, my name is Chanakya. I'm the son of Acharya Chanak of Magadha. I have here a letter for you from Katyayanji, a minister in the Magadha cabinet. He said that he knows you,' explained Chanakya.

Katyayan's name brought an immediate beam to the dean's face. It was quite obvious that the two had been childhood friends. He took off the shawl that was casually thrown on his right shoulder and covered Chanakya with it. He put his arm around the youth in a comforting gesture and took him inside where the warmth of the kitchen hearth was inviting. He quickly instructed his servant to get the boy a tumbler of hot milk and some laddoos. Chanakya realised he was ravenous and wolfed them down between gulps of warm milk.

Pundarikaksha was busy reading the letter Katyayan had written. It spoke of the fact that Chanakya was one of the brightest students of Magadha and was the son of Acharya Chanak, the leading authority in the field of political science and economics. 'Katyayan wants me to get you admission in the university,' said Pundarikaksha. *Doesn't my friend know that princes from all over the world wait for years to get accepted into these hallowed portals?* wondered Pundarikaksha as he continued reading the letter. His mind wandered to the days when Katyayan and he were students in Takshila. Pundarikaksha had been a poor orphan and Katyayan's father had financed his education. The dean knew that his old friend Katyayan was calling in the favour. Refusal of admission for this boy was not an option.

'You must be fatigued, Chanakya. You should rest. I shall ask my manservant to prepare a warm bed for you. I shall be meeting the admissions director to discuss this matter. I may send for you later in case he needs to test your knowledge,' said the perspicacious dean as he rose to leave.

'What is the purpose of good government, Chanakya?' asked the admissions director. They were seated on the floor in his office, a sparsely decorated room filled with musty scrolls, parchments and manuscripts. The room smelt of the eucalyptus oil lamps that illuminated the area in the evening.

The reply from Chanakya was prompt and confident. 'In the happiness of his subjects lies the king's happiness and in their welfare, his own welfare,' he replied emphatically.

'Son, what are the duties of a king?'

'A ruler's duties are three. *Raksha*—protecting the state from external aggression; *palana*—maintenance of law and order within; and finally, *yogakshema*—welfare of the people.'

'O son of Chanak, what are the possible means by which a king can settle political disputes?'

'There are four possible methods, sir. *Sama*—gentle persuasion and praise; *daama*—monetary incentives; *danda*—punishment or war; and *bheda*—intelligence, propaganda and disinformation.'

'What is the difference between a kingdom, a country, and its people?'

'There cannot be a country without people, and there is no kingdom without a country. It's the people who constitute a kingdom; like a barren cow, a kingdom without people yields nothing.'

'What constitutes a state, wise pupil?'

'There are seven constituent elements, learned teacher. The king, the council of ministers, the territory and populace, the fortified towns, the treasury, the armed forces and the allies.'

'Why does a king need ministers at all?'

'One wheel alone does not move a chariot. A king should appoint wise men as ministers and listen to their advice.'

'What is the root of wealth?'

'The root of wealth is economic activity, and lack of it brings material distress. In the absence of fruitful economic activity, both current prosperity and future growth are in danger of destruction. In the manner that elephants are needed to catch elephants so does one need wealth to capture more wealth.'

'What is an appropriate level of taxation on the people of a kingdom?'

'As one plucks fruits from a garden as they ripen, so should a king have revenue collected as it becomes due. Just as one does not collect unripe fruits, he should avoid collecting revenue that is not due because that will make the people angry and spoil the very sources of revenue.'

'To what extent should a king trust his revenue officials?'

'It is impossible to know when a fish swimming in water drinks some of it. Thus it's quite impossible to find out when government servants in charge of under-takings misappropriate money.'

'How important is punishment in the administration of a kingdom?'

'It is the power of punishment alone, when exercised impartially in proportion to the guilt, and irrespective of whether the person punished is the crown prince or an enemy slave, that protects this world and the next.'

'How should a king decide which kings are his friends and which are his enemies?'

'A ruler with contiguous territory is a rival and the ruler next to the adjoining is to be deemed a friend. My enemy's enemy is my friend.'

The admissions director looked at the boy in amazement. He then turned to Pundarikaksha and smiled. 'I have no doubts regarding his knowledge, analytical skills and intelligence, but who will pay his tuition?' he asked. The dean grinned sheepishly. 'My childhood chum Katyayan has called in a loan, my friend. I shall bear the cost personally,' he revealed.

Chanakya prostrated himself before Pundarikaksha and requested him to accept the ten gold panas that remained from the fifty that Katyayan had provided for his trip. 'Keep it, Chanakya. I will call in the loan as and when I deem appropriate,' declared Pundarikaksha. 'You shall unite the whole of Bharat; your brilliance shall be a flame that attracts kings like fireflies until they are humbled into submission; arise, Chanakya, our motherland needs you,' pronounced the dean. The grateful lad touched Pundarikaksha's feet wordlessly and left.

'I wonder whether this one really needs a Takshila education,' whispered the admissions director to the dean as Chanakya left.

◼◻◼

Chanakya's awry front teeth, his gangly limbs, his blemished and cratered face, his charcoal complexion and his patchy skin caused him to stand out as the most ill-favoured of Takshila. Princes and sons of nobility, most of whom placed a premium on being aristocratic and handsome, filled the university. Chanakya's raw intellect and audacious opinion on almost every subject did little to win him friends.

One day, when he was walking from his dormitory to his classes, he yelped in sudden pain as one of the blades of dry *kush* grass growing along the riverbank pierced his right foot. He mechanically lifted up his foot and pulled out the thorny blade of grass that had ventured to challenge him. Having pulled out the thorn and washed away the blood in the river, Chanakya bent down to examine the offending turf. He began uprooting clumps of kush and hurling them into the river.

'Look at Chanakya, friends! He harangues us with accounts of how he will destroy the enemies of the country and look, he cannot even suppress mere grass that attacks his foot!' shouted one of his classmates. Chanakya remained absorbed in the problem before him and ignored the jibes. He continued to pull out the wounding blades of tough kush, oblivious to the laughter and merriment around him. Several minutes and handfuls later, though, he realised that he was not going to be successful in eliminating the adversarial weeds using as unrefined a method as this. He made a mental note of what needed to be done and hurried to class. 'Defeated already!' crowed his compatriots. 'If that were real battle it would have ended without bloodshed. Chanakya would simply have laid down his arms before the enemy,' suggested a young prince. Chanakya had nothing to contribute by way of retort.

The next day, Chanakya's classmates were surprised to see him carrying a pitcher containing a clouded solution. While his compatriots hurried along, Chanakya drizzled the whitish liquid over as wide an area of the turf a possible. Some more sarcastic remarks followed. 'This is Chanakya's new battle strategy. If you can't defeat the enemy, give him milk so that he can become even stronger and decimate you effortlessly,' said one. Another remarked caustically, 'No, no. You don't understand… this is kush grass, revered by our Vedas. Chanakya is making offerings to the grass so that he may please the gods and they, instead of him, may do the dirty work of annihilating the adversary.' As usual, Chanakya did not offer any explanations.

The next day, the boys were shocked to find that large patches of the grass had disappeared. 'Hey Chanakya! What was in that milk you sprayed here yesterday?' asked one of the boys, curiosity piqued.

'The kush was too abundant and vast for me to destroy, so I figured—if my enemy's enemy is my friend— what is this kush's biggest foe? The answer was fungus and ants, both of which attack the grass and feed on it. What I poured yesterday was not milk. It was sweetened whey, my friends. The protein in the whey caused the fungus to grow and the sugar content attracted the ants,' explained the canny youth to his disconcerted companions who were even more surprised to note that Chanakya had brought with him yet another pitcher of whey and was repeating the previous day's procedure.

'You've already killed the grass, Chanakya. What's with the second pitcher?' enquired one of the preceding day's mocking sons of nobility.

'A debt should be paid off till the last pana, and an enemy destroyed till the very last trace,' reasoned the unrelenting Chanakya for the benefit of his new admirers.

'It's unfortunate that the concept of *Bharat*—the common abode and cultural heritage of us Indo-Aryans —has been subjugated by petty rulers and kingdoms. Our scriptures, traditions, culture, prayers, and deities are common. Why is it, then, that we refer to our homes as Magadha, Gandhar, Kashi, Kuru, Kosala, Mallayrajya or Panchala? Why don't we say that we're citizens of Bharat? It's this fundamental divisiveness that will bring about our downfall in the future,' debated Chanakya while tilting his head so that he could partially align his face with that of his host. He was in Sage Dandayan's hut on the outskirts of Takshila. The sage was a yogi and had been standing on his head for the past few days, hence the valiant effort by Chanakya to adjust his own visage with that of the upside-down yogi.

In the past six years, Chanakya had not only excelled at every subject in his curriculum at Takshila but had also been on the merit list each year. His stellar academic performance had earned him the position of *upacharya*— teaching assistant—in his favourite subjects, political science and economics. The meagre but adequate income from the job had allowed him to repay the debt to his guru, Pundarikaksha, in accordance with his sentiment that 'a debt should be paid off till the last pana', although Pundarikaksha had joked that the interest was still due and payable, not in cash, but through the realisation of a united homeland.

Pundarikaksha had introduced Chanakya to the insightful yogi, and Chanakya enjoyed visiting him at his hermitage every once in a while. Dandayan liked the bright young man who seemed to have an opinion on almost every major issue. 'Solitary candles remain centred on their own flames until one applies heat to the vessel that holds them. In the face of a common enemy—heat— they coalesce into a single candle,' revealed the inverted sadhu, his long grey locks and beard forming a pool around his head on the floor.

The sacred ash-smeared yogi continued nonchalantly, 'Unlike the sun which awakes in the east and falls asleep in the west, the Hellenic star has arisen in the west and is travelling eastwards. The fair-skinned god eradicates everyone and everything that confronts him. Your real enemy is not Dhanananda, O learned offspring of Chanak, but the Macedonian divinity whom they call *Alexander the Great*!'

'What shall I do, guruji? My anger towards Dhanananda has not abated. How can I disregard my objectives?' asked a perturbed Chanakya.

'Chanakya. One does not need to pluck fruit from a tree that is about to be chopped down. The fruit will fall by themselves. Focus on the bigger purpose and the rest of your manifesto will follow as a matter of course.'

Chanakya's fame and reputation as a teacher grew. Students vied with one another to be in his class. Every once in a while, Chanakya would break away from learning-by-rote and allow his students to ask him rapid-fire questions which he would answer in his most witty and penetrating manner with little regard for political rectitude.

'Acharya, you're the most learned of teachers. Why shouldn't you become a king?'

'Honestly speaking. I don't mind that I'm not king. I just have a problem that someone else is.'

'Acharya, what is the reason for secrecy in government?'

'If citizens don't know what you're doing, how on earth can they possibly tell what you're doing wrong? That's why secrecy is essential, my boy.'

'Acharya, why do people seem to get away with not respecting the law of the land?'

'If we want people to have respect for the law, then we must first make the law respectable, son.'

'Acharya, isn't the king actually a servant of the people?'

'Correction. In order to become master, a ruler must *profess to be a servant* of the people.'

'Acharya, how can the prime minister reduce the king's burden in times of crisis or panic?'

'Why do that? Rulers must be allowed to panic. They need to be kept busy with lots of crises. It's their measure of achievement!'

'Acharya, is it the sacred duty of the king to always speak the truth?'

'Hah! The king doesn't need the truth. What he most needs is something that he can tell the people, dear lad. After all, a good speech is not one in which you can prove that the king's telling the truth, it's one where no one else can prove he's fibbing.'

'Acharya, which are the freedoms that should be guaranteed to a citizen by the state?'

'Hmm... let me see. It's well known that a hungry man is more interested in four pieces of bread rather than four freedoms.'

'Acharya, why should Brahmins like you be involved in politics?'

'Politics is far too serious a matter to be left to politicians, son.'

'Acharya, is war the only solution to political differences?'

'Wise pupil, politics is war without bloodshed and war is simply politics with bloodshed.'

'Acharya, don't citizens have the right to know how their tax revenues are being used?'

'Dear me. No, no, no. People don't want to know how tax revenue has actually been spent. Does any worshipper ever ask the temple Brahmin what happened to the ritual offering made to the gods?'

'Acharya, isn't good government about acting on principles?'

'Absolutely. Government is about principles. And the principle is, never act on principle.'

'And are principles greater than money?'

'Remember one central tenet, lad. When anybody says, "It isn't the money, it's the principle", they actually mean that it's the money.'

'Acharya, what's the ideal amount of time that should be spent by the king's council debating an issue?'

'Well, if you don't want the council to spend too long over something, make it the last item on their agenda before refreshments.'

'Acharya, should a king go to war to uphold law and justice?'

'The king should always be on the side of law and justice, as long as he doesn't allow it to come in the way of foreign policy.'

'Acharya, what should the punishment be for a prime minister who keeps the king ignorant of happenings in the kingdom?'

'My son, kings are ignorant not because prime ministers do not give them the right answers but because they do not ask their prime ministers the right questions. And here endeth the lesson!'

━◼━

The witty repartee and humour masked an inner melancholy and sense of desolation. Chanakya had left his mother in Magadha on the mere promise of Katyayan. Was she in good health? Would she be missing her son?

How would she be coping with the loss of both husband and son? Over the years, he had tried to send several messages to her through various merchant caravans and wandering bards. No reply had ever come back. It could mean either that the messengers had been unable to locate her... or worse.

It had been over ten years since that dark amavasya night, under the cover of which he had abandoned Magadha. His mentor, Pundarikaksha, had passed away the previous year. On his deathbed, the compassionate dean had urged Chanakya to return to Magadha and bring back his mother to Takshila, so that she could be better cared for. 'Your mother as well as your motherland need looking after, Chanakya, but one's mother comes before one's motherland.'

Pundarikaksha had died leaving three possessions to his beloved disciple—his house, his manuscripts and his loyal manservant. Chanakya quickly installed three of his favourite students, Sinharan, Mehir and Sharangrao in the house to look after his affairs while he was away. Sinharan was the son of the governor of Mallayrajya, one of the handfuls of republics in the region. He had been cheated out of the throne by his uncle who had usurped the throne of Mallayrajya from Sinharan's father. Mehir was a Persian student who had fled his homeland owing to the Macedonian invasion. Sharangrao was the brightest Brahmin boy in the university. All three were his endeared disciples, although they remained consistently at odds with Ambhi, the crown prince of Gandhar—an arrogant and brash freshman in the university. 'Keep him in check, Sinharan,' advised Chanakya, and then having taken permission for a sabbatical from the university chancellor, started preparations for the long march to the city of his birth.

The arduous journey to Magadha brought flashbacks not only of his parents but also of dear Suvasini. She was the daughter of the imprisoned prime minister Shaktar and had been his childhood friend. As a little girl, she had been delicately built, like an exquisitely carved statue. Her rosy cheeks and piercing brown eyes had driven Chanakya quite mad. He had always remained in love with her but had never plucked up the courage to tell her. He knew that she knew, but she had derived mischievous fun from pretending she didn't. As he inched his way towards Magadha, he found himself reminiscing more frequently about his adolescent infatuation.

Pataliputra had not only grown in size but also in indulgence, licentiousness, corruption and debauchery. Betting and gambling halls were on every street corner and it was not uncommon to observe disputes breaking out over claims of loaded dice, sleight of hand or doctored animal fights. Alcohol was consumed to excess and it was a familiar sight to see wine-soaked men staggering out of madiralays, having overindulged in *kinva, asava, maireya, medaka, madhu* or *prasanna*—the wide assortment of cocktails that Magadha pubs had on offer. The other wide assortment consisted of *ganikas, rupajivas* and *pumsachalis*—prostitutes, independent escorts and concubines. Magadha's courtesans offered the finest talent—singing, playing musical instruments, conversing, dancing, performing massages, preparing perfumes, stringing garlands, shampooing, bathing and, of course most importantly, the art of lovemaking. A celebrated guru of Magadha, Vatsyayana, had just published a bestselling treatise, the *Kama Sutra*, with over twelve hundred verses detailing seventy-seven different positions for making love.

When Chanakya arrived at the gates of the capital, Pataliputra, the inebriated immigration officer at the city gates could barely bring himself to cursorily examine his travel documents, leave alone ask him any relevant questions, even though it was only noon. The guards at the city gates seemed dishevelled and red-eyed after heavy drinking the previous night. Magadha was a kingdom in denial—it seemed to be refusing to acknowledge the threat of a Macedonian invasion that loomed large for the bordering kingdoms of Bharat. Both the king and his people simply did not want the party to end even though the night was over.

Most of the city seemed to be unchanged, though, and it was not too difficult for Chanakya to navigate his way to Katyayan's house. The streets, the houses and even the street corner oil-fired lamps looked unchanged. What had changed was the appearance of Katyayan. Ten years had aged him by twenty-five. He instantly recognised Chanakya approaching the house and rushed outside to meet him even though he had last seen him as a mere runt. Tears welled up in his eyes as he hugged Chanakya and refused to let go. As they went inside, he instructed his manservant to wash Chanakya's hands and feet and to have the cook organise the noon meal.

The two men sat down on the floor of the kitchen as the servant placed banana leaves and earthen tumblers of water before them. In Brahmin tradition, they each sprinkled a little water around their leaves, a ritual purification of the earth. Next, the servant brought rice, lentils and vegetables, which he proceeded to place on their banana leaves. As was the custom, both men—before commencing to eat with their hands—removed small morsels of their food from the leaves and left them as symbolic charitable offerings for animals—cows, dogs, crows and ants—to please the gods. Even though they had not seen each other for over a decade, the meal was consumed in silence following Vedic custom.

It was only after they had risen and retired to the courtyard that Chanakya spoke. 'I have come to Pataliputra to take back my mother, Katyayanji. How is she?' he enquired. The silence that followed was protracted and deafening. Finally, Katyayan spoke. 'Vishnu… Chanakya… how do I tell you this? After your father's brutal execution and your departure for Takshila, I did everything to keep her in good stead. At my insistence, she was sent to Kusumpur, your family's ancestral home near Pataliputra. I reasoned that she would be better off away from Pataliputra—a place that she associated with the murder of her husband and the disappearance of her son. I would send her money and provisions regularly and would visit her whenever possible but, my dear Chanakya, she was pining for you and mourning the death of her beloved husband. She stopped eating, and withered away. She passed away around six or seven years ago. Forgive me, Chanakya. I have now been the bearer of bad news twice in your life.'

The blank and distant look that Katyayan had witnessed in Chanakya's eyes when he was told about the slaying of his father seemed to have returned. The old man held Chanakya's hand and tried his best to coax a reaction but failed. The armour of dispassionate determination had once again enveloped Chanakya and he quickly changed the subject, almost as though the demise of a parent was just one among several equally relevant topics for discussion.

'Is prime minister Shaktar alive? How is he?' he asked.

'He's still in prison. Dhanananda destroyed his family. Rakshas and I regularly bribe Girika to keep him alive. You know that it's impossible to leave Nanda's Hell— the prison complex and torture dungeons managed by that monster Girika—alive and well. I'm told by my informants that Shaktarji's life is a living hell and that he dies a thousand deaths each day!'

'So Shaktarji's daughter—Suvasini—is also dead?' asked Chanakya, hesitatingly.

'I know that you always had a soft corner for her, Chanakya. But what can I say? Her life is worse than death. She survived due to the benefaction of that adulterer Rakshas, but ended up his mistress.'

'My dear beloved Suvasini, a harlot? My mother dead! The prime minister in a hellish dungeon! Where is justice in Magadha?'

'The only recompense is that the persecution of Brahmins has ceased. Ever since Rakshas took over as prime minister, he has succeeded in keeping Dhanananda immersed in wine and women. The result has been royal lethargy in the anti-Brahmin policy. Rakshas, being a Brahmin himself, has even convinced Dhanananda to establish an endowment that provides grants to learned Brahmins. Who could have thought that a *Shudra* would ever do anything to even remotely favour Brahmins?'

'So Dhanananda and Rakshas have succeeded in buying the silent acquiescence of the Brahmins through endowments, have they? Mother earth is weeping at the betrayal right now—Brahmins were supposed to be her guardians, the protectors of righteousness, devoutness, godliness, honesty, fairness, truth, virtue, dignity and integrity. Instead we have become common whores, available to the highest bidder for the night!'

'Sshh... Chanakya... not so loud, my son... even walls have ears. Yes, you're right, we're no better than concubines. I also stand guilty before you. It's just that I saw what happened to your father—the illustrious Chanak—when he tried to speak up for what was right. I'm still witnessing the horrors that our erstwhile prime minister Shaktar has to endure for having sought to put the monarch on an appropriate course. There's no point brandishing a bow if your quiver holds no arrows, Chanakya. That's harsh reality for you.'

'I don't blame you, Katyayanji. If it weren't for you, I would never have survived. I shall remain indebted to you for the rest of my life. My anger is due to the hopeless situation. It isn't directed at you.'

'I understand, Chanakya. Let's try to direct this rage to some productive use. If you want Dhanananda ejected from his throne, you need men, materials, allies, and planning… and as you're well aware, at the root of all these is wealth. You need money if you hope to achieve the purge of Magadha.'

<hr>

The *Feast of Wisdom* was the annual banquet hosted by the king for learned Brahmin gurus from all over his kingdom. Their feet would be washed, they would be fed, provided with gifts of gold and, in turn, they would bless the king and his kingdom. Pataliputra Palace was festooned with marigolds and banana leaves for the grand event. Hundreds of cooks slaved within the royal kitchens to prepare choice dishes as offerings to the Brahmins. Outside the palace gates, drummers beat their skins in a frenzied rhythm to announce that the feast of wisdom had begun. Before the feast commenced, however, the list of winners who would be fed by the king and honoured with endowments had to be decided. This was done through a series of open debates in court, with the sovereign in attendance. Those who performed well in these open debates would earn distinction through royal recognition and favours.

Dhanananda was in court, but reluctantly. He was in a foul mood. The fat oaf, the *rajpurohit*—the court astrologer—had been looking at the king's horoscope, and had found his second star, Venus, conjunct with deceptive *Ketu* in the sixth house, to be in close proximity to Saturn. He had warned Dhanananda that the day was not an auspicious one for him and that he should expect trouble. 'You've been in your *Rahu Mahadasha* for the past year, my lord. Mars is the eighth planet, representing death, transformation, and change, from the ascendant, Moon, and Sun. Saturn, the sixth governor of court battles, has also been trailing your Sun and Moon's tenth aspect, and ascendant's third aspect by transit. Be careful of what you say and do today, O King!' exclaimed the astrologer.

≡

'Be careful of what you say and do today, Chanakya,' advised Katyayan, although Chanakya had no intention of participating in any competition. He was far too distinguished a scholar for any such event. He simply wished to observe the proceedings of Dhanananda's court and better understand the equation between the king and his new prime minister, Rakshas. He ensured that he remained suitably hidden within the throng of the palace guests and out of the direct line of sight of Dhanananda. His error, however, was to stand alongside Katyayan and to remain within the sight of Rakshas. Rakshas recognised the ugly Chanakya instantly. Seeing an opportunity to let some sparks fly, he sombrely announced, 'Magadha is honoured to have present here among us today, her illustrious son, Chanakya, who is a revered professor at the renowned Takshila University. The court shall be delighted to kick off today's competitions with a discussion by the acharya.' Polite applause followed and Chanakya reluctantly took centre stage. 'Measure your words and hold your temper,'

Katyayan whispered urgently as Chanakya walked away from him.

'Om! Salutations to Brihaspati and Sukra, the gurus of the gods and antigods, and the originators of the science of politics,' started Chanakya as an opening invocation, facing Dhanananda seated on his royal throne with Rakshas standing at his right hand. 'Om!' chanted the assembly in chorus.

'O enlightened teacher, how can society work in harmony towards the progress of the kingdom?' asked Rakshas.

'By performing one's duty. The duties of a *Brahmin* are studying, teaching and interceding on man's behalf with the gods. The duties of a *Kshatriya* are bearing arms and protecting all life. The duties of a *Vaishya* are trading, manufacturing and producing wealth. The duties of a *Shudra* are to serve the three higher *varnas*,' declared Chanakya, knowing fully well that the king seated at the throne was a Shudra.

Rakshas was malevolently pleased. He had already lit the spark. It would not be too long before an explosion occurred. Surprisingly, Dhanananda maintained his composure and allowed the remark to slip.

'Acharya, what should be the qualities of a king?'

'An ideal king should be eloquent, bold, endowed with sharp intellect, strong memory and keen mind. He should be amenable to guidance. He should be strong and capable of leading the army. He should be just in rewarding and punishing. He should have foresight and avail himself of opportunities. He should be capable of governing in times of peace and times of war. He should know when to fight and when to make peace, when to lie in wait and when to strike. He should preserve his dignity at all times, be sweet in speech, straightforward and amiable. He should eschew passion, anger, greed, obstinacy, fickleness, and backbiting. He should conduct himself in accordance with the advice of elders—'

'Oh shut up! I do not need this sermon!' interrupted Dhanananda in a fit of rage. The court was stunned into a silence one could touch. Rakshas was at a loss for words. He had not expected such an instant result.

'I agree with you, O King. You do not need my advice. My advice is meant for those who have the intrinsic capacity to absorb and implement my advice. You, unfortunately, have neither!' thundered Chanakya. Katyayan cringed inwardly. Why had he brought Chanakya here? He had unwittingly placed his own hand within the lion's jaws.

'Rakshas! Who is this ugly oaf that you deem a revered teacher? He's not fit to be amongst us, leave alone lecture us!' demanded Dhanananda.

'O noble King. He is Chanakya, the son of the dear departed Chanak,' explained Rakshas slyly.

'Ah! I now understand. When I ordered for that impudent dimwit's head to be cut off, I should also have done the same for his son. Rats have a nasty habit of multiplying,' observed Dhanananda.

'Once again, I must agree with you, O King,' said Chanakya, 'you were unwise to leave me alive. An enemy should always be destroyed to the very final trace—just as I shall destroy you and your perverted dynasty one day,' predicted Chanakya calmly.

'Have this wretch arrested and sent to Nanda's Hell. He can think up ways for my downfall under the tongs and probes of the talented Girika! Catch him by his puny pigtail as one catches a rat by its tail!' shrieked Dhanananda as his royal guards moved towards Chanakya.

Chanakya's hands went to his shikha and untied the knot that held the individual strands of hair together. In spite of his fury, Dhanananda's curiosity was piqued and he remarked, 'Untying your tail isn't going to help you! A monkey shall always remain a monkey!'

'O stupid and ignorant King, I have made it my sacred duty to unite the whole of Bharat so that it may stand up to the might of the foreign invaders at our doorstep. My first step shall be to expunge you from history. Today I take a sacred oath! I swear upon the ashes of my wise father and loving mother that I shall not re-tie my shikha until I have expelled you as well as the Macedonian invaders from my country and united it under an able and benevolent ruler!' swore Chanakya as the guards caught hold of him by his now untied hair and dragged him towards Nanda's Hell.

CHAPTER FOUR
Present Day

'Agrawalji, I would like, with your blessings, to relinquish my service in your employment,' said Gangasagar. Over the years he had learned everything that Agrawalji possessed in his bag of tricks. He was grateful but wanted to move on.

'Why, Ganga? You've learned so much under my tutelage. Why throw it all away?'

'Sir, I think that I can help you better from outside than from within.'

'What do you mean?'

'In India's untidy democracy, politics and business shall always need each other. The former is about power but needs money to realise it; the latter is about wealth but needs power to create and sustain it. Let me become your political strength.'

'And what would you want from me?'

'Economic support. I shall repay it with political support when you need it.'

'My blessings are with you, Gangasagar.'

Gupta, the paan vendor, was blissfully smoking his cheroot as he lovingly layered lime, cardamom, areca nuts, and rose-petal paste onto a bright green betel leaf for Gangasagar. The filth surrounding his stall was unbearable, a thick stench of sewage making it impossible to breathe. 'That's why I smoke these cheroots,' said Gupta, 'they make it easier to breath in this foul air. I don't mind the carcinogens!'

Kanpur was home to some of India's biggest tanneries, and the area housed one of them. Hides came to the tannery with animal flesh and hair still hanging on them and the tannery used urine and limestone sludge to remove the residue. The workers then treated the hides with pigeon droppings. A permanent and disgusting smell of rotting flesh, stale urine and pigeon shit hung over the entire area. The poorest of the poor worked in tanneries like this one and they had no alternative but to live in shanties around the area. The result was a burgeoning slum.

For the wealthy of Kanpur, slums like this one were embarrassing boils that needed to be lanced; for those who lived in them, the slum was their only source of sustenance—no matter how wretched. With just one lavatory for every fifteen hundred dwellers, most residents were left with little alternative but to defaecate out in the open drains. Stinking slaughterhouses that supplied the hides to the tanneries discharged bloody remains into the very same open sewers choked with untreated human and industrial waste. Typhoid, cholera and malaria were common conditions in this hellhole.

Along its perimeter were little shops like those of Gupta. The slum was a self-sufficient little community and paan and cigarette stalls, tea shops, grocery stores, and chemists did roaring business because they had captive consumers who lived right there. 'Are there any schools here?' asked Gangasagar, masticating his paan.

'There used to be a municipal school but the teachers ran away. The local mafia thugs wanted the space to set up their bootlegging operation,' said Gupta, blowing a puff of acrid smoke. 'The local politicos are quite happy to wax eloquent about the need for schools to educate our young, but the reality is that they wish to keep us illiterate and uneducated. It's the perfect way to maintain a vote bank,' said Gupta conspiratorially.

'If I open a school here, will parents send their children?' asked Gangasagar.

'I don't know about the others, but I'll send my daughter happily,' said Gupta.

'What's her name?'

'Chandini. She's just ten.'

—◼◻—

He was a rough and uncouth character but his clothes were immaculate. His paan-stained teeth matched the colour of his eyes, blood-red. Not that Ikrambhai ever drank. It was against his religion. He ran extremely profitable ventures in land-grabbing, illegal betting, extortion, and bootlegging. But he refused to drink. His eyes were red because he rarely slept. Hard work was essential, even if you were a slumlord. His swarthy skin boldly contrasted with the pure-white embroidered kurta that he wore. The buttons were sparkling diamonds and on his fingers he wore several rings, each set with a different stone.

He wore a ruby to give him good health and longevity, although his own longevity often meant the reduced life-expectancy of others. He wore a cat's-eye to bestow him with patience, and he often remained exceedingly patient while his thugs beat up a poor sucker who refused to fall in line. That's why he also wore a white pearl, to keep him cool and calm. The yellow sapphire was for increasing his wealth, which seemed to multiply quite miraculously, and the diamond was to keep him sexually potent, not that he needed any aid in the virility department. The green emerald was to enable him to communicate better and the coral was to protect him from the evil eye—of which there were many, given his profession.

'Why aren't you wearing a blue sapphire?' asked Gangasagar as he looked at all the various stones that embellished Ikrambhai's fingers.

'Why? What will that do for me?'

'It will give you power and influence—real power and influence.'

'Bah! I already have that. No one in this slum dare do anything without my say-so,' he said with pride, his eyes boring into Gangasagar.

'But what about the rest of the world? Your universe is this tannery and the slum. There's so much good that someone with your abilities could do for the entire city— even the state perhaps.'

'You mean setting up gambling dens and bootlegging warehouses across the city?' asked Ikrambhai earnestly.

'There's not much difference between running an empire such as yours and running a city administration. I often feel that take-no-shit guys like you would run the city better. That's why I'm here to suggest that you enter politics. I shall be your guru!'

▬▬

Agrawalji had happily advanced the sum needed to finance the school. It wasn't a very large sum though —just enough for lights, fans, a blackboard, basic furniture, a lick of paint and lots of books. Ikrambhai inaugurated it. Gangasagar knew that he needed the support of Ikrambhai.

'Why are you giving him any credit?' asked Agrawalji. 'You're doing all the hard work—including teaching the children history—and I'm coughing up the cash.'

'You can do much more with a kind word and a gun than a kind word alone,' answered Gangasagar. 'Allowing him to take some of the credit for the school has ensured that we're not bothered by his goons. Do you know he's threatened all the parents that he'll thrash them if they don't send their kids to the school?' laughed Gangasagar.

'And what's the catch behind this benevolent attitude of Ikrambhai?' asked Agrawalji.

'He wants to fight the next municipal elections. He wants financial and intellectual support,' explained Gangasagar.

'So you've promised him my money?' asked Agrawalji dryly.

'And my brains,' countered Gangasagar, 'only if he fights on an ABNS ticket, though.'

'What political party is that? I've never heard of it.'

'It doesn't exist as yet. It will by the next municipal elections, though.'

'Should you be handing out tickets of your new outfit to mafia dons, Ganga?'

'The best person to advise one on how to protect a bank is a thief. This one's going to help me build and protect my vote bank.'

'How?'

'I'm a Brahmin. I can do the job of pulling in high-caste Hindu votes but the lower castes and the Muslims view me suspiciously. Ikrambhai will help take care of the Muslim votes.'

'Won't associating with him spoil your reputation, Ganga?'

'Character is what you are. Reputation is what people think you are. As long as he doesn't change my character, I'll be fine.'

'I hope that you know what you're doing. You're making a pact with the devil.'

'God will forgive me. That's his job after all!' said Gangasagar, winking at Agrawalji.

▬◻▬

The Kanpur Municipality had come into existence during the British Raj, but was converted into a corporation— the *Kanpur Nagar Mahapalika*—some years after Independence, with a mayor who was elected every five years. The election was an indirect one in which over a hundred municipal coroporators who were elected from the various geographical wards in the city would choose the mayor. Ikrambhai was contesting only one out of the hundred seats in the municipal council but Gangasagar had also convinced many others to contest the elections on the ABNS platform. He had confidently pronounced that he would make Ikram the mayor.

'The council is hopelessly split along caste and religious lines. Twenty-five per cent of the members are Brahmins, another quarter are the intermediate castes such as the Yadavs, one-fourth are Dalits and the remaining fourth are Muslims,' explained Gangasagar.

'You have no chance,' said Agrawalji helplessly.

But this was politics, not economics. The master of this game was Gangasagar, not Agrawalji.

'Not true. All I need to do is take away five per cent from each of the four blocs. By doing that, I'll have twenty per cent of the total. The fifth bloc.'

'But you'll still be twenty per cent, equal to each of the four other blocs,' argued Agrawalji, not realising that this particular game of chess had already been analysed several moves into its conclusion.

'The other four blocs hate each other. Whoever wants power will have no alternative but to ally themselves with us—the only caste- and religion-neutral outfit,' said Gangasagar triumphantly.

'But they'd only support you if you agreed that their candidate became mayor. How can you expect to make Ikram mayor?'

'The mayor is elected through the system of a single transferable vote. The game theory involved here is different to an ordinary vote,' explained Gangasagar. 'The early bird gets the worm but it's the second mouse that gets the cheese! I don't need Ikrambhai to be the favourite —merely the second favourite.'

'How will that help him?' asked Agrawalji.

'All corporators are required to rank—in order of preference—their choice of all five candidates when they submit their ballot.'

'So?'

'For all the five political blocs, including our own, the first choice will be a candidate from within.'

'Yes. But that merely puts Ikram on equal footing with the other four candidates.'

'Ah, but each corporator must not only indicate his first choice from the five candidates but also indicate his second, third, fourth and fifth preference,' explained Gangasagar. 'Given the intense hatred between the other four parties, they would refuse to endorse each other's candidates as second choice. I simply need to tell them to make Ikram their second choice.'

'How exactly does this process work?' enquired Agrawalji.

'In round one the votes for the first choice candidates are counted. Obviously all five, including Ikram, will be equal. Given the lack of a clear winner, the second-choice votes will be tallied and added to the count of each candidate. At this stage, Ikram becomes the strongest. The second mouse shall bring home the cheese!'

'I just hope that your mouse doesn't turn out to be a cat, Ganga,' said Agrawalji.

■□■

'Can any of you tell me what the core philosophy of Mahatma Gandhi was?'

'Ahimsa,' came the answer from the back. It was a frail and petite thirteen-year-old girl. Her face was rounded and her dark black hair was oiled and pulled back in a plait tied with a red ribbon. Little tendrils that had escaped the torturous ministrations of oiling and being pulled tightly back, hung over her forehead. She wore a dull grey skirt and an insipid blue top—the usual dreary uniform of slum schools. Her complexion, however, was unusually fair for such a setting, and her little white teeth, pink lips and sparkling emerald-green eyes gave her an expression of innocence coupled with intelligence.

She fiddled nervously with her pencil as Gangasagar looked at her. 'Very good, Chandini. Can you tell me what that means?'

'Ahimsa means non-violence.'

'Does that mean refusing to fight?'

'No. Ahimsa is not cowardice. It takes a very brave man to face blows head-on.'

'So it's about getting your way without coming to blows for it?'

'Yes. But you need to have the moral authority to make people understand what you want to achieve. Gandhiji's moral authority was very great.'

'And can you tell me what gave him that moral authority?'

'The personal example that he set for others?' asked Gupta's daughter hesitantly.

'Yes. We Indians continue to adore renunciation. It's a tradition that has come down to us from the ancient yogis. Gandhiji was a modern yogi, in that sense.'

'Because he lived in poverty?' she asked, her emerald-green eyes widening.

'Yes, but his poverty was a symbol. A symbol that gave him the political authority to carry people with him.'

'And it saved the country lots of money?'

'Hah! Sarojini Naidu—our first governor here in Uttar Pradesh—summed it up beautifully when she said that it cost the Indian nation a great deal of money to keep the Mahatma in poverty!'

'Then why did he do it?'

'That's the power of renunciation for you, my dear!'

'Like the way that you renounced becoming mayor so that Uncle Ikram could?'

'Yes,' chuckled Gangasagar, 'something like that.'

━⊏

'We need to clean up this city, Ikram.'

'You mean "clean up" as in "make a killing", right Gangasagarji?'

'No.'

'You don't mean clean up as in sweeping the streets and clearing the garbage, do you?'

'Yes, I do. The city's filthy.'

'Taking control of the municipal corporation is all about making money, not about actually cleaning up.'

'I'd be a fool if I said that corruption isn't a way of life. We're going to need money to strengthen the ABNS, but let's also do some good along the way.'

'Why? Who's ever done any good in local government?'

'We shouldn't do it because we're do-gooders. We should do it because we want to win the next elections without assistance from other political parties.'

'If we make enough money in this term, we won't need another term in the corporation. We'll be rich.'

'Who's talking about the corporation?'

'Huh?'

'My dear Ikram. Real power lies at state level, not in local government. That's where we're all going to be five years from now—the Uttar Pradesh state government.'

'Gangasagarji. The garbage collectors have gone on strike. They say that the new discipline imposed on them has resulted in longer hours—they want more pay and perks.'

'They're already overpaid, Ikram. The corporation can't afford any more hikes.'

'So what do you want me to do? The municipal commissioner phones me every ten minutes for a negotiated settlement.'

'Negotiation must always be done from a position of strength, not weakness. If essential services are disrupted, they'll have the upper hand.'

'What's your advice?'

'Garbage collection mustn't get disrupted. They'll then be forced to negotiate from a position of weakness.'

'So you want me—the mayor—to go around the city collecting garbage?'

'No. But you have hundreds of ragpickers in your slum. Offer them a small daily allowance to do the job. They'll not only do the job but also recycle the waste. It's an economy-friendly and ecology-friendly solution.'

'The garbage collectors will be enraged.'

'Better they than us. Negotiate once they fall in line.'

<hr>

'The municipal hospitals are in shambles, Gangasagarji.'

'Let's improve and upgrade them, Ikram.'

'We don't have the budget. We're in deficit.'

'Then let's rename the hospitals instead.'

'How will renaming anything improve it?'

'Simple. Who are the businessmen in this city who are being prosecuted for tax fraud?'

'There are several. Why?'

'Tell them that their family name will be associated with something charitable. Ask them for a substantial donation to upgrade the facilities and we'll willingly rename the damned hospitals! They get the label of being benefactors and we get the money to upgrade the facilities.'

'What if they don't agree?'

'Tell them that their tax cases will be pursued with double the vigour.'

<hr>

'Gangasagarji, the roads have developed potholes once again.'

'Ikram, why don't we impose penalties on the construction firms that executed the job?'

'They say that the materials used were as per municipal specifications. It isn't their fault that the specifications were substandard.'

'Fine. Announce that we're about to undertake massive road-building projects over the next year. Make a press statement.'

'But we're not.'

'Ah. But they don't know that. Your potholes will get filled for free by the firms that want future business from us.'

'Revenue collections are down this year, Gangasagarji.'

'What are our sources of revenue, Ikram?'

'Property tax, licence fees and rent on municipal lands.'

'Increasing property tax or licence fees is not a viable option. It discourages economic activity, and eventually lowers tax revenues. Increase the rent on municipal lands.'

'But we can't increase municipal rents—even though they are lower than market rates—because of locked-in tenancies.'

'Terminate the tenancies.'

'The tenants will go to court.'

'Let them. Each tenant will need a battery of lawyers whereas a single government attorney will represent the municipal corporation. Our legal costs will be negligible in comparison to theirs.'

'But matters will remain tied up in litigation for years. We'll eventually lose. We're on extremely shaky legal ground.'

'Fine. Threaten to sell the tenanted land as-is-where-is.'

'No one will buy tenanted properties.'

'My dear Ikram, if I recall correctly, you were a slumlord before you were elevated to the exalted position of mayor, am I correct?'

'By your blessings and guidance, sir,' said Ikram glibly.

'So, ask yourself this. If the buyer happens to be an underworld don, will the tenants be comfortable with the thought of having a don as landlord?'

'Obviously not. Mafia lords will use every dirty trick in—and outside—the book to vacate the land. Tenants would be terrorised.'

'So tell the tenants that they have two options. Either negotiate with us for an increased rent or negotiate with a don for decreased life-expectancy. I'm sure they'll mostly opt for the former.'

'I've signed the contract for the sewage disposal system, Gangasagarji.'

'Did you keep five per cent for the party, Ikram?'

'Yes. As you instructed.'

'But did you also make sure that the city saves twenty per cent?'

'Yes. The bidding process ensured that.'

'Good. I know that our party coffers need strengthening before the state assembly elections but I refuse to do it without saving money for the citizens too. There have been too many evil officers inside the municipal corporation who have lined their own pockets without doing anything for ordinary citizens.'

'Alas, money is the root of evil.'

'Yes. And sometimes a man needs roots.'

'Let's cut bureaucracy to the best of our ability, commissioner,' suggested Gangasagar. He was seated in the mayor's plush office meeting with the newly-appointed municipal commissioner. The commissioner knew that the real political power was Gangasagar. The mayor was the television set but Gangasagar was the remote control unit.

To please Gangasagar he asked his deputies to draw up guidelines on how they could reduce red tape. It was a lengthy document written in government legalese. It was returned by Gangasagar to the commissioner the next day with a short note attached on top. It simply said:

Gayatri Mantra: 14 words
Pythagorean Theorem: 24 words
Archimedes' Principle: 67 words
The Ten Commandments: 179 words
Jawaharlal Nehru's inaugural speech: 1,094 words
Your recommendations to reduce red tape: 22,913 words

═══

Ikram, Gangasagar and Agrawalji were in their underwear, sitting crosslegged on the private Agrawal riverbank along the Ganges. Behind each of the men stood a *maalishwallah*. They were all reeking of mustard oil, the preferred lubricant used by Kanpur masseurs. They had drenched the scalps of the three men with warm oil and were vigorously rubbing their customers' heads. Agrawalji was bald but that didn't seem to prevent his maalishwallah from polishing his crown enthusiastically. Intermittently, the masseurs would stray from their primary targets—their heads—and manipulate, squeeze and stroke their patrons' necks, shoulders, arms, and backs. It was an orgy of grease and grunts.

Agrawalji asked, 'Ganga, do you think we're strong enough to fight the next state assembly elections?'

'The moot point is not whether we are strong enough but whether we can make the opposition weak enough,' replied Gangasagar, blissfully aware of the masseur inserting his fingers into his ears and giving his eardrums the Indian version of vibration therapy.

'Knowing how you work, I'd say that you already have a plan,' said Agrawalji, stretching out his arms so that the masseur could give his palms a deep-tissue rub using his thumbs in a circular motion—excellent for blood circulation.

'I'm told that our honourable chief minister has a few not-so-honourable vices,' said Gangasagar shiftily.

'What are they?' asked Ikram.

'The more appropriate question is *who* are they,' replied Gangasagar.

'Fine. Who are they?'

'Shall I recite the ladies' names alphabetically?' joked Gangasagar.

'Anyway, how does this help us?' asked Agrawalji. 'Our chief minister has a good track record of governance. With him at the helm, it will be difficult to dislodge the current administration. With him out of the way, though, things would be different.'

'The problem with men who are extremely zealous at work is that they tend to be equally enthusiastic about other pursuits,' suggested Gangasagar.

'With elections around the corner, he will be cautious. He will not be easy to trip up,' said Ikram.

'Quite often, the only way to get rid of temptation is to yield to it,' said Gangasagar quietly.

<hr />

Gulbadan's *kotha* near Akbari Darwaza in Lucknow was quietly famous. It was one of the very few courtesans' residences that had remained frozen in time. The wealthy madam who owned the kotha wore cashmere wool and brocade shawls, smoked from crystal hookahs, drank from jade goblets, walked in bejewelled slippers, spat into silver spittoons and slept on pure silk bedspreads. She slept with only one man, though.

She was extremely choosy. It wasn't about the money —she had enough of it. It was about power. The only thing that could turn her into a wet and wild woman in bed was the thought that she was in the presence of power. And there was no one more powerful in Lucknow than the state's chief minister.

The reporter standing outside the door to the bedroom was untidy and unkempt. His shirt was drenched in patches of sweat, his cheap trousers were crumpled and the shoelaces of his right shoe were dangerously undone. His Buddy Holly-style glasses were greasy and his thick dark hair sprinkled little specks of dandruff on his shoulders. Around his neck, however, hung a very sleek Agilux camera—manufactured in England—with an uncoupled rangefinder. The payoff to the reporter had been generous—almost one month's pay. The tip-off had been perfect—the venue, date and time typed neatly on a slip of unmarked and unsigned paper. It was going to be the biggest scoop of his life.

The maidservant stationed outside the bedroom signalled for him to try the door handle. He gingerly tiptoed to the door, placed his hand on the doorknob and tried it. It was unlocked. Obviously. The maidservant had unlocked it with her own key. The reason for the maidservant's cooperation lay in his hands—a rather large parcel wrapped in brown paper and tied with string. It contained a new miracle drug to fight tuberculosis—a drug produced and available only in America at the time.

The private detective keeping an eye on Gulbadan's kotha had suggested that the girl could be used. Investigation had revealed that the girl's mother was dying of tuberculosis and that the girl was in financial trouble trying to keep up with medical bills. A new medical breakthrough for tuberculosis patients had been recently discovered and Gangasagar had asked Agrawalji to import the medicine through one of his business contacts in New York. Getting the girl to agree to participate in the sting had been child's play thereafter.

The reporter let go of the doorknob and silently gestured for the girl to grasp the handle while he brought the camera to his eye. He whispered, 'At the count of three, fling open the door—one—two—three!' As she flung open the door, he clicked the camera once intuitively. He then searched for the cavorting couple, directed the viewfinder towards them and clicked again. He wanted to take a third but knew he would not have time. The chief minister yelled for his security. 'Guards!' he shouted, 'catch this impudent dog!' But it was too late.

The reporter's exit route through the servants' entrance had been predetermined in collaboration with the maid-servant while the guards were discreetly seated in the chief minister's Ambassador car in the driveway to the house.

The reporter heaved a sigh of relief as he emerged into one of the dark alleys that ran northwards from the house. He picked up pace as he began planning his story for his editor and the next morning's paper. He thought about the photographs captured on his roll of film. He laughed to himself. *The only fucking difference between erotica and porn is the lighting,* he thought to himself.

'He has resigned!' cried Gangasagar triumphantly, 'I knew that we had to play the man, not the ball.'

'You mean the balls,' said Ikram wryly.

'That too,' said the excited Gangasagar, ignoring the joke. 'With his resignation, his party will be in disarray. The left jab that we have just thrown must be followed in quick succession by a right uppercut. It will ensure that the party is unable to recover and regroup,' he said, popping another paan into his mouth.

'Who's the next most powerful person after the chief minister of the state?'

'The state's home minister,' said Ikram.

'And what's the home minister's job?'

'Maintaining law and order.'

'What happens if law and order deteriorate?'

'His colleagues would be reluctant to project him as their alternative candidate.'

'Ikram, as mayor, you have direct access to the police commissioner, don't you?'

'Rascals like me, and the cops, always have a direct connection,' laughed Ikram. 'What exactly do you want done?'

Rajjo Bhaiya sat in the driver's seat of his rugged Mahindra jeep, wiping his bushy black moustache. In his hand he held a steel mug half-filled with *thandai*. The first half of the mugful of iced milk—flavoured with almonds, sugar, fennel, rose petals, pepper, cardamom, saffron, and a generous lacing of white poppy seeds— was already swirling inside his belly. Under trial in twenty-six criminal cases including several of murder, assault and possession of illegal weapons, Rajjo was a member of the state assembly. A confidant of the chief minister who had been caught with his pants down, Rajjo was the other ugly secret of the state's political underbelly.

Sitting next to him was the police commissioner, an old chum who had specifically asked for the meeting in this isolated location. He could not be seen conversing with Rajjo—supposedly the enemy. The indignant press and a gullible public would never accept the reality that Rajjo and the police chief owed their respective occupations to one another. Men like Rajjo were criminals in civvies and, quite often, cops were simply criminals in uniform. The police commissioner was determinedly picking his nose. Midway through his exploration he realised that his throat was itching and he gurgled a deep, guttural cough, brought the offending lump of phlegm to his mouth and spat it out on the ground. Picking his nose and clearing his throat were his favourite hobbies, it seemed.

'The little cuntface has asked me to investigate all pending cases and to make an example of you,' said the police commissioner at last.

'Has he fucking lost his mind? Doesn't the mother-fucker understand that it will hurt the party's own position? I'm a prominent member of the ruling party, aren't I? How's this going to help him win elections?' demanded an enraged Rajjo.

'At this moment the state home minister's bigger priority is to show his colleagues that he has balls. Once his own position is secure, he'll start worrying about the party's performance!' said the commissioner, successfully plucking a nose hair that was irritating him.

'In that case I'll show the pussyface what I'm capable of,' shouted Rajjo, throwing the rest of the thandai onto the soft ground outside the open jeep door.

'There's one way you could send him a signal without declaring open hostilities that would lead to a complete breakdown of law and order,' suggested the police commissioner helpfully.

'And what's that?' grunted Rajjo.

'You could challenge him politically. Hold a rally in his constituency. That should shake him up a little.'

Rajjo smiled. Two of his front teeth were gold. He flashed what he thought was a winning smile and said, 'Who made you into a paper-pushing police commissioner, eh? You should have been a minister—and I don't mean the praying kind!'

＝＝

'I told him not to hold that rally, sir. I explained that it could cause a law and order problem. He assured me he would reconsider his decision. Obviously he didn't,' explained the police commissioner to a worried home minister of Uttar Pradesh.

'So the whorebanger thinks that I will simply accept his outright rebellion?' shouted the minister. 'I'm worried that he'll have the entire party in disarray. Arrest him today!'

The minister was rocking his chair furiously. 'Worry is like a rocking chair,' thought the police commissioner to himself. 'It keeps you busy but gets you fucking nowhere.' He cut short his musings and spoke up.

'That may not be wise, sir. He has a considerable following from his own caste. They see him as a Robin Hood of sorts. We would be playing into his hands by arresting him,' said the police commissioner conspiratorially.

'I'll end up appearing weak and indecisive if I don't arrest him. How's that going to look? You bureaucrats never have to worry about fighting elections. For you, survival means hanging on until retirement; for politicians like me survival is about making it till Sunday morning!'

'I understand your sentiments, sir. May I make a humble suggestion?'

'Go on,' said the agitated minister.

'Why not round up his known associates instead? We'll release them on bail later. It will send a signal that you will not tolerate insubordination, and yet you'll stop short of lashing out at him directly. You'll take the wind out of his sails, sir. He won't have a leg to stand on.'

The home minister of Uttar Pradesh smiled. He was an old man of seventy-five. His teeth had been replaced by dentures, which moved in every direction other than the one he wanted. Giving the police chief a denture-inspired grin he said, 'Why the fuck aren't you in politics? God knows you're devious enough.'

He had stopped rocking his chair.

⊐⊏

'Look at these warring criminals, my friends. They say that they're serious about your safety and security. The truth is that they're busy protecting each other—your safety be damned!' exploded Ikrambhai to the sound of applause.

'Why is that rascal, Rajjo, free to roam about in spite of twenty-six pending criminal cases?' he thundered. There was applause.

'Why is he allowed to thumb his nose at the home minister by roving around the home minister's own constituency? Doesn't it tell you that they're thick as thieves?' There was louder applause.

'Why is this home minister protecting known criminals? Our efficient police commissioner has rounded up hundreds of Rajjo's associates. In each instance, he has been pressured by his political masters to release these men on bail. Why shouldn't we demand the resignation of this spineless creature that dares to call himself home minister?' Thunderous applause and hoots of approval followed.

⊐⊏

'You have made an instant hero out of Ikram,' commented Agrawalji. 'He could quite easily be a claimant for the position of chief minister if the ABNS performs decently in the elections.'

'That's precisely my problem,' said Gangasagar. 'He's not the right man for the job.'

'Are you mentally unstable, Ganga? You've created him from scratch. Now when he's on the verge of capturing the reins of power in Uttar Pradesh, you want him to back off? Unbelievable!' muttered Agrawalji.

'Have you heard of atropine?' asked Gangasagar.

'No. What is it?'

'It's a poison. It is extracted from a plant called Deadly Nightshade.'

'You plan to poison Ikram, Ganga? Isn't that over-doing things?'

'I'm simply telling you that this dangerous poison—atropine—is also used as an antidote to nerve agents. Even though it's a poison, it can fight a bigger menace when it's used in small doses.'

'So Ikram is the poison that's to be used in small doses?'

'Unfortunately, he's now past the expiry date on the label.'

≡≡

She walked towards her shanty, satchel slung over her shoulder. Her pocket money for the day had been spent on a bag of spiced peanuts—tangy lemon-and-red chilli-flavoured peanuts were her favourite snack. As the teenage girl hummed a tune from the latest Bollywood flick that her father had splurged on the previous week, she thought about flying away to a new world—one in which there was no poverty, disease, decay, and squalor. Chandini did not notice the inebriated goon who had been following her.

She was a few minutes away from home and took a right turn that led her into a windowless alley between two tenements. She was nearing the bend of the isolated stretch when he reached out and grabbed her by her shoulders from behind. She spun around and faced him, the peanuts falling to the ground, scattering around her.

He lunged forward in an attempt to grab her breasts. His stinking breath repelled her and she screamed, but something prevented her voice from carrying. It was his hand. He had managed to spin her around, clamp down a hand on her mouth from behind, leaving his other hand free to molest her. He pressed his hardness into her from behind and she struggled, desperate to free herself from his lecherous clutch.

She opened her mouth and bit down hard, capturing some of the flesh of his fingers. He screamed in anguish and instinctively let go of her. She swung around, looked him in the eyes, smiled at him, took aim and kicked him right between his legs. He doubled over in agony, holding his balls, muttering curses at her.

Chandini smiled. The weak little girl had vanished for that solitary moment. She said, 'The next time you try to touch me, I shall be so powerful, I shall simply order your castration.'

She then ran home sobbing.

![decorative divider]

'I want her,' said Gangasagar. 'I need her badly.'

'But Gangasagarji, little Chandini is already sixteen. I must now get her married. How can I leave her with you?' asked Gupta.

'Haven't I delivered on all the promises I made?' asked Gangasagar, pointing to the new school and hospital in the distance. 'Moreover, she will become immensely powerful one day. You shall be proud of her. I promise!'

'What work will she do within the party?'

'At this moment I want her to complete her education abroad. When she returns she'll be an ordinary party worker. She'll visit constituencies where natural calamities—floods, famine, drought or earthquakes—have displaced populations. She will work along with the party workers to endear herself to them. She must build a political and social platform she can stand on.'

'What else do you want from me, Gangasagarji?'

'I need you to allow her to be adopted.'

'Are you out of your mind, Gangasagarji? She has living parents and you want her to find new ones? What's wrong with the ones that she has?' shouted Gupta, paan-streaked spittle spewing from his mouth.

'I want Ikrambhai to adopt her.'

'You *are* mad! Allow my darling daughter to be adopted by a Muslim? No! A thousand times no!'

'She shall be adopted in name only. She shall continue to be your daughter.'

'But why this outrageous plan?'

'If Ikrambhai adopts her, I shall achieve three significant things. Firstly, the cost of her education abroad shall be borne by Ikrambhai. Second, Ikram will see her as a daughter and natural political successor. And third, it will give her universal acceptability in India—a Hindu girl with Muslim parents. Wonderful political combination,' he mused.

'But if he adopts her, then she will cease to be my daughter!' wailed Gupta.

'*Shariat*—Muslim Personal Law—does not recognise adoption.'

'So how would he adopt her if his own law does not validate it?'

'He must prove in civil court that the adoption is a custom allowed by his specific regional community.'

'And is it allowed?'

'No. Adoption is prevalent amongst many classes of Muslims in Punjab, Sindh, Kashmir, Rajasthan and Madhya Pradesh. But it isn't common among Muslims of Uttar Pradesh. Ikram won't be able to prove anything in court.'

'I don't get it. You want him to adopt her so that his own religious law as well as the civil court can overrule the adoption?'

'Absolutely. The adoption cannot be legalised, so she stays your daughter. But the sentiment is there and politics is all about sentiment and symbolism. She will symbolically represent a union of two great faiths—Hinduism and Islam.'

'Why would Ikrambhai adopt her in the first place?'

'Because she would get him Hindu votes just as he gets her Muslim ones! It shall be a symbiotic relationship.'

━ ━

'No, no, and no. A thousand times—no! I refuse to be adopted by Ikrambhai.'

'Chandini. Listen to—'

'No. Uncle Ganga, I know he's your political ally, but I have a decent father and a caring mother. I will not be adopted by Ikrambhai.'

'I am not asking you to renounce your parents. Your parents will remain your parents. No one can ever change that. I am simply building up your political resumè, my girl—'

'But how can I give up my parents? It's too high a price to pay!'

'You were lucky that you did not get raped, Chandini,' said Gangasagar quietly.

'Luck had nothing to do with it.'

'But what if it had been someone else? Do you know that a woman gets raped every half an hour in India?'

'No. I never—'

'Do you know that a woman gets killed every two hours—usually for not bringing in a large enough dowry?'

'Yes—I mean—no—I don't know—'

'Do you want to be one of those statistics, Chandini?'

'No, Uncle Ganga.'

'Don't you want to rule the country? Be powerful? Never have to be at any man's mercy?'

'Yes.'

'Don't you want to get away from this filth and poverty that surrounds you?'

'Yes.'

'Don't you want the very best international education that could propel your career? Make your life?'

'Yes.'

'Then do what I say! Let Ikram adopt you!'

The girl nodded silently in acquiescence and Ganga-sagar smiled. He would need to ensure that Ikram's goon, who had been given the assignment of following and terrorising the girl, kept his mouth shut.

'*Adi Shakti, Namo Namah; Sarab Shakti, Namo Namah; Prithum Bhagvati, Namo Namah; Kundalini Mata Shakti; Mata Shakti, Namo Namah,*' he muttered softly to himself.

CHAPTER FIVE
About 2300 years ago

The smell of human excrement was overpowering. The harsh stone floor was slick with a thick slime of blood, sweat, urine and faecal matter. The fetid bowels of Dhanananda's prison complex heralded the arrival of the new visitor with the bloodcurdling screams of tortured inmates. The dim light provided by a few flaming torches revealed little of the roughly-hewn rock walls with an assortment of chains and restraints bolted to them.

As the gate to the filthy cell slammed shut, Chanakya felt something slither over his foot, probably a snake. He instinctively slammed down his other foot on the slippery creature and held his foot down until he felt the reptile lying motionless. He stood glued to the spot for quite some time, allowing his eyes to adjust to the dark. As his pupils dilated, he was able to discern a couple of rats fighting over a piece of flesh, quite possibly human.

'One may wash one's anus a hundred times and it will still be vile,' thought Chanakya, 'and Dhanananda may hand out a thousand endowments to Brahmins but he will still remain corrupt!' Chanakya set about finding himself a corner that was least polluted and eventually sat himself down with his back against a damp wall. The cell did not have any windows. There was a complete absence of ventilation. He closed his eyes and began his *pranayama*—the yogic breathing exercises taught by the venerable sage Dandayan—to help him cope with the unhealthy conditions.

Unexpectedly he heard a click and saw a thin dancing sliver of light emerge through the gate. It was a dwarf holding an oil lamp in his hand. He quietly raised his finger to his lips, signalling to Chanakya for complete silence. With a quick jerk of his head he motioned Chanakya to get up and follow him.

The little man led him to an extremely constricted cavity along one of the walls. The midget did not seem to mind the narrow space as he efficiently tied a rope firmly around Chanakya's waist. Chanakya did not know where the other end of the rope was located. Suddenly he felt a tug and found himself being lifted off his feet. He was in some sort of chute that was extremely tight and claustrophobic. During the upward ascent, Chanakya's face, thighs and hands grazed the duct surfaces and either burned from friction or bled from gashes. After what seemed like an eternity, he felt cool air and heard the sound of running water. He was back along the banks of the Ganges.

He was startled to see an entire band of dwarves pulling the rope that held him. Their leader stepped forward and explained. 'Do not be alarmed, acharya. Katyayanji asked us to help. He needed us gnomes to access the ancient escape duct leading from the prison. As you've observed, the passage is very narrow—and that's after we've widened it for you.'

'I am grateful to you and to Katyayanji, but who are you? What is it that you do for a living?' asked Chanakya, intuitively inquisitive even in distress.

'Dwarves have always had a very important function in Magadha, acharya. We've usually been guarders of the royal *kosh*—the treasury. As you know, most royal treasuries are established in concealed spots and have secret corridors not accessible to thieves and bandits. We small people are ideal guards.'

'But you're servants of the king. Why would you help me?'

'Our greater wish was to help our beloved former prime minister, Shaktarji, who created the royal kosh in the first place, and the system of dwarves guarding it. He has remained a prisoner here for many years. We have quietly and determinedly been working on extending this passage for several months now and were able to get him out just moments before you. Getting you out was our next move. Katyayanji and Senapati Maurya assembled us for this mission.'

'Senapati Maurya—the commander-in-chief of Magadha's army? He's working against Dhanananda?'

'It's better that he tells you himself, sir.'

'Where is Prime Minister Shaktarji?'

'He's already been taken to Pipplivan where Senapati Maurya awaits him. He needs to be kept secure from the king and there's no safer place than the camp of Senapati Maurya. Acharya, you're also to proceed to Pipplivan immediately. The alarm will have been sounded and the royal guards will be searching for you. I have a horse waiting.'

'But what of Katyayanji? I have to meet him and apologise for having unleashed my temper in Dhanananda's court,' said Chanakya.

'He knows you too well, sir. He's also on the side of truth and justice. He believes, however, that he can do much more to eradicate Dhanananda and his abominable government by being inside rather than outside. He says that you're the tiger that will attack Dhanananda from the outside while he's simply the germ that will create a storm inside Dhanananda's stomach!'

In the quiet of the dark night—not unlike the dark night when Chanakya had cremated his father and fled—they set off for Pipplivan on horseback.

***

It was still a few hours before dawn when they reached Pipplivan—not much more than a cluster of huts and mud-brick houses located along the banks of a stream. The Lilliputian horsemen led him to one of the slightly larger houses. The senapati was awake and conferring with someone who got up and left the moment their party arrived.

Senapati Maurya was relieved to see Chanakya safe. He bowed before the acharya and said 'Magadha needs you, O wise teacher. Help me rid my motherland of the leeches that are sucking her dry!'

'The time's not yet ripe, Senapati. The only great achievements that make it to the pages of history are those to which tremendous thought and preparation have been given.'

'I await your guidance, revered teacher. But come, you must be tired. And your wounds and scratches need to be cleaned. I'll ask my wife to provide clean garments and some breakfast. Please follow me, I'll show you where you can bathe.'

'Better treatment than I would have expected at the hands of a *vrishala*,' thought Chanakya to himself.

Maurya was considered a vrishala—an outcaste Kshatriya —by upper-caste Brahmins such as Chanakya. Maurya's father had abandoned the strict caste hierarchy of Hinduism to adopt the ways of the great teacher, Gautam Buddha. The senapati had eventually returned to the folds of Hinduism but would permanently bear the mark of Hindu indignation towards the prodigal by being branded a vrishala.

Bathed, dressed, and morning prayers concluded, Chanakya sat on the little terrace outside Maurya's hut. The senapati's wife had placed before him a simple breakfast of millet porridge and hot milk. The sun had just risen and peacocks were dancing in the garden outside, their iridescent blue-green plumage fanning out to reveal their mysteriously beautiful feathered eyes. This was the land of peacocks, and Maurya derived his own family name from them—*mor*—peacock.

Outside the house, a group of young boys was busy in a game of role-playing. One of them had tied a scarf around his head and had tucked a peacock feather into his headband. He was the make-believe emperor, sitting atop a large rock. The other boys standing around him were either subjects or court officials.

'Attention! The court of the wise and benevolent Maharaj Chandragupta, Emperor of the world, is now in session. Come and be heard!' droned a boy playing the role of prime minister and standing by the king's side.

'O great King. I'm in trouble. My neighbour sold me his well but he continues to draw water from it. Please stop him,' pleaded a boy acting the part of the aggrieved.

'Who is the seller of the well?' asked the miniature king.

'I am, my lord. But I sold him the well, not the water inside it. Please let your justice prevail,' replied another boy, slightly older.

Addressing the senior one, the king grandly pronounced, 'You're right. You sold the well, not the water. This would mean that you're wrongly keeping water in someone else's well. Please empty it! Next case!'

Chanakya chuckled to himself. He was watching this little drama with great interest. He decided to join the fun. He got up from the terrace where he was seated, walked up and stood before the king with folded hands.

'Yes, Brahmin? What is it that you want?' asked the boy seriously.

'O illustrious King, I'm a poor Brahmin. I need milk and ghee for the *yajnas*—the rituals—that I perform but I have no cow. Please assist me, O protector of the land,' said Chanakya earnestly.

'Treasurer! Give this Brahmin a cow,' commanded the king as the mock official came forward to hand Chanakya a pebble—the substitute cow.

'But I don't have any money to pay for it, my king,' explained Chanakya.

'O Brahmin. If your offerings to the gods are inadequate, how will the bounty of my kingdom be adequate? And if my kingdom is not prosperous, from where will I collect taxes? And if there are no taxes, what will happen to the treasury and the army? Who will defend the kingdom if there is no army? So, you see, I am not doing you a favour. I'm simply guaranteeing my own prosperity!' explained the intellectual giant of a boy.

Chanakya smiled and blessed the boy. 'Who are you, child?' he asked.

'I am Chandragupta. The son of Senapati Maurya.'

'Shall I take you to meet Shaktarji?' enquired the senapati emerging from the house. Chanakya nodded. It was time to meet his departed father's dearest friend —a comrade for whom Chanak had laid down his very life.

The old man that Chanakya saw was frail and battered. Years of deprivation, foul living conditions, food unfit for human consumption, sickness, and brutal repression had taken their toll on the former prime minister. Chanakya's memories of Shaktar were of an aristocratic and sophisticated noble, always impeccably dressed in the finest silks and adorned with the richest of gold and diamond amulets, rings and necklaces. He could barely recognise what once used to be the second-most powerful man in the kingdom.

Chanakya prostrated himself before Shaktar and the old man asked him to rise. When Chanakya got up and saw Shaktar's face, the octogenarian had tears in his eyes. He reached out his hand to place it on Chanakya's head to bless him affectionately.

'You're the only son that I have left, Chanakya. My real sons are all dead. And my daughter—Suvasini— whom you loved so dearly, is worse than dead. Your father never broached the topic but I knew that he wanted you and my daughter to eventually marry, merging both families into one.'

Chanakya remained silent.

'What terrible conjunction of planets in my horo-scope has produced this endless nightmare? My wife, dead; my best friend Chanak, dead; my sons, dead; my daughter, a concubine of Rakshas; my body, shattered and weak; the kingdom—in the hands of a psychopath!' continued the old man as his misery flooded over.

Chanakya gripped Shaktar's hand and said, 'The nightmare shall end soon. I promise. But you need to stir yourself from this troubled slumber. One must awake, see the rays of the sun, and realise that it was all just a terrible dream. Help me, Shaktarji and senapatiji.'

'What do I possess that can help you, Chanakya?' asked Senapati Maurya.

'Chandragupta.'

'And what do I have that can possibly help?' asked Shaktar.

'The dwarves.'

<hr />

The kings of Magadha knew that an army moves on its stomach. The royal treasury—the *rajakosh*—was even more critical than the army itself because the treasury was the fuel that propelled the fighting machine. Mining was a state monopoly so all the gold, silver or precious stones mined in the land automatically found their way to the rajakosh.

The protection and security of the rajakosh was achieved in various ways. The official state treasury would always be located in the capital but be built in such a way that access to the prized metals and gems would be through three underground floors of trapdoors and removable ladders. The wall and floors of the underground structure would lie encased in an extra-thick layer of stone so that any ambitious tunnel thief would find his access permanently blocked. The treasury would usually be located in the northern quarter of the capital, sandwiched between the royal residence and the city's main temple. Concentric circles of guards would police the treasury day and night, while sharpshooters with bows and poisoned arrows would man the innumerable towers that surrounded the rajakosh. It was instant death for any thug seeking material gratification.

The other measure of security was to decentralise the rajakosh and to create secret troves in remote locations. Usually, condemned prisoners would build such remote treasure hides and would be executed shortly thereafter. With the exception of the king and his prime minister, no one would know the whereabouts of such clandestine stores. Very often, the actual storehouse would be built in a pit underground with narrow secret passages for access. On purpose, many of these would be built to prevent access to a full-grown adult and, often, the only way to reach the store would be by sending down trained dwarves. The hoard would usually be camouflaged with dense vegetation, snakes, scorpions and wild animals let loose in the environs to discourage bounty-seekers.

Chanakya knew that the previous prime minister, Shaktar, would be aware of any covert repository of Dhanananda, and that the key to accessing the prize would be Katyayan's dwarves.

The jungles to the north of Pipplivan were vast and foreboding. Arranged in concentric circles like the layers of an onion, each peeled away to reveal another, even more dark and isolated. The outermost skin was that of productive thickets used for producing timber, herbs and medicinal plants; further inside lay the ascetic woodlands reserved for holy men's ashrams and penances; travelling inwards one reached the hunting parks used by kings and nobles for sport; another peel and one reached the elephant reserves managed by the state for breeding of elephants that would be used in the army; and finally, the innermost circle consisted of wildlife sanctuaries, where lions, tigers, leopards and cheetahs roamed free. The secret rajakosh revealed by Shaktar was located within this core.

The horses had been left with a rather relieved band of guards at least one *yojana*—about four miles—back. The dense vegetation and the virtual absence of any pathway had made it impossible for the beasts to travel any further. Chanakya, Senapati Maurya and Jeevasiddhi —a trusted aide of Katyayan—and their band of dwarves made slow but steady progress. The map provided by Shaktar was proving to be quite useful and most of the key landmarks had been found in spite of the constantly changing forest environment.

The team had been chosen very carefully for the expedition. If one took too many people on a treasure hunt one risked the possibility of information reaching the ears of Dhanananda. If the team was pared, one ran the risk of being killed by wild animals or being left with inadequate hands to cart the loot.

They were nearing a pile of boulders overrun by vines that had aggressively taken over territory in their amorous embrace. Chanakya's calculations told him he was very near the final destination, but before he could consult his map he heard the whoosh of an arrow and felt the heat of the missile graze his left cheek. Immediately alert, he raised his sword to engage in combat with the offender, and found that it was none other than Jeevasiddhi, who was still pointing another arrow—duly loaded in his taut and tense bow—in his direction.

Any ordinary man would have viewed Jeevasiddhi suspiciously, but not Chanakya. From Jeevasiddhi's eyes he could discern that even though his weapons were pointed at him, his eyes were looking beyond him. Chanakya calmly swung around with his back to Jeevasiddhi and saw the body of an enormous tiger that had been caught mid-leap by his protector's projectile. The beautiful beast lay on the ground with the arrow half-piercing his neck.

Chanakya turned around, placed his sword back in its sheath, and raised his hand in a gesture of blessing towards Jeevasiddhi. No words were exchanged but the silent pantomime had conveyed the full import of a thousand words. From that day onwards, Jeevasiddhi would be one of the acharya's trusted lieutenants.

They stealthily crept towards the boulders, thick with a carpet of moss and creepers. Chanakya instructed Senapati Maurya to remove from his cloth pouch a dry powder he had supervised the mixing of. Maurya handed it over to the dwarves who went about sprinkling small quantities of the substance all around the rubble. It was actually a dry rhizome of mint oil, putrescent eggs, garlic, thyme oil and sulphur and smelled positively putrid. Brahmins traditionally shunned many of the ingredients such as eggs and garlic but Chanakya had nonetheless remained present while the dwarves ground and dried the mixture.

As the air filled with the stench of the terrible compound, there was a sudden rustle as scores of snakes slithered out of the stones and fled from Chanakya's reptile repellant. Chanakya nodded, and Senapati Maurya and Jeevasiddhi moved in to clear a path to the trapdoor that would lead to a maze of underground tunnels.

Camouflaged with boulders and overgrown vegetation, the trapdoor was very small—certainly no more than around fifteen *angulas* wide—around a foot. Senapati Maurya's mace shattered the ancient copper locking mechanism and within a few minutes they could see a dark and narrow vertical duct that led into the depths. A long rope was secured to one of the boulders and a dwarf cautiously made his way inside with a small flaming torch strapped to his head. A few minutes later he yelled, 'It's empty! I need to search for another door. Send down the next man.' A second dwarf followed the first, carrying carpenter's tools. A while later the sounds of hammering revealed that they had located the trapdoor inside the first level. A third dwarf scampered down holding a loop of rope that would be used to go down the second trapdoor.

'Praise Lakshmi!' shouted a dwarf from within. 'We've hit the mother lode!' Chanakya, Senapati Maurya and Jeevasiddhi looked at each other and smiled. A few more dwarves were sent down the passage so that a relay team could be set up for conveying instructions and materials. 'Send up small quantities of whatever lies within,' instructed Chanakya. 'We do not have enough men to carry everything away. We should concentrate our efforts on the richest and lightest material.' An assortment of treasures began to appear before them—diamonds, pearls, rubies, sapphires, pure crystal, beryl, silver panas and copper *kakani*.

'Search for cow dung and sesame oil,' instructed Chanakya.

The senapati and Jeevasiddhi looked at the acharya wondering whether he had gone mad. Apparently he hadn't, because very soon, bricks of cow dung mixed with sesame oil began to appear via the relay team. 'Don't be fooled by the cow dung,' explained Chanakya to his accomplices. 'All gold is purified with lead and the excess lead is removed using cow dung. If the gold is brittle, it is softened in sesame oil. Thus, the ideal way to store gold is by encasing it in a mixture of cow dung and sesame oil. What you're seeing before you is pure gold!'

'The first preference is to be given to gold, which is high in value and also easily monetised. The next priority should be silver panas, and finally diamonds and rubies. We do not wish to carry copper, pearls, sapphire, or crystal. Please also ignore other treasury commodities such as sandalwood, aloe, incense, and camphor,' continued

Chanakya. Maurya and Jeevasiddhi were amazed at Chanakya's depth of knowledge in matters of treasure and asked, 'Acharya, you're a holy man—a revered teacher. Why do you concern yourself with articles of wealth?'

Chanakya answered them, while keeping one eye firmly glued to the little mountain of precious articles that was taking shape before them. 'What should a man strive for? *Kama*—love, *dharma*—duty, *artha*—wealth, and *moksha*—salvation. But the fact is that neither your wife nor your children will love you if you're poor, no single citizen will ever perform his duty if he's not motivated by financial incentives or penalties, and which man can renounce his worldly life in quest of salvation if he does not have wealth to support the family he leaves behind? I'm a teacher—but a teacher of *arthashastra*, the science of wealth. The source of livelihood of men is wealth, and the science of the means of attaining and protecting it is politics!'

Chanakya and his accomplices headed back to Pipplivan, their horses laden with abundant treasures and armed guards in tow. That evening, sitting outside with a campfire for warmth, Chanakya broached the topic. 'Senapati, you have done your duty and lived your life. But your vision of a grand and prosperous Magadha can only be realised through Chandragupta, who has all the traits of a king. Let me take him to Takshila where I can prepare him for kingship. In the meantime, you can start using the treasury that we've just gained to help me build an army.'

The commander reflected on Chanakya's words and spoke. 'Acharya. He's my only son. I can't bear to be parted from him. Can't you stay here with us instead?' Chanakya smiled. 'I wish it were that easy to unite a kingdom, Senapati. As we speak, the borders at Gandhar are in imminent danger of being attacked by Alexander's battalions. If Gandhar falls, the rest of Bharat will follow. How does one keep the enemy out if the door has already been forced open? The army that I wish to raise from the wealth that we've acquired is to fight the Macedonian intrusions, as well as to create a glue that can consolidate the fractious petty kingdoms that never seem to unite on any issue—not even critical ones,' he elucidated.

'In that case, should my wife and I come along with you and Chandragupta to Takshila?' asked Maurya. 'I don't think that's a good idea,' argued Chanakya. 'Chandragupta has far greater chance of success if you're not with him. You're a direct enemy of Dhanananda and his spies will always be on the lookout for you. Studying among hundreds of students at Takshila will keep Chandragupta anonymous and out of danger. Above all, I need you, Shaktarji and Katyayanji, to be in or around Magadha so that we have adequate feet on the street to give Dhanananda the trouble he deserves by the time Chandragupta returns.'

The senapati called out to his wife who had been listening to the conversation from within the house. As she came out and warmed her hands from the campfire, Maurya asked her what she thought of the acharya's suggestion. Her words bore the stamp of a true *Kshatrayin*—the wife of a warrior. 'We were among the few lucky ones to receive some of Buddha's ashes. Let's remember that our revered lord renounced his entire kingdom in his quest for moksha. As Kshatriyas, our duty lies in protecting all life. If we must renounce our son for a greater purpose, so be it,' she said simply. 'A Brahmin without knowledge or a Kshatriya without courage is of little use to society.'

Senapati Maurya was born of the union of Mahanandin, the powerful Shishunga ruler of Magadha, and his wife Mura, the only daughter of the chief of the *Moriyas*—the warrior tribes of Pipplivan. Although Senapati Maurya would have made an excellent successor to Mahanandin, the old king had many other sons who were considered more appropriate for the role. As it turned out, none of his better-qualified sons would ever make it to the throne. Old Mahanandin was very fond of his barber, a shrewd, smooth-talking fellow called Mahapadma. Mahapadma was the illegitimate child of a Kshatriya father and a Shudra mother.

The wily barber Mahapadma ingratiated himself not only with the king but also his queen, Sunanda. Before long he had graduated from shaving the king to fornicating with the queen. Having screwed the queen, the barber, with the help of the queen, decided to screw the king as well, by bumping him off and all other claimants to the throne. The only one left alive was a little boy—Maurya—who was simply too young to be perceived as a threat.

Although Mahapadma was a mere barber, he possessed an uncanny raw intelligence. He recognised the talent of Senapati Maurya and eventually made him the commander of his armed forces. Mahapadma was a tyrant, but a benevolent one. Under his reign, crime became virtually nonexistent and the petty nobles who had become tyrants during Mahanandin's reign were ruthlessly put down. Mahapadma conquered most of north Bharat and the Deccan, and brought vast tracts of land, from the Himalayas to Kuntala, and from the Jamuna to the Brahmaputra, under his authority and made Magadha into the most powerful state in north Bharat. Though he was a Kshatriya-Shudra, he patronised Brahmins and learned gurus such as Vararuchi,

Vyadi and Varsha. High levels of efficiency, strong military authority, fair taxation, massive irrigation projects, and an overall attitude of benevolence and tolerance characterised his reign.

The golden period would change dramatically under his son Dhanananda. Senapati Maurya was seen as a liability rather than an asset by the twisted son. The man who had helped Mahapadma conquer most of Bharat was now a fugitive himself—and was seething with anger for having been made one.

Chanakya loved anger. It was a wonderfully energetic emotion and could be used very productively if channelled in the right direction.

CHAPTER SIX
Present Day

Miss Feversham slowly looked her up and down. 'I'm going to be brutally honest. Your shoulders are rounded, your knees are tight and your tummy's sticking out.' It was another excruciating hour of intensive instruction. Chandini instinctively pulled in her tummy and tried lifting her shoulders. The result was even more awkward. Miss Feversham sighed. This was going to be very difficult indeed. Chandini was in Miss Feversham's finishing school in London—and was utterly finished. 'You have one shoulder higher than the other and your feet roll outwards. Your slouch is unladylike.'

Chandini was made to stand up and sit down several times, and her movements were observed in excruciating detail. 'You're taking up a lot of space. And look at all those angles when you stand up. You also fidget too much with your hands. You look a bit like a mouse. A mouse is a humble thing. When you walk you must lead with the solar plexus, situated somewhere around the bottom of your bra. Hold your head up and keep your neck elongated!' said Miss Feversham, running a stick between Chandini's arms and back to keep her shoulders down, and straight.

Over the past month, Miss Feversham had focused on the girl's English. Chandini's English skills, acquired in a slum school of Kanpur, were fine for impressing her own parents but were of no help in communicating in England. Miss Feversham's lessons concentrated on helping Chandini communicate effectively and confidently in everyday, idiomatic English. The wide-ranging syllabus was geared to improving her listening, reading, writing and speaking abilities.

But knowing the language was insufficient. Chandini needed to be taught how to use a fork and knife—*if there are several pieces of cutlery, use forks, knives or spoons on the outside first;* how to order food in a pub—*could you tell me what the soup of the day is, please;* how to attend a party—*take a bottle of wine or some flowers or chocolates to present to the host;* how to pay a restaurant bill—*if the bill says service not included, it's usual to add about ten per cent by way of a tip;* how to drink tea—*if the teapot contains loose tea, place the tea strainer onto the cup before pouring;* and how to eat scones the proper way—*use a knife to cut the scone into two halves, put jam on each side, there's no need to add butter first, then spread clotted cream on top carefully. Eat the top and bottom halves separately and please do not try to make them into a sandwich.*

'When you speak, keep your hand movements slow and graceful. And when you are about to sit, stand at right angles to the front of the chair, twist your upper half, lower yourself down and tuck one leg behind the other. It must be done slowly and with no accompanying sound,' explained Miss Feversham to the girl.

'When it comes to physical contact, the English are still deeply reserved. The preferred English handshake has no hint of lingering. "How do you do?" signals the end of the greeting and there should not be any deviation from this. Women who know each other well may kiss each other on one or both cheeks. When women do, the "miss kiss" is to be used, the kisser making a kissing gesture with the appropriate sound in the air in the general region of the recipient's ears. Men may kiss women in greeting, but only on one cheek, not both,' explained Miss Feversham to the bewildered girl.

The English were crazy.

<hr />

Oxfordshire was one of England's most picturesque cities. Chandini was awed by the architectural grandeur and historical import of the university, established eight hundred years ago. The glorious buildings of the Bodleian Library, the Radcliffe Camera, the Sheldonian Theatre and the Ashmolean Museum blended together seamlessly to create a heady mix of history, culture, liberated thought and intellectual freedom. Like all newbies, Chandini walked up to the top of Carfax Tower and then panted her way up the steps of the University Church located on High Street, both of which provided uninterrupted vistas of the breathtaking city.

Among all the colleges that dotted the Oxford University campus, Christ Church College was the largest and most magnificent. In fact, the grand college church doubled as the Oxford Cathedral. Towards the eastern side of Oxford ran the most beautiful street in Europe— the alluring High Street, located close to two of Oxford's most idyllic parks—Headington Hill and South Park. It wasn't merely the buildings of Oxford that were impressive. God seemed to have bestowed all of nature's abundance and splendour on a single city. Acres of undulating meadows, grazing farm animals and sparkling streams of the Thames created a virtual Eden.

Miss Feversham's finishing school had increased Chandini's confidence, but the awkwardness of a shy and introverted girl from a Kanpur slum suddenly transplanted into the rarefied atmosphere of Oxford would remain for some more time. Her trip from Paddington to St Hilda's—the all-women's college at Oxford—had been terrifying on account of her over-whelming fear that everyone that she encountered in Oxford would be intellectually, financially and socially superior. The friendly family atmosphere of St Hilda's Junior Common Room, however, put her at ease from the very first moment. She had been allotted a room in Garden Building, Wolfson, a part of St Hilda's grounds. As she lugged her suitcase up to her room, a tall lanky blonde stepped up to help her with her luggage. 'Hello. My name's Josephine Richardson—I'm an art major. I think you're the Indian girl who has been allotted the room next to mine.'

'Nice to meet you,' said Chandini, plucking up her courage from Miss Feversham's feverish drills, 'and thanks for helping me with my luggage.'

'No problem. Shall we head over to the Buttery when you're done settling in?' asked Josephine.

'The Butt—the what?' asked Chandini.

'The Buttery is St Hilda's tuck shop that sells toasties, chips, hot chocolate, and tea. You'll find most of us girls there. I'll wait for you. Ah! Here we are. The standard issue room comes with a single bed and blanket, a desk, two chairs, a sink, a wardrobe, and a chest-of-drawers—you'll need your own bed linen, though. If you want I can show you a nice place to buy some.' Chandini's fears and depression began to wear off rather quickly in the presence of juiced-up Josephine.

The world's most renowned debating society had been established in 1823. It was called the Oxford Union and stayed the focal point of contentious debates unparalleled in their content and influence. The famous 1933 motion, 'This House will under no circumstances fight for King and Country' had been passed by 275 votes to 153 in the Oxford Union and had ignited national indignation in the media. Winston Churchill had condemned the 'ever shameful motion' as an 'abject, squalid, shameless avowal'. Many believed that the vote had played a significant role in reinforcing Hitler's decision to invade Europe. Members of the Oxford Union couldn't care less what Churchill and the media thought. Divergence and forthrightness remained central to the Union's founding philosophy.

Josephine and Chandini were attending an event organised by the Union to welcome its latest batch of members. As they were introduced to the president, Chandini complimented him on the work done by the Union in maintaining a free society through open debate. The president smiled at her as he shook her hand and said, 'A free society is one where it's safe to be unpopular, but then, freedom of speech also carries with it the freedom not to listen!'

At that moment, Chandini decided that this was going to be her forte, as she along with the rest of the novices began the journey into the fascinating world of political argument.

The chairman for the debate opened the Thursday-night event with a few words on the debate and voting procedures. 'Ladies and gentlemen. It's a pleasure for me to chair this debate, because there's no issue which has been as long running or as divisive across the world.

The motion for today is, *this House believes that women must be legally guaranteed equal pay.*' He then called on the first speaker, Geoffrey Hemingford, to begin the debate.

It was the duty of the first speaker for the proposition to introduce the other speakers. 'Mr Chairman, as the first speaker it is my honour to introduce your guests this evening. The first speaker for the opposition, Chandini Gupta is—possibly—Oxford's next prime ministerial candidate for India. In the past few years she has established an unblemished track record for winning arguments irrespective of whether she actually believes them—an important trait for any politician—and I daresay that her personal views might possibly be at variance with the official line that she takes tonight. I'm delighted to be sparring with her. Supporting me is the second speaker for the proposition, Elizabeth Lytton. Elizabeth's own job at Lytton, Tryon & Yarborough is already guaranteed and deservedly so, I might add. One of the brightest young minds of Oxford, Elizabeth will argue for the motion. The second speaker for the opposition, Victor Walsingham, shall follow. Victor has spent the last twelve months of his self-imposed sabbatical travelling America and shall bring us refreshing insights from his observations of our cousins across the pond. Mr Chairman, these are your guests and they are most welcome.' Polite applause from the audience of around five hundred followed.

'Mr Chairman,' began Geoffrey, 'the Representation of the People Act, 1918, granted women the right to vote in Great Britain. But funnily enough, only women who were over the age of thirty and owned houses were deemed intelligent enough to place a mark on ballot slips. Ten years later the law was amended and all women over twenty-one were given the right to vote. Should we have stood back and waited for natural forces to right the wrong?'

Geoffrey noticed several women in the audience nodding their heads in agreement and pushed on. 'For most women the blessings in the years that followed the end of the war were mixed indeed. Women who had held jobs of metalworkers and ironworkers in aircraft and munitions factories suddenly found that their *man's job* and *man's pay* had vanished. Rosie the Riveter reluctantly went back to waiting on tables as Rosie the Waitress. At lower than pre-war levels of pay! Equal pay, in effect, implied seventy-five per cent of the male rate. This fundamental discrimination has carried through into our generation. Should we allow this gross injustice to prevail?' he demanded.

'Mr Chairman, it is argued that if parliamentary intervention were needed, the majority of our honourable Members of Parliament would indeed have voted in favour of such a motion by now. The argument offered is that the majority has not. I would like to remind this audience that sometimes a majority only means that all the fools are on the same side. This is the present case,' said Geoffrey. He smiled acknowledging the loud applause from the women present and sat down.

Chandini arose and surveyed her audience. Men made up more than half, so she knew she had to get them on her side. She began by introducing the first speaker for the proposition, Geoffrey Hemingford, who had just spoken. Geoffrey was extremely popular, having been instrumental in Oxford's victory over Cambridge in the boat race the previous year. On race day, a quarter of a million spectators had crowded the banks of the Thames from Putney to Mortlake to witness Geoffrey's team win the race. Chandini knew that she needed to get votes—there was no point in winning an argument and losing the case.

'Mr Chairman, as the first speaker for the opposition it is my pleasant duty to introduce the first speaker for the proposition, Mr Geoffrey Hemingford, not that he needs any introduction. You all know the old tale about our friends from North Fens Polytechnic,' she said, using the derogative term used by Oxonians for Cambridge, 'and their decision to field a rowing team. Even though they'd practise for hours each day, they never managed to beat Oxford. Finally, the team decided to send a spy. Their spy hid in the bushes and carefully watched the Oxford team—led by Geoffrey—at their daily practice. After two weeks the spy returned and announced that he'd discovered their rivals' secret. "What? Tell us!" his teammates said. "We should have just one guy yelling. The other eight should be rowing!" said the spy.' There was loud applause and appreciation for Chandini's compliment to the Oxonian rowing hero. She moved on, having won the affection of most of the men in the audience.

'Mr Chairman, it has been said that married men live significantly longer than single men. This in itself should be an argument in favour of women in the workplace. Their mere presence would increase the longevity of their male colleagues. But I'm also given to understand that while married men live significantly longer than single men, they're apparently a lot more willing to die.'

There was laughter from the audience. 'And that's one of the reasons that when a man steals your wife, there's no better revenge than to let him keep her,' she said. There were even more laughs. She knew that she had the male audience—which constituted the majority— firmly by their balls.

'As a woman from India, I can tell you that a woman's intrinsic value depends entirely on what she's compared with—men. The solution to greater equality does not lie in artificial legislation to prop up women's salaries. It lies in changing the very basis of the comparison. There are some jobs to which men are better suited than women—let's pay the men more there. And conversely, there are several jobs to which women are better suited than men—let's pay these women more. But who should decide how much either gets paid? Not a bunch of paper-pushing bureaucrats in Westminster! That would be the equivalent of telling my honourable opponent to have a team of ten rowers instead of eight!' she said as she sat down to thunderous applause and left Geoffrey wondering whether he had been used or abused.

She smiled at him demurely. He seemed smitten.

'They've announced the elections,' said Gangasagar triumphantly, 'they had no bloody option. The ruling party is split right down the middle. The Uttar Pradesh home minister and Rajjo Bhaiya's dispute has achieved what we could never have achieved ourselves!'

'Our victory is certain,' said Agrawalji, stuffing another spoonful of the delectable malai-makkhan—saffron-flavoured cream lovingly whipped from hung butter—into his eagerly awaiting mouth. The light and fluffy soufflé vanished as it hit his tongue, teasing his taste buds.

'The only certainty in life is death,' said Gangasagar slipping back into one of his philosophical moods, 'and I plan to be the death of this present regime.'

'But you wanted Ikram out of the way,' began Agrawalji leaning back contentedly as the confection settled in his belly.

'There's no one in this world who cannot be defeated or cheated,' said Gangasagar taking another gulp. They were seated on the steps of Thaggu Ke Laddoo—an eatery of Kanpur—famous for its desserts. The owner's grand-father, Thaggu, had acquired his name by using sugar—an item to be boycotted as per Mahatma Gandhi's directive—to produce his world-famous sweets. He had been branded a thug, hence the name Thaggu. *Aisa koi sagaa nahin, jisko humne thaga nahi*—there's no one, not even a family member, who hasn't been cheated by us—was the motto of the eatery, a line that epitomised the swagger of Kanpur and its politics.

Gangasagar was merely a reflection of it.

'They've announced the elections,' said Chandini triumphantly, 'they had no bloody option. The rift bet-ween Elizabeth and Victor left no room for compromise in the presidential race.'

'You are supposed to sit still for a portrait,' complained Josephine. Her art teacher had asked her to do an oil-on-canvas as her next assignment. Josephine put down her paintbrush, a welcome relief from the struggle to complete a portrait of someone who could never sit still. 'Both candidates claimed foul play, right? The grapevine's been abuzz with charges of electoral misconduct.'

Chandini nodded. 'Victor Walsingham, our twenty-three-year-old sociology student at Merton College, formally won the election in November for the summer term of the Oxford Union. He defeated Elizabeth Lytton, a twenty-one-year-old politics and law major at Balliol College, by 961 votes to 656,' explained Chandini excitedly. 'Victor, who had served as the Union's treasurer, was disqualified and forbidden from contesting again by a university tribunal after Elizabeth complained that he'd organised an eve-of-poll get-together for thirty-five people in a specially reserved room, in violation of Union regulations that banned campaigning.'

'So who won eventually?' asked Josephine, wiping her brushes.

'Neither. Victor's group accused Elizabeth, the Union's librarian, of breaking with tradition by requesting a London barrister—from her own father's firm, Lytton, Tryon & Yarborough—to represent her. She was expecting that she would be declared president by default, but the Union ordered a new election instead,' said Chandini.

'Why don't you contest instead?' asked Josephine.

'I can't do that. Both Elizabeth and Victor are my friends,' said Chandini.

'That's the problem with friends in politics,' said Josephine.

'What's that?'

'Friends come and go. Enemies accumulate.'

'I've figured it out,' declared Gangasagar.

'What?' asked Agrawalji.

'Section eight, subsection three of the Representation of the People Act.'

'What?' asked Agrawalji again, even more confused.

'It says that a person convicted of any criminal offence shall be disqualified from the date of such conviction and shall continue to be disqualified for a further period of six years.'

'But Ikram has no convictions. Everyone—including you—knows that he's a don but he's managed to steer clear of convictions. His friend, the police commissioner, ensures that.'

'Ah! But what if the home minister of Uttar Pradesh were to be enlightened on the devious scheme by which the police commissioner ignited the fire of discord between him and Rajjo Bhaiya?' asked Gangasagar mischievously.

'It would be man overboard,' said Agrawalji, 'but such a situation wouldn't help the ABNS either, Ganga. The party would lose its main candidate—Ikram.'

'You're right. That's why Ikram must understand that he can continue to exercise power through a nominee who is not barred from contesting elections under the law.'

'And who would that be?'

'Who better than a daughter?' asked the naughty Gangasagar.

Agrawalji laughed.

'*Adi Shakti, Namo Namah; Sarab Shakti, Namo Namah; Prithum Bhagvati, Namo Namah; Kundalini Mata Shakti; Mata Shakti, Namo Namah*,' said Gangasagar.

<hr />

'He's decided not to contest,' said Chandini deliriously to Josephine, 'Victor's decided to throw his weight behind me instead.'

'Why?' asked Josephine, happy for her friend.

'He thinks I'm a frail and nervous little girl from a poor third-world country. He'll be able to control me and run the Union through me.'

'Poor sucker,' chuckled Josephine, 'he should ask Geoffrey.'

<hr />

They were sitting at a table in the Eagle & Child, Oxford's favourite watering hole where the likes of C. S. Lewis and J. R. R. Tolkien had met to discuss literature, love and life. A memorial plaque on a prominent wall bore signed photographs and autographs of theirs with their inebriated affirmations that they had drunk to the landlord's health.

The affair had blossomed instantly after her demure smile at the end of the debate. Geoffrey had hesitantly asked her out, not sure whether it was acceptable for an Indian woman to date. She had been hoping that he would ask her and agreed instantly.

After several hours of uninterrupted conversation and a few bottles of wine, they both fell quiet. She thought to herself, *a man on a date wonders if he'll get lucky but the woman already knows.*

— ◼ —

Hurrying back to Geoffrey's bachelor pad, they had melted into each other's arms almost as though they had been created specifically for this one single moment. He kissed her and she kissed him back even harder. It was almost as though she wanted to consume him and, in turn, be consumed by him.

The next morning when she awoke, he was in the kitchen, brewing tea and frying eggs. They ate breakfast in bed and then decided that some mistakes were simply too delicious to make just once.

— ◼ —

It was a Sunday morning and Chandini and Geoffrey were seated in the Holywell Music Room, the oldest purpose-built concert hall in Europe. Opened in 1748, the elegant hall had hosted some of the world's greatest musicians and composers, including Haydn and Handel. Sunday mornings saw Holywell playing host to the Oxford Coffee Concerts. The very best musicians and ensembles from around the world performed in the absolutely stunning setting.

Chandini's taste in music had been influenced by the rhythms of Bollywood and she had initially found Geoffrey's appetite for Bach, Beethoven and Mozart rather insipid. But she soon fell in love with the simple and unadulterated sounds of the organ and violin.

The violinist was performing Vivaldi's *Concerto in A Minor* accompanied by a string quartet and an organist. Geoffrey grazed her hand lightly. The artiste then went into a beautiful rendition of Bruch's *Scottish Fantasy*. Geoffrey took her hand in his and held it tightly. By the time the performance had moved on to Beethoven's *Violin Concerto in D Major*, his hand was on her thigh. They did not stay on for Bach's *Chaconne* from *Partita in D Minor*.

<hr>

The fan creaked as it completed one more strenuous revolution but threw off no air. The man seated under it threw off lots. He was seated on a dirty white plastic chair that had seen better days. In front of him stood a shaky table, covered with a sheet of soiled yellow plastic. Another two even more squalid plastic chairs— supposedly for visitors—sat opposite him.

Sub-inspector Brij Lal ran his police station like his personal fiefdom. To the left of his durbar was the men's lockup, from which a foul stench emanated. To the right was the women's lockup, dark and isolated. Towards the centre of his office was a steel storage cabinet bursting with case files that had been partially eaten—and digested—by rats. On his plastic-covered desk was an ancient rotary phone that didn't work and a bottle of whisky that did. Brij Lal took another gulp from his glass and wondered how he should approach the problem.

Instructions had travelled from the home minister of Uttar Pradesh to the director-general of police. The latter had relayed them to the deputy inspector-general who, in turn, had briefed the senior superintendent of police.

The chain of command had descended to the additional superintendent who had instructed the deputy super-intendent who had ordered the circle officer who had commanded the senior inspector who had directed sub-inspector Brij Lal—at the very end of the food chain—to do whatever was necessary to get the inmate to talk. The inmate was a known associate of Ikrambhai—the mayor of Kanpur—and had run Ikram's extortion racket for him.

During the reign of Ikram's buddy, the police commissioner, no one would have dared to pick up any of Ikram's men, but now things were different. The Uttar Pradesh home minister possessed definite infor-mation that the police commissioner had purposely screwed around and allowed the political conflagration between himself and Rajjo Bhaiya to flare up. The police commissioner had been unceremoniously booted out. The home minister now wanted a conviction to screw Ikram, no matter how many balls had to be crushed in the process.

Sub-inspector Brij Lal took another swig, stretched back in his chair and farted. The food in the police canteen did not augur well for his system—the grub was full of germs. That's why he needed liberal doses of whisky to kill the bacteria in his intestines. At length, he got up, yelled at one of his constables to accompany him and sauntered over to the solitary-confinement cell where Ikram's unfortunate henchman was being hosted. The cell, a ten-by-ten room without even a light bulb, had a worm-eaten blanket thrown in one corner, upon which sat the nervous and naked inmate. In one corner stood a wall, three feet in height, separating the cell from the latrine. Its well-planned location inside an unventilated lockup provided the unmistakable stink of piss.

Brij Lal held in his hand what he called his *samaaj sudharak*—the Hindi phrase for 'social reformer'. His social reformer was a two-foot-long rubber belt attached to a wooden handle. He caught hold of his prisoner's hair and hissed into his ears, 'When we carry out our social reform programme with this, there are no fractures, no blood, no major peeling of the skin. Nothing will show up in your post mortem. But the pain will be excruciating. You will appeal to God repeatedly but He won't listen. So, my friend, are you ready to be reformed?'

The confession was written up and signed within an hour. Gangasagar's tip-off had done the trick—in addition to the samaaj sudharak.

'Saar,' began the young Keralite, his oily black hair slicked back carefully, 'I am aa-nerd tomit you.'

'You are aa-nerd tomit me?' repeated Gangsagar, not too sure of what the young, dark, polite man had just said. He then realised that the south Indian was saying that he was *honoured to meet him*.

'I studied in ko-liage yin Kerala, now looking to yearn many in job with you.'

Gangasagar did a mental translation. *I studied in a college in Kerala and am now looking to earn money in a job with you.*

'Why did you leave Kerala?' asked Gangasagar.

'I zimbly jembed at the chance of baying here in Yindian pulley-ticks.' *I simply jumped at the chance of being here in Indian politics*, translated Gangasagar to himself, as he smiled at the earnest young man.

'What qualifications do you have?'

'Yum Beey Yay.'

'Ah! An MBA—good. I need someone who has management skills.'

'I know, saar. You are very bissee man.'

'Yes. I am busy but I still do manage fairly well on my own. I'll give you a shot—something tells me that I won't be sorry. Thousand rupees salary okay?'

'Will it attract yingum tax?'

'Income tax? I don't think so. It would be below the minimum threshold,' said Gangasagar smiling at his new secretary.

'Sir. I have this friend. He's a waiter. He's waiting to meet you.'

'Why would I want to meet him, Menon?' asked Gangasagar, ignoring the accent. After several months, Gangasagar now found that he was speaking almost like Menon himself.

'Sir. I think you should meet him. He can be very valuable.'

'Why on earth would a waiter be of any value to me?' asked Gangasagar.

'Sir. He wants to join you.'

'I have no need for a butler. Tell him to find someone else.'

'No, no, sir. He doesn't want a job. He wants to sell you something.'

'What?'

'Information.'

Gangasagar's ears perked up.

'Can I bring him inside? He's been waiting for an hour,' asked Menon.

'Sure. Let's meet him,' said Gangasagar.

A young man—a Muslim from Kerala—was ushered in by the enthusiastic Menon. 'Sir. This is Hameed. He's a waiter at the Golden Gate bar here in Kanpur. Go on Hameed—tell sir your story,' urged Menon.

The sub-judicial district magistrate yawned. It had been a long day hearing bail applications of inmates. He heard another defence lawyer argue a case that he knew nothing about and shouted 'Bail denied!' mid-sentence. The startled lawyer looked at him quizzically wondering why he hadn't been given due hearing. He didn't realise that the magistrate had made up his mind well before the hearing ever started.

The magistrate had a nasty little secret. He was married to a loving wife and had two sons, but his wife had ceased to excite him anymore. He had tried ayurvedic remedies to help his sagging libido but nothing worked. He visited brothels thinking that a little action on the side would kickstart things. The girls had ended up laughing at him. Fed up of his miserable existence, he sauntered into a bar and ordered himself a whisky-soda on ice. The waiter not only brought him his drink but also lots of peanuts and crisps. He left the bar that night along with the waiter only to realise that his brain was wired differently. His machinery was still in working order but it needed alternative current, not the straight kind. He was suddenly happy—and gay.

The waiter had soon realised that there was a profitable opportunity awaiting exploitation—his days of waiting tables, washing dishes and pacifying disgruntled customers at the Golden Gate bar seemed to be over. He was now the secret lover of the sub-judicial magistrate.

The magistrate's nasty little secret wasn't that he was a closet homosexual. The nasty little secret was that any case heard by the magistrate could be fixed for a price. His agent was the efficient waiter who had graduated from serving peanuts to delivering sentences—Hameed.

It was definite. The telltale signs were all there. It was certain that it was that time of the month when she had come to expect pain in her lower abdomen, spasms in her uterus, dizziness in her head, and bloating everywhere else. But the symptoms hadn't arrived. She was quite definitely pregnant.

Terrified of the consequences, Chandini ran to Geoffrey's college and waited for him outside until his lecture ended. He saw the expression in her green eyes and knew. Panic was written all over her face. He held her hand as they strolled into Headington Hill and allowed their feet to squelch the autumn leaves on the ground.

At length, she asked, 'What shall we do, Geoffrey?'

The emphasis was on *we*.

'I'm really not sure what you can do,' was his reply.

The emphasis was on *you*.

'Here's the five quid I owe you,' said Victor to Geoffrey as he handed over the note.

'Hemingfords never lose bets,' said Geoffrey smugly, 'but you owe me ten'.

'Why?'

'Five if I got the Paki into bed, another five if she got banged up,' said Geoffrey slyly.

'So she's pregnant?' asked Victor.

'Let's just say that you can now safely claim the presidency of the Oxford Union,' said Geoffrey, accepting the second note from Victor.

The telegram in front of Gangasagar told him more than he wanted to know. It was the usual monthly report that came to him from a gentleman in England—a Mr Harvey Richardson. He conveyed regular updates regarding her grades, her progress, her debates, her friendships and her extra-curricular activities—and she'd had more than her fair share of those.

Mr Richardson was not an affluent man but a man who could get things done on occasion. He had originally been a business associate of Agrawalji and, during Gangasagar's employment with Agrawalji, had helped Gangasagar import manufactured goods from England and export commodities to England. He had been delighted when Gangasagar had offered to sponsor his daughter, Josephine Richardson, to Oxford. It was an incredibly generous gesture.

But generous gestures usually came with some strings attached. In his case—and Josephine's—it was to look out for the Indian girl at St Hilda's in Oxford.

<hr/>

The critical elements were the syringe and formula containing shavings of carbolic soap. Her power douche would eventually result in a pregnant girl shedding her uterine lining within forty-eight hours, after which everything would be bright and sunny once again. The house to which Josephine accompanied Chandini was a modest low-income home in which the nameless resident, a middle-aged and matronly lady, would administer the douche to terrified girls. She had performed over a hundred back-alley abortions and operated one of the most hygienic illegal clinics from her home.

Josephine had ferretted out the lady's name from another girl. Chandini, who was petrified that her father—Guptaji—would somehow get wind of her condition, and brave all odds to reach the shores of

England to strangle her for bringing shame and dishonour upon the family, was relieved when Josephine took all the planning out of her hands and into her own.

The matron asked Chandini to undress and lie down on the wooden table, putting her feet in the stirrups one at a time. She positioned herself between Chandini's legs and asked the girl to open them, but try as she would, Chandini's knees refused to budge. They remained glued together almost as though a voice within her was telling her not to abort.

⚏

The Mother & Baby home at Grasmere was secluded enough to filter out unwanted attention. Moreover, it was unlike the usual ones managed by nuns where 'errant unmarried mothers' were sent to deliver illegitimate children who would subsequently be put up for adoption. This was, on the contrary, a private home that charged substantial fees from wealthy families who sent their pregnant daughters to its care. Grasmere was the loveliest spot that man had ever found, according to William Wordsworth, who had lived there for fourteen years of his life. Located in the centre of the charming Lake District, Grasmere was ethereal—surrounded by misty hills, unending lakes, and undulating farmlands. Harvey Richardson had instructed Josephine to take Chandini there without letting on that anyone—including Gangasagar or Harvey himself—knew of her condition.

Josephine bought a gramophone that she installed in one corner of Chandini's room. She managed to source long-playing records of Chandini's favourite music—violin concertos by Bach, Beethoven, Brahms, Tchaikovsky, and Paganini. Chandini would sit by the window gazing out at the serene Grasmere surrounded

119

by gentle walks and craggy peaks. Josephine would often go to the market while Chandini meditated to the sounds of the violin. Sometimes, when Josephine returned, she would notice that Chandini's eyes were moist and her face stained with dried tears. Sounds of the violin reminded her too much of Geoffrey. Josephine tried to cheer her up by placing a vase of fresh pink chrysanthemums on the windowsill every few days—they were Chandini's favourite flowers.

Eight weeks after moving in, Chandini was ready to deliver. She had not realised that it would be the equivalent of pushing a bowling ball through a nostril. Josephine held her hand while the matron checked her cervix for dilation. Blood and amniotic fluid were seeping out as the nurse urged her to push. Chandini pushed and blacked out as she felt a body covered in slippery gob gush out of her.

When Chandini awoke, she realised that she had been cleaned up and wheeled back into her room with the flower-patterned curtains that framed a picture postcard view of the lake. Josephine was sitting by her side, gently running her fingers through Chandini's hair. Chandini took one look at Josephine and she knew instantly.

'I'm so sorry, honey,' Josephine whispered, 'the doctor says you can have others but this one was stillborn.'

▰◧▰

Another telegram a few days later informed Gangasagar in Kanpur that the needful had been done. Gangasagar did not inform either of the fathers—Guptaji or Ikram. The telegram also informed him that the two girls had rented a cottage in the Lake District and were spending a few more weeks in the country before Chandini returned home.

'One down, one more to go,' thought Gangasagar as he dropped in to meet Agrawalji for an evening walk along the riverbank.

━━○━

The Air-India Boeing 707-420 on the bus-stop route of London-Cairo-Geneva-Mumbai had a hundred and sixty passengers on board. Chandini was airsick as they landed turbulently in Geneva in the middle of a thunderstorm. By the time they reached Mumbai airport, she was relieved to be back home.

She could never forgive Geoffrey for the games he had played with her life. She could try to forget—but she would never forgive. Neither would Gangasagar.

━━○━

London's hip Esmeralda's Barn was located in Wilton Place, a fashionable street running off Knightsbridge. One of the first clubs to open after the new Gaming Act, it had the best croupiers, waiters, hostesses and chefs in town. A narrow and dimly-lit passage led to the large office that accommodated two giant antique desks, each illuminated by a green lawyers' lamp. The two men that sat behind the desks smoking Cubans had been separated by just ten minutes. Ted had been born ten minutes before Fred. The twins had gone on to create and ruthlessly manage England's largest crime syndicate— the Payne Brothers.

Born in Hoxton, East London, to Jack Payne, a scrap gold dealer, the twins had exhibited none of their future ruthless tendencies at school. Their grandfather had led them into the world of amateur boxing, and the brothers never lost a single bout. The problem was that they were more interested in throwing punches outside the ring than inside it. They soon bought a run-down local snooker club in Bethnal Green, where they started several rackets—protection, hijacking, armed robbery, arson, betting, and prostitution. Their most high-profile acquisition had been Esmeralda's Barn.

Harvey Richardson headed over to the roulette wheel. The croupier was stacking chips while customers were placing their coloured chips on the playing field. The croupier expertly flicked the small white roulette ball between his thumb and index finger towards the rim and the ball went into frenzied orbit. Harvey placed a fiver on black. As the ball lost momentum and slowed down, it wobbled and fell gently into the still revolving wheel. 'Double zero,' said the croupier, 'no winners.'

'Fuck!' said Harvey as he got up. The bouncer was nodding at him. The brothers were ready to see him. He was nervous but tried not showing it. It was rumoured that the brothers had once fed a drugged man to pigs on a farm. When either Ted or Fred entered Harrods, the queues at the tills would instantly part, like the Red Sea before Moses, to let them through. In return, the brothers would 'look after' the community. The previous year they had even spent thousands on a Guy Fawkes fireworks extravaganza for London.

Harvey knew them because of the help they had extended to him when his house had been burgled. Josephine had been in Oxford, at St Hilda's, when the break-in occurred. They reported it to the police but nothing happened. Then a well-dressed man representing the brothers had come around to see the Richardsons. He had listened to their tale and said that he was sorry to hear about the theft and that he would do everything he could to ferret out those responsible. Within a week, Harvey's wife had all her jewellery back and almost everything else that had been taken.

What Gangasagar wanted done could not be handled by anyone else. It had to be the Payne Brothers— social workers in the real sense. Gangasagar requested Harvey to finalise the terms of engagement, including the final price.

The OUBC—the Oxford University Boat Club—was waking up to an early start as usual. The OUBC owned a boathouse on the Thames and the first few boats had already left by six in the morning. An hour later the serenity and predictable routine of the club was shattered as the junior team's boat collided with the floating corpse of a naked man. The club boat had bumped into the body at seven that morning, just past the green spit post near the jetty. The police were immediately summoned. The body was of a white male aged between twenty and twenty-five, extremely fit. His face had been beaten to a pulp, hence facial recognition was not possible.

Thirty minutes later the seven policemen and the coroner were joined by a police boat to search for the unidentified man's clothes and belongings along the stretch of the riverbank. A few hours later they located the bloody sleeveless dark blue vest of an Oxford Eight. Near it was the distinctive blue-bladed oar of the OUBC covered in bloody gore. It had been used to smash the victim's face into mush. The dark blue vest located on the riverbank had an identifying label stitched on at the back. It bore the name 'Geoffrey'.

CHAPTER SEVEN

About 2300 years ago

Draped in a dark blanket and wearing a blue turban, the man could have been mistaken for any of the thousands of citizenry walking on the streets of Takshila. His gold amulets would have conveyed the air of a merchant, but his twirled moustache and long hair gave him the appearance of a warrior. It was late evening. By his calculation it was ten *muhurtas* into the night, day and night each being fifteen muhurtas long. He walked purposefully but not briskly. He did not wish to attract attention to himself at this late hour. Within his vision lay her house—Jalakrida. The name was derived from *jala*—or water, and *krida*—or pleasure. This house was a pleasure palace with a swimming pool reserved for wealthy and influential men. It was owned by one of the most famous ganikas—courtesans—in all of Takshila. Her name was Mainika.

The blanket-draped stranger reached Jalakrida and after ascertaining that there was no one watching, went up to the door and knocked—one, one-two, one-two, one—a pattern recognised by the lady of the establishment. The door half-opened and she led him directly into her bedchamber. Once in, she locked the door from inside. But this was certainly not a nocturnal rendezvous to explore the pleasures of Mainika's secret garden. The man remained standing and whispered, 'I have news.'

'How much more stress do I need to take?' she caustically asked.

'Bear with me for just a couple of days. The army of Gandhar, disguised as cattle herders, keeps attacking Kaikey's border farms. They loot cattle and grain and we do nothing. Well, we have finally decided to do something!'

'But when? And what is it that you want me to do?' asked Mainika.

'In this winter month of Magha, during the third day of Bakula—the waning fortnight of the moon—the forces of Kaikey shall attack Gandhar. You must make sure that the commander-in-chief of Gandhar is with you on that day.'

'He's utterly captivated by the pleasures that I provide. He's here every night to bathe in the warm waters. But how do I keep him here for the entire duration of the attack? My skills lie in teasing a man to the very highest peak of bliss, but I can't keep him here with me after the moment of ecstasy has passed!' she argued.

'It's absolutely essential that the commander-in-chief must not be in a position to direct Gandhar forces when we attack—we need to elicit shock and awe. Do whatever is necessary. If you have cannabis incense, use it!' he snapped.

'But—uh… why are we doing this? Can't the politicians talk to one another and resolve the dispute amicably?' asked Mainika.

'Gandharraj, the aged king of Gandhar, wants to have good neighbourly relations with Paurus, our lord and master of Kaikey, but Gandharraj's brash and headstrong prince—Ambhi—is intent on destroying his neighbour even if it means getting into bed with the Macedonians! In these circumstances, attack is the best form of defence,' argued the Kaikey intelligence operative.

'But Ambhi is studying in Takshila University. How can he possibly influence state policy?' asked the bewildered courtesan.

'He has been expelled from the university owing to his misbehaviour. The university authorities hushed up the matter and Gandharraj has requested that the prince's tutoring continue at the palace itself. The arrogant and foolish youth now wants to depose his own father and take control of Gandhar with the help of Alexander's bastards—'

'Sshh,' she hissed, 'this may be the house of a ganika, but we do not use foul language within the precincts of my sacred love nest!'

'A thousand apologies, dear Mainika. I forgot that in our ancient scriptures, Mainika was the most beautiful of the celestial apsaras, sent by Lord Indra to break the severe penance undertaken by Sage Vishwamitra,' he joked.

'Don't forget that Vishwamitra's penance was indeed broken and his lust awakened when he saw Mainika swimming in a lake near his hermitage, which is precisely what you want me to do with the commander-in-chief!' she retorted.

'The only difference being that you have your own lake!' he quipped as he slipped away into the wintry darkness of Takshila's streets.

Chanakya introduced his newest protégé to his students, Sinharan, Mehir and Sharangrao. 'This is Chandragupta. He's the son of Senapati Maurya and I have brought him with me so that he may be tutored in the subjects of kingship—combat, warfare, politics, economics, languages, mathematics and the sciences. Sinharan, I need you to be his best friend.'

'It shall be done, acharya,' said Sinharan as he put his arm around the young Chandragupta. 'In the past few years, the acharya has been training me in the very same subjects, Chandragupta. My father is the governor of Mallayrajya and we too face the Macedonian threat. With my help, you will absorb what the acharya has to teach you at twice the pace,' he bantered, trying to make the new boy, who was quite obviously missing his parents, feel at home.

Sinharan continued. 'This is my friend Mehir. He's from Persia. I've been learning Persian—cusswords mostly—from him! When Ambhi, the crown prince of Gandhar, was a student here, he was always curious about what we were saying about him, little realising that a string of the choicest Persian expletives was being let loose! And this is Sharangrao—be careful about what you say in his presence. He has the memory of an elephant!'

The trip from Magadha, at the eastern tip of Bharat, to Gandhar, along its northwest frontiers, had been tiring but efficiently completed. They had managed the journey in about six months. Unlike on his previous journey, this time Chanakya had the advantage of fresh horses and an entourage of attendants. Some of the treasure had been left with Senapati Maurya to raise an army that would eventually help overthrow Dhanananda and keep external aggression at bay. 'The senapati will not double-cross me,' thought the game theory-inspired

Brahmin. 'After all, I have his son with me, and that son is the future king of Magadha and, possibly, the emperor of a united Bharat.'

Chanakya and Chandragupta had brought back with them a significant amount of gold. This would be used to raise a student force that could assist in repelling the Macedonians at the doorstep of Gandhar. During the long and arduous journey they had been under constant threat from gangs of thugs and thieves. Had it not been for the presence of a large contingent of specially trained men sent along by Senapati Maurya, they would never have been able to return to Takshila safely and with treasure chest intact.

—◼◼—

'Let's understand the dynamics at play here. Gandhar is a powerful kingdom, but the king is old and weak. His son, Ambhi, is impatient and ambitious. Time will prove me right but I'm sure that he'll sleep with the enemy— Alexander—to usurp the throne. Attacking Gandhar at this moment would be foolish because you'll precipitate matters and push him into the arms of the Macedonians,' cautioned Chanakya to his friend Indradutt, the prime minister of Kaikey.

They were seated on a thick jute rug by the banks of the Indus. Indradutt's wife had provided them with fruits, yoghurt and a few savouries for their little picnic. Their horses were tethered to a tree close by. Meetings between Indradutt and Chanakya necessarily had to remain secret lest Ambhi accuse Chanakya of conspiring with the enemy.

Indradutt knew that what Chanakya was saying made sense. There was no point in weakening the hinges of a gate when the enemy was standing just outside. But he also knew that his own king, Paurus, was an old-world honour-guts-and-glory kind of guy. He saw himself as a knight in shining armour who would teach the rascal Ambhi a lesson that he would never forget.

'I agree with you, Vishnu'—he was one of the few people who still had the liberty of calling him by his birth name, Vishnugupta—'but Ambhi has provoked the situation through perpetual border skirmishes. Sending military men dressed as cattle herders and looting livestock has made the whole of Kaikey very angry. Maharaj Paurus has been pushed into a corner. If he doesn't act against Gandhar, he fears that his own people may call him a coward,' explained Indradutt, biting into an apple absentmindedly.

'Very often, one does not need to act, but simply give the impression that one is acting. Let Paurus make a speech against Gandhar. Let him cut off diplomatic ties with Takshila. Let him send a strongly-worded note of caution. In short, let him act as though he's acting without really acting!' said Chanakya, tossing a pebble into the mighty river.

Indradutt sighed. He knew that the clever fox was, as usual, on the mark. It would be better to let Gandhar keep the Macedonians out rather than pushing Ambhi into their arms. Gandhar would, quite unnecessarily, become the fortress from the safety of which the Macedonian soldiers would fight Kaikey. 'I shall speak to Paurus about the implications, Vishnu, but don't hold your breath. I know my king better than he knows himself!'

***

God was pleased. In this particular instance, God was Macedonian, and his name was Alexander. He didn't look divine though. For one thing, he was a little too short to be God. His long, blond hair reaching down to his neck, his perfectly straight nose, prominent forehead, and noble protruding chin, however, more than compensated for his short stature. The celestial deity had raised a terrifying dust storm as his army ran over Syria, Egypt, Mesopotamia, Persia and Bactria. His mother, Olympias, on the night before the consummation of her marriage to King Philip of Macedonia, had dreamed that her womb had been struck by a thunderbolt. And the product of that mystical union between Olympias and Philip had produced a son who was no less than a thunderbolt.

The thunderbolt then had his cousin executed, two Macedonian princes murdered, his general poisoned, and his stepmother and her daughter burned alive in order to ensure his accession to the throne. The thunderbolt had then taken forty-two thousand men on a long trek to defeat the no-less-magnificent Darius III of Persia who had been forced to offer his own daughter as war repatriation to Alexander before the omnipotent godling marched into Persepolis and declared himself *shahenshah*—the king of kings—having crucified all captured men of military age and having sold their women and children into slavery.

The king of kings was copulating with his latest wife, Roxana, a stunning Uzbek princess, a change in diet from his usual menu of young men, when the thought of invading Bharat crossed his mind. He decided that Ambhi was the key.

≡

The thousands of horsemen galloping through the dusty fields was an awe-inspiring sight. The *chaturangbala*—the four-limbed army of Kaikey—was formidable, but this one-limbed monster was even more terrifying. In usual military combat, the four limbs of the army consisted of the infantry, cavalry, elephants and chariots.

However, to capitalise on the elements of speed and surprise, Kaikey had decided to use only cavalry to pulverize Gandhar into submission.

Inside the Jalakrida of Mainika, lay a comatose commander-in-chief. He had been delicately bathed, erotically massaged, and tenderly fed by the seductive Mainika. As he fell into a gentle and peaceful slumber, she lit the cannabis incense near the bed in her boudoir and left the room briskly, locking the door behind her. He would be out like an oil-starved lamp for several hours.

The alarm had been sounded and Takshila's gate pulleys were being overworked to shut the monster barriers, but it was too late. Kaikey horsemen poured into Takshila, surrounded the local garrison, rode up to Gandharraj's palace and blocked ingress and egress. Gandhar's royal family sat in their gilded cage, prisoners of Kaikey's cavalry. Gandhar's commander-in-chief lay unconscious in the bedchamber of Gandhar's most expensive whore, as the citadel of Takshila capitulated to the sudden influx of hordes of ferocious riders.

Inside the palace, the old king Gandharraj received a message. The prime minister of King Paurus, Indradutt, wished to pay his respects whenever Gandharraj was willing to spare his time. Spare his time! The bastard was being sarcastic. He had absolutely nothing to do with his time—his palace was under siege!

'Bring the prime minister to the council hall. I shall meet him there shortly,' said the weak and exhausted emperor to the messenger as he was helped to his feet by his attendants. *O my imprudent son Ambhi, I had always warned you about your foolish incursions into Kaikey. The result is plain to see,* thought the monarch as he allowed his servants to cover him with his silk stole and adorn him with his thirty-three-carat diamond-studded amulets in preparation for the meeting with the emissary of Paurus.

≡

Indradutt bowed down low before Gandharraj and began, 'O Mighty Emperor, Lord and Master of the valley of Gandhar, Benefactor of Takshila, O Benevolent Father of the citizens of Gandhar, O Wise, Learned, Brave—'

Gandharraj interrupted him mid-sentence. 'It is kind of you to accord me this courtesy, Indradutt, but the truth is that you're the victor, and I the vanquished,' said the greybeard motioning for his subjugator to sit down. Indradutt did not instal himself on the chair offered to him. Instead, as a gesture of respect towards the aged monarch, he sat down cross-legged on the floor next to his feet.

'Why are you being so respectful to me?' asked Gandharraj, 'I am your prisoner and have been defeated in one fatal swoop.'

'Gandharraj, the kingdom of Kaikey has always held you in high regard. Our king, Paurus, has always spoken about you with affection and respect. He knows that you're wise, just and honest. The decision to attack your kingdom was a very difficult one, but we were left with little alternative. Your son, Ambhi, has been sending disguised militia and mercenaries to Kaikey to stir up trouble along the border areas. We tried our best to ignore minor skirmishes, but the unprovoked aggression remained undiminished,' explained Indradutt to the tired and venerable sovereign.

'I understand your predicament, Indradutt. I am willing to do everything that is within the realm of my earthly powers to rein in Ambhi, but he's fool-hardy and reckless. Ask Paurus to forgive him, for me,' pleaded Gandharraj.

Indradutt hesitated before he spoke. 'O sagacious King, please do not embarrass me. I'm your humble servant and my own master, Paurus, has been clear that his difficulties do not lie with you but with Ambhi. He's also worried that your son has been secretly negotiating a treaty with Alexander. If Gandhar allows Alexander passage to Bharat, then all our kingdoms shall be at risk,' he said.

'That's impossible! Even Ambhi knows that he does not have the authority to enter into an accord with anyone without my seal of approval,' asserted Gandharraj, more hopeful than convinced.

'How do I convince you of Ambhi's actions, maharaj?' wondered Indradutt. Without waiting for an answer to the rhetorical question he shouted 'Abhaya! Please come within.'

Within moments the intelligence operative who had been having late night consultations with Mainika at her pleasure pool walked in. He folded his hands in a gesture of greeting to both men but remained silent as he stood awaiting further instructions from Indradutt.

'Abhaya, have your men been following Crown Prince Ambhi?' asked Indradutt, almost in courtroom fashion.

'Yes, my lord,' replied Abhaya.

'And has the prince remained under your observation for all fifteen muhurtas of the day and all fifteen muhurtas of the night?'

'Yes, my lord. He has never been out of our sight.'

'Has the prince remained in Takshila for every single day of the last *shuklapaksha*?'

'No, my lord. He went hunting and crossed over into Kamboja on the second day of shuklapaksha.'

'When the prince crossed into Kamboja, did he camp there?'

'Yes, my lord. He remained in his Kamboja camp for three days and three nights.'

'Did any special guests drop in to meet the prince?'

'Only one, my lord. Seleucus dropped in and spent a few hours with him.'

'Seleucus, the trusted general of Alexander?'

'Yes, my lord. The Macedonian insignia on the horses seemed to indicate as much.'

'And did your agent hear what was discussed?'

'No. But Seleucus' secretary did step out of the meeting tent to arrange for hot wax and the general's signet ring.'

'So it would seem that this was certainly not a friendly hunting expedition, unless it's now fashionable to brand one's hunting trophies with wax seals,' commented Indradutt caustically as he observed Gandharraj's worried expression. 'Thank you, Abhaya, you may leave,' said Indradutt.

'Alas! What has my foolish son done? How shall I repair the damage, Indradutt?' asked Gandharraj as Abhaya left.

Indradutt had no words to offer. He knew that Chanakya had been right. Paurus had achieved absolutely nothing by attacking Gandhar except for propelling Ambhi into Alexander's arms.

<hr/>

The figure was clad in loose black pyjamas and a black cotton vest. A black mask was tied around the lower half of his face, leaving only his head and eyes uncovered. A long jute rope was wound around his waist. His face and hands were coated in soot so that any exposed flesh would blend in with the dark night. To one side of his waist hung a small dagger and on the other side a well-polished bamboo tube resembling a flute. He was barefoot and his feet made no sound as he gently trod the cool and well-worn stone slabs along the palace corridor. Some minutes later, he stopped by a window, unwound the rope, tied it firmly to one of the pillars nearby, and threw the remaining cord outside. He grasped the rope firmly and began lowering himself to the window ledge that was a floor below. Having reached it, he swung inside, landed inside the unending passage, balanced himself and looked in the distance at the ornate door that led to the royal bedchamber.

Two guards stood outside holding lances that crossed one another across the doorway. A row of pillars ran along the length of the hallway, which led to the door of the chamber and the guards outside it. The black figure skipped lightly towards his goal using the massive columns to hide himself from the vision of the guards. He measured his final steps carefully to satisfy himself that he was within shooting distance and knelt down behind one of the pillars. He unclasped the flute-like tube from his waist and sucked in a long deep breath.

Bringing the tube to his lips he aimed the flute at the more alert of the two sentinels and blew hard into the pipe. An exceedingly small dart, coated with the juice of aconite tubers and snake venom, hurtled through the dark alley until it punctured a microscopic hole in the sentry's neck. It was no more than a mosquito sting but produced a devastating effect. Before he could collapse to the floor and alert his companion, another little pea-sized spur left the peashooter's aperture and caught the second guard between his eyes. Both men collapsed in a matter of seconds, the sound of their spears falling to the floor reverberating eerily in the sombre corridor.

He leapt up, jogged over to the two dead bodyguards and dropped down on his knees to efficiently check their carotid arteries. Having satisfied himself that they were well and truly dead, he unclasped his dagger and cautiously opened the door. The room was silent except for arrhythmic snores emerging from the silhouette that lay on the giant bed towards the eastern end. The room was dim, the only light being that of a single oil lamp near the entrance door.

The assassin advanced towards the snoring individual until he reached the bed. He looked down at his father's face, raised his knife and with one fatal blow, plunged it into Gandharraj's chest. Arterial blood squirted in arcs as the old king's left ventricle contracted, leaving the bed drenched in wine-coloured gore. The sovereign's eyes opened for a fraction of a second as the image of his murdering heir was captured on his retinas. His terror-struck expression soon gave way to a look of relief as he realised that his humiliating life was finally over.

'I had warned you, Indradutt,' said Chanakya as he watched Chandragupta wrestle Sinharan inside the mud *akhada*—the wrestling arena on the Takshila campus. Both wrestlers were wearing muddy loincloths and were slick from a mixture of sesame oil and sweat. Their methodology was a freestyle of all four types of wrestling prevailing in Bharat, *Hanumanti, Jambuvanti, Jarasandhi* and *Bhimaseni*. But this was no mild wrestling match. Just as one contestant would succeed in holding down his adversary, a team of monstrous-looking men wielding batons would attack him. This would give his opponent a chance to recover while his rival fought off the attacking horde.

Indradutt winced at the remark. 'I know, I know. You have the luxury of saying "I told you so" but Paurus gave me no alternative. I withdrew Kaikey's troops from Gandhar upon Gandharraj's assurance that he would rein in his son. How was one to know that the wretch Ambhi would decide to murder his own father! We've created a mess. Now Ambhi is free to pursue his treaty with Alexander. They say he looks like a god!' he complained as he looked at Chandragupta pinning down Sinharan in a submission hold.

Over the years, Chandragupta had grown into a fine specimen of masculinity. Broad shoulders, muscular arms and wrestler's thighs contrasted with his gentle face, aristocratic nose and thick, curly, dark hair that fell in cascading waves to his shoulders. His fitness instructors had trained him in wrestling, archery, horseback riding and swordsmanship.

His daily regimen was more difficult than that of the most punishing and austere monkhood. In a day and night of thirty muhurtas, the first two muhurtas after sunrise were used for exercise, physical and combat training. The next two muhurtas were for mastering kingly subjects—economics, politics, history and geography. The ensuing two muhurtas were allocated for his personal time—bathing and early lunch. The two muhurtas following noon were used for studying other subjects—mathematics, general science and languages. The succeeding two muhurtas were designated for equestrian activities including horse-mounted combat. The two muhurtas before sunset were reserved for spiritual discourse and learning the ancient scriptures followed by a two-muhurta break for bathing and dinner. The two muhurtas after dinnertime were for homework and revision of everything learned during the day. The final two muhurtas were used for meditation and contemplation before he took his forty winks and the cycle started all over again at dawn.

'I am not worried, Indradutt. And if I were you, the best strategy would be to do absolutely nothing,' said

Chanakya looking over at other wrestlers wearing *garnals*—circular stone neck weights—and practising their squats.

'I don't understand you, Vishnu. You lecture us on the perils facing our nation from the Macedonian war machine and when they succeed in getting their foot into the door you preach masterly inactivity!' burst out Indradutt, ignoring the three wrestlers who were performing *dhakulis*—twisting rotations—with maces in hand.

'Mehir! Come over here. Please explain to Indraduttji why I am so confident,' called out Chanakya, motioning his Persian student over. Mehir, also dripping with sweat, dropped his weights and walked over to them. He folded his hands in a gesture of greeting to both men.

'Tell the prime minister of Kaikey why I recommend that he do nothing,' said Chanakya.

'Upon the advice of the acharya, I have cultivated a network of Persian merchants who keep me informed regarding the developments in Persepolis. I had left the great city just after it had fallen to the Macedonians and it seems that a few months later there was a great drunken orgy hosted by Alexander at the palace, which set off a massive fire. Most of Persepolis including its wondrous treasures was destroyed. The thrust provided to Alexander's war efforts by Persia's wealth has been neutralised,' explained Mehir.

'What it means, Indradutt, is that Alexander's progress will be slow. Most of his troops are mercenaries. If they are not paid, they will not fight. It will be difficult for Alexander to defeat the mighty army of Kaikey in his diminished capacity,' said Chanakya, taking some sesame oil from a large earthen pot next to them and rubbing it into his dry elbows absentmindedly.

'So what should I tell my king?' asked Indradutt.

'Tell him that he should sleep peacefully,' said the ingenious Brahmin.

'The burning down of Persepolis has not blunted the edge of Alexander's sword, yet you asked me to lie to the prime minister of Kaikey. Why, acharya?' asked Mehir as Indradutt left.

'Mehir, I need you to think very carefully before answering the questions that I am about to ask you. Which is the strongest kingdom in Bharat?'

'Magadha, without doubt.'

'And who rules Magadha?'

'Dhanananda.'

'To wrest Magadha from Dhanananda, we shall need the help of the next most powerful kingdom. Which do you think that is?'

'Kaikey.'

'And who rules Kaikey?'

'Paurus.'

'But why will Paurus help us acquire Magadha if he doesn't feel the need to? Under what circumstances would he feel obliged to throw in his lot with us?'

'If he were under attack.'

'And who is his sworn enemy?'

'Ambhi, the king of Gandhar.'

'And is Ambhi capable of taking on Paurus alone?'

'Obviously not. His own capital was captured by Kaikey effortlessly!'

'So how does one make Ambhi strong enough to attack Kaikey?'

'Alexander!'

'Precisely.'

'But acharya, you said that the Macedonians are poison and that we need to ensure that this poison does not spread.'

'We often use poisons in small quantities to treat ailments, don't we? If the dosage is correctly calibrated, the very toxin that can kill becomes a saviour. We need to use the Macedonians in precisely the same way.'

'If Alexander is friends with Ambhi and they jointly attack Paurus, there exists the possibility that Alexander may become emperor of all of Bharat!'

'Once again, Mehir, I urge you to think this through very carefully before replying. Before planning a campaign in Bharat, which countries did Alexander conquer?'

'Persia, Syria, Egypt, Assyria, Babylonia—'

'Yes, yes, I know. But how many Alexanders are there? One? Two? Ten?'

'Only one,' said Mehir smiling.

'Only one Alexander and tens of conquered territories. He will fight and move on. He cannot be in ten places at once!'

'But his generals may remain. He may appoint governors.'

'What was the size of Alexander's army when he left on his military conquest?'

'My sources say that he had around forty-two thousand troops when he left Macedonia.'

'And have your sources told you how many men he currently has?'

'Around the same.'

'Strange. If he had left some of his own troops in Persia, Syria, Egypt, Assyria, Babylonia, Bactria, and other conquered territories, his present troop numbers should have been lower. What does this tell you?'

'That he isn't leaving behind large contingents to maintain control over conquered territories?'

'And that he depends on local allies to protect his conquered interests.'

'So we should sit back and allow Paurus to be defeated by the combined forces of Ambhi and Alexander, acharya? I would much rather die for my country.'

'It's foolish men who die for their country. The intelligent ones make others die for their country instead. Remember, he who plans and runs away, lives to fight another day. That's not cowardice, it's chess—and the board belongs to me! Alexander's campaign will leave Paurus as well as Ambhi weak. Having weakened them he will appoint one of his generals—probably Seleucus—as his governor and move on. That shall be our moment. Chandragupta's moment! Bharat's moment!'

'And we do nothing to prevent Paurus from losing?'

'Battles are won or lost before they are ever fought. Paurus has already lost.'

'And what do we do till then?' asked Mehir, looking at his mentor intently.

'We build our forces and wait—patiently.'

'And Indradutt?'

'I have already burnt that bridge by lying to him today.'

CHAPTER EIGHT

Present Day

The bailiff was elocuting. 'The sub-judicial district magistrate's court of Kanpur is now in session. The honourable judge S. C. Pande presiding. Order and silence is commanded. God protect this honourable court!'

The honourable sub-judicial district magistrate S. C. Pande looked at the lawyer who stood before him. 'Where's your client?' he asked. The lawyer looked around as though he expected to find his client under the desks of the courtroom. The magistrate sighed. He didn't want to be here in court. He would have preferred to be in the hotel room on the outskirts of the city experiencing the pleasures of Hameed's sublime body. A faint smile crossed his lips as he thought of him.

'Sir, I don't know. He had said that he would be here ten minutes before the appointed hour,' explained the harried lawyer, breaking Mr Pande's carnal reverie. 'In that case, I'm issuing orders for his arrest. Bailiff, please issue an arrest warrant and see to it that Mr Ikram Shaikh is produced before me at the earliest.'

━■━

'The lowly bastard had the balls to issue an arrest warrant for me,' said Ikram angrily.

'Ikram—Ikram—calm down! What happened?' asked Gangasagar, feigning complete ignorance of the situation.

'As you know, the police commissioner was booted out by the state home minister. With his departure, I was no longer a VIP. They started investigating me and my businesses, even though I'm the mayor of this goddamn town!'

'But what's the problem with that? You've dealt with enough investigations, I imagine. All investigators have their price,' suggested Gangasagar.

'But this time it's different. They beat up Ahmed— my extortion racket-fixer—and got him to admit a pack of lies against me!' sputtered Ikrambhai, visibly shaken.

'Even then—when the matter comes before the magistrate, I'm sure that matters can be handled, right?' asked Gangasagar shrewdly.

'I've tried everything with this sonofabitch. He just won't budge. There's nothing that I haven't offered the asshole but he refuses to let me off. I can't even get him kicked in the face because all my men are being watched by a hostile police force!' complained Ikram, bemoaning the injustice of it all.

'You know, Ikram, you're my closest friend. And as your friend, I advise that you must maintain a low profile. As mayor—and chief ministerial aspirant—everyone has it in for you,' recommended Gangasagar quietly, omitting to mention himself in the list of 'everyone'.

'But state elections are around the corner,' said Ikram. 'Who will represent the party if not myself? We have worked so hard to make the ABNS relevant. It isn't about my personal glory—heaven forbid—it's about a sense of duty towards you and the ABNS,' pleaded Ikram.

'I shall hate losing you, Ikram,' said Gangasagar, 'but I value our friendship too much to risk losing you entirely. I think you should drop out of the chief ministerial race and put your weight behind someone else.'

'What's your suggestion?' asked Ikram.

'I know someone who can get the magistrate to do what we want him to. But you'll have to lie low so that the government machinery stops working against you. Chandini's returned. Why not anoint her your political successor? She's just a poor helpless girl—she'll still be in your control,' counselled Gangasagar.

'He's decided not to contest,' said Gangasagar to Agrawalji. 'Ikram's decided to throw his weight behind his adopted daughter instead.'

'What convinced him?' asked Agrawalji.

'When you're holding a man by the balls, his heart and mind will follow,' said Gangasagar, laughing as he silently thanked his secretary, Menon, for bringing him Hameed.

'Chandini, I would like you to meet some extremely good students. This is Upendra Kashyap from Lucknow University; this is Brijmohan Rai from Allahabad University; Iqbal Azmi from Aligarh Muslim University; Girish Bajpai from Banaras Hindu University—'

Chandini looked at the thirty men from various universities around the state of Uttar Pradesh. They didn't look like students. Most of them seemed to be in their thirties and forties. The first one, Upendra Kashyap from Lucknow University, stepped up and greeted Chandini, his palms pressed together in front of him in a gesture of respect. 'I know what you're thinking, Chandiniji.

We seem too old to be students! But under the tutelage of Pandit Gangasagarji we have all devoted our entire lives to earning degrees.'

'So which field are you studying?' asked Chandini curiously.

'Oh, I joined the university fifteen years ago. I first obtained a BA in philosophy and then decided to complete a double degree, a BA (Honours) in English. Having taken two basic degrees at the bachelor's level, I then worked towards an MA in anthropology. I am now completing my PhD in linguistics.'

'Why are so many young men staying on in universities earning multiple degrees—and that, too, in liberal arts?' whispered Chandini to Gangasagar.

'So that they continue to remain as students on the campus,' explained Gangasagar.

'But why do you need them there?' asked Chandini.

'So that they can contest the elections,' explained Gangasagar.

'Which elections?'

'Students' Union elections.'

'Why does the ABNS need to involve itself in Students' Union activities across the thirty-odd universities of Uttar Pradesh?'

'Because if our young men control the Students' Unions of the universities, we—the ABNS—control the youth, a key constituency in the state's power balance.'

'And then what will they do?'

'A liberal arts education is general enough for the IAS—the Indian Administrative Service or the IRS—the Indian Revenue Service.'

'So they'll enter the bureaucracy?' asked Chandini.

'Some of them will become trade union leaders, others income-tax commissioners, secretaries within the Reserve Bank of India—there are so many jobs that need us to have our own people!'

Some paces away, thirty policemen, armed with rifles, stood near jeeps and police vans. 'Why are there so many policemen around our Students' Union presidents?' asked Chandini.

'Protection,' answered her mentor.

'Protection?' asked Chandini, confused.

'Half of our Students' Union leaders have to be protected from candidates of other parties who are keen to dislodge them.'

'And the other half?'

'Others need to be protected from them,' he guffawed.

<hr/>

'You need a major victory,' said Gangasagar, as Chandini walked in.

'But I don't know the first thing about fighting elections,' she said.

'I don't mean an electoral victory, dear girl. I mean that you need a huge public relations coup. It should propel you into instant fame so that you're seen as the true inheritor of Ikram's legacy!'

'You obviously have something planned, Uncle Ganga,' she said astutely.

He smiled. He knew he had made the right choice.

'Did you know that Rungta & Somany are putting up a huge steel plant on the outskirts of the city?' he asked.

'Yes. I read about it. It's good for the state. More than twenty-five thousand jobs will be created upstream and downstream. The project is being put up in collaboration with a Japanese multinational and will be India's largest integrated steel plant, surpassing all that have been built till date,' said Chandini.

'Any idea how much land they need?' asked Gangasagar.

'I'm told that it will be spread over a thousand acres. The Uttar Pradesh government has offered it free. Various state governments across the country have been falling over themselves to woo R&S. An instant GDP booster shot,' said Chandini, gesturing.

'And who owns the land on which the plant is being built?'

'It's mostly agricultural land. Owned by subsistence farmers. They're delighted to surrender their land because they've all been guaranteed jobs by R&S.'

'What if the farmers were to revolt? What if they were to announce that they were being cheated out of their meagre holdings?'

'The press would have a field day,' she responded, 'but it wouldn't be good for the state's economy if R&S pulled out.'

'I want you to meet a few of the farmers. Get them to make you their spokesperson. Then I want you to sit outside the gates of that proposed plant and announce that you're going on an indefinite hunger strike—a fast unto death—until the plight of these poor unfortunate farmers isn't remedied!'

'But I'll be hungry!' she exclaimed.

'The power of renunciation, Chandini. Remember our history lessons and Mahatma Gandhi?'

'But I'm not used to starving myself. My sugar level falls within twenty-four hours,' she whined as she gratefully accepted the sweet cardamom tea offered to her. There was no beverage better than sweet cardamom tea in Chandini's world.

'Trust me. You'll have your victory within a day!'

'How? We haven't even negotiated with the management as yet.'

'Ah! I forgot to tell you that I had a meeting with Mr Somany—the vice-chairman of R&S—and...'

'What?'

'—he agreed to increase the compensation to farmers.'

'Firm commitment?'

'Unfortunately, his partner, the chairman—Mr Rungta —backed out. He said they couldn't afford to pay more.'

'So what have you told them?'

'I've said that we would be willing to give R&S a complete sales-tax holiday for twenty years—an offer that they're delighted with—if the ABNS came to power in Uttar Pradesh.'

'And how much is the sales-tax holiday worth?' she asked shrewdly.

'Several billions,' he replied.

'So you've negotiated to *increase* what the state government has *already* offered them?' she asked incredulously.

'Yes. But they've agreed to channel this money back to the farmers as compensation for the land.'

'So they don't have to spend a dime more but can still show that they've bowed down to your wishes and paid a hefty settlement for the land?'

'Precisely. Everyone's happy and we have an election victory!'

'But—but—why am I going on hunger strike? If we've got their agreement we could simply make an announcement to the press,' proposed Chandini.

'My precious girl. The press is not interested in problems that are already solved! They first need a dramatic problem with insurmountable odds. That's what they want to talk about. They'll lap it up! After we've given them an unsolvable problem, we then give them a miraculous solution. You'll be an instant heroine!'

Chandini looked at her Uncle Ganga, dazed. She realised that she had a lot to learn. 'Go eat a hearty meal.

You're not getting any food tomorrow,' said Gangasagar as she got up to leave.

＝

The former police commissioner was seated with Gangasagar in his little Birhana Road flat. 'I helped Ikram widen the rift between the home minister and Rajjo Bhaiya—on your instructions. I've now been booted out. You owe me,' he said.

'I agree,' said Gangasagar. 'I'll arrange an even better post—I'll use my influence in New Delhi. But before that you need to do something more for me.'

'What?' asked the police commissioner curiously.

'Shoot Chandini,' said Gangasagar simply.

＝

The press took an instant liking to the fresh young face that was braving the searing heat to sit outside the plant on a hunger strike. 'Chandini the Champion' said the *Times of India*; 'Chandini Changes the Deal' said the *Dainik*; 'Chandini Takes a Chance—and Wins!' screamed the *Lokbharti*.

The reporter, who had stood outside Gulbadan's kotha and engineered the fall of the previous chief minister, was reading the headlines. He looked at the photographs of the petite young woman, wearing a plain white cotton saree, looking positively radiant as she sat in silent hunger protest with hundreds of farmers. His scoop on the ex-chief minister had made him famous too. He wondered how long Chandini's honeymoon with the press would last. *A little bit of powder, a little bit of paint, makes a girl seem what she ain't*, he thought to himself. Where was the dirt? He decided to look under the carpet.

＝

'Your daughter is amazing,' said Gangasagar to Ikrambhai as they sat in his veranda sipping iced lemonade.

'Technically speaking, she's not my daughter. I was unable to adopt her. Muslim Personal Law didn't recognise it and the courts were unwilling to ratify it, as you well know,' replied Ikram wryly.

'It's the thought that counts. Everyone sees her as your natural successor—your legacy,' remarked Gangasagar.

'That's funny,' said Ikram.

'What?' asked Gangasagar, putting his glass down on the table in front of him.

'To be succeeded when one hasn't even succeeded!' he burst out, as Gangasagar laughed.

＝

'So what is it that you want me to do?' asked Ikram as they drained their glasses.

'I'll handle the vote-gathering but you handle the counting,' said Gangasagar.

'The Election Commission does the counting—not me!'

'But what if there's vote-rigging? Electoral malpractices are rampant, Ikram. I need you to handle it.'

'You want me to go around the state in an SUV capturing polling stations and stuffing ballots favouring the ABNS?' asked Ikram, relishing the thought of some good old-fashioned muscle power.

'No. I simply need you to station your lookouts at every polling station. The slightest sign of electoral malpractice and you phone me.'

'And you'll come flying in, like Superman, and ensure that the polling station is not captured?' asked Ikram sarcastically.

'No. But at least we'll know if we need to compensate by capturing some other polling station elsewhere!'

===

'Who's the Opposition's main candidate in Pilibhit constituency?' asked Gangasagar.

'Ramprasad Trivedi,' replied Chandini.

'Find me someone else with the same name. And who is the primary competition in Bisalpur?'

'Rafiq Ahmed Hussain.'

'That shouldn't be hard. Let's get someone with an identical name to contest in Bisalpur. Any idea who the strongest aspirant in Puranpur is?'

'Prakash Yadav.'

'Find me another Prakash Yadav.'

'You want us to hand out ABNS tickets to people who have no qualifications, no experience, no vote-share, simply because they have names that are identical to those of their strongest opponents?'

'No. Not ABNS tickets. We'll fund them but they'll contest as independents.'

'And why are we doing this?'

'Because the votes of the primary Opposition candidates will then get split. From the confusion in the similar-sounding names, some of their rightful votes will get logged as favouring the identically-named independents financed by us.'

'Is this a worthwhile exercise? Finding hundreds of independents to contest against the Opposition?'

'Winning is not only about strengthening yourself; it's also about weakening the enemy. Anything that reduces the Opposition's vote-share must be done if we're to win.'

'But the opposing parties may adopt the same strategy with us,' argued Chandini.

'When is the notification of elections expected from the Election Commission?'

'April twenty-first.'

'And the last date for filing nominations would be a week thereafter—April twenty-eighth, right?'

'Yes.'

'What's the deadline for filing nominations on April twenty-eighth?'

'6.30 pm.'

'I want all our independents to file their nominations from various constituencies at six pm on April twenty-eighth. Let's not give the opposition any time to react.'

＝＝

The phone bill would be enormous and his editor would be furious. But everything would be accepted once the story was splashed as headlines across their front page. 'Chandini's Love Child' would be sensational. The investigative reporter silently thanked God for giving him a sensitive nose—he could sniff dirt a mile away.

Everyone has a past, he thought. And this beloved idol of the youth, this new sensation, Chandini, was no different. Acting on this assumption, he had made a few phone calls to one of his cousins, a teacher who had emigrated to England a few years previously. The cousin had promised to make a few discreet enquiries in the Oxford area. The cousin's friend—a doctor—had checked with the National Health Service. A few days later he phoned to say that Chandini's assigned GP in Oxford had indeed issued her a medical certificate in order to get leave of absence from classes at St Hilda's. The reason provided on the certificate was 'intense menstrual cramps'. No one took eight weeks off because of menstrual cramps, reasoned the curious doctor. A quiet word with the local GP had led to the matronly abortive douche lady, and from her to the Mother & Baby home in Grasmere.

He looked at the first draft of the story that lay before him. 'The sacred goddess being worshipped in temples across Uttar Pradesh, and indeed in many other parts of India, is not Lakshmi, Saraswati or Durga, but a new sensation called Chandini. The refreshingly young and attractive politician has won the hearts and minds of voters and now looks poised to seriously contend for the coveted chief minister's post. She fasts unto death for farmers, preaches honesty, integrity and lofty values of moral and ethical conduct. But how many are actually aware of the background of this debutante? Not many, as it turns out. All that we seem to know is that she wears off-white sarees and looks good in them. But a little research led this reporter to find the dirt that has stained her pure and pristine snow-white image. He was shocked with what he discovered.'

Perfect start. He looked over the rest of his story that he had typed using his trusted Remington electric typewriter, and walked over to the editor's desk. 'You'll find that my expense log is justified once you read what I've just submitted,' he said as he walked back to his desk and covered his typewriter with a grey plastic dust cover.

'You need to go to England and verify the facts,' said the editor as he read the story.

'Wh—what? Since when does this rag have the budget for a reporter to travel across continents to verify his facts?' he asked. 'You crib if I take a cab!'

'The budget appeared after we decided that we don't wish to get our asses kicked by her adoptive father—Ikrambhai—or our asses sued by her godfather, Gangasagar.'

'Gangasagar can't touch me. He knows that I helped him with the expose on the last chief minister. He wouldn't be figuring out ways to place his protégé on the throne if it weren't for my story having destroyed the last poor sucker!'

'And we can't be seen as a rag that's keen to carry out a moral crusade against every chief minister or aspirant. That's why we need you to go verify the facts for yourself. The story is too explosive to be based on the hearsay of a cousin!'

———

The flight to London via Cairo and Geneva was to take off from New Delhi two hours later. An economy-class ticket had been provided to him along with a frugal travel allowance. He would need to stay in rat-infested hellholes to survive on that. Having checked in his suitcase, he headed over to passport control where the officer cursorily looked over and stamped his travel papers. He took back his passport and placed it in the leather duffel bag he had slung over his shoulders. He reached the departure area and went through security.

'What's this, sir?' asked the security officer as he unzipped the duffel bag. At the bottom of the bag was a little parcel wrapped in grey plastic and held together by duct tape. 'That's not mine,' said the reporter, wondering how the parcel had gotten into his bag. The security officer, a burly Jat from Haryana, ignored the answer and took out a penknife with which he proceeded to puncture the parcel.

A white, crystal-like powder spilled out. The security officer touched the powder with his forefinger and dabbed it lightly on his tongue. It was odourless but bitter. It was definitely heroin. 'Are you aware of the provisions of the Dangerous Drugs Act, 1930, read with the relevant provisions of the Opium Act, 1878, sir?' asked the security officer as he signalled one of his colleagues to cuff the offender.

'That's not mine! I'm telling you that I don't know how it got there—' he protested but it was of no avail. The muscular Jat already had him bent him over the security check counter, with his arms pulled tightly behind his back, and with a pair of cuffs on his wrists. 'If this is not your parcel, how are your fingerprints on the plastic, eh?' he shouted. The officer pulled him by the scruff of his neck, pushed him against a wall and asked him to spread his legs. He quickly patted him down and also gave him a sly pinch on his ass. 'Just checking to see whether your ass can take the treatment that it's gonna get in prison,' he growled.

As the reporter was loaded into the police jeep outside the airport en route to custodial lockup, he wondered, 'How the fuck did the security chap know that my fingerprints were on the plastic without having it dusted or examined?' He then remembered the grey plastic dust cover on his Remington electric typewriter in the newspaper office.

He cursed Gangasagar, his editor, and his luck—in that order.

■C■

Anjali arrived in her chauffeured silver Jaguar XJS, wearing a chic lemon cotton saree. The Bollywood sex symbol had tied back her long auburn hair with a white Hermès scarf and her eyes were hidden behind an extremely expensive pair of Versace sunglasses. She gently dabbed her kerchief under the sunglasses and the paparazzi contingent immediately burnt up their flash bulbs taking photos of the sultry goddess, looking positively delicious in her designer election ensemble—excellent breakfast material for the pathetic, inquisitive masses.

The streets leading up to the rally site were festooned with bunting and flags and a hundred thousand people lined up waiting for a glimpse of two female deities—one political and the other filmic. The rally ground was an expanse of saffron, green and red—the three colours of the ABNS flag. Saffron for Hindus, green for Muslims and red for the Dalits. Towards one corner was a massive stage adorned like the rest of the rally grounds with banners and flowers. Anjali walked up to the stage where Chandini awaited her. The women hugged each other as though they were the best of friends. They were actually meeting each other for the very first time. Behind them were massive rose-pink cut-outs of their images, almost fifteen feet high—Bollywood movie poster-style. The image of Chandini showed her with an angelic expression on her face, holding the scales of justice in one hand and a sword in the other. The poster of Anjali showed her holding a Statue of Liberty-inspired flaming torch.

Both women stood on stage as party workers brought out massive six-inch-thick garlands fashioned from marigolds and red-green ribbons—another reminder of the party colours—and garlanded them as though they were indeed manifestations of deities. Both women continued to remain standing, waving to the adoring crowds.

'I promise you that I shall deliver pure, unadulterated justice to you, my beloved people. And if this hand ever needs to hold a sword to deliver justice, it shall rise for one reason alone—to defend the poor and downtrodden of this state!' shouted Chandini emotionally into the microphone as echoes of her words bounced off massive speakers located all over the rally ground. Thousands of her supporters roared in glee and chanted, 'Till the sun and moon shall be, Chandini's name immortal be!'

'I am humbled by your love. I am honoured by your respect. I am blessed by your support. I am energised by your enthusiasm. I am motivated by your confidence in me. I shall not let you down—ever!' she thundered as the crowd burst into deafening applause. Police had cordoned off the stage where the two women were standing. Hundreds of baton-wielding khaki-clad cops wearing riot helmets were preventing the surge of humanity from clambering up the platform.

Chandini sat down and Anjali arose to speak. She was nervous. It was one thing to utter the lines of a screenplay in front of a movie camera, and quite another to deliver a speech to hundreds of thousands of screaming political activists. She was only here because her special nocturnal friend—Somany—had insisted that her endorsement of Chandini was vital.

'In a state that has remained enveloped by the darkness of poverty, disease, illiteracy and feudalism, there is a single light that shines bright! I see the light! Do you?' she yelled, and the grounds reverberated with approval. 'The light is intense, it's incandescent, it's the brightest light I've ever seen. This light can illuminate, this light is pure, this light is unadulterated energy, this light is the light that shall envelope Uttar Pradesh— Chandini!'

As the multitude went berserk and howled their approval, a shot rang out. It would not have been heard if it were not for the fact that the gun had been fired near an open microphone. Chandini fell to the ground clutching her right shoulder. Blood was trickling through her fingers and a large red stain had developed on her off-white blouse and saree. Anjali threw herself to the ground and cradled Chandini's head in her lap as the security officers rushed to prevent the frenzied crowds from reaching them. The Doordarshan television camera and the hundred press photographers beautifully captured the sentiment of the moment.

'*Adi Shakti, Namo Namah; Sarab Shakti, Namo Namah; Prithum Bhagvati, Namo Namah; Kundalini Mata Shakti; Mata Shakti, Namo Namah,*' whispered Gangasagar as he watched the proceedings from a distance.

They were standing in the hospital corridor outside her room. Members of the press had been barred from entering the premises. They had created a makeshift camp outside the hospital gates and were snapping photos of everyone—including startled patients—as they came and went.

'How is she,' asked Gangasagar.

'Fine,' said Menon, 'the bullet grazed her right shoulder. A few stitches, some dressing and antibiotics—and she should be ready to go.'

'Did you meet the former police commissioner?' asked Gangasagar.

'Yes. He's a crack shot—I'd told him that it should be her right side, not left. Too much risk of her heart being in the vicinity,' explained Menon.

'Sometimes I wonder whether the girl has a heart,' murmured Gangasagar, 'she reminds me so much of myself. Did you also tell him that you didn't want the bullet to actually pierce her but only graze her?'

'I did. He told me that there were no guarantees on that one, though. We'd asked him to shoot near an open microphone so that the shot would be heard. He performed well—he's waiting for you to put in a word so that he gets a fresh assignment in New Delhi.'

'Yes, I promised him. She doesn't know anything, does she?'

'No.'

'How many times has the scene been replayed on Doordarshan?'

'Around fifty times.'

'Get the press photos of Chandini's head being cradled in Anjali's lap. Put it on posters with the slogan—*I am willing to shed every drop of my blood in the service of my people*. Have thousands of posters printed and plastered over the city. I want her to be a martyr without having died!'

'But the doctor will be letting her leave pretty soon. She doesn't require hospitalisation—it's a surface wound only,' argued Menon.

'Get the doctor over here. I want him to announce that she's being kept overnight for observation.'

'And?'

'And nothing else. Never tell a lie unless it's absolutely necessary.'

'Should he reveal that she's in no danger?'

'He should say that she's out of danger, but only tomorrow morning. There's a significant difference between lying and delaying the truth!'

= =

'Uncle Ganga, stop fussing over me. I need to get up, leave this miserable hospital and get back to my election rallies,' she protested.

'Chandini. You're not going back to any election rally. Battles are won or lost before they are ever fought. This one has already been won.'

'So I do nothing till polling day?'

'Ah! You shall be busy. I have arranged an aircraft that will take you from here to Tirumala. From Tirumala you shall proceed to Goa, and onwards to Ajmer. The same aircraft will then take you to Amritsar and you'll be back here in three days.'

'But why am I going to all these places? There are no elections being held in any of them!' she argued.

'In Tirumala you shall bow down before Lord Venkateshwara and make the Hindus happy. In Goa you shall light a candle at Bom Jesus and make the Christians happy. You shall next go place a chador of flowers at the Dargah of Moinuddin Chisti in Ajmer, making the Muslims happy. Finally, you shall offer prayers at the Golden Temple in Amritsar, making the Sikhs happy. After you have made everyone happy, they will make you happy—by electing your party to government.'

<hr />

In Mumbai's hip Bandra suburb sat the homes of Bollywood's rich and famous. Bollywood siren Anajali's home was a beautiful palatial sea-facing house, guarded by a massive iron gate and tight security. She needed the last. Not because she faced a threat, but because of the very special friend—Somany—who visited her most nights.

After her emotional speech in support of Chandini at the rally, Gangasagar had taken her aside. 'You are endowed with special gifts,' he said.

'I know,' she said, 'many people have told me that both are spectacular.'

Nothing flustered the old man. 'Yes, I understand that. But I was talking about your ability to express yourself—to influence people and their emotions. Have you ever considered joining politics?'

'I would love to sit in Parliament, but I don't have the patience for elections. Alas, I'm resigned to my fate as a Bollywood sex symbol.'

'Not necessarily. Because of the public support you brought us, we shall soon be in government in Uttar Pradesh. We shall be happy to nominate you to the Rajya Sabha—the Upper House. You get to sit in Parliament, and that too without undergoing elections!'

'And what's the catch? You're not one of those dirty old men, are you?' she smiled.

'My dear Anjali. I'm a dirty man—but not in the field of love. Only politics. And all politics is dirty. Clean politics is an oxymoron.'

'So what is it that you want from me if not a cuddle?' she asked, her eyes twinkling.

'Let's just say that I'll call in the favour whenever I need it. In the meantime, do continue to have fun with your special nocturnal friend.'

= =

'And it now seems clear that the Uttar Pradesh assembly elections are likely to throw up an unclear mandate with no single party being able to form the government on its own,' droned the news anchor. Agrawalji, Ikrambhai, Menon and Gangasagar were seated in Agrawalji's living room watching the polling results as they were flowing in.

'I thought you said Chandini would become chief minister,' said a visibly worried Agrawalji. He had spent millions financing the ABNS and was seeing his investment being washed down the drain.

'I never said that Chandini would become chief minister. I said that the ABNS would hold the reigns of power.'

'How in heaven's name are you so damn flippant about such things, Gangasagarji?' exclaimed Ikram.

'Menon, how many seats does the Uttar Pradesh assembly have?' asked Gangasagar.

'Four hundred and three,' replied Menon.

'And how many of those seats are with the ABNS?'

'One hundred and sixty.'

'So we're forty-two short of the halfway mark for a majority, right?'

'Yes.'

'Is there any party in the state that has won more seats than the ABNS?'

'No. The next highest has ninety-nine.'

'And as per the Constitution of the country, the governor of the state must invite the leader of the party that has obtained the maximum number of seats in the assembly to form a government. Right?'

'Right.'

'The problem, of course, is that if the governor invites the ABNS to form the next government, we would need to entice opposition MLAs to cross over to our side.'

'So what?'

'They'll want cabinet berths. Our own members will be deprived of positions. We'll have disciplinary problems.'

'So you *don't* want the governor to invite us?' asked the perplexed Agrawalji.

'If we don't produce adequate letters of support from MLAs of other parties, he'll have to ask the next largest party to try cobbling together a government.'

'Yes, but if they need to reach the halfway mark they'll need a hundred and three allies in addition to the ninety-nine MLAs that they already have. They would need our ABNS MLAs to get a working majority in the house.'

'Suppose we offer them our entire strength?' asked Gangasagar quietly.

'What? Are you out of your fucking mind?' yelled Ikram.

'My price for ABNS support is that I want each and every cabinet berth for my MLAs. All the portfolios—home, finance, revenue, industries, human resources—must be allotted to us. They can have their chief minister.'

'And what happens to Chandini?'

'She waits for the government to go into paralysis.'

'Paralysis?'

'What will their chief minister do when all his decisions get stalled? All the portfolios shall be with us.'

'But what if the paralysis prompts the governor to ask New Delhi to step in and impose President's Rule?' asked Agrawalji.

'The governor won't ask for President's Rule.'

'Why?'

'Because the president will advise him against it.'

'Why?'

'Because the prime minister will not recommend it to the president.'

'And you have direct access to the prime minister of India?'

'Well, almost.'



The sadhvi was dressed in a simple, pale saffron saree and chose to remain barefoot. Around her neck was a string of *rudraksha* prayer beads. She was a beautiful woman, and not in the physical sense alone. True, she was fair-complexioned, shapely and her smiling face was framed by her open shoulder-length hair. But these aside, her face reflected deep spiritual contentment. Her presence was almost magical—radiating quiet confidence and divine serenity.

She sat on a comfortable sofa facing a large picture window that framed a rose garden. It was summer and the searing heat of New Delhi was kept at bay by the quiet hum of air-conditioning within. To her left sat the prime minister of India, on an armchair slightly lower than the sadhvi's sofa—in deference to the sadhvi's enlightened soul.

'What is bothering you, child?' she asked him.

'I'm rather worried, blessed mother,' he replied.

It was ironic. He was sixty, and she barely thirty, but she insisted on addressing him as 'child' and being addressed as 'mother'. Anyone listening in on their conversation would have laughed but their conversations were always entirely private. The prime minister's secretary was not allowed to make any entry either in the official entry log or in the prime ministerial diary.

'I know—I can tell. A mother always knows when her child is in trouble,' she commented softly.

'The situation in Uttar Pradesh is confusing. The ABNS emerged as the single largest party. The governor had asked us—informally—if he should invite them to form the next state government. We felt that there were sufficient grounds not to invite them.'

'Such as?'

'They did not have a clear majority.'

'Neither did your party—you had fewer numbers than them!'

'But they did not even attempt to muster letters of support from legislators outside their party. They made it painfully easy for us to convince the governor to invite the second-largest formation—our own party—to form the government.'

'So what seems to be the trouble? Aren't you happy that your party is in government in Uttar Pradesh?'

'At what price? We had only ninety-nine legislators of our own. The balance hundred and three had to be pulled in from the ABNS to get a working majority. None of them wanted any monetary reward, only ministerial berths.'

'And you obliged?'

'Yes. But it meant making the cabinet gigantic—sixty members! The entire cabinet—with the exception of the chief minister—is drawn from the ABNS. The tail is wagging the dog!'

'And this troubles you?'

'O blessed mother, we shall soon have a revolt within our ranks in Uttar Pradesh. Our own MLAs—who have been denied cabinet positions to accommodate the ABNS—are up in arms.'

'Do you believe that your state government in Uttar Pradesh will fall, child?'

'Yes, blessed mother, I do.'

'And what will be the implications of this elsewhere in the country?'

'State elections are due in several states over the next year. A problem in Uttar Pradesh will send out a very negative signal to the rest of India. It will suggest that our party is not in control of things.'

'What are your political options, child?'

'I'm damned either way. If I don't do anything, we'll have a rebellion, the government will fall and the Opposition will slide easily into power. If I ask the president to declare President's Rule—government by New Delhi—I'll be called a traitor to the Constitution, a backdoor manipulator.'

'Come over here, child,' she commanded suddenly. He rose and walked over to her and knelt before her.

She placed a hand on his head and chanted some prayers fervently, with her eyes closed. A minute later, she opened her eyes and directed, 'Your answer will be with you by tomorrow!'

'But blessed mother—' he began.

'Sshh!' she admonished him, placing a finger upon his lips. Her touch was electrifying. 'Haven't I guided you correctly in the past?' she asked.

He nodded quietly.

'Then do as I say!' she instructed.

special camp had been set up along the border of Gandhar. Luxurious tents, overflowing with food, wine, perfume, musicians and dancing girls, were buzzing with activity, the event managers desperately keeping up with the demands of Ambhi. He certainly knew how to throw a party. 'Alexander is no less than a god who shall help me crush that devil—Paurus! Alexander's welcome to Gandhar should reflect his exalted status,' said Ambhi to his new ministers—handpicked loyalists who had no ties to his dead father.

The cacophony of marching drums and bugles accompanied by the ominous stomping of thousands of feet was deafening. The Alexander war machine marched like a swarm of killer ants ready for a feeding frenzy. As their feet trampled the ground, the dull vibration of the infantry's advance sounded a sinister warning to those who ventured near. The main body of the army had traversed the Khyber Pass while a smaller contingent directly under the command of Alexander had taken the more circuitous northern route, capturing the fort of Pir-sar in a victory that had eluded the great Heracles before him.

Hearing the approach of the Graeco-Macedonian monster, Ambhi's camp fell into a silent hush. The Gandhar musicians stopped blowing trumpets and beating drums, the dancing girls stopped gyrating their bellies and hips as the music ceased. The sound of the approaching Macedonian army was dull, a bit like the lumbering tread of a giant that shook the earth each time it placed another foot forward.

'Maybe we've been duped,' whispered one minister excitedly to another. 'Isn't it possible that we've dropped our dhotis in humble obeisance only to be raped?' His colleague gestured for him to shut up. Both of them would be roasted on the skewers that were being used to cook meat for the flesh-loving visitors if Ambhi heard them. He silently muttered a few expletives as he maintained a plastic smile for the benefit of his monarch.

A special platform had been constructed at a huge height. It was to be used by the two leaders to be seen embracing one another in order to send out a signal of their mutual friendship to the men. Ambhi climbed the stairs that led to it, to get a better view of the approaching behemoth, slightly out of breath. His eyes were blood-shot from excessive drinking, though his physique continued to remain fit and firm. His face had a permanent scowl that looked even more menacing when he smiled or flashed his teeth. He was always attired impeccably, with colour-coordinated turban, dhoti, wrap, slippers and jewellery. If his outfit was of a reddish hue, his jewellery would consist of rubies or pink diamonds; if his clothes were green, the jewels were emeralds; if his ensemble was blue, the gems would be sapphires; of course, diamonds went with any colour. Ambhi squinted as he tried to gaze into the distance. All he could see was what looked like a gathering storm in the distance. It was actually the dust being kicked up from the earth as Alexander's phalanxes marched inexorably to the beat of the drummers.

After an interminable wait, Ambhi could eventually discern the infantry wearing protective bronze armour, including bronze leg-guarding greaves and helmets with cheek guards and decorated with plumed crests of horsehair. All of them were carrying bronze and leather shields, long spears and shorter swords. Flanking the infantry on either side was the companion cavalry of around three thousand, which had been divided into groups of two hundred each. The horses seemed oversized and well-fed, each animal draped with thick felt over its sides. The beasts were armoured with breast and head plating and their riders, wearing bronze cuirasses, shoulder guards and Boeotian helmets, carried xystons and shorter curved slashing swords. Alexander's army was a sight to behold. Ambhi gulped nervously and wondered whether he had bitten off more than he could chew.

Quite unexpectedly, there was silence. The drums and bugles ceased. Alexander halted his battalions and rode up to Ambhi's camp alone. 'Horse shit! Why are these things not choreographed in advance,' Ambhi muttered to himself as he ran down the stairs frantically to mount his own steed and ride towards the Macedonian divinity. Both horses slowed towards the final stretch, each of the riders not wishing to appear over-eager. Ambhi was wondering what Alexander would say to him. *Ambhi, I think you're a great big bloodsucking leech. I don't need you to fight my battles for me. Fuck with someone else?*

Trailing behind each rider were four or five other horsemen—bodyguards, interpreters, scribes and advisors.

At length, when they drew up before one another, Alexander spoke first. 'Ambhi. I think you're a great—'

Ambhi broke out in a cold sweat. Was Alexander about to humiliate him?

'—friend of Alexander. I too extend my hand of friendship to you. Together we shall create a formidable alliance!' declared Alexander through Sasigupta, his Afghan lieutenant who was playing interpreter. Ambhi heaved a sigh of relief. It was working out as planned— his moment of triumph. A grand alliance with the greatest warrior on earth!

Ambhi was at his humble best. 'Why should we battle one another, O Alexander? It is evident to me that you do not wish to rob us of our food or water, the only two necessities of life for which intelligent men will feel compelled to fight. As for wealth, I have more than I can possibly use and I shall be happy to share it with you, O fortunate one!'

Both men having dismounted, Alexander embraced Ambhi and jokingly said, 'Do you think that your courtesy, charm and impeccable manners will prevent a fight between us? You're mistaken. I shall fight you, O Ambhi, to determine who can be a better friend and I promise you that you shall not have the better of me!'

◼️

The Jhelum was in full flood. Monsoon winds had lashed the Punjab landscape mercilessly, and the men and their equipment were soaked. An endless stream of thick muddy water flowed down the hills and made it impossible to walk even a few steps without slipping. There was water everywhere—in the river, in the rains, in the Macedonian army's food, in their tents, even in their cooking fires! Damn the water!

Worsening the situation, Alexander kept insisting that they move several miles up and down the riverbank each day so as to keep the other side guessing about the possible crossing point. The brilliant military strategist in Alexander knew that every move made by his forces stationed on the right bank of the Jhelum was being shadowed by Paurus's troops on the left bank. He also knew that the massive Kaikey forces—fifty thousand infantry, five thousand cavalry, three hundred war chariots and over two hundred war elephants—vastly out-numbered his.

He would need to play this game meticulously. 'Seleucus!' he called out to his trusted general.

'Yes, my lord,' said Seleucus, walking up briskly to Alexander, ignoring the aide who had been buffing his armour.

'Can you look like me?' asked Alexander in all earnestness.

'No one can look like you, O lord, you're divine!' exclaimed Seleucus laying on a thick layer of buttery praise. He knew it had worked when Alexander smiled at him. *Flattery will get you everywhere*, thought Seleucus.

'No, no. I mean from a distance. Suppose we leave the royal tent in place, leave the bulk of the infantry along with it, leave the royal pavilion untouched and have someone who looks like me parading every once in a while wearing my royal robes. Would it be enough to convince the other side that we've not moved?' asked the ingenious tactician. Seleucus smiled. He knew what Alexander was thinking. It was the classic pincer move that he was famous for—leave the enemy open to attack on both flanks.

'Better than me, would be Phillipos. He has more of your build, my lord. As I see it, we should be able to convince Paurus's lookouts that we've not moved. The more critical question is, what then? How do we cross the Jhelum and where?' asked Seleucus, knowing fully well that his boss already knew the answer.

'Remember those rafts we used to build the pontoon bridge across the Indus? What if we cut them into pieces, carry them quietly to a spot some miles upstream and reassemble them there? We could then use the rafts to cross,' explained Alexander.

'Chopping up and putting together rafts for forty thousand men and three thousand horses? That's impossible!' spluttered Seleucus incredulously. His men were already complaining that they were wet and weary.

'Ah! You and I shall take the entire cavalry of three thousand but only ten thousand of the infantry. The vast remainder will stay right here with Phillipos. Once we have crossed the river with our secret forces, we shall attack Paurus from the rear,' explained Alexander triumphantly.

'But he may turn around and attack us with his full might,' argued Seleucus. 'We'll be vastly outnumbered, my lord. He has hundreds of elephants,' he said nervously.

'That's the moment for Phillipos to cross, my friend!' reasoned Alexander.

'Either way Paurus would be compelled to fight on two fronts,' rationalised Seleucus as the full import of his master's strategy sunk in.

'We're being attacked,' yelled the vanguard of Kaikey's massive army. Like an echo, the message was relayed through a series of shouts until it reached the ears of the towering Paurus. His name was derived from *Purushottam* —*Supreme Being*—and he looked nothing less than that. Standing over six-and-a-half feet in height, the king had a radiant glow on his face that was accentuated by his curled and oiled moustache, in the typical fashion of Rajput warriors. He wore his military armour and regalia as though it were an intrinsic part of his royal personage. His muscles rippled with every move that he made, his chest puffed out with muscular pride. His fair skin was wet from the rains but each droplet clung to his frame as though it were in love with his body, refusing to let go of the physical contact. His jet-black hair hung down to his shoulders and was held in place by a ruby-encrusted helmet that covered half his face. He was the mighty Paurus. Having subdued the hill kingdoms of Kashmir, Mallayrajya, Kuluta, and Sindh, he was rightly entitled to the title of *Parvateshwar*—Conqueror of the Mountains.

'How can that be?' Paurus asked his prime minister, Indradutt. 'Hadn't your lookouts told us that Alexander's army continues to remain stationed across the Jhelum right before our very eyes?'

'Yes, my lord. In fact, Abhaya's spies also chatted with the local farmers who told them that Alexander had surveyed the river yesterday and had blurted out that the river was just too deep and wide to think of an immediate crossing,' answered Indradutt.

'O Indradutt, my trusted advisor. We've been tricked by that crafty devil. Tell the charioteers and archers to swing around and teach Alexander a lesson that he will never forget!' thundered Paurus, as monsoon rains continued to lash down on him. Indradutt nodded and went over to convey the message to the commander-in-chief who was in utter panic. His chariots were slipping in the smooth clayey soil and they had already lost several of them. The archers' two-metre highbows—monstrous weapons that could shoot spears instead of arrows—needed firm ground on which to be anchored and in this weather firm ground was an impossibility.

Kaikey's elephants were their biggest strength. Desperate to relieve the rear that was bearing the brunt of the attack, Paurus commanded that the elephants be called into action. As the giant pachyderms lumbered towards the terrified Macedonian forces, they were suddenly attacked by axes and spears hurled by horrendous catapults. As the hatchets and lances began to meet their mark, the tuskers went wild and, in the ensuing stampede, trampled Kaikey's own battalions. Just when things couldn't possibly get worse, news came in that the attack from the rear had been carried out by only a small contingent of Alexander's troops and that the remaining troops commanded by Phillipos were now crossing the Jhelum and attacking the front.

The valiant Paurus seated on the howdah of his elephant towards the centre of the battlefield then received devastating news. Both his sons had been killed, one defending the tail and the other the head of Kaikey's army. With nothing left to lose, Paurus asked his mahout to charge towards Alexander so that he could put a spear through the invader's heart. It was the opportunity that Alexander had been waiting for. He ordered his phalanx to move and surround Paurus and his personal battalion. The mayhem that followed was pure butchery. Rivulets of blood flowed down the banks to meet the mighty Jhelum as thousands of Kaikey's soldiers were massacred.

Having pulled out a javelin piercing his right shoulder, the brave Paurus, now weak from loss of blood, staggered off his elephant and was instantly surrounded by Alexander's men who took him captive. The magnificent and proud warrior had lost none of his dignity as he was brought before Alexander who was flanked by Ambhi. 'How shall I treat you, O Paurus,' asked a bloody Alexander with the swagger of a victor. Ambhi smiled smugly—this was going to be fun.

'Treat me, O Alexander, as befits a king!' replied Paurus as he stood in chains before his subjugator, defeated but not dispirited, wounded but not vanquished, chained but no less proud.

The stately answer brought a smile to Alexander's face. 'For my own sake, I would do that, O Paurus,' said Alexander, and the smile disappeared from Ambhi's face. 'Ask for any boon and it shall be yours,' said Alexander grandly and Paurus replied, 'All that I want is included in that request.'

Alexander was not immune to acts of bravery, chivalry and stateliness. He walked up to Paurus, embraced him, and said, 'From this day on, you're my friend, my ally. I give you back your kingdom and your lands. Make peace with Ambhi and rule in my name!'

The tearful Paurus threw away the last vestiges of his reserve and made peace with Alexander and Ambhi.

Chanakya was sitting with Chandragupta on the floor of his hut eating *poha*—flattened and roasted rice. 'What have we achieved, wise teacher?' asked Chandragupta, baffled by the sudden turn of events.

'Everything that we wanted,' said the Brahmin taking a handful of poha from the leaf.

Outside the hut, there were sounds of men going through their mid-morning drill. The official supervising them was calling them a bunch of sissies for not running fast enough, jumping high enough, hitting hard enough or throwing far enough. He pushed them harder each day. He wanted a small but extremely effective and overwhelmingly powerful force—one that would be able to capitalise on strength, speed, flexibility and surprise.

Ignoring the harsh and sometimes unholy language being used by the drill sergeant outside, Chanakya calmly continued. 'Alexander defeated Paurus. Paurus lost twenty-three thousand troops. He's now a mere vassal of Alexander. We could never have achieved that by ourselves,' reasoned Chanakya.

'But we've created a stronger Alexander,' exclaimed Chandragupta, popping some more of the spicy rice mixture into his eager mouth.

'Exactly the opposite, dear Chandragupta. Alexander's men were tired and weary even before the battle with Paurus began. The Jhelum victory came at a very high price. Our undercover operatives tell us that Alexander's men are refusing to march further. The world could not stop Alexander's advance but a single battle with the courageous but foolish Paurus has halted him in his tracks!' laughed Chanakya.

'I continue to have reservations about what we did. We should have fought for what was right!'

'Chandragupta, my son, a battle is never about who's right. It's mostly about who's left!'

'So what happens now, acharya?'

'Alexander will turn back. He'll leave Bharat soon. He'll probably designate Seleucus as governor in charge of the conquered territories. That's when we'll make our move,' said Chanakya.

From outside sounds of hundreds of batons crashing against one another accentuated Chanakya's words. *Silambam*—bamboo staff combat—was on. The trainer had studied ancient martial arts from all over Bharat and had incorporated these into the exercises of his men.

'We're lucky to have him with us,' commented Chandragupta as he heard the sounds of bamboo shafts being thrashed against each other.

'As long as he remains away from the arms of Mainika, we should be fine,' commented Chanakya with a roguish grin on his face.

'I'll never understand how you managed to convince Ambhi's commander-in-chief to become our trainer!' burst out Chandragupta.

'He had no choice but to join us. He was having a siesta in his harlot's bedroom while Takshila was being taken over by Kaikey's forces. He couldn't expect to be welcomed back by Gandharraj or Ambhi. They would have had his head impaled on a spike and paraded for his folly! I offered him an alternative.'

'Hah! He didn't have an alternative!'

'True. Always remember that a conjurer will offer you alternatives to choose from but you always end up picking the one that he wants you to!'

'I don't understand. You talk in riddles sometimes, acharya!' complained Chandragupta.

'Who is Mainika? How did she acquire the jalakrida for the commander's aquatic delights? How did Abhaya, the intelligence operative of Indradutt, get a whiff of this news and decide to use it to Kaikey's advantage?' asked the crafty teacher quietly.

Chandragupta bowed down before his guru and touched his feet. He knew that he was in the presence of the ultimate master—not of the martial arts that were being taught outside but of the craft that was taught inside.

'Protect me, O wise guru, for I have sinned,' pleaded Ambhi as he prostrated himself before Chanakya. 'Rise, O King of Gandhar. I'm not aware of any sin committed by you. You seem to be under the mistaken impression that I am omniscient and omnipresent!' joked Chanakya. The young king rose and straightened himself. With hands still folded in a gesture of obeisance, he said, 'I should never have extended my hand of friendship to

Alexander. All that I gained was the wrath of my own people. Even the defeat of Paurus was no victory because Alexander made Paurus his satrap instead of handing over his kingdom to me.'

'Gandhar is big enough for the ambitions of Ambhi, isn't it?' asked Chanakya slyly, eyes twinkling.

'Yes, but it rankles me. Paurus and I are now equals before Alexander. We're both his vassals. The title that I gained without spilling my people's blood is the same title that Paurus obtained after allowing thousands of his people to be slaughtered. Yet, history will record him as the hero and Ambhi as the coward!' said a forlorn Ambhi.

Chanakya put on his best false smile and asked, 'And what can Chanakya do for you, O King?'

'I need your wise counsel, acharya. I need you by my side. I'm aware that my former commander-in-chief is helping train your anti-Macedonian forces. I do not mind that. I know that you're training Chandragupta to be king of Magadha. I do not have any objection to that either. I simply need your guidance and wise counsel so that I can make Gandhar economically and politically strong and resilient,' pleaded Ambhi.

'And what would that involve?' asked Chanakya cautiously.

'I would like you to be my *rajguru*—royal advisor—and would like you to reside next to my palace. I've built a marvellous official residence for the rajguru. I want you and your disciples to move in there. No expense will be spared and you'll be well looked after. Grace this house with your august presence, O acharya. It will give me the advantage of meeting you whenever I need your wise counsel!' urged Ambhi.

'O King, I'm but a poor Brahmin. Of what use are palaces and mansions to me? I'll be uncomfortable in such lavish surroundings!' commented the man wrily, knowing full well that maintaining his poverty cost him an arm and a leg. Tears in his eyes, Ambhi prostrated himself once again before Chanakya and pleaded, 'Please, acharya, do not let me wander through the political jungle all by myself. Please be my guide. I shall not leave until you agree!'

'Very well, O Ambhi. You're indeed persuasive. I accept, but on one condition,' said Chanakya.

'And what's that?' asked Ambhi looking up from his prostrated position awkwardly. 'If the stars are not auspicious, you shall allow me to relinquish the position,' stated the Brahmin. Ambhi acquiesced and requested the new rajguru to visit his official residence along with an architect so that his personal requirements could be met.

==

The villa built by Ambhi for Chanakya had bright and airy rooms, high ceilings, polished stone floors, thick hardwood beams, and lots of space. The house was built around a splendid courtyard and was located on the banks of a babbling brook. It had open gardens dotted with wild flowers and fruit trees that sent wafts of scented breeze through the doors and windows.

Chanakya was taking a tour of the premises along with Chandragupta, Sinharan, Mehir and Sharangrao. His disciples were frustrated. Why had their teacher allowed himself to be misled by the fanciful claims of that rogue Ambhi? How could he agree to ally himself with a scoundrel who had lent his very soul to Alexander? As they wandered from one room to the next, being guided by the architect, the disciples could not help wondering what they were doing there. For his part, Chanakya seemed a little too obsessed with the glamour of the mansion. He was actually running his hands over the wooden doors and windows and lying down on the floors to marvel at the excellent finish wrought by the stonemasons! Tour over, Chanakya thanked the architect profusely and announced that he would move in along with his disciples the next day. They mounted the royal chariots sent by Ambhi and set off for their ashram.

'Acharya, what are you doing? We can't move in—' began Chandragupta. Chanakya silenced him with a gesture requesting that they maintain silence until it was safe to discuss matters privately.

Back in the confines of Chanakya's simple hut, the ugly Brahmin spoke. 'Sinharan. I need you to burn down that house tonight. But be careful, no one should know that it was you.'

'But why—' began Sinharan.

Chandragupta interrupted him. 'Acharya, you obviously have a very good reason for what you want done. It shall be done. But please tell us why,' he said.

'Dear Chandragupta, I wasn't fooled by the false ingratiating tone of that snake Ambhi. The rogue thinks that he can destroy me! The fact is that he's uncomfort- able having me sitting inside his kingdom with militia trained by his former commander-in-chief, and enough money-power to finance it!' hissed Chanakya.

'But why not simply refuse to be his rajguru? Don't shift residence. Why burn the place down?' asked Mehir.

'Because the place is booby-trapped. You thought that I was admiring the quality of the stonemasonry when I lay down on the floor? I was actually observing a row of ants carrying cooked rice through cracks in the floor. You assumed that I was feeling the smooth finish of the doors and windows, while I was busy studying the lacquer!' laughed the Brahmin, mighty pleased with the confusion on their faces.

'Need an explanation?' he asked at length. Without waiting for an answer he launched into one. 'If ants are observed carrying boiled rice through the floor cracks of an uninhabited house, it must mean that there is cooked food beneath the floor. Where there are provisions, there would be men. It was evident to me that the house had a concealed basement filled with troops. They're quietly awaiting our arrival and will strike when we're asleep. In one fell swoop Ambhi would have wiped us off the face of the earth!'

Chandragupta was bewildered. 'But why were you so interested in the doors and windows?' he asked.

His teacher replied, 'They were lacquered. Seeing that his answer had not cleared their confusion, he continued, '*Lac* is a sticky secretion of a tiny insect. The female insect, globular in form, lives on twigs and young branches in cells of resin created from its excretions. Mostly one will find these insects in kusum trees. Collecting the twigs along with the living insects inside and extracting the secretions using hot water creates resin dye. The dye is called *lac* because *lakhs*—hundreds of thousands—of insects have to be gathered to produce just a single pound of the dye. When applied to doors and windows, lac provides a smooth finished look—something that you thought I was busy admiring! The problem with lac, however, is that it's highly inflammable. That house will go up in flames like a fireball if it were to accidentally ignite. Probably that was Ambhi's intent—to kill us using the soldiers in the concealed basement and then burn down the house attributing our deaths to an accident. Sinharan, that's why I want that house burned down with Ambhi's men packed inside it! Tonight!'

≡

Chanakya was back in Sage Dandayan's hermitage. The acharya had requested the sage to let him stay at the ashram, and the venerable rishi had been delighted to have some company. A few days later, Ambhi dropped in to see him. 'Ambhi, my son, the great fire that enveloped the official residence reserved for me a few days ago is a divine message that I should not be your rajguru. My stars are not in favour and I would not like Gandhar's future to be dragged down with my own. I'm quite sure that you'll be able to find someone much more capable than me,' said Chanakya smoothly.

He waited for a reaction. He could sense the inner rage within Ambhi but he did a fairly good job of keeping it bottled in. 'O acharya, it's my loss. I hope that you'll continue to stay in Takshila so that I may take your advice from time to time,' said Ambhi.

And eventually kill me, thought Chanakya. 'Absolutely. I shall always be available to assist you, O King. Please do not hesitate to call for me,' lied Chanakya.

As Ambhi left, Chandragupta asked 'What now, acharya? Alexander's forces are in retreat. Do we plan for making war?' Chanakya thought for a moment and answered with a roguish expression, 'Leave the task of making war to me, Chandragupta. I need you to focus on making love!'

She was always dressed simply but elegantly—a cream-coloured sleeveless linen chiton that reached her feet, light thong sandals, her long blonde hair tied back with filet mesh, and a delicate gold and diamond tiara perched atop. She wore no jewellery other than the tiara and simple earrings. The absence of royal trappings only served to accentuate her classic beauty and her unpretentious charm. Her skin was fair with a light golden hue and the sleeveless chiton was perfect to show off her delicate arms and graceful shoulders. Her eyes were the colour of clear blue oceans, and like those waters, ran deep. Her slender face, full lips, aquiline nose and high cheekbones were the perfect combination of allure and innocence. Her name was Cornelia, and she was the daughter of the second-most powerful man in Bharat—Seleucus.

The most powerful man, Alexander, was planning to return home, leaving his trusted general—Seleucus—in charge of his Asian dominions. Born in northern Macedonia, Seleucus had been told by his mother that his real father was actually the god, Apollo. Apollo had left with her an anchor insignia ring to be given to his son when he grew up to be a man. The same anchor was also present as a birthmark on Seleucus' thigh. 'Go fight the Persians along with Alexander and may you be called Nicator—*the Victorious One!*' she had said as she gave him the ring.

He had not only been victorious in war but also in love. Having helped Alexander conquer Persia, Seleucus had married Apama, the ravishing daughter of a Persian nobleman, in a grand marriage ceremony at Susa, during which Alexander had also married the daughter of the Persian king Darius III. Seleucus and Apama's passionate affair earlier had produced a bastard son. Their marriage a year later produced a legitimate daughter. Cornelia was grateful that she was born on the right side of her parents' marriage ceremony.

Cornelia was staying in Takshila as a state guest of Ambhi. The girl was an Indophile and found herself more comfortable in Gandhar than in Greece. She would visit Sage Dandayan's ashram each morning to learn yoga. A retinue of nervous Macedonian guards, who knew that Seleucus would have their testicles ripped off if anything untoward happened to her, would follow.

Seeing the great yogi leading an austere life she would ask Chanakya—who was also living with Dandayan—

'Learned acharya, why is renunciation so important in Bharat? Sage Dandayan lives here in the forest with no protection from heat, cold or rain. He still seems at peace, having renounced the very things that we Macedonians value—power and wealth.'

Chanakya laughed heartily, frightening the poor confused Cornelia as he bared his crooked teeth. As his laughter subsided, he spoke. 'Lord Rama renounced his kingdom and became the most powerful king in the land. Buddha renounced the world and the world fell at his feet. Cornelia, my innocent girl, please do not believe that renunciation is to forsake power. Rather, it's the very means to power!'

Chandragupta was walking briskly towards Dandayan's hut when he saw her conversing with Chanakya. *She looks like a goddess*, he thought to himself. He had been quite angry when his teacher had told him that he wanted him to woo the girl. What was he, a gigolo? Why had he spent his life training for kingship? Just to chase a Macedonian girl in a gown? But now he was smitten. There could be no one lovelier than this princess, he thought.

'Ah! Chandragupta, I see that you have arrived,' called out Chanakya, deftly pulling Chandragupta into the conversation. 'This is Cornelia, the daughter of the honourable Seleucus. She's here to study yoga from Sage Dandayan. Unfortunately, her lessons keep getting interrupted by our profound deliberations on the renunciation of power!'

Chandragupta strode confidently over to them. 'Cornelia, my guru is not one who can teach you about the renunciation of power, but he can certainly teach you about the power of renunciation!' Chanakya had helpfully prepared the witty one-liner for him in advance so that Chandragupta could make the right first impression.

Chandragupta was accoutred in his finest ensemble, some of it hastily borrowed from Sinharan. A royal purple dhoti flowed from his waist, and he had thrown a blue silk wrap casually around his shoulders. Around his neck he wore a heavy necklace of pearls. His gold earrings accentuated his sidelocks, defining his kind and gentle face, clean-shaven except for his warrior moustache. Long black hair curled down to broad shoulders that led to rippling muscular upper arms adorned with gold armlets. He looked every inch a prince even though he had no kingdom.

Cornelia smiled. Chandragupta beamed. Chanakya chuckled. He knew that the wheels were in motion. Love conquered all. He thought of Suvasini, his childhood flame, and decided that the time had come.

◼◼

Chanakya wandered over to the elevated bamboo latticed lofts constructed by his disciples in a clearing just outside Sage Dandayan's hermitage. As he approached the raised enclosure, the soft chirping and cooing of his winged charges greeted him. Their trainer ran up to the acharya and greeted him. 'Are the pigeons in good form today, Siddharthaka?' asked Chanakya casually.

'Absolutely, my lord. They have been fed and watered and are eagerly awaiting some exercise,' replied Siddharthaka, as he took from the acharya a little capsule with a light but firm string attached to it. He opened one of the enormous coops using a rope that hung down from the gate and his call was immediately answered by a beautiful white Rock Pigeon that flew over and perched itself on Siddharthaka's outstretched leather-encased arm. The bird had made journeys of more than a hundred and eleven yojanas at speeds exceeding five yojanas per muhurta and could remain in sustained flight for several muhurtas without resting.

The critical element was training, and Siddharthaka was an accomplished master in the science. Each bird would be transported in a bamboo cage some distance from home each day and released. The birds would immediately fly back to their remembered home using the earth's magnetic field as an inbuilt compass for navigation. These birds were called 'homing pigeons' for a very precise reason—their ability to fly back the way they'd been transported, no matter what the distance. With each training trip, the distance would be increased using a network of trainers along the route, and each bird's experience, strength and ability to navigate longer and longer distances would increase. Siddharthaka's pigeons were extremely strong on the wing, able to fly even against powerful countercurrents of air. Each of his birds had keen eyesight, being able to see much further than any normal human. Despite their gentle demeanour, his birds possessed incredible endurance and were trained to withstand prolonged aerial voyages.

Siddharthaka expertly tied the capsule proffered by Chanakya to the bird's left leg and whistled. With a strong flutter of its wings, the bird rose straight up in the air, gained altitude and then, circling around a few times to get its bearings, headed off directly in a straight line towards its destination—in this case Pataliputra, where Jeevasiddhi awaited.

CHAPTER TEN
Present Day

The reporter had spent over a month in the malodorous cell. His bail applications kept coming up before the sub-judicial district magistrate but were equal times denied without even the courtesy of a hearing.

His hair was full of lice. His skin was red and blotchy from the insect bites that plagued him every night. On his left ear was a surgical bandage applied by the prison doctor to a wound caused by a rat that had nibbled on his ear. He had lost several pounds and his cheeks had sunken in. His face looked gaunt and tired, his eyes lifeless. He was dehydrated due to the diarrhoea caused by the terrible jail food. On several occasions he found cockroaches in the lentils. When he complained, the warden had joked, 'Sshh! Not so loud. If your cellmates hear you they'll want non-vegetarian food too.'

The visit by a dark, oily-haired Keralite was curious. His mere presence seemed to open doors and command respect. They sat across from each other in the warden's office. Sugary tea had been arranged for them. The tea boy left two glasses of the syrupy mixture before them and disappeared.

'I can make all your problems disappear,' said Menon.

'Who are you?' asked the prisoner.

'It isn't important. You're a very intelligent man. You know why you've landed up here—you've been very naughty!' he admonished, wagging his finger like a head-master at an errant schoolboy.

'That son of a whore—Gangasagar—wants me to back off, is it? Leave his pure little Barbie doll untouched? Well, it seems that she isn't all that virginal!' he shouted, his red eyes blazing with indignation.

Menon stayed cool. 'My friend, if you behave decently with me, I shall deal even more generously with you. Yes, you do need to back off from the media hunt, but what if I point you in the direction of an even juicier story, eh?'

'Go on. I'm listening,' said the reporter disinterestedly but Menon knew that he had his attention.

'Did you know that the prime minister of this country has a very close advisor?'

'You mean the general secretary of his party?'

'No.'

'The finance minister of India?'

'No.'

'The home minister of India?'

'No.'

'Then who?'

'She apparently visits his residence every month. Her visits are kept off the record—no notations are made either in the visitors' log or in the prime minister's diary.'

'He has a mistress?'

'Use your grey cells, my intelligent friend. If he had a mistress, would he bonk her at his official residence?'

'Then who?'

'She's simply known as the sadhvi. He apparently consults her on all major decisions.'

'And what is it that you want me to do?'

'Get me leverage on her.'

'My nose is like a bloodhound's—it can sniff out anything anywhere. But why should I help you?'

'You could be a free man in the next ten minutes. Think about how good a long bath, a decent meal, a stiff drink and a warm woman in your bed would feel.'

'Not good enough. You'll have to do better,' growled the reporter, negotiating but ready to lap up the offer as long as another bone was thrown his way.

'How about if I arrange the biggest sting operation of your life?' suggested Menon calmly.

***

'She has ambitions—' he began.

'Not interested in the future,' said Menon.

'The sadhvi visits him almost weekly—' he said.

'Not interested in the present,' said Menon.

'Then what the fuck are you interested in?' asked the reporter.

'Her past.'

***

'We've hit the mother lode,' the reporter said excitedly.

'Do tell,' said Menon coolly.

'When our prime minister was chief minister, a lady used to visit him. Often late at night.'

'Big deal. If I laid end to end the women who screw around with businessmen or politicians, we'd circle the fucking globe.'

'If you laid them end to end you'd be very tired,' joked the reporter.

Menon ignored the joke. The reporter cleared his throat and continued. 'Well, it seems that this lady—very pretty she was apparently—used to visit him, but one fine day she disappeared. Poof! Gone.'

'So?'

'The same lady appeared at a Hindu shelter two months later, pregnant.'

'How do you know this?'

'The orphanage accepted the pregnant lady on the formal recommendation of the chief minister—our present prime minister.'

'And did this lady deliver?'

'Sure. A little girl.'

'Whatever happened to the mother and daughter?' asked Menon, suddenly very interested.

'The mother packed up and left. The daughter was brought up by the Hindu nunnery attached to the shelter.'

'What's to say that the girl's got anything to do with the prime minister?'

'In her hurry, the mother left behind a postcard. It was from the father enquiring about the mother and child. The purohit was happy to share it with me when I told him that I could arrange for his son's admission to a medical college.'

Menon made a note. A favour promised was always to be honoured. 'And?'

'It was the prime minister. He's the father.'

<hr />

'So the sadhvi is his illegitimate daughter?' asked Gangasagar incredulously.

'He was already married, with three kids in tow and a rosy political career ahead of him—he couldn't accept her,' replied Menon.

'But where's the proof?' asked Gangasagar.

'That weasel reporter has a postcard in which the prime minister writes to her asking after her and the child.'

'But that's hardly clinching evidence,' said Gangasagar, then reflected before thoughtfully resuming. 'It could be enough for a sensation though. And this child—she grew up to become a nun herself?'

'Yes. Father and daughter never refer to one another as being related. Apparently, she calls him *child*. A joke.'

'And what the fuck does he call her—*mother*?'

'Actually, yes.'

<hr/>

'It's time I met her,' said Gangasagar as he put down his newspaper.

'What will you tell her?' asked Menon.

'I'll tell her that if she wants Mother's Rule in Delhi, she must make sure that there's no damn President's Rule in Uttar Pradesh.'

<hr/>

'Your instructions have arrived, child,' she said as she placed her hand on his head and began chanting some more prayers with her eyes closed. A minute later, she opened her eyes and directed, 'Do not impose President's Rule on Uttar Pradesh.'

'But blessed mother—' began the prime minister.

'Sshh!' she admonished him, placing her palm in front of her in a gesture for him to halt. 'Have my divine messages ever gone wrong?' she asked.

'No,' he acknowledged quietly.

'Then do as I say!' she instructed.

<hr/>

'Fine. So you've managed to bring things to a halt and prevented President's Rule. But now what?' asked Agrawalji.

'We tell the chief minister to step down and let Chandini take over,' said Gangasagar.

'But their party would want portfolios for supporting our chief minister in the same way that we demanded portfolios for supporting theirs. Why would their chief minister step down without a deal?' asked Menon.

'Changing the topic completely, Menon, weren't you supposed to organise a sting for that press worm?' asked Gangasagar.

Menon smiled. 'You want the chief minister to take a walk, don't you?' he asked. 'So that you don't have to offer any Cabinet berths to him?'

'I like long walks—especially when they're taken by people who annoy me,' said Gangasagar.

◼◼

The gentleman from Mumbai was well-dressed, immaculate, suave and soft-spoken. He arrived in a black Mercedes-Benz at the residence of the chief engineer of the PWD—the Public Works Department. In one hand he carried a bunch of lilies for the chief engineer's wife, and in the other he held a box of Swiss chocolates for his kids and an expensive Mont Blanc pen for the man himself. The appointment had been fixed a week earlier at the behest of the chief engineer's nephew.

Preliminary introductions over, the man from Mumbai said, 'This is a massive project—upgrading and widening priority state highways, constructing four new bypasses, and three major bridges. Who's picking up the tab?'

The chief engineer answered. 'Civil work, supervision, project management support, consulting contracts, land acquisition and cash compensation shall be funded entirely by the government of Uttar Pradesh, while other costs of resettlement and rehabilitation will be eligible for World Bank financing.'

'So the entire cost is borne either by the state government or the World Bank, right?'

'That is correct.' replied the chief engineer.

'We have carried out our own internal budgeting and believe that the actual cost should be around one point five billion,' said the man from Mumbai.

'Ah!'

'But we could inflate or deflate it, as required,' added the Mumbai man smoothly, 'that's why I'm here. We want to be sure that our bids are submitted in the manner that you want.'

'You'll have to meet the principal secretary for that,' said the chief engineer.

'When can we arrange a meeting?' asked the man from Mumbai, smiling.

⌗

The well-dressed, immaculate, suave and soft-spoken man from Mumbai arrived in his black Mercedes-Benz at the Nirman Bhawan office of the principal secretary in Lucknow. In one hand he carried a bunch of tulips for the principal secretary, and in the other he held a plain vanilla Mont Blanc pen for the executive assistant to the principal secretary. The appointment had been fixed two days earlier at the behest of the chief engineer.

'As you know, the tender process can be handled in three ways—percentage rate, item rate or lump sum. Under the first method, we would do the costing and you would bid by quoting a percentage above or below our estimates. In the second alternative, we would give you a schedule of quantities and you would quote individually on each item. Under the third mechanism, you would quote a lump sum for the entire project based upon our specifications,' explained the principal secretary.

'How can you swing it so that we get it?' asked the Mumbai man.

'Do you have subsidiaries and affiliate companies?' asked the principal secretary.

The man nodded. 'Lots.'

'Then we'll do it this way. The prequalification bids will ask for your background, technical expertise, and track record. Make sure that all your subsidiaries and associates bid individually.'

'How will that help?'

'We will find qualitative reasons to eliminate other bidders at this stage. But it would look very strange if only one party were left uneliminated. That's why we need you to have at least five to six prequalification bids.'

'So we'll be the only bidders by the time it gets down to commercial bids?'

'Yes.'

'And how much will this cost us?'

'You'll have to meet the chief minister for that,' said the principal secretary.

'When can we arrange a meeting?' smiled the man from Mumbai.

ᴈ⊏

The well-dressed man from Mumbai arrived in his black Mercedes-Benz at 5, Kalidas Marg, the official residence of the chief minister of Uttar Pradesh. In one hand he carried a bunch of orchids for the chief minister, and in the other he carried a ten-*tola*—a hundred-and-sixteen-gramme gold bar—for the personal assistant to the chief minister. The appointment had been fixed a few hours earlier at the behest of the principal secretary.

'I'm told you've already discussed the details with the principal secretary,' said the chief minister, shaking his hand.

'Yes. I have come here only to seek your blessings.'

'My blessings are expensive.'

'How expensive?'

'Fifteen per cent.'

'Cancel one blessing and give me two.'

'Ten per cent?'

'Yes.'

'I would not do that under normal circumstances. But then, you brought me orchids,' laughed the chief minister, getting up to seal the deal with the smiling man from Mumbai.

❧

The well-dressed man from Mumbai arrived in his black Mercedes-Benz at the Birhana Road residence of Pandit Gangasagar Mishra. In one hand he carried a roll of photographic film and in the other he carried a small pocket-recording device with the tape still inside it. Menon smiled as he took his reporter friend inside to meet Pandit Gangasagar Mishra.

'With this scoop, you shall graduate from weasel to eagle,' said Menon to the journalist as they walked towards Gangasagar's living room.

'I would rather remain a weasel,' said the reporter.

'Why?' asked Menon.

'Eagles may soar but weasels don't get sucked into jet engines!'

❧

On the dusty Birhana Road of Kanpur, inside one of its bylanes, in a building that had seen better days, the rickety staircase to the second floor flat occupied by Pandit Gangasagar Mishra was groaning under the weight of hundreds of feet. It was 11 am and Chandini Gupta had arrived at Panditji's residence. Accompanying her were MLAs from the Opposition who were willing to defect.

The sting operation had forced the chief minister to reconsider whether he should hang on to his chair. Good counsel had prevailed and he had resigned. 'You're happy that he's gone?' enquired the weary Menon.

'My dear Menon, some cause happiness wherever they go. Others whenever they go.'

'*Pranam*, Uncle Ganga,' said Chandini, as she folded her hands in respectful obeisance to the kingmaker. 'God bless you, my dear,' said the old man as she sat down on the chair next to him. He paused for a moment as he placed a hand on her head, closed his eyes and chanted something under his breath. '*Adi Shakti, Namo Namah; Sarab Shakti, Namo Namah; Prithum Bhagvati, Namo Namah; Kundalini Mata Shakti; Mata Shakti, Namo Namah.*'

'Are you ready to go to Governor House to stake your claim to form the state government?' he asked as he opened his eyes.

She nodded, smiling. 'The chief minister's MLAs are outside. They've agreed to support us without any cabinet positions—they didn't have much of a choice,' she laughed.

'Your first task as chief minister—' he began.

'Yes?'

'Award the World Bank contract to a nominee of Agrawalji's choosing, but make sure that there are no open microphones! He has pulled out all his remaining hair financing these elections. He needs something to calm him down.'

≡

The Uttar Pradesh chief minister's office was on the fifth floor of Lal Bahadur Shastri Bhawan in Lucknow. The reception area was extra large—in anticipation of the large number of waiting visitors. Two secretaries were stationed in the reception area, assigned with the single task of managing the crowd.

The inner office was smaller than the reception but much more imposing. The room was wood-panelled, dominated by an oversized mahogany desk behind which was an imposing swivel chair done up in aged maroon leather—the most powerful chair in the state. On the wall behind the desk was a large portrait of Mahatma Gandhi. The visitors' chairs, also in maroon, were lower and smaller, instantly putting any guest in a slightly subordinate position. To the right of the desk was a large window with a cabinet below it polished to a mirror. Chandini noticed the vase of pink chrysanthemums on the cabinet as she walked into her new office.

'Good morning, ma'am,' said her assistant, a pleasant young man. 'I'm your principal private secretary—your executive assistant. My name's Shankar.'

'Did you organise the pink chrysanthemums, Shankar?' asked Chandini.

'Yes,' said the slightly embarrassed young man, 'I do hope you like them.'

'How did you know pink chrysanthemums were my favourite?' asked Chandini.

'Ma'am, I'm your secretary—it's my job to know your preferences,' he quipped. 'Shall we go through your diary?'

⚊⚊

The stream of visitors, phone calls, letters, meetings and files had been endless. It was past 5 pm and Chandini had not been able to leave her desk, even for lunch.

'Send in the delegation from the builders' federation,' she instructed Shankar on the intercom. A minute later, he walked in carrying a tray. 'Where are they?' she asked, not looking up from the file before her. Her secretary put the tray down in front of her with a look of concern and said, 'Ma'am it's been a long day. I asked them to reschedule. I think you should take a break.' Chandini looked up at him realising he was right—she was famished. She smiled when she noticed her favourite sweet cardamom tea and tangy peanuts in lime juice on the tray.

⬛

'Have you begun to gain her confidence?' asked Ganga-sagar.

'With the background information that you gave me, it was rather easy,' admitted Shankar. 'She depends on me for almost everything.'

'Good. Keep me informed of her activities. She's a single woman in a male-dominated society. I can't afford to have any malicious gossip about male friends—real or imagined!' growled Gangasagar.

⬛

'It seems that there's trouble brewing already,' said Menon.

'What? She's been chief minister for barely a few weeks,' said Gangasagar.

'There's a rebellion in the ranks. Our dear Ram Shankar Dwivedi is spearheading the effort. There have been secret meetings and parleys.'

'Ask Ikrambhai to meet me. This situation needs his brand of assistance,' said Gangasagar.

⬛

Entire families crowded every available inch of space. A cow sat nonchalantly chewing cud in the centre of the railway platform, as a man, with wife, three children—including a newborn baby—mother-in-law and chickens in tow, attempted to create floor space for their luggage. Flies and mosquitoes buzzed around, excited by the abundance of garbage piled up on the tracks. Young boys employed by the prosperous tea stall-owner ran up and down the platform yelling, '*Chai, garam chai!*' and serving hot, sugary, milky tea in little glasses. Other vendors—selling cheap plastic toys, newspapers, fruit, deep-fried samosas, toothbrushes, herbal remedies, and even baby clothes—harangued those waiting on the platform for the much awaited train. Eventually, the shrieking and puffing iron monster arrived, causing everyone to go into general hysteria as the passengers waged the inevitable battle to board.

Ikrambhai's man was not waiting to board, though. He was awaiting the arrival of a very special lady who was to be whisked off to the Durbar Club.

━❐━

At the Durbar Club opposite the Lucknow railway station, the ambient temperature was almost ten degrees below. The smell of fresh jasmine flowers pervaded the air. The interior décor was of dark wood and deep-red velvet. In the centre of the room was a dance floor where, some fifteen young girls clad in extravagant lehengas gyrated to popular Bollywood songs. Around the perimeter sat lecherous men drinking whisky. Smitten patrons showered notes on girls who caught their fancy, drowning them in a cascade of crisp currency. The cash would be efficiently mopped up from the floor by the waiter on hand. Fifty per cent for the establishment, fifty per cent for the girl being fêted.

Eesha was lost in her own world—shutting out the leers of the men inside the club—allowing herself to get immersed in the music. Her penchant for jewellery was evident in the glittering bangles, chains, earrings and nose ring that adorned her. Her make-up had been professionally applied but was not overdone. She was just twenty-one and oozing sex appeal. She had been dancing for the past three hours but wasn't tired. The spliff of cannabis had taken care of that. The train journey had been long but drugs had been on hand to remove the fatigue and boredom. Thank God she needed to be here only for this single assignment. The city was a dump!

One of the men seated near where she was dancing had already sprayed her with cash and winked at her, indicating that he was ready to pay for some one-on-one action outside. She smiled at him, sizing him up. He was obviously loaded. She glanced over at the bar where Ikram's man was standing, sipping a Coke. He nodded at her. The prey had taken the bait.

As they made their way to one of the seedy little rooms upstairs, Ram Shankar Dwivedi stared at her lustfully, like a dog with his tongue hanging out for a bone. Eesha would give him the bone he wanted, although, judging by the bulge in his trousers he seemed to have one of his own.

The room was a small windowless twelve-by-twelve-foot number. Towards the centre of the main wall stood a queensize bed, draped in a floral bedspread that bore patches and stains that could not be attributed to the pattern alone. To one corner was a single chair that faced a mirror—an oddity in this crummy room. Mercifully, an air-conditioner installed in lieu of a window was working and the room was cool.

'So shall I tell you what's on the menu?' Eesha asked as she sat on the edge of the bed and patted the space next to her. He nodded mutely, intoxicated by her blandishments.

'BBBJ, BDSM, Bareback, GFE, DT, HJ—'

'I don't understand any of this—' he began.

'Hush. You don't need to. I'll show you everything,' she said as she began to help him off with his clothes.

The photographer arranged by Ikram's man stood in a dark room behind the two-way mirror on the other side of the bedroom wall. He had set his camera to manual mode and the shutter to thirty seconds. The photographer's finger was firmly frozen on the button of the camera, mounted on a tripod. The shutter kept clicking and whirring over and over again as Ram Shankar Dwivedi chose items from Eesha's extensive menu.

▬ ▬

'The road contract we handed over to Agrawalji's nominee—' began Chandini.

'Yes?' asked Gangasagar.

'His nominee turned out to be Rungta & Somany, the conglomerate, you know, the one with whom we negotiated on the farmers' land.'

'Somany was also the one who supported us by sending that Bollywood bimbo—Anjali—to campaign for you,' reminded Gangasagar.

'Precisely,' acknowledged Chandini, 'but we now have a problem'.

'What?'

'The R&S fortune is in dispute. The World Bank project was allotted to a private company belonging to the senior partner, Rungta.'

'And?'

'The junior partner—Somany—is now claiming that it should have been allotted in the name of the parent company in which he holds an equal share.'

'How does this concern us? I'm sure you floated an open tender following all the *apparent* norms of transparency and fairness, right?' asked her devious mentor.

'Obviously. But now Somany has threatened to go to court. If he does, the resulting attack on Rungta will drag the state government into this mess.'

'We can't afford to antagonise either one of them. Let's schedule a meeting with Somany to talk some sense into him.'

'You don't need to schedule a meeting.'

'Why?'

'He's waiting outside to meet us.'

=○=

'I have been cheated of what should have rightfully belonged to both partners fifty-fifty. How can you allow this injustice?' asked Somany as he strode in dispensing with all formalities.

'Nice to meet you too,' said Gangasagar saracastically.

'Madam, I beseech you. Remedy this mistake and I will not drag this issue to court,' pleaded Somany of Chandini.

'How can we get involved in a squabble between partners?' asked Chandini.

'You have no alternative. If this dispute goes to court, all the sordid details of how the contract was awarded are bound to spill into the public domain,' said Somany.

'Are you threatening the state government of Uttar Pradesh and its chief minister?' asked Chandini angrily.

'I am not, madam, but I shall be left with no option but to wash dirty linen in public if you do nothing,' said Somany.

'Then be prepared for the entire might of the state government to come down on you! You should not defaecate where you dine, Mr Somany!' snapped Chandini, her voice rising.

'Now, now, let us not argue with one another. We're all decent folk who are gathered here to arrive at a mutually amicable solution, right?' asked Gangasagar, gesturing for Chandini to calm down. 'Changing the topic completely, am I correct in believing that you have a personal stake in Majestic Munitions PLC, Mr Somany?'

'H—how do you know that?' asked the startled scion of a business house.

'It's my job to know everything,' said Gangasagar. 'As I understand it, a large chunk of shares in Majestic Munitions PLC—a company quoted on the London Stock Exchange—was acquired by a Dubai-based investment bank in which—or so my sources tell me—you have a substantial stake.'

'Let's say that you're hypothetically right, so what?' asked the flustered businessman.

'Talking hypothetically, how would you react if I told you that your hypothetical stake in this hypothetical investment bank that holds a hypothetical share in this hypothetical armaments company could be multiplied six times over in value?'

'How?'

'Are we *still* talking hypothetically?' sneered Gangasagar. 'I am given to understand that a large order for semi-automatic rifles is to be released to Majestic Munitions but the file is held up in the prime minister's office. If this proposal were to be cleared, the value of your stake in Majestic would increase in value almost six times.'

'But we've tried everything—' began Somany.

'Leave it to me. You shall only have to do six things to get your six-fold return.'

'And what are these six things?'

'The first thing you will do is allot two per cent of the shares to a charitable trust. It belongs to a simple sadhvi—a lovely lady.' *Whom I also need to reward for preventing President's Rule.*

'Done. What else?'

'Second. Sell the shares of Majestic and book your profit no sooner than the deal is awarded. I cannot guarantee what happens in the future.'

'Fine. And?'

'Third. There's a young boy from a very poor family. He's the son of the purohit of a Hindu shelter. You shall have him admitted to a medical college that you're a trustee of.' *A debt must always be repaid entirely.*

'Easily done. Fourth?'

'Your friend in New Delhi—the defence minister who is lobbying for your Majestic Munitions deal—make him available to me as an ally when I need him in the future.'

'I shall talk to him. Fifth?'

'Majestic Munitions has a stake in Strategic Asia Research Defence—SARD—an American think-tank on Asian military matters. I may require a word put in.'

'Fine. And finally?'

'Drop the case against your partner—Rungta—so that we can all fucking get on with the fucking business of running this fucking government! And I'm not speaking hypothetically anymore!'

◨◧

'Thank you for handling Somany,' said Chandini.

'You're welcome. I'm happy that you followed my advice and yelled at him,' said Gangasagar.

'Why did you ask me to be so tough?'

'If there's no bad cop, how's the good cop to get his work done?' asked Gangasagar.

◨◧

The chief minister was on her way to inaugurate a primary school in Nutpurwa, a small village about a hundred kilometres from Lucknow. They were to have left Lucknow at 1 pm but meeting overruns had delayed them by a couple of hours. Shankar had suggested cancelling the visit but Chandini was determined to go even though the state government's helicopter was out of service. Meetings with businessmen and bureaucrats were urgent but not as important as meetings with humble villagers and children for whom a simple school meant the world.

Winter had arrived and sunset kicked in early. She sat in the rear seat of her official Ambassador car wearing her trademark cream-coloured saree with an elegant beige pashmina shawl wrapped around her shoulders. Shankar sat next to her, helping her clear the backlog of files they carried with them. Ahead of their car were two motorbike-mounted pilot policemen and behind them was a police jeep carrying the chief minister's bodyguards. The road between Lucknow and Nutpurwa was bumpy and dusty and the convoy made progress in fits and starts.

As dusk approached, the convoy paused momentarily to allow a herd of buffalo to cross the road. The lumbering beasts took their own time, ignoring the impatient honking of Chandini's police-deputed driver. The herd was extensive and the occupants of the chief minister's car suddenly found themselves surrounded by hundreds of buffalo. Five minutes later, when the animals had moved on, neither the police jeep nor the bike-mounted cops were anywhere to be seen.

As the dust kicked up by the animals settled, three riders emerged on horseback and within moments the chief minister's car was surrounded. One of the riders steered his steed towards the driver's window, pointed his .303 calibre rifle at the driver's head and shot him dead through the glass which shattered into tiny splinters. 'It's Rajjo Bhaiya,' whispered Shankar to

Chandini. 'He'll kill us if we don't make a run for it'. Chandini was paralysed with fear. Her pale complexion had turned snow-white as she nodded mutely in response to Shankar's words. Another rider used his rifle butt to smash open the car window on Shankar's side and was now pointing his rifle at him.

'That son of a whore, Gangasagar, thought he could play politics with me, eh? Instal his pretty girl on the throne and rule by proxy? He fucked me, now I'm going to fuck his pretty little lady and have me some fun. Boys, are you ready for some group action?' laughed Rajjo Bhaiya, and his men laughed with him—evil and menacing cackles.

Both Chandini and Shankar stayed seated, their windows shattered into shards that lay all over the seats and floor. Two .303 barrels pointed at them from each side. Rajjo's men were in no hurry to get them out of the car. Having eliminated the bodyguards in the rear, the bike riders in the front, and the driver, they knew that Chandini and Shankar were helpless prey.

'At the count of three,' whispered Shankar to Chandini as he gestured for her to pick up a dagger-shaped shard of glass that lay near her hand. He was already holding one—the blood from his palm dripping on the seat. 'One—two—three—' he whispered and, in unison, both Chandini and Shankar thrust out their hands wildly, stabbing the two horses that stood on either side of their car.

The stallions went wild, whinnying and neighing as they bucked and reared. 'Motherfucker!' shouted Rajjo Bhaiya in disgust as he and his accomplices concentrated their attentions on bringing their mounts under control. The rifle barrels were withdrawn momentarily from the car's interior. 'Now!' hissed Shankar as he pulled open his door and dragged Chandini out with him. He knew that the bucking steeds had bought them less than a minute.

As they stumbled out, Shankar took another stab at the horse next to him and the animal went berserk. Shankar grabbed hold of the gun that fell to the ground, picked it up, aimed for the thug's head and fired. He wasn't sure what he was doing but his mind and body were on autopilot. He realised that he had killed a man only when the horseman's lifeless body fell from his horse, one foot still in the stirrup. The horse went into a crazed gallop, dragging the corpse with it into the dusty horizon.

Falling to his hands and knees, Shankar pulled Chandini down with him and they crawled under the car. He silently thanked the Government of India, which continued to insist that all officials and ministers use an Ambassador car for their official duties. Based on the Morris Oxford III of 1956, the Ambassador had changed little over the years and had the highest ground clearance among passenger cars, making it easy to slip underneath it. 'Why the fuck don't you come out and fight like a man, cuntface?' yelled Rajjo Bhaiya.

'In the same macho way that you held us at gunpoint?' taunted Shankar. He could see the horses' hooves and knew that they needed to act before Rajjo Bhaiya dismounted. He pulled Chandini close to him and gave her hand a brief squeeze, to comfort and reassure her that they would get out of the mess alive. He pointed his gun towards the space underneath the left side rear door and hastily told Chandini to fire a few shots, being careful to avoid the tyres. His aim was to distract Rajjo and his remaining accomplice while he crawled out below the front right door—the door to the driver's seat.

Chandini's shots had brought both horsemen to the rear left of the car and in that instant, Shankar yanked open the door, wildly dragged out the driver's body, and pulled the policeman's IOFB Mark I revolver from his holster. Standing up he aimed his revolver at Rajjo Bhaiya—whose attention was still focused on the shots from the rear left—and fired. Rajjo Bhaiya dropped his rifle and clutched his heart from which blood was spurting. He had a dazed expression on his face before the second shot caught him between the eyes.

The third horseman, realising that his master was dead, steered his horse away from the car and galloped away into the surrounding hills. Shankar crawled underneath the car once again, and held on to Chandini who was still attempting to fire the rifle mechanically although it had run out of ammunition. She was trembling as she clutched the gun. He reached out and gently unclasped her hand that had been wrapped like a vice around the trigger. He offered her his other hand and nudged her out from the under the car. Putting his arm around her, he sat her in the front passenger's seat and then, running around to the other side, got into the driver's seat, started the ignition, shifted the gear from neutral and put his foot on the gas. He did not lift his foot from the accelerator until they reached the government circuit house on the outskirts of Nutpurwa.

It was past 10 pm when they arrived at the circuit house, a small two-bedroom bungalow constructed by the district collector. The caretaker—a gentle, toothless old man—came out running when he noticed the car with the chief ministerial numberplate. 'What happened?' he asked with anxiety, as he saw Shankar emerge from the car, his clothes bloodied and soiled. 'There was an attack on the chief minister. I need you to help me get her inside—she's in shock,' explained Shankar.

The two men helped Chandini out of the car, and placing her arms around their shoulders helped her up the circuit house steps and into one of the rooms. By standards of government accommodation, the house was surprisingly well-maintained. Shankar allowed Chandini to slump onto the bed and then, turning to the caretaker said, 'Please make us some tea. And do you have a sedative? After that, I'll need to use the phone.'

The worried caretaker nodded and headed off to get the tea and sedative but his trailing voice said, 'The phone line's been dead since this morning, sir. The only other phone's five miles away!'

Shankar propped up Chandini against a couple of pillows, sat beside her on the bed, and forced her to take a few sips of the hot, sugary brew that the caretaker brought them. He then made her swallow the tranquilliser. 'I'm not comfortable driving you back to Lucknow in this state,' he told her gently. 'Ideally, I'd like a police escort. If you're hungry I'll drive down to the village and get something to eat.'

She shook her head. 'I'm not hungry. Let's leave in the morning—by then the control room in Lucknow will have realised that they need to send a team here.'

'Fine. I'll tell the caretaker to stay awake and sit near the front porch. I'm in the room next door—' he began, as he got up.

'Shankar,' said Chandini holding on to his hand and looking directly into his eyes, 'don't leave me. Please stay.' It was a simple request loaded with meaning and he found himself falling in love with the tragically beautiful and vulnerable woman.

'You were supposed to watch over her, not bloody sleep with her!' roared Gangasagar. The attack on the chief minister's convoy had been all over the news and they had been brought back to the safety of Lucknow under armed escort in the morning. Shankar had bathed, hurriedly grabbed a bite to eat and rushed over to meet Gangasagar. There was no point in keeping any secrets from the old man—he would find out anyway.

Shankar's mind was whirling. He was a mess. 'I never meant for it to happen. It was just so sudden. She needed me and—'

'—and you obliged by performing gymnastics with her in bed?' shouted Gangasagar.

'It wasn't like that at all. It was an intense, emotional, momentary—' began Shankar.

'Please! Spare me the details!' said Gangasagar as he strode up and down his living room, hands clasped behind his back.

'I—I—I think that I'm in l—love with her,' stammered Shankar. 'I don't know if I can really do what you want me to. How do I watch and report on a w—w—woman that I have fallen for?'

Gangasagar smiled. It was a gentle, reassuring smile. He walked up to the chair that Shankar was sitting on, placed a hand affectionately on the young man's shoulder and said, 'You're brave and honest, Shankar. I'm proud of you for telling me the truth.'

Shankar heaved a sigh of relief. 'I suggest that you go home and get some rest. We'll talk about how to pull you out of this assignment a couple of days later.'

Shankar fell to Gangasagar's feet and touched them. 'I am grateful to you for everything that you have done for me—including getting me the secretaryship. You're my mentor, sir, and I'm ever grateful.'

'Cheer up, Shankar. Love's not such a bad thing, after all,' chuckled Gangasagar. 'Without it, neither you nor I would have been born!'

Shankar awoke early, shaved, bathed and dressed. His small bachelor's flat smelt of coffee, a daily indulgence that required grinding fresh beans and brewing them. Ignoring the freshly-brewed coffee, he grabbed his brief-case, ran down the stairs and headed over to the bus stop. There was a spring in his step as he thought about his phone conversation the previous night with Chandini.

'I don't know how to thank you,' she said.

'Hush! You know that no thanks are needed,' he admonished.

'I know. Listen, about what happened between us—'

'Yes?'

'I don't know how to say this. If it was just casual for you, I'll understand—'

'What are you talking about? Casual? I—'

'I'm glad it meant something to you. I want you to know that it still means a lot to me.'

'I think I'm falling in love with you,' he said.

'That makes the two of us,' she said simply.

Shankar had reached the bus stop that lay across the street. He looked to his right and left before crossing the street. Without warning, the Tata truck wheeled up, the driver having apparently lost control of his vehicle. The massive twenty-five-tonne monster smashed into Shankar, crushing his bones into dusty death. Shankar's mangled body lay in a mess of blood and pulpy gore as the truck driver looked in his rearview mirror and drove on.

CHAPTER ELEVEN
About 2300 years ago

'I love you,' said Suvasini, Chanakya's childhood crush, to Rakshas, Magadha's prime minister, as she kneaded his neck and shoulders.

Suvasini was the ideal spark that could set off a conflagration in Magadha, Chanakya had decided. For one thing, she was sexy. For another, she loved playing games. In Magadha's political landscape, carnal desires were paramount drivers of the key protagonists—the lustful king Dhanananda and his lecherous prime minister Rakshas.

Suvasini had a dusky quality to her skin, which made her mysterious and desirable. She could not be called beautiful in the traditional sense, but there was a parti-cular quality in her that simply set the fertile imagination of any testosterone-bearing man into overdrive. She had curves in all the right places and this, combined with her tawny complexion, full lips, deep back eyes and thick black hair made her look tangy, saucy and sensual.

'I love you,' said Suvasini to Rakshas, 'but the king has put me in a very delicate position, darling. He wants me to become his queen.'

She felt the muscles in Rakshas' neck go taut as he stiffened. 'Is that what you also want?' he asked cautiously.

She put her arms around his neck, leaned forward and whispered into his ear, 'You know what happens when you and I are in bed together. Do you really think he'd be able to satisfy me?'

'But once he has his eyes on a woman, he gets her at any cost. No one can argue with him—he's the goddamn king! How are we going to handle it?' demanded Rakshas, his face flushed from her breathing into his ear.

'I shall be clear with him. If it means my head, so be it,' said Suvasini.

'My worry is that it isn't your *head* that he's after,' mused Rakshas.

■━■

'I love you,' said Suvasini to Dhanananda as she gently ran her fingers through the king's hair as he rested his head on her lap, 'but your prime minister has put me in a very delicate position, sweetheart. He wants me to be his wife.' She felt his temples throb.

'What is it that Rakshas can give you that I—emperor of Magadha—cannot?' he thundered.

She lowered her fingers to his chest and playfully traced light circular patterns around his nipples, lowered her own face into his and whispered, 'You know how I love what we have between us. You also know that I really don't care for your power or wealth. I simply adore *you*, my lord.'

'What I like about you, Suvasini, is that you can be a caring mother in the morning, a doting sister in the afternoon, and a whore at night!' he coarsely muttered.

She shuddered inwardly and closed her eyes. Why had Vishnugupta asked her to create this dangerous triangle?

'I shall be clear with him. If it breaks his heart, so be it,' said Suvasini.

'It isn't his heart that will break but something much lower down,' laughed Dhanananda.

It was the last muhurta before midnight and the palace was quiet at this hour. Inside the council chamber, Dhanananda was having a meeting with his prime minister, Rakshas. Several torches were blazing, held by clamps along the pillars, and the room was full of dancing shadows.

'Go meet Alexander as my emissary, Rakshas. Meet him before he leaves for Persia and tell him that Dhanananda would like to be his friend and that Magadha would like to welcome him as an honoured guest,' said Dhanananda.

'Maharaj, it's a long journey to Gandhar. Are you sure it's worthwhile? Who will help you run the administration while I'm away?' asked Rakshas.

'I shall miss you, my friend. But I cannot entrust this sensitive mission to anyone else. We can't afford to have Alexander being friends with Ambhi and Paurus, but not with Dhanananda. What if they all gang up against me?' asked Dhanananda.

'I shall need an armed contingent to accompany me—most of our neighbouring kingdoms are in tumult,' requested Rakshas. 'Also, if I am to be your ambassador of goodwill to Alexander, I shall need to carry precious gifts.'

'Absolutely. Please arrange it, Rakshas. I'm confident that you shall be successful in your endeavour. And don't worry about your loved ones. Dhanananda shall keep them close so that they shall want for nothing,' said Dha-nananda foxily.

I'm sure you shall, you bastard, thought Rakshas to himself as he bowed before the king.

◼━◼

At a decrepit temple in the city, the sultry Suvasini was meeting yet another man surreptitiously. His name was Jeevasiddhi, the lieutenant of Katyayanji who had saved Chanakya from an attacking tiger. He was now also Chanakya's trusted agent in Pataliputra.

The forsaken temple had stood in solitude for several generations, the colossal pillars crumbled and lying around in heaps of rubble. Years of looting and neglect had robbed, pilfered or destroyed anything of value. In the night of a full moon, the ruins were bathed in cool silvery light and the broken and jagged temple ruins seemed like a lunar landscape. The flaming torch being carried by Jeevasiddhi was not really required. The forbidding temple had been out of use for several generations owing to a curse by an enraged sage who had been prevented from sleeping in the temple premises by the local priests.

'You have something for me?' asked Jeevasiddhi. She nodded as she handed over two silken pouches to him. One contained a ring with the royal insignia of Dhana-nanda. The other contained a ring that had been given to Rakshas by his father and bore his family crest.

'I hope Vishnugupta rots in hell,' she said angrily to Jeevasiddhi. 'He has made me whore myself to achieve his own political ambitions.'

'There's always a greater purpose to everything we do, Suvasiniji,' said Jeevasiddhi. 'Acharya Chanakaya has asked me to read out this message to you and destroy the parchment afterwards.'

'What? A message from Vishnu? Why didn't you say so earlier? Tell me what it says,' urged Suvasini. Jeevasiddhi took out a small scroll from his waistband, unfurled it and began to read.

'My dear Suvasini. It's no secret that I've always loved you. But I've been pragmatic enough to bear in mind that you were always beyond my reach. You have been my one and only true love, but in my present world of power politics—to secure the unity and security of Bharat—I know there's no place for any woman in my life. I have taken the vows of *Brahmacharya*—celibacy— till such time as I achieve my dream of uniting a strong Bharat. Who knows, by that time I may be so old that the expiration of my vow may be of no consequence! I'm grateful for what you've done for me—it was a difficult decision to ask you to do it. I need you to remember that you've done it for a noble reason and I promise not to forget. Chanakya thanks you and Vishnugupta loves you. God bless you.'

Her eyes turned moist as she heard the words but before she could ask him to read it aloud to her again, Jeevasiddhi placed the scroll in the mouth of the flaming torch and held it till it was completely ablaze. 'Good night, Suvasiniji,' said Jeevasiddhi as he turned around and hurried away into the dark night, his torch leaving a trail of smoke behind him. Suvasini shuddered. She so wanted Chanakya to succeed. She began praying to Shiva to grant him victory. '*Om tryambhakam yajamahe, sugandhim pushtivardhanam; urvarukamiva bandhanam, mrityor mukshiya maamrital*,' she chanted. It was an ancient mantra from the Rigveda and meant '*O praise to the Three-Eyed One, who increases prosperity, who has a sweet fragrance, who frees the world from all diseases and death! Liberate—as the fruit from the wine. Shiva, grant immortality!*' Suvasini would find herself repeating the mantra many thousands of times for her beloved Vishnugupta as future events played out in Magadha.

The spymaster standing before Dhanananda was nervous. How had he allowed himself to be suckered into this double game, he wondered. He anxiously adjusted his wrap as he waited for Dhanananda to finish reading the note that had purportedly been seized from a messenger leaving Rakshas's camp and heading out to Kaikey. The expression on Dhanananda's face was one of seething wrath. His lips seemed to be mouthing the words written on the scroll in order to convince himself that they were real.

'O great King Paurus. Magadha's prime minister, Rakshas, sends greetings. I am on my way to your land. I come in my personal capacity, not as a senior functionary of the Magadha government. I have heard wonderful stories of your bravery, wisdom, and honour. If you deem fit, I would like to discuss an alliance between us that could be to our mutual advantage. It would allow me to grow in stature while expanding your borders significantly. It is critical, however, that this conversation remains confidential. I look forward to receiving your invitation for a meeting at the soonest. Your humble servant, Rakshas.'

'How do we know that the letter is genuine?' asked Dhanananda, hoping that it would turn out to be a forgery.

'There can be no doubting the authenticity, my lord,' said the spymaster. He stepped forward and handed over Rakshas's ring. 'This was enclosed in the scroll to prove his credentials to the king of Kaikey.'

'That traitorous fiend!' Dhanananda screamed. 'I want the scoundrel captured and brought back here to stand trial. He betrayed my trust and friendship. I made him the most powerful official in the kingdom and this is how he repays me. The ungrateful wretch! Even if it means sending the army to get him, do it!' he ordered.

⚊⚌

'My dearest Suvasini. I have succeeded in my efforts to get Rakshas out of Magadha. With him gone for several months, there's now no obstacle to our sweet union. I long to kiss you and hold you in my arms. Do not have any fear. Rakshas shall not return from his trip. My men have orders to kill him before he returns to Magadha. What are you waiting for? Come quickly. Your servant in love, Dhanananda.'

The message was clear. Rakshas looked at the ring bearing Dhanananda's royal insignia, which had been found inside the rolled parchment. He knew it! The priapic bastard wanted him dead so that he could claim Suvasini for himself. He had gifted him the finest cunts in the kingdom but the lascivious rascal only wanted the one woman that Rakshas coveted—his Suvasini.

Enough! He had spent his life pimping for Dhanananda and instead of being appreciated he was being hounded like a wild animal. He thought about how he could get even and then had a brilliant flash—Chanakya!

⚊⚌

'You're a fool! When eating hot porridge you should always start from the outer edges which are cooler, and not from the centre which is steaming hot,' the mother chided her little son as she nursed his scalded fingers. Chanakya, sitting outside Dandayan's hermitage, watched the little drama unfold as Dandayan's housekeeper scolded her child.

Dandayan's ashram was a quiet example of nature's bounty. Surrounded by dense trees, the hermitage was located on the banks of a sparkling stream and the air had a magical quality that was difficult to describe—a mystical combination of fresh air, the scent of pine, eucalyptus, and the sacred smoke of holy fires. Seated next to Chanakya was Chandragupta who was also fascinated by the theatrics of this simple everyday occurrence. When he looked away, he saw Chanakya smiling at him. 'What is it, acharya?' asked Chandragupta. A smile from Chanakya usually meant that he was plotting something. It made Chandragupta uneasy.

'I've been strategising this all wrong,' said Chanakya at length. 'This uneducated and illiterate mother is more intelligent than me. She's expounded the perfect military strategy that I, the wise and learned Chanakya, could not define.' Chandragupta was confused but he decided to stay quiet. Usually his teacher would explain himself without further prodding.

'Until today, my focus has been on Magadha and the coronation of you, Chandragupta, as its emperor, but now I see that I was mistaken. Magadha is the centre of the porridge. We first need to tuck into the smaller kingdoms along the peripheries. Magadha will follow much more easily,' explained Chanakya. 'The only two large kingdoms that could have posed a challenge to Magadha are Kaikey and Gandhar. Both have now been neutralised owing to our strategy of divide-and-rule. And within Magadha, Suvasini has succeeded in driving a wedge between Dhanananda and Rakshas. I expect to see Rakshas here with us in a few days. He sent me intimation of his imminent arrival a few days ago. Who could have thought that the manipulative Rakshas would one day be our ally? Politics makes strange bedfellows!' laughed Chanakya.

'But acharya, Magadha still remains the most powerful kingdom in north Bharat. With over two hundred thousand infantry, eighty thousand cavalry, eight thousand chariots and six thousand war elephants, it will be difficult to capture Magadha. Even Alexander's own men are afraid to cross the Ganges!' exclaimed Chandragupta.

'Ten soldiers wisely led will beat a hundred without a head,' said Chanakya. 'War is all about deception. Direct force is a poor solution to any problem. That's why it's used only by little children!'

Their deliberations were suddenly interrupted by the sound of trumpets and the dull thud of marching soldiers. 'Sinharan!' called out Chanakya. 'See who it is. Quick!' he whispered urgently as Sinharan drew near.

'It's the mighty Alexander himself,' said Sinharan clambering down the lookout tree. 'He's come to pay his respects to Sage Dandayan.' Alexander was atop his favourite horse, Boukephalus. A Thessalian horse-breeder had offered the steed to Alexander's father, King Philip II, for three thousand talents, but not one of Philip's horse-trainers had been able to mount the untamed stallion who would buck and throw any rider that attempted to scale him. Alexander was the only one who had succeeded. He had kept the horse ever since. Boukephalus had seen more countries and wars than most of Alexander's lieutenants.

Alexander dismounted as his retinue reached the ashram, and they were led to Dandayan and his followers, who were performing their yogic exercises. One particular routine involved stamping their feet on the ground. They continued with their routine, oblivious to the arrival of the godlike Alexander. Sitting at a distance, Chanakya chuckled to himself. This would be fun.

Alexander was dressed in a short Sicilian-style tunic with a heavily embossed leather belt wrapped around his quilted linen breastplate. He wore a highly polished helmet with a great white plume, and a matching gorget embedded with gems around his slender throat. His sword, a toughened yet agile blade, a gift from a Cyprian emperor, hung casually by his side. Through interpretation by Sasigupta, an Afghan tribal leader and now a key lieutenant in the Macedonian army, Alexander asked Dandayan what the significance of their stamping the earth was. Dandayan's reply was explicit. 'O great King of kings, a man can possess only so much of the earth's surface as this, the extent that one steps on. You are mortal, like the rest of us, and yet wish to possess more and more ground. You will soon be dead, and in that state you will own just enough earth as needed for your burial.'

Alexander went pale. His lieutenants gasped at the temerity of the sage and braced themselves for the worst. Instead, a moment later, Alexander pulled himself together and shrugged the words off. He knelt before the wise and naked Dandayan who was now sitting in a lotus position. 'Please come with me, O wise sage. Be my personal advisor. I shall cover you in gold and you shall not want for anything,' he pleaded. Alexander knew the importance of enlightened teachers. His mother, Olympia, had appointed Leonidas, a stern relative of hers, as his tutor, and his father, Philip, had put the adolescent prince under the tutelage of the Greek philosopher, Aristotle. Alexander had always maintained that his father and mother had given him life but that Leonidas and Aristotle had taught him how to live.

'Alexander, if you're the son of God, then why, so am I. I want nothing from you, for what I have suffices. I desire nothing that you can give me; I fear no exclusion from any blessings, which may perhaps be yours. Bharat, with the fruits of her soil in due season, is enough for me while I live. And when I die, I shall be rid of my poor body—my unseemly dwelling!' replied the sage. Alexander had finally met his match.

He rose, hands still folded in obeisance before Dandayan. 'I still need your blessing, great sage. I need you to bless me that I may be victorious in battle,' asked Alexander.

'My son, you have my blessing. May you be victorious in the battle that rages within you!' declared the sage, knowing that it wasn't exactly the blessing that Alexander had asked for.

The battle that raged within had deeply affected morale in his troops. Alexander's men had left Macedonia to teach Persia a lesson. They had not only conquered it but also subjugated it. They had silently accepted Alexander's transformation into a Persian shahenshah and had tolerated his whims and fancies. They had pushed onward into Bharat, had overcome Gandhar and Kaikey, but now their king wanted them to fight battles in faraway Magadha, never even part of the Achaemenid Empire, and to march through the intolerable rains in the excruciating summer heat. Mutiny was as as inevitable as Alexander's turning his back on Bharat.

▬▬

'Chanakya, my friend, how wonderful to see you again,' lied Rakshas, as he embraced his nemesis.

'Rakshas, your mere presence gives me confidence and happiness,' the Brahmin fabricated in his turn.

'Dhanananda has crossed all limits of decency,' complained Rakshas.

And you're such a decent human being, it goes against your moral conscience, thought Chanakya caustically to himself. 'Dhanananda's court is no place for honourable people like you—those who wish to lead an honourable but pleasurable life,' Chanakya said aloud, silkily.

'The problem is that most things in life that are pleasurable are usually illegal, immoral or fattening,' joked Rakshas as he sat down on the mattress proffered to him.

'The lesson for today, dear Rakshas, is that between two evils you should always pick the one that you haven't yet tried. I happen to be that particular evil,' suggested a smiling Chanakya. 'Now, let's examine, what it is that I can do for you, and then we can calculate what it is that you can do for me.'

'Always the teacher!' laughed Rakshas.

'And always right,' interjected Chanakya seriously. 'Dhanananda covets the love of your life,' he began.

'Yours too, as I understand it,' commented Rakshas warily.

'I'm not your competition, Rakshas. Look at me. Can I, a dark, ill-featured, pockmarked, crooked-toothed, uncouth Brahmin compete with you—the immaculate, suave, and cultured prime minister? You have my promise that I do not fancy Suvasini. She's yours, provided that Dhanananda's out of the way.'

'But how will that happen? He's firmly entrenched on the throne. He has Bharat's largest armed force at his command—a force so terrifying that even Alexander is being forced to turn back.'

'Battles needn't be fought on battlefields, my friend. I've always believed that wars are better fought without soldiers and unnecessary bloodshed,' said Chanakya softly.

'Do you have a plan to end all wars, acharya?' asked Rakshas.

'O Rakshas, everything is always all right in the end. If it isn't all right, then it isn't the end,' said Chanakya simply as he looked into his new ally's eyes.

＝

The house on Shiva street, in the eastern district of Pataliputra, was an unassuming structure. The neighbours knew it to be a dancing school run by a former courtesan. The simple single-storey house was built around a covered courtyard used by the girls who stayed within to practise their art. The principal of the institution was an elegant lady in her fifties. It was said that she had once been the chief courtesan of Dhanananda and that a wealthy patron had paid more than twenty-four thousand panas to secure her release from royal employment.

The students were girls from modest backgrounds who needed a vocation to support themselves and their families. They would usually enter the institution at ages six to eight and would be taught a variety of arts including painting, poetry, music, dancing, singing, cooking, and drama. No expense was spared either on their training or in their living standards. They were provided with the best accommodation, clothing, food and comforts. Their principal and their teachers were kind and understanding.

However, there was one golden rule that could never be broken. They each had to drink a glass of specially formulated milk every evening. The milk would be of varying colours, textures, and taste. Each lactic potion was specifically mixed for a given girl and the principal herself maintained detailed records of who drank how much of what. The girls could lead a pampered and sheltered existence provided they did not question this single stricture that applied to them automatically the moment they walked through the portals of the school.

Between ages six and eight, the girls who showed no visible signs of pubertal development would be given one *kuduba* of powder-blue milk formula each day. As they progressed to ages eight to ten and their breast buds began to appear, they would be given two kudubas of a saffron-orange brew every day. From ten to twelve, as their pubic hair began to grow, the daily dosage of the concoction went up to three kudubas of a pistachio-green mixture each evening. During the twelve to fourteen period, as their underarm hair began growing and their hips started widening in relation to their waists, the daily ration went up to one *prastha* of a cherry-pink milk sherbet. Between ages fourteen and sixteen, as they went into ovulation and menstruation, they would be fed two *adhakas* of an almond-brown lactic potion daily.

Anyone researching the institute closely would have come upon an even more interesting fact: all the girls, without exception, were born on Tuesdays during the seventh lunar day of *vishaka*. They possessed unfortunately potent horoscopes that guaranteed that any man they cohabited with would die. They were known as vishakanyas—or poison maidens.

An audit investigation into the largesse that funded the establishment would have revealed something even more curious. The entire corpus had been donated by a foundation called The Peacock Trust, the founders of which were Chanakya and Senapati Maurya. An apt name, given that Maurya owed his name to the peacock—*mor*.

'We need control over Mallayrajya,' said Chanakya. 'And we have the perfect candidate in Sinharan, whose father—the legitimate ruler—was murdered by his brother so that he could ally with Paurus. If Sinharan were in power, it would give us a much-needed base to station our troops.'

'We have sufficient hands, acharya. Let's mount an attack,' suggested Chandragupta quite predictably.

'That would be foolish. Never interrupt the enemy while he's in the process of making a mistake,' counselled the shadowy Brahmin.

'And what mistake is Mallayrajya making?' asked a puzzled Chandragupta.

'Not making. About to make.'

'About to make? Acharya, as usual you're talking in riddles.'

'The kingdom of Mallayrajya is about to surrender itself to us,' said Chanakya, leaving Chandragupta dumbfounded.

The cottage of Nipunaka was eerie. For one thing, it was built at the edge of a deserted cremation ground. For another, it was surrounded by ghostly banyan trees from which hung numerous symbols of the black arts—skulls, dead animals, earthen jars of alcohol, knives smeared in vermilion blood, and other offerings to the countless unexplained negative forces that ruled Nipunaka's dark world. An eccentric practitioner of esoteric medicine, pharmacology, sorcery, astrology and psychology, Nipunaka wore black robes and a garland fashioned from the skulls of infants. His rituals supposedly involved human sacrifice and tantric sex.

Chanakya was not impressed by the trappings of magic. He couldn't give a horse's fart if Nipunaka wanted to dance upon a corpse in the middle of the night while pouring wine into a ritualistic fire. To each his own, he reasoned. What Chanakya did believe in was the power of fools and the folly of group psychology.

'What brings the renowned Chanakya to my humble abode?' asked Nipunaka, bowing low.

'Don't be humble, Nipunaka. You're not that great. Humility is better left to kings!' Chanakya advised him.

Nipunaka laughed. It was a sinister, menacing laugh that seemed to echo through the dark forest. 'You obviously have one of your naughty schemes taking shape inside that fertile mind of yours,' chuckled Nipunaka. 'Will I get to sacrifice a virgin?'

'No one's a virgin, Nipunaka. Life screws them all,' said Chanakya playfully. Nipunaka laughed again. The sound that emerged was even more dreadful as the weird doctor of ghoulish sciences expressed his enjoyment of the joke. Chanakya had the uncanny ability to plumb the lowest depths of the human mind. It was his greatest asset.

'This is my disciple, Sinharan,' Chanakya said indicating his companion. 'He's the rightful heir to the throne of Mallayrajya. I need your help to win it back for him.'

'I am a simple tantric, O acharya. I can perform a sacred ritual so that he's able to ascend the throne,' suggested Nipunaka helpfully.

'I don't really give a rat's ass about those perverted orgies you organise every once in a while at some poor fool's expense,' commented Chanakya. 'I need your skills in psychology, drama, theatrics. Not your usual evil incantations,' he continued while placing a bag of gold panas in front of the mad scientist.

Nipunaka smiled, quietly this time. 'What exactly do you have in mind, acharya?' he asked as he picked up and tucked away the bag of gold deftly in a swift, well-practised motion.

'Sinharan here would like to share some secrets about Mallayrajya with you. Listen to him very carefully and memorise whatever it is that he has to tell you,' instructed the sagacious Brahmin.

'And then what?' enquired Nipunaka.

'Ah! Then you shall go to Mallayrajya, draw upon your wondrous powers, and do some good old-fashioned fortune-telling!'

The court of the king of Mallayrajya was deathly quiet. All eyes were focused on the strange tantric godman dressed in black robes with a necklace of human skulls around his neck. In his right hand, he held a long staff that also had a skull tied atop. In his other hand he held a blood-red earthen pot, supposedly filled with gore.

'O King, hear the words of the omniscient Nipunaka!' yelled the bordering-on-insane charlatan as he mentally reviewed the intimate secrets of Mallayrajya provided to him by Sinharan. 'Within your palace exists a room—a musty and unused chamber which remains locked most of the time. In the floor of that room lies buried the body of a Brahmin who was murdered here. Have it dug out and interred outside the borders of your kingdom. The spirit of that Brahmin continues to curse your dynasty and is an obstacle to your progress!'

Sinharan had known that his aunt had been having a torrid illicit affair with one of the palace guards—a Brahmin. Caught in the act of frenzied copulation, the guard had been murdered by Sinharan's furious cousin who had witnessed his mother's royal fornication. The son had then proceeded to bury the body in an unused storage closet for want of an alternative means of disposing of it. He had taken Sinharan's help, drawing on his sympathy and moral outrage. Two parties to the secrecy—Sinharan's aunt and her angry son—died a few years later when Paurus attacked the capital of Mallayrajya, taking the secret of the buried corpse to their pyres.

The king and his courtiers were mesmerised by the sheer audacity of the madman who stood before them. The king struggled to maintain his composure and asked, 'Powerful guru, can you tell us where this Brahmin's body is located? The palace complex covers more than a hundred acres and finding it without divine intervention would be impossible.'

The half-crazed Nipunaka shut his eyes and started mumbling—loudly enough to be audible to most present at court—'I prostrate myself before Bali, the son of Vairochana. I pray to Sambara, the master of a hundred magical mantras. I kneel before Nikumbha, Naraka, Kumbha, and Tantukachha, the powerful beast. O Chandali, Kumbhi, Tumba, Katuka, Saraga, I beg you, point me in the direction of those bones!' He suddenly opened his eyes wide and with an air of hysteria shouted aloud, 'I have it! Follow me!'

He started running wildly towards the room, the location of which had been explained in detail by Sinharan. As he approached the seventh door, situated along the west-facing passage on the second floor, he stopped. He closed his eyes once again and mustered up all the preternatural energy that he could possibly hope to gather and remarked, 'I can feel the negative energy of the Brahmin's ghost right here. I'm not wrong! Nipunaka is never wrong! By the power of Chandali, excavate that room and get rid of Mallayrajya's worries.'

As the bones were exposed from the shovelled earthen floor, the king went up to Nipunaka and bowed to him, overpowered by the intensity of the tantric's unearthly power. Nipunaka blessed the king by smearing consecrated ash on the ruler's forehead. The king took off his sapphire necklace and offered it to the mystic, who picked it up and threw it into the grave that had been uncovered. 'Of what use are precious gems to me, O King? If I wanted, all the world's riches could be mine but I neither possess nor desire material wealth,' he said, meticulously though reluctantly following Chanakya's instructions to appear incorruptible. There was a hushed, respectful silence as the gathered spectators mulled over the selfless attitude of the profound master.

A day later, the king fell ill. High fever accompanied by chills and convulsions made him weak and unable to attend court. His feverish state made him delusional, too, and in his state of temporary insanity, he hurled filthy abuse at all around him. Nipunaka knew that the sacred ash applied to the sovereign's head had worked. It had contained powdered *dhatura* seeds, a known formula for inducing hallucinations. The worried queen called Nipunaka back to the palace. 'Please find a remedy for the sudden inexplicable state of the monarch,' she pleaded.

'Do not worry, O Queen. Make the king drink a glass of milk with this unique formulation that I have prepared. You have my word that he shall be healthy by the morning,' the artful fraud reassured her. His antidote contained powdered *chitrak* roots and black pepper, prepared in advance by Chanakya.

The king's remarkable recovery the next day propelled Nipunaka to godman status. This was the guru's second extraordinary achievement in two days. But there wasn't any time to celebrate. Armed mercenaries, led by a young upstart known as Chandragupta, and assisted by Sinharan—claimant to the throne of Mallayrajya—surrounded the city, and the fortified capital came officially under siege. The siege continued for the entire duration of the waxing of the moon and the city began to run low on critical supplies and provisions. At a hastily convened council meeting, the decision to launch an outright frontal assault on Sinharan and Chandragupta's forces was being pondered over, when Nipunaka made another grand entrance.

'King! I have an important message for you,' began the trickster, blissfully aware that the gullible Cabinet was lapping up his every word. 'Inside the palace temple stands a statue of Kubera. The daily prayers performed by your royal priests before the deity were flawed and it is precisely for this reason that you face the threat of extinction. Rectify the fault and you shall see the enemy retreat!'

Following his orders and accompanied by a series of incantations and rituals, the earthen idol of Kubera was duly removed and allowed to melt away inside the royal lake while hymns and invocations prescribed by the pre-eminent Nipunaka continued. At that very moment, Chanakya ordered Sinharan and Chandragupta to withdraw their troops and retire to a hideout a few miles away from the fortified capital. As news of the miraculous withdrawal filtered in, celebrations began and nobles and commoners alike flooded the streets. As music, wine and women took over and the revelry reached its climax, Chanakya's soldiers of fortune crept back to the fortifications and stormed the unsuspecting town. It was a bloodless coup—sudden, dramatic, and smooth, typical of the Brahmin who had choreographed it all.

The coronation of Sinharan as king of Mallayrajya was magnificent. 'Always keep your words soft and sweet, O Sinharan. Just in case you ever have to take them back,' advised his mentor as he blessed the new sovereign.

Sinharan knelt before his teacher and said 'Acharya, I feel guilty about what happened to my uncle and his family. I had simply exiled him after our takeover of the kingdom, as you advised. I feel terrible that he and his family were murdered by dacoits thereafter. I fear that his death will haunt me for the rest of my life.'

'Everyone leaves the world a better place, some merely by leaving. Your uncle was one of those!' said a victorious Chanakya as he gloated over his memory of the events of the previous day when the inhabitants of the city had capitulated to them.

'I do not wish to burden Sinharan with the odious task of eliminating challengers to his throne,' he had confided to Mehir. 'I shall ask Sinharan to banish his uncle from Mallayrajya. Our effort, Mehir, must be to ensure that the former king leaves the borders of the kingdom absolutely unharmed.'

'But is it wise to exile him? He's an ally of Paurus, and will flee to Kaikey with a view to raising troops. Paurus will only be too happy to support his endeavour. Afer all, Sinharan's ascension to the throne means that Mallayrajya is no longer a vassal of Kaikey,' Mehir had exclaimed.

'You're absolutely right, Mehir. And that's why I need him eliminated—but not officially. The population of Mallayrajya must love their new ruler, Sinharan. He should appear kind, fair, just, truthful and benevolent. It's vital that Sinharan's uncle be seen leaving the kingdom—unharmed and unhindered—along with his family and supporters.'

'And then?' asked Mehir, knowing the answer and also knowing that it was an answer that would remain unspoken.

CHAPTER TWELVE
Present Day

The suite at the Hotel Clarks in Lucknow was cool and dark. The curtains had been partly drawn to block out the harsh afternoon sun, and the air-conditioning had been set to the lowest possible temperature. Sitting inside were two men—Pandit Gangasagar Mishra and Ram Shankar Dwivedi. Dwivedi was nervous. He kept adjusting his spectacles and straightening his hair. He was dressed like any other Indian politician—white homespun kurta and pyjama—but the accessories that embellished his Gandhian outfit were not all that humble. His spectacle frames were Gucci, the pen in his pocket a solid silver Mont Blanc, his wristwatch a yellow gold Rolex, and his feet were comfortably encased in Bally loafers.

Why had the party patriarch decided to call him for a one-on-one meeting in a luxury suite, he asked himself. A trickle of sweat left his upper back and dripped down his spine in spite of the freezing room. It caused him to shudder. This was not good. Pandit Gangasagar Mishra was a cold-blooded killer when it came to politics, thought Dwivedi. What did he know? Was he being called for a dressing-down by the ABNS patriarch?

Gangasagar stared at him in silence for what seemed like an eternity. Talk, damn you, thought Dwivedi to himself. Unknown to Dwivedi, Gangasagar was wearing a woollen vest inside his kurta and sat comfortably snug, unaffected by the sub-zero chill of the room. *Let him shiver*, thought Gangasagar. *If he's cold, he'll want to pee, and that will make him even more nervous.*

'I'm told that you're rather sociable these days, Dwivediji,' said Gangasagar at length. 'Everyone I meet tells me they have visited your house.'

'It is my misfortune that you have not had the time to be my guest, Panditji, I would love to have you over for dinner,' replied Dwivedi anxiously.

'Let me rephrase the statement. To be precise, twenty-four of our ABNS MLAs have been observed regularly visiting your house—and please don't tell me that they came just for whisky and samosas!'

Dwivedi fidgeted some more. He took a deep breath and said, 'I'm a loyal party worker, Panditji. Some disgruntled elements were trying to ignite a rebellion. I thought that it was my paramount duty to convince them otherwise.'

'I'm proud of you, Dwivediji. I should have realised that these photos were doctored,' declared Gangasagar as he tossed a bunch of glossy 4 x 6-inch photos on the glass coffee table before them. The colour drained from Dwivedi's face as he stared at the obscene photographs showing him in various *Kama Sutra*-inspired positions along with Eesha. He mumbled incoherently, but no words emerged.

'Relax, Dwivediji. Don't worry. She said that you were quite good in bed,' Gangasagar laughed maniacally as he went in for the kill. 'I have forty-nine negatives with me—one for each month of the remaining term of this government. If Chandini is still chief minister in the forty-ninth month, all the negatives shall be returned to you, deal?'

Dwivedi nodded dumbly, his very life having been sucked out of him. Pandit Gangasagar Mishra got up from his chair. 'Ah! One more request. Please remember that it's now in your interest to ensure that this government lasts. It shall be your personal responsibility to keep me informed if there are any murmurs of dissent, is that understood?' he demanded before walking out of the hotel suite, turning off the air conditioner as he left.

'*Adi Shakti, Namo Namah; Sarab Shakti, Namo Namah; Prithum Bhagvati, Namo Namah; Kundalini Mata Shakti; Mata Shakti, Namo Namah,*' he said to himself.

***

Chandini was devastated. Shankar had been a breath of fresh air, her only indulgence after Geoffrey. She looked at herself in the mirror, holding back tears that wanted to breach the dam. She would not cry. It seemed that it was not in her destiny to either love or be loved. She dabbed a tissue under her deep-green eyes, flushed it down the aircraft toilet and stepped out to join Gangasagar.

The flight from Lucknow to Delhi was short but uncomfortable. Take-off had been delayed by over an hour due to a faulty auxiliary power supply unit and by the time that had been rectified, air traffic control had denied permission to leave, owing to inclement weather. Gangasagar had phoned the civil aviation minister in New Delhi to have a word put in to Lucknow's air traffic control to grant them permission to take off. The rest of the passengers on the flight were unaware that they were the lucky recipients of political largesse—a take-off that would have probably been aborted if not for the presence of Gangasagar. Chandini, Ikram, Gangasagar and Menon were seated in the front row of the aircraft. The usually grumpy airhostess had suddenly perked up and was making an extra effort to be warm and caring towards her VIP guests although her attitude of general indifference returned the moment that she reached the second row.

'What do we expect to achieve in New Delhi?' asked Ikram.

'Do you remember our conversation when you had just taken over as mayor, Ikram?' asked Gangasagar.

'Which one? There were so many,' joked Ikram.

'The one when I told you that we should be do-gooders because we want to win the next elections. That real power lay at state level, not in local government.'

'Yes. I do remember.'

'Well, I want to tell you that I was wrong.'

'What do you mean? We hold the reigns of power in Uttar Pradesh. Our own dear Chandini is the chief minister. I, Ikram Shaikh, am mayor of Kanpur.'

'Yes. But real power lies at the Centre in New Delhi and that's where we're all going to be some years from now. This is orientation week.'

'But we could have had this discussion in Lucknow. Why are we going to Delhi to discuss these matters?' asked Chandini.

'To meet Major Jaspal Singh Bedi,' replied Gangasagar.

'Who's he?' asked Ikram.

'He's the man who will ensure that we win sixty-five out of the eighty-five Lok Sabha seats in Uttar Pradesh.'

◧▬◧

The suave and dapper Sikh was over six feet tall. He wore a navy-blue suit, and his deep crimson turban was meticulously colour-coordinated with his pocket kerchief and tie. The double cuffs of his starched white Egyptian cotton shirt peeped the correct inch from his suit sleeves and bore solid silver cufflinks emblazoned with the crest of the Indian armed forces. His salt-and-pepper beard, moustache and eyebrows were immaculately groomed, not a single hair out of place.

Major Jaspal Singh Bedi had been born to a middle-class family in Punjab and had been wild and unruly throughout his childhood and youth. He was the leader of a gang that had perfected the art of stealing sweets from unsuspecting customers just as they emerged from popular sweet shops. Jaspal's accomplices would cause a ruckus by fighting amongst themselves. The hapless customers carrying shopping bags would attempt to intervene and resolve matters while Jaspal would courteously offer to hold their parcels for them while they did. Five minutes later the customers would have succeeded in reconciliation but Jaspal would have vanished—along with their parcels.

Jaspal's worried father had eventually requested one of his cousins, a lieutenant-colonel in the Indian Army to convince Jaspal to take up a ten-year short service commission in the army. Jaspal refused—he was having too much fun stealing sweets. The officer had called the boy to his cowshed and given him the thrashing of his life. No options were offered. Jaspal left for the Officers Training Academy in Chennai for fifty weeks the very next morning. His father hoped the army would discipline the reckless youth and give his life a sense of purpose.

It did. The discipline of army life suited Jaspal. His stint with the army empowered him with analytical thinking, planning skills, and team-playing abilities. He rapidly worked his way up from lieutenant to captain to major. Having completed his ten-year commission, he joined a small market research agency employed by the Government of India to carry out surveys of rural populations in conjunction with the ten-year population census. Jaspal had spent the next ten years mapping population demographics across India, a gargantuan task, methodically implemented by the disciplined soldier in him. He left the firm having reached the position of Country Head—Rural Research, to set up his own consultancy, which would combine two sciences that were symbiotic—polling and politics.

'The Lok Sabha is the directly elected lower house of the Parliament of India. Five hundred and fifty-two members are directly elected by an electorate of over seven hundred million voters, an electorate larger than that of America and Europe combined,' began Major Bedi. 'The reason I am here with you today is that your state—Uttar Pradesh—sends eighty-five members to the Lok Sabha. That is a significant number. Why? Because if this number were to ever be controlled by a single party, that party—even if just a regional player—would play a crucial role in forming a government at the Centre.'

'But that dream is far-fetched, Major Bedi. Uttar Pradesh is not a homogenous monolith. It consists of people who vote based on religion, caste, gender and economic strata. One size does not fit all!' said Menon.

'You're right, Mr Menon. And that's the reason why a single formula will never work in Uttar Pradesh. The single formula is to have no single formula. Some seats will be fought along caste lines—Dalits versus Brahmins or Yadavs versus Banias; other seats will be fought along religious divisions—Hindus versus Muslims. Yet others may be fought on economic grounds—poor versus the rich. That's where the ABNS scores,' explained the Major, taking a sip of water to lubricate his throat.

'How?' wondered Ikram, dipping a sugar-coated biscuit into his tea and taking a bite.

'All other parties in Uttar Pradesh seem to have a core constituency. The ABNS has none,' replied Jaspal confidently.

'So we're screwed?' asked Ikram slurping his tea loudly.

'On the contrary. Your strength lies in *not* having a core constituency. The very criteria that is perceived as a strength in one region is usually a weakness in another. For example, if the ABNS were perceived as a party of Dalits, that would help the party in Dalit strongholds but it would be a drawback in Brahmin-dominated areas,' reasoned Major Bedi.

'So you want us to ally ourselves with Hindus *and* Muslims, Brahmins *and* Dalits, Yadavs *and* Thakurs, landlords *and* farmers, rich *and* poor, men *and* women, old *and* young... don't we run the risk of becoming a *khichdi* with no single dominant flavour?' asked Chandini.

'The other parties already have candidates who have represented these constituencies for years. You have the advantage of a clean slate. You can cherry-pick your own candidates, accurately tailored to the specific require- ments of the constituency in question,' said Major Bedi, 'and that's where I come into the picture'.

'What will you do?' asked Chandini.

'Have done,' corrected Bedi. 'I was assigned by Gangasagarji the job of determining the ideal profile of a candidate for each of the eighty-five Uttar Pradesh constituencies a year ago. I am here to apprise you of my findings.'

━❑━

'You have eighty-five constituencies—Kheri, Dhaurahra, Bijnor, Amroha, Moradabad, Rampur, Sambhal, Budaun—'

He continued rattling off all the names methodically from his list. Along with each name he described its population, the literacy rate, age demographics, gender split, percentage composition of castes, religions and ethnicities, and the primary occupations of the population. Facts and figures poured forth effortlessly from Major Bedi. He was the human equivalent of a computer.

As he reached the last constituency he said, 'In Uttar Pradesh the electoral contest is still about settling the primary questions of social dominance. I have analysed each of the eighty-five constituencies on this parameter.'

'Social dominance? You mean caste!' exclaimed Ikram.

'Not merely caste. Social dominance is influenced by caste, gender, religion, age *and* economic strength. Please understand that there is no single constituency where a single dominant group can win an election! For example, in western Uttar Pradesh—Meerut—you have a concentration of Jats, the region often being called Jatland. How many Jats are there in Meerut? Ten per cent! Can you win an election with ten per cent?' asked Bedi.

'So how does one win, for example, Meerut?' asked Gangasagar.

'Look beyond the caste equations, Gangasagarji,' suggested Bedi. 'Meerut has a population of half a million. The city is sixty-two per cent Hindu, thirty-five per cent Muslim, three per cent Sikh, half per cent Christian and half per cent Jain; fifty-three per cent of the population is male, and the average literacy rate is seventy-two per cent, quite high for Uttar Pradesh.'

'So our ideal candidate is an educated Hindu male?' asked Chandini.

'On the contrary, Hindus tend not to vote en bloc. Their votes get split along caste lines or on other considerations. Instead, if one was to try to forge an alliance of Jats and Muslims one could, theoretically, capture forty-five per cent of the votes,' answered Bedi.

'But why would Jats and Muslims vote for the same candidate?' asked Chandini.

'Good question. You assume that these two groups have been opposed to one another historically and hence correctly figure that the possibility of finding someone who appeals to both groups is remote. But I have succeeded in identifying potential candidates from the Chhachhar community,' said Major Bedi proudly.

'Why Chhachhar?' asked a confused Menon.

'Chhachars are a tribe of Jats who converted to Islam many years ago. Their descendants are Muslim Jats. A Muslim Jat is your perfect combination to win this constituency,' declared the dapper sardar.

'What would further strengthen his chances of winning?' asked Gangasagar quietly.

'Meerut is an important industrial town. It has eleven sugar-processing mills and more than seventy per cent of the population is engaged in sugarcane cultivation. If our Chhachhar candidate were to be a sugarcane farmer, he would be much more acceptable—even to other castes and communities—because of economic considerations.'

'But you said that by doing all of this we would have forty-five per cent of the votes. That would still leave fifty-five per cent!' said Menon.

'The fifty-five per cent is only dangerous if it is left concentrated in the hands of a single opposition candidate. That brings me to the next part of my strategy,' said Bedi, flipping through his notes.

'And what is that?' asked Gangasagar.

'The second part of the strategy is to ensure that the remaining fifty-five per cent votes get split.'

'And how would you achieve this?' asked Ikram.

'Simple. Map the profile of the existing sitting MP and find a replica to put up as an additional independent candidate in each contest. The job of this candidate is simply to play spoiler and split the competition's vote bank.'

'So we need to find ourselves a Muslim Jat sugarcane farmer? We then need to find ourselves a spoiler who closely matches the profile of the present MP from Meerut constituency?' spluttered Ikram.

'I have already found the former for you. His name is Daula Hassan Bhatti. He's fifty-three years old, a Muslim Jat—his family migrated to Meerut three generations ago—and owns a five-acre sugarcane farm along with a crushing facility. He's a natural choice,' explained Bedi.

'But—but are we expected to go around begging such people to contest elections on our ticket? We already have party workers queuing up for Lok Sabha tickets, why not make it easier by choosing from amongst them?' asked Ikram.

'Do you want to win or not? Never make the mistake of choosing from a suboptimal pool. Identify the perfect candidate according to the constituency. Now, shall I tell you about the remaining eighty-four ideal candidates from the other constituencies?' asked Bedi, as Gangasagar sat quietly through the exchange, smiling.

'The traders of Uttar Pradesh are going on strike,' said Chandini.

'Why?' asked Gangasagar.

'They say that the sales-tax rate in Uttar Pradesh is too high. They want it reduced.'

'You don't simply go around giving away tax revenue because someone wants it! Do you give whisky to an alcoholic because he just happens to want it?'

'I agree. But what should I do? The strike will bring all economic activity to a halt. Prices of essential commodities will skyrocket. Our constituents will be angry.'

'Hike sales tax by another five per cent!'

'We can't do that! They're already in a combative mood—'

'They have already taken the ultimate step of going on strike, right? What more can they do?'

'And how will we ever get them to call it off?'

'Give them a three-per-cent cut as concession to halt the strike. You still gain two,' the Pandit chuckled.

———

'The bus drivers of the state transport corporation continue to drive rashly under the influence of alcohol— this has been the fourth road accident in a fortnight,' complained Chandini, pointing out the newspaper report to Gangasagar.

'Why don't we sack the drivers if they are found guilty?' asked Gangasagar.

'They have to be convicted first. The court cases drag on for years.'

'There's a perfect solution to solve the problem.'

'And that is?'

'Pay drivers' salaries directly to their wives. They'll never part with a penny for tipple! Tell the transport commissioner to ensure that all salary payments are made out to the wives. You'll halve the drunk-driving rate!'

———

'Loan defaults plague our regional banks,' said Chandini as she pushed across the financial statements compiled by the state comptroller.

'Who are the defaulters?'

'Farmers, businessmen, traders, home-owners, as well as people who run up hefty bills on their credit cards. If we don't recover these amounts, Uttar Pradesh's banks may collapse one day.'

'Leave the farmers. Scant rains have resulted in poor harvests this year. Give them more time to pay up and write off the interest on their loans.'

'And the others?'

'They should have no difficulty paying. They are simply taking advantage of the sloppy debt-recovery mechanism of our state-owned banks.'

'But the only action that we can take is to go to court. That's expensive and time-consuming. It could be years before one sees results.'

'Tell Sachla Devi to recover your loans.'

'Who?'

'Sachla Devi. She's a famous eunuch in Lucknow. I can ask her to help you.'

'Why on earth should I take help from a eunuch?'

'Because she has bands of wandering eunuchs who do absolutely nothing productive all day, besides standing outside homes and shops and clapping and shouting loudly.'

'They only do that on happy occasions—marriages, births, inaugurations. Donating to eunuchs is supposed to bring good luck!'

'But people don't cough up cash to eunuchs because they want good luck. They simply want good riddance.'

'So?'

'Sachla Devi will organise her gangs to stand outside defaulters' homes and offices. They will clap loudly and embarrass them before their friends and neighbours. They'll get fed up and pay up. Tell Sachla Devi that she will get ten per cent of the loans recovered by her team!'

The cabinet meeting was excessively long, the tea luke-warm, the snacks insipid. The agenda was fiery, though. The cabinet room located inside the PMO—the Prime Minister's Office—at South Block, Raisina Hill, was an ornate room in which cut flowers were changed each day and sniffer dogs were led into corners to check for explosives every few hours. The PMO had an uncompli-cated occupancy plan with six joint secretaries housed on the ground floor and the prime minister and his key lieutenants on the first. The only noticeable feature of the PMO was the presence of a paper-shredder in almost every room. This prime minister was obsessive about secrecy, and rightly so. They were sitting for a marathon Cabinet session simply because some nitwit had forgotten to use the damned shredder.

The offending paragraph was read and reread several times. 'Articles 15 and 16 of the Constitution guarantee every Indian citizen freedom as well as equality before the laws of the land. Reservation for those who had been left behind by Indian society was indeed part of the Constitution when it was framed and adopted in 1950. Those who framed the Constitution themselves believed that it was a temporary measure and would last for ten years. But several decades later we still find reservation in place. Doesn't this tell us that India has made very little progress in bringing the scheduled castes, scheduled tribes and other backward classes into the mainstream of India? Is it time to take another look at the policy and decide whether it has actually worked?'

The prime minister never had any intention of reviewing the policy on reservation. It was a powder keg that would explode irrespective of which way one went. If one came down in favour of ending reservation, the streets would be filled with protestors—those who were the beneficiaries of the reservation policy. If one expressed a view that reservation should be continued, the streets would also be filled with protestors—this time with those whom the policy had discriminated against. It was a no-win situation. This prime minister's policy was *not* to have a policy on the matter.

The infernal document had been drafted by his policy advisors who had believed that the prime minister might be forced by the Opposition to make a statement on the issue in the Lok Sabha. They wanted to be prepared. But why hadn't they used the damn shredder thereafter? The offending paragraph had travelled from South Block, to North Block, and further to the editorial offices of the *Hindustan Times*. The next morning the prime minister was fried for the country's breakfast.

'The press is asking for our views on the story,' said the cabinet secretary.

'Of course they are. I send them stories about foundation stones laid for new hospitals—they don't care. I send them material on the new education reform policy— they don't care. I send them photographs of our foreign delegations that are ushering in a new era of peace and stability—they don't care. But they get one paragraph from that infernal memo that should never have been written up in the first place and they come flocking like vultures smelling blood!' retorted the premier angrily.

'Er… ahem… ' began the finance minister.

'Yes, what is it? Say what you want, let's not have you clearing your throat in perpetuity,' demanded the irritated PM.

'Er… ah! Yes. I do believe that the only way that we can limit the damage is by giving them an even bigger story—one that would simply overshadow this one,' said the greying finance minister.

'And what would that be?' asked the prime minister.

'A war with Pakistan perhaps?' interjected the external afffairs minister.

'You want me to declare war on Pakistan so we can kill a newspaper story? Has everyone lost their minds?' shouted the prime minister.

After an interminable pause, the home minister spoke up. 'We do not have to declare war. Simply convey the impression that there are skirmishes along the Indo-Pakistan border. The press will lap it up.'

'It takes two to tango,' said the Prime Minister. 'What gives you gentlemen the impression that Pakistan will go along with it?'

'Pakistan will always go along with it. Their own internal politics is a mess. It will be a welcome relief for them to get back to doing what they do best, whipping up war hysteria and dishing it out to unsuspecting suckers—the ordinary citizens of Pakistan,' said the minister for external affairs.

'Couldn't we be hauled up later by the press for dishing out precisely the same sort of drivel to our citizens?' asked the prime minister.

'A little inaccuracy sometimes saves a ton of explanation, sir,' said the cabinet secretary. The finance minister, the home minister and the minister for external affairs nodded their heads sagely. The defence minister was conspicuously silent.

***

'If a war-like situation persists, public sentiment will be with the government of the day. It always happens. People who would love to pull down the government's pants suddenly become patriotic!' said Agrawalji to Gangasagar as they sat in his garden eating lunch. Chandini and Ikram were the only other invitees.

'He's covering his ass! Nothing more,' exclaimed Ikram, stuffing a *gobi paratha* into his eagerly awaiting mouth.

'A wise man covers his ass. An even wiser man leaves his pants on,' said Gangasagar.

'Huh?'

'The reservations leak that we arranged from the Prime Minister's Office did its job. The prime minister has played into our hands by creating war hysteria. Every defence contract will now be under scrutiny—Majestic Munitions in particular.'

'Why?'

'Because Majestic Munitions was awarded a very large contract for rifles, and two per cent of the firm now belongs to the sadhvi as per our instructions to Somany. And the sadhvi is the prime minister's illegitimate daughter. A case of impropriety, wouldn't you say?' asked Gangasagar, draining his glass of salted lassi.

'But we would end up hurting Somany. He holds a stake in Majestic,' argued Chandini. 'He'll come back wanting his losses recouped.'

'I'd asked him to sell the shares of Majestic no sooner the deal was inked. I'm given to understand that his block of shares was sold three days ago,' said the Pandit, suppressing a little burp in appreciation of the wonderful food that was served at Agrawalji's house.

'So how do we play this?' asked Ikram, digging into the famous Agrawal rice pudding.

'We get our weasel reporter back and offer him the opportunity to shake the Prime Minister's throne. After all, he has been sitting impatiently awaiting our nod to use the sadhvi material, right?'

'Right.'

'But no talk about her being an illegitimate daughter,' said Gangasagar.

'Why Ganga, I didn't realise that you had a soft spot for her,' said Agrawalji in jest.

'I don't. I believe that information is like money. Better to retain it like a bank balance than spend it unwisely,' said Gangasagar. 'Chandini, I think Lok Sabha elections may happen sooner than we expected!' Gangasagar laughed. The laugh tickled his throat and he coughed. He gulped some water and laughed again, uncontrollably. Agrawalji, Chandini and Ikram looked at him curiously. It was disconcerting to see the Pandit out of control.

'What's the joke?' asked Ikram.

'The prime minister. I'm imagining him with no pants on!'

<hr>

'It's said that she visits you every day! Your side of the story, sir.'

'No comment.'

'They say you awarded defence contracts to Majestic because she was a shareholder. Is that true?'

'No comment.'

'Is it true that she has divine powers and that she used them to make you prime minister?'

'No comment.'

'Do both of you practise black magic together when you're alone?'

'No comment.'

'Does she attend cabinet meetings to influence decisions?'

'No comment.'

'Is she your mistress?'

'No comment.'

The prime minister got into the waiting car and sighed. This was not turning out to be a good day.

<hr>

'The prime minister will have no alternative but to resign. There shall be a power struggle for the top job with the finance minister, home minister and the minister for external affairs battling it out for the position,' said Gangasagar.

'And who shall win?' asked Chandini.

'None. When lions fight over a goat, it's usually the hyena that gets away with the prize.'

'And who's the hyena?'

'The defence minister.'

'But he's a fool!' sputtered Chandini.

'I don't care. All that I want is for him to finalise his party's candidate list for Uttar Pradesh.'

'And whom do you want on that list?'

'All his existing MPs.'

'Why?'

'Politicians are like diapers—they need to be changed frequently! Anti-incumbency will work beautifully against them.'

'Shouldn't the ABNS get into a pre-poll alliance with the ruling party in New Delhi?' asked Chandini.

'Of course not!' exclaimed Gangasagar.

'Why not? Doesn't the defence minister want it?'

'Of course he does. But we'll decide later.'

'Why? Haven't we decided which side we're on?'

'Of course we have.'

'And which side is that?'

'The winning side, my girl, the winning side.'

'He must have a victory, something that enables him to become the centre of attention,' said Gangasagar.

'You mean the defence minister? He's been saying that he has no ambitions to become the prime minister,' said Chandini.

'That's not the same as saying he won't allow his name to go forward if he's persuaded by his well-wishers!'

'The prime minister, the finance minister, the minister for external affairs, the home minister and the defence minister—they are all members of the same ruling party in New Delhi. Why should it matter to us which one eventually wins?'

'There is one significant reason, Chandini.'

'And what's that?'

'Our young tycoon, Somany, has an excellent equation with the defence minister. Remember Majestic Munitions? It's in our interest that our man gets the job.'

'So you think you can swing the prime minister's job towards the defence minister?'

'Yes, but he's not seen as a serious contender for the top job. If he's to emerge as an alternative he must do something dramatic, something that gives him instant credibility and recognition.'

'Like what?'

'We could ask him to win a war.'

'Where?'

'NJ9842.'

'Never heard of it.'

'Precisely why it's the perfect location.'

⸻

Coordinate NJ9842 was the point from where the boundary dispute between India and Pakistan stretched into the highest battlefield in the world. Both countries' troops were stationed eyeball to eyeball at a height of over twenty thousand feet above sea level at sub-zero temperatures. The Siachen Glacier—located in the Karakoram mountain range containing some of the highest peaks in the world—was one of the world's most inhospitable regions. Temperatures hovered at around minus forty degrees centigrade and if one's exposed skin touched metal, it would instantly bind as though with crazy glue. The glacier received ten metres of snow annually and blizzards reached one hundred and fifty knots.

Despite having been fitted with five layers of clothing, the defence minister shivered as he stepped off the special AN-32A military aircraft from Leh. A military advanced light helicopter was waiting to fly him to Point Sonam, the world's highest helipad, built by the Indian army. The chopper pilot remained quiet. He didn't wish to scare the minister by telling him that landing a chopper at Point Sonam was a hair-raising experience.

As the shuddering metal beast began its descent on the microscopic helipad perched atop a needle of ice, the rotor blades struggled to extract even minimal lift from the rarefied air. The decision to lower the minister via rope ladder when there was no need to do so was foolish, thought the pilot. But who was he to argue with the intellectual might of the bureaucracy at Sena Bhavan—defence ministry headquarters.

He turned around to look behind. He saw the nervous and bundled-up defence minister shivering, his teeth chattering. The pilot didn't know that the defence minister was cursing his friend—Somany—under his breath as he got ready to descend the rope ladder. The minister didn't know that the idea wasn't Somany's but Gangasagar's.

⊒⊏

'There's no war to be won,' said Chandini.

'There's always a war if you look closely enough,' said Gangasagar.

'And where are you searching for it?'

'In the newspapers,' said Gangasagar.

'Huh?'

'The war to be won is on paper—a war of words! Not soldiers fighting! We don't need anything that messy.'

'I'm still confused.'

'We'll leak the story that Indian and Pakistani troops stationed in Siachen have exchanged fire.'

'Have they?' asked Chandini.

'They *might* have,' answered Gangasagar. 'We can't be sure that they didn't. Exchange of random fire happens almost every day in Siachen.'

'You could say that almost anything *might* be possible, using that particular theory!'

'Precisely. They *might* have. They *might not* have. Who's to say what's the truth?'

'And then?'

'We tell Somany to ask the defence minister to visit the Indian troops in Siachen. Wonderful publicity with the minister of defence clambering down a rope ladder from a chopper. The ultimate protector of India's sovereignty and integrity! Superman and Spiderman morphed into one!'

'And then?'

'Another leak that the situation was rapidly brought under control as a result of the defence minister's personal initiative to visit the troops and the consequent lifting of their morale.'

'The newspapers won't fall for it—they'll see it as a publicity stunt.'

'They'll believe it if a leaked secret report of an American defence think-tank says so.'

'How will you get an American defence think-tank to say what you want it to?'

'Majestic Munitions has a stake in Strategic Asia Research Defence—SARD—an American think-tank on Asian military matters. Somany has promised me a SARD report as and when I ask for it.'

'And the report would be true?'

'It *might* be. Who's to say that the Pakistani troops *didn't* withdraw!'

'But they never *attacked* in the first place!'

'Really? I didn't know that. They *might* have.'

'So it's all one big lie?'

'It *might* be. But then again, it *might not!*'

———

'So what does Somany want in return for having swung the prime minister's job the defence minister's way?' asked Chandini.

'Nothing. He's gained by having his own friend inside South Block. He will now use his newly acquired status to teach his senior partner—Rungta—a lesson,' replied Gangasagar.

'And we're fine with that?'

'In politics there are no permanent friends or enemies.'

'Uncle Ganga, you shall definitely go to hell when you die!'

'I'm entirely prepared for that eventuality, dear girl. I shall be delighted to go meet my maker. Luckily for me, my maker doesn't seem to be in a hurry to meet me!'

———

Chandini was seated at her desk in her spacious office at Lal Bahadur Shastri Bhavan. Gangasagar was sitting on the sofa in the informal corner of her suite. They were watching the news. The anchor was saying:

'The President of India on Wednesday dissolved the Lok Sabha with immediate effect, paving the way for constitution of the new House, which is expected later this month. The president signed an order to this effect following a recommendation from the new prime minister, the erstwhile minister of defence. Soon after a meeting of the Union Cabinet the prime minister drove to Rashtrapati Bhavan to submit the resignation of his council of ministers to the president in person. The president asked him to continue until a new ministry was formed. The meeting between the president and the prime minister lasted for thirty min—'

Gangasagar switched off the television, cutting the anchor in mid-sentence. 'The bastard has called for early elections thinking that his newly-won national fame in Siachen will help him personally,' said Gangasagar.

'We're ready for the ballot,' said Chandini. 'It does not matter that the date has been advanced by six months. We've spent the last two years doing nothing but preparing for this.'

'Even so, it's now crucial that the early opinion polls put us in the lead in Uttar Pradesh,' said Gangasagar.

'We don't control public opinion,' said Chandini.

'There's no such thing as public opinion. There's only published opinion and we must ensure that it's in our favour.'

'How can we ensure that?' asked Chandini, 'Polls are carried out by newspapers and magazines. We don't own them!'

'Get your own private agency to carry out a poll. Newspapers that are starved for content shall be quite happy to publish the results as long as they can claim that they commissioned the study themselves.'

'Even so, we can't control the outcome!'

'Use the conjurer's fourth card.'

'Huh? What's that?'

'When a conjurer shuffles the cards and asks you to pick a card, he already knows which card he wants you to pick—and you do, in fact, end up picking the card that he wants you to. Opinion polls are like that. You structure them such that the respondent answers exactly the way you want him to.'

'But what's the fourth card?'

'Surveys should be conducted as four-question polls specifically tailored to the subject being interviewed. Never publish the preceding three questions—only the results of the fourth. They're the only answers that are relevant!'

The woman pollster stopped the shopper just as she was exiting the grocery store.

'Question One: As a woman, do you think our gender has been exploited and discriminated against by men?'

'Yes.'

'Question Two: Do you think men have monopolised power to the detriment of women?'

'Yes.'

'Question Three: Do you think it's high time a strong woman was at the helm of affairs, not just in the state, but also at the Centre?'

'Yes.'

'Question Four: Do I take it that you would be willing to support a bid by Chandini Gupta to give greater representation to women?'

'Yes.'

The Brahmin interviewer was asking a Brahmin teacher:

'Question One: As a Brahmin, do you think upper castes have been left uncared for by politicians?'

'Yes.'

'Question Two: Do you think reservations in education and employment have resulted in Brahmins being left out from remunerative opportunities?'

'Yes.'

'Question Three: Do you believe it's time for someone to speak up for the rights of Brahmins?'

'Yes.'

'Question Four: Do I take it that you would be willing to support a bid by Chandini Gupta to give greater voice to Brahmins?'

'Yes.'

<hr>

The Dalit survey agent was in the slum. He asked his Dalit subject:

'Question One: As a Dalit, do you think years of discrimination and untouchability have resulted in Dalits continuing to be inadequately protected?'

'Yes.'

'Question Two: Do you think reservations in education and employment need to be increased for scheduled castes and tribes?'

'Yes.'

'Question Three: Do you believe it's time for someone to demand greater representation for the Dalits?'

'Yes.'

'Question Four: Do I take it you would be willing to support a bid by Chandini Gupta to give greater impetus to Dalit progress?'

'Yes.'

<hr>

The young polling executive approached the university student.

'Question One: As a youngster, do you think the youth of our country have been denied sufficient voice in the future of our nation?'

'Yes.'

'Question Two: Do you think the financial security of your generation is being mortgaged by older politicians running up massive deficits?'

'Yes.'

'Question Three: Do you believe it's time for the next generation to be in the driver's seat?'

'Yes.'

'Question Four: Do I take it you would be willing to support a bid by Chandini Gupta to put the youth of this country in control?'

'Yes.'

◆

The Muslim interviewer was outside the mosque. Friday prayers had just concluded.

'Question One: As a Muslim, are you worried about the fact that you're a minority in a Hindu-majority nation?'

'Yes.'

'Question Two: Do you believe that successive governments have ignored Muslim progress?'

'Yes.'

'Question Three: Do you think it's time for Muslims to elect someone who speaks for them?'

'Yes.'

'Question Four: Do I take it you would be willing to support a bid by Chandini Gupta to put Muslim issues on the table?

'Yes.'

◆

Chandini smiled as she watched the evening news. 'Earlier this week, the *Observer* published the results of a CFC opinion poll it commissioned regarding the general mood of Uttar Pradesh voters on the eve of Lok Sabha polls. The survey found that a majority were dissatisfied by government apathy in New Delhi and believed that the ABNS and Chandini Gupta's bid to play a role at the Centre must be supported. This is the first time ever that identical results have been obtained across castes, communities, genders and ages. "An overwhelming majority of the electorate seems to think the ABNS under Chandini Gupta can deliver better results by having a voice at the Centre," said the CFC spokesman releasing the opinion poll results yesterday.'

'What kind of agency is CFC?' Chandini asked her secretary.

'I have no idea. Shall I check with Menon?'

'Yes. He would know. Gangasagarji had spearheaded the effort,' said Chandini.

A few minutes later the secretary entered Chandini's office smiling.

'I found out the full name of CFC for you. Menon had it.'

'What is it?'

'Conjurer's Fourth Card.'

'I need astrologers like you to predict a massive win for our party,' explained Gangasagar to the startled man. He had been pulled off the pavement where he sat conning poor suckers into believing that incredible riches, unbelievable good luck, fame and fortune were on the way.

'I am not famous, sir. No one will believe me,' pleaded the astrologer.

'Leave that to me. I have arranged an interview for you today with a prominent newspaper in Lucknow. You need to predict that a cabinet reshuffle is on the way in Uttar Pradesh.'

'But I don't know that!'

'Now you do. I'm speaking to the chief minister today and she will ensure that a minor reshuffle happens tomorrow. Unlike your kind, I always avoid prophesying too soon beforehand. It's much better to prophesy after the event has already been ensured. Now, once the reshuffle happens, you shall give another interview.'

'And what shall I say?' asked the bewildered man.

'You shall predict a bumper harvest this year.'

'But I don't know that!'

'Now you do. I have a confidential report of the agriculture ministry. The report shall be made public the day after your interview. That's when you shall give your third interview.'

'And what shall I say then?' he asked predictably.

'You shall predict unexpected rains in Allahabad.'

'But I don't know that!'

'Yes you do. I have arranged for a small aircraft to seed the clouds over the Ganges with silver iodide. There shall be unexpected showers on the day after your prediction. The press and public shall believe anything and everything you say by then. That's when you shall offer your fourth interview.'

'And what shall I say during this fourth interview?'

'You shall predict an overwhelming victory for the ABNS and Chandini.'

'But I don't know that!'

'Neither do I, but I hope that your prediction comes true.'

Allahabad, situated at the confluence of the Ganges and Yamuna rivers, was tense. Inside the Old City, revelling Hindu youngsters had thrown alcohol on Muslims. In anger, some ill-advised Muslim boys had left cuts of beef on the steps of the Ganges riverbank. The spark ignited, Allahbad had roared into a frenzy of violence.

The chief minister of Uttar Pradesh—Chandini Gupta—had summoned the new police chief. Chandini wanted to know what action was being taken by the police to prevent further rioting. Gangasagar sat on one of the visitors' chairs while the chief occupied the other.

'The situation is in control, ma'am,' said the police chief. 'Three battalions of riot police wearing riot gear marched into the city and used teargas to disperse unruly mobs. They were attacked by stones and bricks but were quickly able to gain control over key areas of the city. Most of the area is in control except for the Old City, where it may take us another few days to restore normalcy.'

'Deaths or casualties?' asked Chandini.

'No deaths, a few casualties though. The toll would have been higher if an anonymous tip-off had not resulted in us sending the battalions into the Old City in advance.'

'Fear,' said Gangasagar suddenly changing the direction of the conversation.

'What was that, sir?' asked the chief.

'Fear! We need order to be restored today—not tomorrow or the day after. Create fear. Fear of the law,' said Gangasagar emphatically.

'But sir, curfew has been declared and we await your orders for lifting restrictions. We can achieve results without resorting to drastic measures.'

'Do what I say. I need the chief minister to address a public meeting in Allahabad by tomorrow.'

'But sir—'

'I think that the new police chief has done a commendable job, chief minister,' said Gangasagar smoothly, 'but sometimes situations like these require an emotional appeal rather than batons and teargas.'

'Sir, it would not be advisable to visit Allahabad at this moment. It is a powder keg that can explode,' spluttered the chief.

'You're there to protect the chief minister, aren't you, chief? Or do we need to search for a new man who can adequately ensure the safety and security of the chief minister when she wishes to meet her beloved citizens?' asked Gangasagar in almost a whisper.

'We shall protect her, sir,' said the police chief as he realised that the decision had been already taken.

'O beloved people of Prayag—the great city where Brahma offered a sacrifice after creating the world. O favoured citizens of Allahabad—the city renamed by Akbar after his own great new religion, Din-i-Ilahi. O great men and women of Kosambi—the greatest centre of Buddhism. I am honoured to be here among all of you today,' she said, cleverly addressing the Hindu, Muslim and Buddhist elements of the city. 'I stand before you today as a shining secular example of a daughter of a Hindu biological father and a Muslim adoptive father. I represent the two great faiths of this land and it is my honest pledge to you that I shall die before allowing anyone to ever split this great nation along religious lines!' Chandini thundered.

The chief of the ABNS Allahabad district committee had organised the rally. Upon the dais sat Ikram, Gangasagar, the ABNS Lok Sabha candidate for Allahabad, as well as several assorted functionaries. A local band played soul-stirring and patriotic Bollywood songs as local party workers came up on stage one by one and garlanded the bigwigs seated alongside the rostrum. Tens of thousands of supporters had braved the blazing heat and the fear of riots to sit in the open field and hear promises from their beloved representatives—promises that would in all probability be broken.

Across the field, exactly opposite the stage upon which the politicos sat was another stage that had been set up with effigies of the major Opposition leaders. Unbeknownst to the public was the fact that each of the likenesses had been built with firecrackers. Welcoming ceremonies over, Chandini stood up and walked forward to centre stage. An assistant brought her an ornate bow and arrow that she lifted and held up as though she were aiming it at the statues across the field. As she aimed, the pyrotechnics were unleashed and each of the effigies was methodically exploded. The crowd went wild—cheering Chandini and howling with approval as she shouted, 'Let's direct our energy towards destroying those who would like to divide us. Let's usher in a new era of peace and brotherhood. Let's avoid a quarrel between the past and the present—it can only end up destroying the future!'

Gangasagar glowed with optimism. He winked at Ikram. So much could be achieved with a quart of rum and a pound of beef. And people thought that elections were expensive! He took a deep breath and began chanting softly, '*Adi Shakti, Namo Namah; Sarab Shakti, Namo Namah; Prithum Bhagvati, Namo Namah; Kundalini Mata Shakti; Mata Shakti, Namo Namah.*'

CHAPTER THIRTEEN
About 2300 years ago

'With Sinharan on the throne of Mallayrajya, we now have a kingdom in which we can station our soldiers,' said Chanakya.

'Yes,' answered Chandragupta sadly, 'with my father's passing away in Pipplivan last year, we should now consolidate our forces under Ambhi's former commander.'

Chanakya understood the grief of a son who had lost his father. At least Chanakya had been able to perform the last rites of his own. Chandragupta had not. But Chanakya also knew that they did not have the luxury of grief. 'Chandragupta, we cannot afford to lose Paurus as an ally. You will need his help to fight Dhanananda,' he said.

'But Paurus is angry with us. We've snatched away Mallayrajya, part of his network of vassal states. Why will he discuss any strategic alliance with us?' asked Chandragupta incredulously.

'Because he's aristocratic, angry, proud and vain. These are qualities which make it rather easy to manipulate a human being,' replied Chandragupta's acharya complacently.

'So we flatter him into an alliance?' asked Chandragupta.

'If a man tells a woman she's beautiful, she'll overlook most of his other lies! We simply need to treat Paurus as one would a beautiful woman,' laughed Chanakya.

'And what if he doesn't take the bait?' asked Chandragupta, prodding Chanakya for explanation.

'We then pander to his ambitions of power, fame and glory—his burning desire to be the most powerful ruler in Bharat.'

'And how will we do that? We don't have anything of substance to bribe him with,' observed Chandragupta grimly.

'Simple. I can offer him the throne of Magadha, instead of offering it to you,' said Chanakya slyly.

Chandragupta knelt before his teacher and said sombrely, 'I shall willingly serve you in whatever capacity you deem fit. But I refuse to serve under the vain and petty Paurus!'

Chanakya burst out laughing at this display of principled anguish. 'I only said that I would offer it to him. I never said that I would give it to him. You should pay more attention to my choice of words, Chandragupta. This is a treaty with Paurus that I shall knowingly break!' he said.

The utterly perplexed Chandragupta spoke up hesitantly. 'Wouldn't it be better to be honest with him and tell him that we need his support to take Magadha? We could offer him a few provinces but not the throne.'

'He sees you as an upstart, O Chandragupta. He will not value you as an ally. It's better to sign a treaty with him and let him build castles in the air, thinking that he shall rule Magadha. Once our goal has been achieved, Paurus will become expendable.'

'And how will you explain your betrayal to him,' asked Chandragupta.

'Remember that it's often easier to get forgiveness rather than permission!' said Chanakya, a wide grin on his ugly face. 'I shall speak to my good friend Indradutt, Paurus's prime minister, to intercede on my behalf and convince the great king that it's in his best interest to ally with Chanakya.'

'Doesn't an alliance with Chanakya mean an alliance with Chandragupta?' asked the puzzled prince.

'Ah. We need to change that. You and I shall fight and go our separate ways,' responded Chanakya.

'I could never fight with you, acharya. Your wish is my command. Even if you asked me to lay down my life for you, I would. How can I ever dream of going against your wishes?'

'Relax, Chandragupta. I'm talking about the power of illusion. We must create the illusion that you and I have fallen apart—a difference of opinion. This will allow me to convince Paurus that I truly intend to instal him on the seat of Magadha's power!'

'And what do I do till such time?' asked Chandragupta uncomfortably.

'Stir up a revolt!' said Chanakya, thumping the ground where he was seated and sending up a little dust storm.

'Stir up a revolt? Where?' asked the hapless Chandragupta.

'The Macedonian provinces—the ones ruled directly by Alexander's satraps.'

'Which ones?'

'All of them. As you know, most of northern Bharat is either part of Magadha, Kaikey or Gandhar. But what about the small states that aren't part of these three large blocs? Alexander's satrap Phillipos, who reports to the powerful Seleucus—Alexander's chosen successor in Bharat—directly rules all of them. If Phillipos were to die, their provinces would fall into our laps without effort on our part.'

'Acharya, are you suggesting what I think you're suggesting?' asked the weary and wary Chandragupta. These strategising sessions with his guru sapped him of all his energy.

'No, no, dear Chandragupta. We shall not kill Phillipos. We shall merely identify his worst enemies and provide them with just cause to assassinate him!'

'And who is his biggest enemy?' asked Chandragupta, aware that the question was unnecessary.

'His biggest friend and ally.'

'Ambhi?'

'No.'

'Paurus?'

'No.'

'Then who?'

'Sasigupta.'

'Who?'

'Magadha covers a substantial portion of eastern Bharat. To its west lies Kaikey. Travel further westwards and you reach Gandhar. But who lives beyond Gandhar, to the extreme northwest—beyond the Indus?' asked Chanakya.

'The Ashvakans—the tribal horsemen of the Kabul River region.'

'Correct. They are strong and fierce warriors. Their primary strength lies not only in their innate capacity to carry on a sustained fight with very little food, water or rest, but also in their talent to breed, raise and train the finest *ashvas*—horses—in the region. Their leader is Sasigupta. Do you remember the day Alexander came to Sage Dandayan's hermitage? Sasigupta was with him—helping him interpret the sage's words.'

'You want me to go enlist his support?' asked Chandragupta innocently.

'No, my brave warrior, no! The Ashvakans are mercenaries. For a price, they will provide thousands of cavalry to anyone, irrespective of their own political beliefs. They fought on behalf of the Persians and subsequently also fought for the Macedonians. They have no permanent loyalty to any one side. Training horses and fighting battles is simply an occupation, nothing more, nothing less.'

'Which side are they fighting for presently?'

'The Macedonian side. But not too long ago they were allied with the Persians. So why should they hesitate to switch sides again?' asked Chanakya.

'But what would cause Sasigupta to rebel? As I understand, he was also present at Alexander's Jhelum victory over Paurus. When Ambhi failed to bring Paurus before Alexander after the battle was over, it was Sasigupta who succeeded in doing so.'

'But on whose orders did Sasigupta fight for Alexander?' asked Chanakya.

Chandragupta was stumped. Chanakya smiled and resumed. 'The Ashvakans are fierce warriors but they take their orders from women! Their chief is always a queen. The present one is a stunning beauty called Kalapini. Any danger or threat to her and you'd have thousands of enraged Ashvakans ready to die in a blink!'

'You want me to kidnap their queen?' asked Chandragupta, half expecting an affirmative response. He knew that his cunning teacher was capable of almost anything as long as it advanced his aims of installing him on Magadha's throne.

'More than that! I need you to arrange for her to have an affair with Phillipos, the Macedonian satrap. Nothing will get Ashvakan blood boiling as much as the thought of their queen sleeping with a Macedonian man!'

'And how do I arrange that? By kidnapping them both and barricading them inside a tent?' asked an exasperated Chandragupta.

'Do you want a one-word answer?'

'That would be nice.'

'Cornelia.'

Cornelia and Chandragupta were lying on a soft cotton sheet that had been spread under the wide branches of a giant simsapa tree in a corner of a sylvan grove with ashoka, bhavya, champaka and nagara trees in blossom. The ground lay heaped with fragrant flowers that had fallen off the branches. Chandragupta and Cornelia lay side by side. The bodyguards that accompanied Cornelia wherever she went had been offered some cold milk sweetened with honey by Chandragupta's men. The light refreshing drink had been seasoned with crushed hemp for the extra zing. Within minutes, they had passed out under a banyan, snoring peacefully.

'I simply adore you,' murmured Chandragupta into her ear as he absentmindedly ran his fingers through her golden hair.

She smiled at him. 'Liar! You adore being with me so that you can play your naughty games,' she admonished.

Chandragupta thought about it for a moment, smiled wickedly and said, 'That too!' as she playfully slapped his cheek in mock punishment.

'Darling, I cannot bear to be away from you for even a moment,' said Cornelia as she reached up to hold him even closer. 'It worries me that my father will find out about us and will call me back to Babylonia. How will I live without you?'

'Seleucus is stationed far away, darling. It's hardly likely that he would know about the wanton life of his precious daughter who decided to stay back in Bharat,' offered Chandragupta comfortingly.

'I wish to marry you, Chandragupta. There's no man I've loved more. Why must we go through this unbearable secrecy each time to be with one another?'

'Your father will have no option but to offer your hand in marriage to me—I shall make sure of that. But for that to happen, I must be king of Magadha. You shall be part of a political treaty—the prize that I long for, my sweet Cornelia.'

'And how will that happen? Besides installing your classmate Sinharan on the throne of a modest kingdom, what else have you and the acharya actually achieved? It may take ages for you to become emperor and by that time you may not even be able to perform!' she teased.

'Sweetheart. Let's get married right here, right now!' said Chandragupta suddenly serious, taking her completely by surprise.

'How? No fire? No priest? No guests?' asked an intrigued Cornelia.

'In our ancient Hindu scriptures there are eight types of marriage. One of them—legally recognised by the scribes—is known as a *Gandharva Vivah*. It's a simple secret ceremony between man and woman with no third party present. We simply garland each other, exchange vows, kiss, and there you have it. It's done!'

'But I can't come and live with you, Chandragupta. My father will slay us both. He'll get very angry if I'm seen to be going against his wishes,' argued Cornelia.

'I agree. Our marriage should remain secret. You should continue to live your life independently until we get married officially. At least we'll live in the comfort of knowing that we're betrothed,' said Chandragupta with a twinkle in his eyes. He quickly took off his silken shoulder wrap and efficiently tore from it two thin strips. He began picking up the flowers that lay strewn on the grass and tying them, using small knots to the silk. Cornelia started on the second garland. Within a few minutes they were both holding crude but love-inspired garlands, eagerly waiting to put them around each other's necks.

Both stood up and faced one another. Chandragupta tenderly placed his garland around Cornelia's neck and, holding her face, said, 'My dearest, sweetest love. I promise to worship you for the rest of my life. I shall protect you with my life and shall always honour and cherish you. From this day onwards you're my wife, before the eyes of God.' With tears in her eyes at the intensity of the moment, Cornelia placed her garland around Chandragupta and whispered, 'My husband, my life, my love. Nothing has ever given me more joy than to wed you. I promise to be ever faithful to you and to always respect and obey you. You are, and always shall be, my one and only true love.'

Chandragupta pulled her towards him, took her in his arms and kissed her with ardent passion. He hadn't comprehended that obeying his acharya's wishes would be so much fun. He wondered at what point the acharya's instructions had ended and his love for Cornelia had begun.

❖

As husband and wife embraced under the simsapa tree, Cornelia asked, 'Now that we're married secretly, what needs to be done to make it official?'

'A political treaty between Chandragupta and Seleucus,' replied her husband.

'Why would my father sign such an alliance with you?'

'If he saw himself losing his grip on his provinces in Bharat. Better to be friend than foe to the king who's gaining control.'

'And why would my father lose control over his Bharat dominions?'

'Because of Ambhi's fear, Paurus's greed and Sasigupta's anger.'

'Ambhi's fear?'

'Ambhi lies sandwiched between Sasigupta and Paurus. He will be fearful of another battle.'

'And Paurus's greed?'

'His insatiable pride that needs to be fed. His lust for the throne of Magadha shall be his downfall.'

'And Sasigupta's anger?'

'Over his betrayal.'

'Betrayal by who?'

'Phillipos, the Macedonian governor appointed by your father.'

'But Phillipos has not betrayed him.'

'He will though.'

'Why?'

'If Phillipos were to fall in love with Kalapini, the Ashvakan queen, the Ashvakans headed by Sasigupta would revolt. They would see it as the ultimate betrayal.'

'But my darling Chandragupta, how can one make people fall in love? Love simply happens. It can't be forced!'

'But one can make a start by getting two people to meet each other. I'm told that Phillipos has a roving eye. Get them to meet and let destiny take over!'

'You want me to get involved in this roguish scheme?'

'Hah! You're right. I'm using you. But I do need you to help them meet, Cornelia. You know everyone in society. Visit Phillipos and take Kalapini along as a friend. She's supposed to be gorgeous,' said Chandragupta.

'I thought that we just took vows that we would be faithful to one another,' she joked, mildly annoyed to hear another woman being described as beautiful by her own husband.

'That's why it's better that you organise her engagement so that she becomes unavailable to me,' quipped Chandragupta.

≡

'Get out at once! I should never have spent my life trying to tutor you—you're an ungrateful wretch!' shouted Chanakya, smiling broadly at Chandragupta.

'You've trained me well, O guru. In fact, my training shall now be used for one purpose alone—to bring about your downfall!' shouted back Chandragupta, trying his best not to laugh.

'How dare you speak to me like that? I'm your teacher. I have every right to be angry. Sinharan has been like your brother and you have the temerity to question his right over the throne of Mallayrajya?' shot back Chanakya, gesturing to Chandragupta that he should stick to the prepared script in front of him.

'You promised me that I would be king. Instead you're busy striking up an alliance between Paurus and Sinharan. Shame on you, acharya! I hadn't realised that you would stoop so low. Is there no limit to the depths you can sink to? You would swindle your own disciple and offer the throne to the haughty Paurus? Damn you, my lord. Curses be upon you!' roared Chandragupta as he tried to keep pace with the dialogue prepared by his guru.

'I want you to leave immediately. You have no place here. Forget your dreams about becoming emperor of Magadha. You're unfit, unwise, uncouth and ungrateful. Get out!' shrieked Chanakya, as he signalled for Chandragupta to leave the room.

Chandragupta stormed out of his teacher's room as the men looked on. The end of a promising partnership, they thought to themselves, as they saw their military leader stomping off and their strategic leader sulking in a corner.

Within minutes, a young man scurried out of Chanakya's camp to meet Abhaya, the intelligence chief of Paurus. This was startling news. He would be paid very well for information of such magnitude. What he couldn't understand was why the acharya had allowed Chandragupta to take with him his entire garrison of soldiers of fortune.

'O glorious King, Chanakya comes before you to seek your help,' said the hideous Brahmin, as he sat down on the seat offered by the majestic and suave Paurus opposite him. Indradutt sat next to Chanakya.

'Acharya, I've heard wonderful stories about your razor-sharp intelligence, your expansive knowledge, your uncanny ability to predict outcomes as well as your unbounded determination. But aren't you here because you've simply fallen out with Chandragupta?' asked Paurus, feeling rather grand for being aware of such vital information.

Chanakya put on his best forlorn look and said, 'There can be no secrets from you, O mighty Paurus. You have eyes and ears everywhere. Yes, indeed I've had a difference of opinion with Chandragupta. But I am not here because

I fell out with Chandragupta; rather, I fell out with him because I planned to meet you.'

Paurus nodded sagely. He was sure Chanakya was telling him the truth. Abhaya had revealed that the cause of the dispute between the acharya and his star pupil was the fact that Chanakya wanted to offer the throne of Magadha to him—the illustrious Paurus—and not to Chandragupta.

'Why should I trust you, acharya? Your machinations resulted in my ally, the king of Mallayrajya, being overthrown by his nephew Sinharan,' goaded Paurus, hoping to elicit an outburst.

'Yes, indomitable king. I took back for Sinharan what was rightfully his. In my place, you would have done exactly the same. However, to answer your question— why should you trust me—please call for the visitor who waits outside,' said Chanakya.

Indradutt asked the orderly to bring inside the acharya's guest. Within a few moments, the orderly ushered in a young man, attired in silken robes, precious gems and all the usual trappings of royalty. It was the newly crowned king of Mallayrajya—Sinharan. He walked up to Paurus, knelt before him, and said 'O magnificent Emperor, I have no quarrel with you. Mallayrajya was, and shall continue to remain, your unflinching ally. My conflict was with my uncle who had usurped the throne in a treacherous manner. That matter has since been resolved. Please let me have your blessings, O heroic King.'

Paurus was trying his best to maintain his indifferent and impartial manner, but Chanakya knew that he had succeeded in pandering to the king's vanity. If Paurus had been a peacock, his feathers would have puffed out entirely! It was so much easier to handle conceited and arrogant monarchs than the ones who had no pretensions of greatness. 'Rise, Sinharan. Come and sit next to me,' said Paurus, completely swayed by events.

'What is it that you have in mind, acharya?' asked Paurus, once Sinharan was seated.

'With over two hundred thousand infantry, eighty thousand cavalry, eight thousand chariots and six thousand war elephants, Magadha remains the most powerful military might in the world. Even the combined strength of the great Paurus and his allies—including Sinharan—will be inadequate to force Magadha into a state of submission. If the magnificent Parvateshwar is to occupy the throne of Magadha, we shall need your might and my cunning,' began Chanakya.

'I have no use for cunning,' interrupted the haughty Paurus.

'Of what use was your might before Alexander?' reminded Chanakya gently. 'Take my advice, magnificent conqueror of the mountains, and you shall certainly be emperor of Magadha.'

'And Chandragupta?'

'I've no use for disciples who do not respect their teachers. I've taught him everything that he knows and this is the thanks I get? Let him rot in hell!'

'All right, acharya, I commit myself to your goals. We shall either take Magadha or attain heaven while attempting to do so!' announced Paurus grandly.

'Everyone wants to go to heaven, but no one wants to die,' said Chanakya simply.

'Let him rot in hell!' shouted Sasigupta, as the news was confirmed. He was seated in the grand hall of his fort at Pir-Sar, in the heart of the Swat valley. He had helped Alexander take the fort and this was the thanks that the Macedonian bastards gave him? News had filtered in that their queen, Kalapini, had decided to stay on with Phillipos—Alexander's satrap in Bharat. He had been informed of their torrid affair some weeks ago by his spies but had imagined that it was one of Kalapini's temporary bouts of sexual insatiability. Her decision to stay on with Phillipos was an entirely different matter though.

He looked across the low beaten-silver table at his new friend and comrade, Chandragupta, as they each took a gulp of *maireya* from their goblets. The potent brew had started affecting Sasigupta's speech, and his words were slurred.

'D—d—do you know, Ch—Chandragupta, that y—you and I actually have the very same name? Sss—sasi m—m—m—means m—m—moon, and sss—so d—does Ch—chandra. We're b—b—brothers!' said Sasigupta, banging down his goblet so hard that the maireya splashed out on the silver tabletop. Chandragupta, who had only consumed a few sips, was stone sober. This was an excellent opportunity to stoke the fire of rebellion.

The grand old fort at Pir-Sar was rich but gloomy. It had been a terrible winter during which Alexander had decided to take Pir-Sar once and for all. As a boy growing up in Macedonia, Alexander had been narrated the story of his illustrious ancestor, Heracles, who had marched as far as Pir-Sar but had eventually been unable to capture the fort. Alexander was determined that he would outdo Heracles and become a historical legend. Besides, capturing Pir-Sar would help neutralise the threat to his supply lines, which were painfully stretched over the Hindu Kush to Balkh. The fort of Pir-Sar lay north of Attock in the Punjab, on a mountain spur above narrow gorges in a bend of the upper Indus. The mountain was gifted with a flat summit irrigated by natural springs and was certainly broad enough to grow adequate crops. Pir-Sar could not be starved into submission.

Had it not been for Sasigupta, Alexander would never have been able to capture it. At his suggestion, Alexander had reinforced a neighbouring spur to the west. Using this as a base, Alexander had asked his men to bridge the ravine along the northern face of the fort—which happened to be the most vulnerable side as revealed by Sasigupta. After three days of intense battle, which included massive boulders being flung down upon the Macedonian army by soldiers within the fort, Alexander and Sasigupta had finally succeeded in hauling themselves up over the last and final rock face as the rest of the Macedonian army went about massacring fugitives. Alexander had erected victory altars to Athena and Nike and then pursued his onward journey to battle Paurus.

Pir-Sar had been critical to his success because it had established Alexander's reputation for invincibility. More often than not, it was people's awe of his immortality and tenacity that preceded him in further conquests into Bharat.

Sasigupta stammered 'I h—h—handed over th—th—this f—f—fucking f—f—fort and the r—rest of Bharat to the Macedonians on a p—p—platter and the p—p—pieces of sh—sh—shit reward m—m—me by f—f—f—fucking the queen of the Ashvakans?' The Ashvakan queen, after all, was a living female deity that the fierce tribal warriors sought inspiration and guidance from. Sasigupta was their commander, but their source of strength was Kalapini.

Wise men think all they say, fools say all they think. Chandragupta could almost hear Chanakya mouthing the words into his ears. Chandragupta measured his words carefully and after some deliberation he spoke. 'Sasigupta, you're my friend. I have a plan, if you're interested.'

The fierce, independent, strong and resilient Afghans who inhabited the rugged mountains along the Kabul River derived their name from their ancestors who lived there—the Ashvakans. They were Indo-Aryans who specialised in breeding and training horses—known as *Ashva* in Sanskrit. Their strength in battle as well as their skill in riding horses was in demand from all sides—Persia, Greece and Bharat. Sasigupta was their leader. He had altered the course of Alexander's campaign in Bharat by switching sides—having originally fought for Darius on the Persian front.

Sasigupta was a ruggedly handsome man. Tall and muscular, with a stomach a taut as a drum, he had extremely fair skin and green eyes. His long chestnut-brown hair was intertwined with lengths of silk and was tied up in a conch-shell-shaped knot towards the front of his head. His rich beard and warrior moustache gave him a military bearing. His high turban embellished with rubies was a dark midnight-blue and covered his knotted tuft. It matched his flowing woollen robe of the same colour. Strung around his neck were strings of pearls. He wore a thick crimson sash around his waist in which was tucked a diamond-handled scimitar. He was indeed a formidable example of male beauty.

His masculinity was a gift from his ancestors who had instituted a special ritual known as the *Ashvamedha Yajna*. A strong horse would be prayed to by the king and would then be left free to gallop through various lands with the king's army following in close pursuit. Chiefs of the lands that were wandered into by the horse could either submit to the king or choose to fight. If defeated, they had to accept his suzerainty.

When Alexander first tried to subdue Sasigupta and his ferocious combatants, he knew that he had finally met his match. In a letter to his mother, Alexander wrote,

'I am in a land of a lion-like brave people, where every inch of ground is like a wall of steel, confronting my soldiers. You have brought only one Alexander into the world, but each man in this land can be called an Alexander.' Alexander had thought it prudent to win over Sasigupta and his untamed champions rather than fight them. His decision had not proved wrong. Sasigupta not only helped him acquire Pir-Sar but also provided thousands of cavalrymen to serve in the Macedonian army, for a price of course.

'You have thousands of cavalrymen serving under Phillipos. Get them to revolt. Let them refuse to serve a master who defiles their goddess,' suggested Chandragupta. The idea had been Chanakya's, but Chandragupta was quite happy to pass it off as his own.

'But Phillipos might order executions in order to enforce discipline,' countered Sasigupta.

'That's precisely what we want him to do,' remarked Chandragupta smiling at his new friend.

▬▭▬

Phillipos's fortified military camp lay quiet at this hour. All four gates to the massive rectangular raised enclosure were sealed shut for the night. The perimeter of the camp, protected by a ditch three metres wide and two metres deep, consisted of a very high palisade constructed from sharpened wooden stakes. Sentinels stood on guard at multiple points around the fencing while duty sergeants took frequent rounds to check that sentinels were not dozing off on the job.

From the main gate in the centre of one of the two shorter walls ran the principal road of the camp, eighteen metres wide, bisecting the camp into two long, rectangular halves. Running at ninety degrees to this avenue was a subsidiary road, fifteen metres wide, which effectively quartered the camp. At the intersection of these two thoroughfares, at the centre of the camp, stood its largest tent—that of the commanding general, Phillipos. In close proximity to Phillipos's tent stood those of his immediate subordinates. Beyond lay rows and rows of barracks shared by the enlisted men, two hundred and twenty men to an acre.

The entrance to Phillipos's tent was illuminated by two massive flaming torches that were fastened in the ground on either side of the entry flap. Two expressionless Hoplite sentinels, holding six-feet-long spears with sharp iron heads fixed on shafts of ash wood, guarded the tent zealously. Their faces did not register or react to the sounds that emanated from within as Phillipos made hectic love to his newest conquest, the Ashvakan queen, Kalapini.

The loyal Macedonian guards could hear in the distance a low rumble that seemed to get louder every few minutes. Although they were curious about the distant roar, their training prevented them from moving away from their duty-roster-designated spots. Every few minutes their attention would alternate between the moans from within the tent and the growling from the camp's invisible horizons.

Phillipos's guards, who were on duty at the sole west-facing entrance, did not realise that their master's tent was on fire until the heat from the blaze seared the hairs on their necks. They turned around quickly to respond to the startled cries from within but fell backwards as a volley of arrows caught them in the back. As a naked and frightened Phillipos ran out, followed by an equally nude Kalapini, the gathered Ashvakan cavalrymen surrounded the Macedonian satrap, caught hold of him, tied his hands behind his back and blindfolded him. Meanwhile, another lot covered Kalapini with a blanket to protect her modesty and threw her into the arms of a mounted horseman who immediately galloped away towards the camp exit.

'Filthy son of a whore!' shouted the men angrily at Phillipos. 'You thought you could get away with banging our queen and executing our comrades? You shall die for this!' Phillipos struggled desperately, trying to free his hands from the ropes that cut into his wrists. He tried to explain that his relationship with Kalapini was one of mutual love, but the fierce Ashvakan warriors were in no mood to be lectured on the subtle differences between rape and fornication. The news of Phillipos being attacked by the furious mercenaries of Sasigupta spread like wildfire among the Macedonian troops. They rallied to the defence of their general but were no match for the enraged tribesmen. A Macedonian commander managed to break the cordon of Ashvakans surrounding Phillipos. He lunged forward to liberate Phillipos, wrapped his arms around the general and started furiously cutting away at the ropes that bound Phillipos's hands. Before he could release Phillipos, he coughed blood into the satrap's face as a javelin brutally pierced his lungs from behind.

The camp was thundering with the sound of hoofbeats as Ashvakan horsemen rode through the main avenue hurling flaming bunches of grass into tents. Several quarters were already ablaze as confused Macedonian soldiers ran outside only to be hacked mercilessly to death.

A few yards away, standing atop a small hill, a band of horsemen observed the flames in the Macedonian camp and listened to the shouts and cries of the men who were being slaughtered. Mounted on a muscular grey Kamboja steed, Sasigupta looked at Chandragupta who was seated on an Ucchaisrava stallion, white and of immense muscular beauty. 'I'm not sure whether we did the right thing, Chandragupta,' said Sasigupta, thoughtfully stroking his beard. 'This is not in the Ashvakan tradition of a formal call to arms. This is bloodshed without honour!'

'My dear friend, Sasigupta, where was the honour when you fought for Darius? Where was the honour when you sold yourself to Alexander? Face the truth—Ashvakan bravery has been more about commercial interest than honour. What's happening now is probably the most honourable thing that you've ever done—raising your sword against an alien invader and protecting the dignity of your queen,' said Chandragupta, fully briefed by Chanakya on how to deal with such last minute change of heart.

Chandragupta signalled to his expert archer whose all-metal arrow had been following Phillipos's movements for the past few minutes. Upon receiving a nod from Chandragupta, he pulled back on the taut hemp string that held his massive multilayered bamboo bow in shape, ensured that the target was momentarily stationary and released his feathered missile. It whizzed past Chandragupta, countless trees, the camp perimeter, Macedonian soldiers, and Ashvakan cavalrymen, before it met its mark. The sharp tip pierced the skin of the intended victim and drew blood. Thirsty for more, it plunged deeper until it could find a beating heart or pumping lung to lodge in. The arrow wound to his chest succeeded in rupturing his lungs, rapidly flooding them with his own blood, effectively drowning him in his own plasma. As his heart continued to pump, his blood was forced up through his airways and spurted from his mouth and nose. His eyes rolled back and he fell backwards desperately wishing that his life would end soon—and it did. Phillipos was dead.

CHAPTER FOURTEEN
Present Day

Menon was reading the morning newspaper aloud to Ikrambhai. Major Bedi, looking relaxed after six months of incessant electioneering, sat in Ganga-sagar's living room sipping tea.

'With a working majority in the Lok Sabha, the chairman of the victorious alliance shall meet the President of India at 4 pm on Tuesday to stake claim to form the new government. This was decided unanimously at a meeting of the alliance partners. The chairman's name was proposed by the ruling party and was seconded by Pandit Gangasagar Mishra, the president of the ABNS, one of the largest alliance partners of the ruling party.'

'Hah! *The* largest, not *one of* the largest!' exclaimed Ikram as Major Bedi smiled. His formula of having no formula had worked. He took the newspaper from Menon and continued reading. 'The ABNS, with sixty-five MPs from Uttar Pradesh, is the largest constituent of the coalition after the ruling party, which won two hundred seats. The coalition has received letters of support from several smaller parties and now has the backing of around three hundred MPs, much more than the two hundred and seventy-two required for a basic majority in the Lok Sabha. The chairman of the alliance shall present a letter to the president providing details of the re-election of the prime minister—the former defence minister—as leader of the ruling party's delegation to Parliament. He's also expected to hand over letters of support received by his party from its coalition partners. The president is likely to extend an invitation to the alliance to form the next government at the Centre. The oath-taking ceremony is likely to be fixed for Friday at Rashtrapati Bhavan.'

'It's good that the total number of MPs supporting this government are three hundred,' said Ikram.

'Why? Because that puts them at twenty-eight more than the halfway mark?' asked Menon.

'No, because it puts them thirty-seven short of the halfway mark if the ABNS decides to withdraw support!' said Ikram, chewing on his paan contentedly while Bedi chuckled.

He sat in the first row—next to Somany's victorious Prime Minister—watching the scene unfolding at Rashtrapati Bhavan. The President was administering the oath of office to Chandini. She was saying 'I, Chandini Gupta, do swear in the name of God that I will bear true faith and allegiance to the Constitution of India as by law established, that I will uphold the sovereignty and integrity of India, that I will faithfully and conscientiously discharge my duties as cabinet minister and that I will do right to all manner of people in accordance with the Constitution and the law without fear or favour, affection or ill will.'

Her moving from state to central politics had created a vacuum in Uttar Pradesh. Agrawalji had asked, 'Who shall we make chief minister? I'm sure Ikram's still hoping that you'll offer the position to him.'

Gangasagar had replied, 'Ikram knows that I plan on acquiring the home portfolio eventually for the ABNS— and him in particular. I've told him to lie low for a while. He'll accept someone else from the ABNS taking the chief minister's post in Uttar Pradesh.'

'So whom do we appoint as chief minister for the remaining term of the state government?' asked Agrawalji.

'Ram Shankar Dwivedi,' answered Gangasagar.

'But that's preposterous! The lecherous rogue inspired the local rebellion against Chandini. He can't be trusted!'

'On the contrary, Agrawalji. I trust him completely.'

'Why?'

'Because I still have twenty more photographs to return to him,' laughed Gangasagar.

<hr />

'Gangasagarji, what are you thinking?' whispered the former defence minister—now new Prime Minister— to him. Gangasagar realised his mind had wandered. 'I am wondering where Rungta is hiding. I can see our mutual friend, Somany, in the audience. Didn't you invite Rungta for the ceremony?' he asked the premier.

'I did, but I guess he's busy.'

'With what?'

'Finding some other minister to send down a rope-ladder. If Somany can get me to do it, Rungta can find someone too,' said the prime minister, smiling at the old man who had been the reason behind his clambering down the chopper's ladder in Siachen. Gangasagar laughed loudly. Everyone turned to look. He wasn't bothered. He laughed some more.

≡

'The scumbag refuses to part with the finance, external affairs, defence or home portfolios—the four key ministries. He says that the senior partner of the ruling alliance always holds these four posts along with the post of prime minister. Doesn't he realise he wouldn't be in government if it weren't for the support of the ABNS? So much for having Somany's man as PM!' complained Gangasagar as he got up from his chair and paced the room.

'What do you want?' asked Ikram.

'I want Chandini to be minister for external affairs. The global exposure would give her both national and international stature,' said Gangasagar.

'There's only one way you can achieve that. Create a crisis within the ministry of external affairs. A crisis that forces the minister to resign,' suggested Ikram.

'That doesn't seem possible or probable. The minister for external affairs is an old warhorse—and a careful one. He doesn't even cough without first checking to see if anyone is within earshot. Moreover, he's stark honest. Honesty is a most dreadful quality—it makes people difficult to manipulate,' said an exasperated Gangasagar. He sat down again and began to drum the arms of his chair with his fingers.

'There is another way,' he said after a moment. 'Sometimes, to score a goal you have to kick the ball away from the goalpost. The present minister for external affairs is the only one who could realistically take over the finance portfolio if the finance minister were to suddenly resign.'

'And why would the finance minister do that?' asked Ikram.

'Ah! You see, unlike the minister for external affairs, he's not too honest. It seems that while our friend Somany supported the previous defence minister's bid for the top job, Rungta supported the finance minister. Our present PM hates the finance minister and will be delighted to lose him from the cabinet. We simply need to provide him with the opportunity. Ikram, put your best boys on the job—discreetly. The finance minister is dangerous to mess with. He'll feed us to the crocodiles if he gets to know!'

The allocation of the rest of the ministerial portfolios, too, was a tug-of-war. Gangasagar demanded ten berths for the ABNS. He had wanted external affairs for Chandini but was willing to let her remain a minister without portfolio until it could be arranged. In the meantime, he wanted cabinet positions in commerce, telecom, petroleum and agriculture although he was willing to settle for minister of state positions for the other five ABNS MPs whose names were being put forward.

Menon had asked him, 'Why are you willing to settle for state positions for fifty per cent of your ministerial strength? You should insist on ten cabinet berths.'

'I'd rather negotiate for the positions that matter. By settling for five I'm now in a position to negotiate for getting our own people into other positions of power—not necessarily within the cabinet,' said Gangasagar.

'Such as?'

'The directorship of the Intelligence Bureau; governorship of the Reserve Bank of India; and the chairman's position in the Central Board of Direct Taxes. So many of our erstwhile student leaders are now senior enough within the bureaucracy—Brijmohan Rai from Allahabad

University, Iqbal Azmi from Aligarh Muslim University, Girish Bajpai from Banaras Hindu University... but more importantly, I want to leave the door open for Chandini to get external affairs.'

'And why do you particularly want Cabinet positions in commerce, telecom, petroleum and agriculture?'

'Because our cabinet ministers shall spend the next two weeks sniffing around for every deal that was ever made within their departments, thus giving me ammunition to use against the finance minister!'

Gangasagar and Chandini were at Udyog Bhawan, the headquarters of the department of commerce. An ABNS man was now heading the department as cabinet minister.

'Land for Special Economic Zones was allotted to private companies at meagre rates,' said the commerce minister.

'So what?' asked Gangasagar, 'That was as per government policy, right?'

'Yes. Quantitatively, but not qualitatively.'

'You've lost me,' said Chandini.

'The quantity of land acquired and passed on to developers was as per the policy.'

'But?' asked a curious Gangasagar.

'The SEZ policy was framed in order to bring about development of arid wasteland. The building of transport links, power plants, water supply systems, and the addition of concentrated industrial and commercial hubs were supposed to enhance land value. Instead, prime land that was already well connected and developed was given away by the commerce ministry without considering its intrinsic value. Thousands of acres of land were given away to a single company,' disclosed the commerce minister.

≡

Gangasagar and Chandini were at Sanchar Bhawan, the headquarters of the department of telecom. 'Telecom licences were issued in an arbitrary fashion at fees that were low, even going by ten-year-old benchmarks,' revealed the telecom minister, an old hand of the ABNS.

'Big deal. One could argue that one individual's perception of value is different to another's,' argued Gangasagar.

'But subsequently, the company that obtained the new spectrum allocations sold their stake to outside investors for a huge profit,' said the telecom minister.

'Isn't it possible they enhanced shareholder value by building a business in the interim?' suggested Chandini.

'In twenty-four hours?' asked the telecom minister quizzically.

≡

Gangasagar and Chandini were at Shastri Bhawan, the headquarters of the ministry of petroleum and natural gas. 'Oil exploration rights were handed out to a single company for a value prescribed as per law,' said the petroleum minister, an ABNS winner from Bijnor constituency.

'What's wrong with that?' asked Gangasagar.

'The exploration rights were handed out on 24 July.'

'So?'

'An internal memo shows that the exploration basin had already been drilled by the public sector oil cor-poration.'

'And?'

'They had already discovered oil there on 23 July.'

━━

Gangasagar and Chandini were at Krishi Bhawan, the headquarters of the ministry of agriculture. The minister was Daula Hassan Bhatti, Major Bedi's Muslim-Jat experiment in Meerut. He had won his election with a margin of over two hundred thousand votes.

'Large quantities of fodder and fertiliser were procured during the term of the previous government,' said the agriculture minister quietly, afraid of being overheard by his secretary.

'That would be expected,' send Chandini. 'Any government that wishes to hang on to votes must subsidise fodder and fertiliser to keep farmers happy.'

'But did we subsidise fodder for cattle in America and western Europe too?' asked the agriculture minister.

'What do you mean?' asked Gangasagar.

'If I count the total head of cattle subsidised by the government, it adds up to the total cattle population of India, America and western Europe added together! They subsidised farmers and cattle that did not exist!' revealed the agriculture minister.

━━

'Could any of these deals have happened without the finance minister's complicity?' asked Chandini. Ikram and Agrawalji shook their heads. That would have been impossible. Chandini and Gangasagar mulled over the revelations in silence. At length she asked him, 'What do you intend to do with this information? Reveal it to the press and bring down the government?'

'On the contrary. Of what value is it to bring down this government when we are in it? And that, too, so early in the day? Information is only of value when it isn't in the public domain. I shall safeguard it and use it to bargain,' said the shrewd Pandit.

'So you'll talk to the Prime Minister and secure the finance minister's resignation on account of the four scams?' asked Chandini.

'No. I shall not secure the finance minister's resignation on account of the four scams,' said Gangasagar, blandly.

'Why not?' asked Chandini, wondering why they had spent a fortnight digging up dirt if it wasn't to be used.

'I shall secure the finance minister's resignation on account of one scam, not four! I shall use the remaining information only as and when I deem appropriate. When a full house is adequate, why should I use straight flush?'

⚊⚌⚊

'Congratulations on taking over as minister for external affairs, Chandiniji. I know that you will work hard and go even higher,' said a wellwisher as Chandini moved around the room shaking hands.

Gangasagar was standing within earshot. He turned around to his faithful patron Agrawalji who was munching on a stuffed potato. 'Funny isn't it?' he said to Agrawalji.

'What's funny about you having realised your dream of making this humble girl into India's minister for external affairs?' asked Agrawalji.

'Here's what's funny, my friend. She goes to an *external* country for an education, has an *affair*, gets pregnant, and as a reward I make her minister for *external affairs*!'

⚊⚌⚊

'Is the honourable minister for external affairs aware that our national flag was displayed even after sundown at the Indian Embassy in Poland in violation of Section 2.2 subsection (xi) of the Flag Code of India? Will the honourable minister assure this House that she shall take corrective action.'

'Mr Speaker, sir, I can assure the House that I might definitely take action.'

'Mr Speaker, sir, is the honourable minister for external affairs ready to admit that we have allowed Pakistan to gain the upper hand in the recent foreign secretary-level talks in Geneva? Has the minister learnt anything from the mistakes made there?'

'Mr Speaker, sir, I respectfully submit that I'm willing to make some more mistakes if the honourable member is willing to learn from them.'

'With permission of the Chair, is the honourable minister for external affairs aware that alcoholic beverages were served within the premises of her ministry's South Block offices even though it was on a dry day?'

'Mr Speaker, my own view is that alcohol is certainly not the answer to anything. It simply makes one forget the question. By the way, what was the honourable member's question?'

'Mr Speaker. The ministry of external affairs seems to be picking its way through a minefield of international diplomacy. Unfortunately, the honourable minister lacks experience and is stumbling like a child in the dark.'

'Mr Speaker, it is my understanding that children in the dark make accidents whereas accidents in the dark make children. I presume that's how we've all reached here!'

Chandini sat down as the entire Lok Sabha erupted in an explosion of laughter. It was evident that the new girl was not someone to be messed around with. Geoffrey Hemingford had tried, much to his regret.

The chairman of the Central Board of Direct Taxes—the CBDT—sent two files to the finance minister prior to the latter's resignation. These issues were hot potatoes and he wanted them signed off by the minister himself.

The first file related to R&S, and given the close relationship between the minister and Rungta, the chairman of the CBDT decided to get a clearance from the finance minister directly.

Hon'ble Finance Minister. Investigations into the activities of R&S have revealed several instances of financial irregularity. Various items on the expense side seem to have been inflated, specifically with the intention of reducing their taxable income. In addition, it seems that private partnerships have been created with a view to parking of profits. Various items on the income side have been deferred, seemingly with a view to deprive the tax authorities of revenue. Certain transactions—particularly sale and purchase of assets—have been carried out at questionable valuations, thus further reducing their tax liability, at least on paper.

The memo was double-spaced and continued on the next page.

Given the circumstances, I seek your advice on how the above matter should be handled. Thanking you. Chairman, Central Board of Direct Taxes.

The second file concerned overall tax rates for the common man—a political decision—and once again, the chairman of the CBDT had decided that seeking ministerial clearance would be was prudent.

Hon'ble Finance Minister. Income-tax returns filed for the last fiscal year have shown that the present burden of income tax on the lowest income-earners seems to be the hardest. Last year's economic slump has resulted in several taxpayers going into bankruptcy or insolvency. The above is particularly true of salary-earners who also have loan commitments such as home mortgages to be met. During internal deliberations with income-tax commissioners it has been felt that the department ought to take a lenient view with ordinary wage-earners this year.

As before, the memo was double-spaced and it continued on the next page.

Given the circumstances, I seek your advice on how the above matter should be handled. Thanking you. Chairman, Central Board of Direct Taxes.

The files arrived at North Block an hour later. The finance minister pulled out his fourteen-carat gold Waterman from his homespun cotton shirt pocket and made a note below the first memo. He knew that he could not protect R&S officially. He needed to be perceived as impartial, at least on paper. His jotting below the memo read:

I suggest they be investigated thoroughly and you should take whatever action you deem appropriate to recover taxes that are legitimately due to the government. Regards. Finance Minister.

The second one was relatively easy. He had discussed the matter with the prime minister and it was evident that they would need to give some concessions and tax breaks to salary-earners. His jotting below the second memo read:

We need to be sympathetic and gentle in our dealings with them. Without their support, no government can hope to remain in power. Suggest that adequate flexibility be shown. Regards. Finance Minister.

———

A few hours later, both memos were in Gangasagar's hands, having been helpfully forwarded to him by his protégé, the CBDT chairman. He carefully removed the staple that held the two pages of the first memo together and then repeated the procedure with the two pages of the second memo.

He then attached the first page of the R&S memo with the second page of the memo requesting relief for ordinary salary-earners, and stapled the two pages together. He contentedly surveyed the result of his handiwork.

Hon'ble Finance Minister. Investigations into the activities of R&S have revealed several instances of financial irregularity. Various items on the expense side seem to have been inflated, specifically with the intention of reducing their taxable income. In addition, it seems that private partnerships have been created with a view to parking of profits. Various items on the income side have been deferred, seemingly with a view to deprive the tax authorities of revenue. Certain transactions—particularly sale and purchase of assets—have been carried out at questionable valuations thus further reducing their tax liability, at least on paper. Given the circumstances, I seek your advice on how the above matter should be handled. Thanking you. Chairman, Central Board of Direct Taxes.

The memo was followed by the finance minister's handwritten remark.

We need to be sympathetic and gentle in our dealings with them. Without their support no government can hope to remain in power. Suggest that adequate flexibility be shown. Regards. Finance Minister.

Gangasagar showed the memo to Agrawalji. He was astounded. 'What do you plan to do with it?' he asked.

'Nothing,' replied Gangasagar, 'I have enough ammunition with the scams to destroy him.'

'Then why have you gone through this elaborate ritual with your appointee—the CBDT chairman?' asked Agrawalji.

'When you take out an insurance policy, do you hope for a fire soon?' asked Gangasagar.

'The Chinese ambassador has sought an audience with you, madam,' said the foreign secretary.

'But he has just made a statement supporting the Pakistani position. He says that militants crossing the Line of Control in Kashmir are independent non-state actors. We know that the Pakistan intelligence establishment is involved and yet the Chinese choose to look the other way. Why should I meet him?' asked Chandini angrily.

'We can't afford a confrontation with China, madam. We have always believed that China has unlawfully occupied around fifteen thousand square miles of our territory ever since they invaded us in 1962. Beijing, on its part, claims Arunachal Pradesh—in our north-east— as their own. Diplomatic relations between the two nations are critical.'

'I shall meet the ambassador, but on my own terms… after I'm done with my trip,' said Chandini.

'Your trip? I didn't know that there was anything on the agenda for the next two days.'

'There wasn't, but there is now. Please arrange an aircraft to take me to Gaggal.'

'Gaggal?'

'The airport near Dharamsala. In the state of Himachal Pradesh.'

'Dharamsala? You can't possibly go meet the Dalai Lama. The Chinese ambassador will be extremely upset.'

'Yes. And once he's adequately rattled, I shall have my meeting with him.'

—◼—

Lodhi Road in the heart of Lutyens' Delhi was home to the famous Lodhi Gardens. The tombs of the Mughal emperors Humayun and Safdarjung marked its eastern and western limits. Headquartered there, the Research and Analysis Wing—RAW—was not an agency but a wing of the Prime Minister's Office. This allowed it to remain outside the purview of the Parliament's budget allocations even though it was rumoured to employ over twelve thousand agents. The chief of RAW reported directly to the prime minister of India.

Earlier in the morning, the chief—known by the unpretentious title of Secretary (Research)—had left his office on Lodhi Road and driven in his chauffeured white Ambassador car through the gates of South Block. He was to brief the prime minister and the minister for external affairs on an assignment. It had been the brainchild of Chandini.

'Have we made progress?' asked Chandini eagerly as the RAW veteran settled down in the chair facing the premier's desk.

'I am happy to inform you that Makhmud has been arrested,' said the RAW chief to Chandini.

'Arrested? By whom?' asked the prime minister.

'The Chinese authorities in Xinjiang,' he replied.

'I thought that Makhmud was our agent operating in Pakistan,' said the premier.

'That's true, sir,' explained the chief, 'but Chandiniji's suggestion was that Makhmud be prepared, briefed and transferred to the Xinjiang Uyghur Autonomous Region of the People's Republic of China.'

'And you're happy that he's arrested?' asked the premier. The RAW chief smiled at Chandini. He then looked at the prime minister and said calmly, 'He didn't know that he'd be arrested. He was sent there to liaise with Uyghurs, but we ensured that the Chinese were tipped off.'

'And what has been achieved by this arrest?' asked the confused prime minister, wondering whether he should have allowed Chandini to directly coordinate an assignment with RAW.

'As you know, Makhmud is Pakistani and is one of our secret assets in Karachi. He acts as a militant cleric and trains jihadis who operate in Kashmir,' said the man from RAW.

'We pay agents who train thugs to infiltrate Kashmir and cause death and destruction?' asked the naïve prime minister.

The RAW man spoke up. 'If I may, Prime Minister, I would like to address your concerns. For years we have known that Pakistan finances and trains terrorists to cross the porous border between India and Pakistan. These trained mercenaries enter Kashmir and give impetus to acts of terrorism. Makhmud—and others like him—are RAW's moles within these jihadi groups. We know that Pakistan will continue to send these jihadis anyway. It's useful to have spies within their outfits.'

'But what does this have to do with Xinjiang?' asked the prime minister.

'The Xinjiang Uyghur Autonomous Region is claimed by the People's Republic of China as an integral part of China. The Uyghurs are the local Muslim population who are fighting to break away from China. They're demanding independence,' explained Chandini.

'And what have we achieved by sending a strategic asset to Xinjiang and having him arrested?' asked the prime minister.

'Lots, actually. The Chinese have been supporting Pakistan's anti-India stance in recent years. China sees Pakistan as India's enemy and, of course, "an enemy's enemy is a friend". Chinese support for Pakistan has also crept into the Kashmir debate, with the Chinese often supporting the Pakistani claim that the conflict in Kashmir is a homegrown freedom struggle and is not financed and encouraged by Pakistan,' said Chandini.

'But that narrow view could dramatically change if China finds that Pakistan is also financing other Islamic movements—especially the one in Xinjiang,' said the RAW chief, eager to get back into the conversation.

'So why did we get Makhmud arrested?' asked the Prime Minister.

'Given that he's a deep undercover RAW agent, he's truly viewed as a jihadi himself. He has a rich resumé, having personally been the recipient of largesse from the Pakistani intelligence establishment. He was sent by us to Xinjiang to liaise with other Islamic militants and to assist them,' explained the RAW chief. 'He did not know that he would be arrested. Now that he has, he'll be interrogated by the Chinese MSS—the ministry of state security—and his Pakistani establishment links will become known to the Chinese. The Chinese will not be as supportive to the Pakistani cause now.'

'But what if Makhmud is killed?' asked the PM.

'That's the price we pay for Kashmir,' explained the Secretary (Research).

'I'm assuming that my meeting with the Chinese ambassador next week and my visit to China the week thereafter should be extremely warm and cordial. After all, both nations have common issues!' exulted Chandini.

▭▭

The Great Hall of the People, running along the western edge of Tiananmen Square, covered an area of one point eight million square feet. The political hub of Beijing, the Great Hall had hosted many historic meetings, including a famous one by US President Richard Nixon. The northern part of the building contained the State Banquet Hall that could seat over seven thousand guests.

The hon'ble Indian minister for external affairs, Chandini Gupta, arrived in Beijing on Sunday morning, starting her three-day official visit to China. It was Chandini's first-ever visit to China and during her stay there, Chandini would meet with the Chinese premier as well as top legislators—besides holding talks with her counterpart. Chandini would also attend a ceremony marking the establishment of a joint China-India medical team to handle natural disasters. She would then deliver a speech at the Chinese Academy of Social Sciences, a Beijing-based government think-tank. Talking to *Xinhua News*, Chandini said that she came to China 'with an open mind to hold free and frank discussions on all issues of common interests with a view to shaping a relationship that befits our two countries and our future generations.'

The Chinese foreign minister hosted a banquet in her honour on the last night of her trip. Also attending the banquet were Chinese party and state leaders. The national flags of China and India had been hung in the hall, and the banquet began with the military band playing the national anthems of the two countries. The Chinese minister arose from his chair and welcomed Chandini and her official delegation. He went on to say, 'Even though China and India had their fair share of differences, the sagacity and wisdom of the Hon'ble Indian minister for external affairs has resulted in greater understanding and appreciation of issues of common concern to our two great nations.'

Chandini smiled graciously. The Chinese minister thought that she was basking in his compliments. She was actually thinking about Makhmud and his perfectly timed arrest. Chandini returned the compliment by raising a toast to her host. She quoted, in his honour, two lines from a poem by the great English poet John Dryden, 'A man so various he seemed to be, not one but all mankind's epitome.' The minister thanked her for the kind words. He might not have been as gracious if he had read the rest of Dryden's poem left unread by Chandini.

It said, 'A man so various he seemed to be, not one but all mankind's epitome; stiff in opinions, always in the wrong; was everything but starts and nothing long; but in the course of revolving moon, was chemist, fiddler, statesman and buffoon!'

<hr />

'The leader of the Opposition on a point of order?' asked the Speaker.

'Yes, Mr Speaker, sir. Relevance. My question was put to the minister for external affairs regarding the Indo-China détente. The answer by the Hon'ble Prime Minister is not relevant—' began the leader of the Opposition.

'The leader of the Opposition shall resume his seat. The prime minister has just begun his speech and he is indeed relevant,' the Speaker cut him short.

'On a point of order, Mr Speaker. The question put forth by the leader of the Opposition is incorrectly framed—' argued Chandini.

'The minister for external affairs is debating the issue. Does the hon'ble minister have a point of order?' asked the Speaker.

'My point of order is that disorderly points of order are being taken up by the leader of the Opposition,' said Chandini as the Opposition benches joined her in the joke.

'The minister will resume her seat, please,' said the Speaker indulgently. The girl was a star.

'The girl's a star,' said his wife as she watched the recorded debate on *Lok Sabha Television*. 'You'd better watch out, she may become more popular than you. The diplomatic victory she pulled off in China has made her visibility soar!' The Prime Minister nodded as he sipped the bubbling antacid from the glass in his hand. Lok Sabha sessions always gave him indigestion and caused his stomach ulcers to act up. His wife was right, as always. Gangasagar's stunning victory in the Uttar Pradesh elections and Chandini Gupta's equally stunning coup in China had made them a potent combination. He would have to play his cards carefully.

'Sir, we seem to have a problem on our hands,' said Menon uncomfortably.

'What is it, Menon?' asked Gangasagar, looking up from his morning papers.

'Hameed—the waiter—you know, the one who gave us access to the magistrate. He wants more money.'

'But hadn't we paid him for getting the magistrate to issue an arrest warrant for Ikram?'

'Yes. He wanted more, though.'

'Didn't we pay him some more for having the warrant withdrawn when Ikram renounced the chief minister's post?'

'Yes. But the magistrate has tired of him and found himself another pretty boy. Apparently, Hameed's in financial distress.'

'What, specifically, does he want more money for?'

'For keeping quiet.'

<hr/>

Ikram had just finished Friday afternoon prayers at Jami Masjid, Lucknow's largest mosque. Ikram was a bit of a hero here. He had helped hundreds of people with little things—a job recommendation, a school admission, sorting out a property dispute, advancing cash for a daughter's dowry. Ikram was no less than a Robin Hood amongst the regular Friday worshippers at Jami Masjid.

Prayers over, Ikram wandered over from one of the fifteen arched domes of the yellow sandstone mosque in the heart of Lucknow into its massive open courtyard, fifty thousand square feet in size. He was instantly surrounded by a gang of adoring fans. He noticed a dark young man gazing at him. In fact, he was pretty darn certain that the boy had followed him into the mosque too. Not one for pleasantries, Ikram beckoned him, 'Boy! Do you wish to meet me? Out with it!' The young man glanced furtively around him, almost like a frightened mouse facing a cat. Ikram asked his acquaintances to leave them alone for a moment.

'Sir, I've heard many wonderful things about you. It's because of your reputation as a fair and compassionate man that I have plucked up the courage to meet you. I have some information that could be of interest to you,' said the young man.

'Information, eh? What sort of information?' asked Ikram.

'Sir, please promise me that you won't hurt me when I reveal it to you—'

'Why on earth should I want to hurt a pretty boy like you?' Ikram asked sarcastically.

'Sir, I needed the money and, in the process, ended up hurting your interests. By Allah, I swear I never meant to—'

He broke down, weeping.

'Son. Why don't we start at the beginning, eh? What's your name and what do you do?' asked Ikram, putting an arm around the youth's shoulders.

'My name's Hameed and I used to be a waiter at the Golden Gate bar in Kanpur...'

'And what's your connection to me?'

'I used to be the gay lover of the magistrate who issued an arrest warrant against you.'

'Ah. I see,' said Ikram scratching his chin.

'Gangasagarji's secretary, Menon, approached me to have the warrant for you issued and then subsequently cancelled—I did as he asked.'

'But if you're so influential, why are you in this pitiable state? You seem to have fallen on hard times.'

'I gave up my job as a waiter—it was more lucrative to fix cases. But then Pande—the magistrate—tired of me and dumped me.'

'And what do you want from me?' asked Ikram.

'I am told that you recently got a job for Rashid, a member of your Friday congregation, at R&S Aviation. Could you put in a word for me also?'

'And why would I want to do that? You helped the Brahmin fox, Gangasagar, trick me out of the chief minister's post!'

'But sir, I would be at close proximity to all key politicians—including Chandiniji—because R&S Aviation provides aircraft and helicopter charters to various government departments. I can be your eyes and ears. As you know, in politics the only relevant currency is information,' pleaded Hameed.

Ikram scratched his chin while he thought about what Hameed had just said. At length, he said, 'Go meet Rashid. Tell him I sent you.'

▬◻▬

The steward wearing a dark grey uniform was on his way to the restaurant. Being a flight attendant for government-chartered aircrafts was a no-win job—one was anonymous if one performed one's tasks well and handed out ignominious treatment if one didn't. The fact that he was attached to the aviation company that handled the ministry of external affairs' choppers and airplanes was an even greater pain. The ministry operated several aircraft for the bigwigs—both visiting and homegrown. The big cheeses could not afford to lose a single moment of their oh so precious time and needed to be ferried on the multi-million dollar machines so that they could be in time for their spoilt children's birthday parties. The pompous hotshots never even thanked him—he was just a nameless, unacknowledged and overlooked lackey who cleared their used tissues and candy wrappers from the interiors of the craft. But it was still better than being the gay lover of a sub-magistrate.

Thanks to Ikrambhai, Hameed would now be able to rise in his mother's esteem. She was so difficult to please. She was always humiliating him about his humble position and meagre pay. She would constantly compare him with other members of his family who had been more successful, more enterprising, more achieving. He'd had enough. He needed to move on with his life and R&S Aviation—the private air charter company servicing the ministry of external affairs—had been just the right opportunity at the right time.

'Good to see you again, my friend,' said the nice man—Rashid—who had initially interviewed and appointed Hameed upon the instructions of Ikrambhai, as they sat down and ordered some tea. 'Your confirmation letter is ready and waiting,' began the man as they sipped their tea. 'I just need a small favour from you before we can move forward.'

The minister for external affairs was expected at a conclave in a hotel near the Taj Mahal, in Agra, with a visiting delegation of Russian businessmen within a few hours of her arrival, and the Bell 400 Twin Ranger helicopter was ready, awaiting her. Pre-take-off checks had been completed and the pilot had received clearance from Air Traffic Control to take off in five minutes. Several minutes before her Ambassador car with the red cherry light on the roof appeared, a fleet of police cars— lights flashing and sirens blaring—surrounded the chopper. Policemen jumped out of their vehicles and quickly took Hameed, who was standing by, into custody. The baffled pilot abandoned his chopper and climbed down, wondering what the commotion was about.

One of the policemen drew the pilot's attention to the filler cap. The pilot reached out and opened the cap in order to refit it correctly but still couldn't understand the reason for the fuss. It was only when the cap came off that he saw the pebbles and gravel in the filler neck. It was debris that could have been fatal. It would have allowed the chopper to take off but would eventually have entered the gearbox and cut power, thus bringing down the machine and its ministerial occupant. Lights still flashing and sirens still blaring, the cops handcuffed Hameed and bundled him into one of the jeeps and sped off. The pilot did not notice that the number plates on the police cars were not government series and the rifles that they held were not standard police issue.

The man who had appointed Hameed—Rashid— looked at the happenings through his binoculars from a safe distance. It was time to leave.

'Hameed could not have planned the sabotage by himself. Someone else guided and influenced him. We must get to the bottom of it,' said Agrawalji worriedly.

'No one messes with Chandini and gets away with it, Menon!' hissed Gangasagar as he turned towards his secretary. 'If anyone thinks he has the balls to fuck with me, I want his balls!'

'Hameed was appointed to his post on the recommendation of Ikram, it seems,' said Agrawalji.

'It was Intelligence Bureau men, dressed up as cops, who were sent to grab Hameed. Hameed must now be made to talk—he can tell us who wants Chandiniji out of the way. Shall I tell the director of the Intelligence Bureau to make him talk?' asked Menon.

'No. I have asked the director to pass Hameed on to Sachla Devi—she'll do the needful,' said Gangasagar.

'Sachla Devi? But she's a eunuch. What will she do?' asked Agrawalji.

'I want his balls. She'll find them for me.'

<hr>

Hameed looked around him furtively, terrified by the ferocious eunuchs that surrounded him. He had been forced to drink a mild mixture of milk and opium, just enough to get him to open up, but not enough to lessen the fear. He lay spread-eagled and naked on a hard-surfaced bed, his hands and feet bound to the posts. A cord had been tied tightly around his testicles to halt the flow of blood to his genitals. Every few hours, the head eunuch would tighten the cord causing him to faint. They would throw water on his face to revive him and he would again feel the intense searing pain from the cord around his privates.

The eunuchs surrounding him were praying to Bahucharamata—an avatar of Durga. They were holding him down as their leader, Sachla Devi, took out a sharp, gleaming surgical scalpel, its edges twinkling under the overhead light. She recited some prayers with her eyes closed, holding the scalpel in her cupped hands and outstretched arms, almost as if she were offering the blade to a higher power. She then opened her eyes and said to him, 'It seems that you aren't much of a man. I've been assigned the task of donating your testicles to a more deserving one!'

Hameed screamed a gut-wrenching wail. Tears poured down his face as he pleaded, 'Please, I'll tell you whatever you want! Take whatever money I have! Just don't hurt me! Please! Mercy!'

'Hush, little one, hush,' said Sachla Devi, as she walked over to his face and wiped his tears with her kerchief. 'This should be the happiest day of your life.

Not many people achieve the honour of serving Bahu-charamata for the rest of their lives. You are indeed blessed. Stop crying, blessed one.'

'Why are you doing this to me?' shrieked Hameed. 'I just wanted a better life for myself. I would never have sabotaged the chopper. I am a good, decent and honest man—'

'You're not a man! You shall never be a man! If you want my blessings, you shall tell me the truth. Who is the scoundrel who convinced you to perform this vile act? Attempting to assassinate the very incarnation of Devi!'

'I'll tell you everything! Please don't castrate me! Please! Oh God, please! The man who put me up to it called himself Rashid—he works for R&S Aviation. I've even kept Ikrambhai informed. I've told you everything, please let me go!'

'I'm happy that you've told me the truth, blessed one. It is important to make this journey with a clean heart,' said Sachla Devi, as the scalpel severed his genitals in one single swift movement. Hameed was unable to scream because the intense, incandescent pain caused him to black out. He only awoke when they inserted the wooden plug into where his genitals had once been and poured hot oil in to cauterise the wound.

CHAPTER FIFTEEN
About 2300 years ago

The palace of Nebuchadrezzar II in Babylon was a study in opulence. The king had spared no detail in cedar wood, bronze, gold, silver or precious stones. An underground passage connected the two halves of the city that lay divided by the river Euphrates. A short distance away from the palace stood the verdant Hanging Gardens of Babylon built by the king to heal his ailing wife Amytis. Nebuchadrezzar was the greatest builder of all. Magnificent temples in honour of the various gods of the Babylonian pantheon dotted the city landscape. A marvellous bridge across the Euphrates had been built, supported on asphalt-covered brick piers that were engineered to reduce resistance from and turbulence in the river. The city was virtually impregnable through a triple-layered wall defence system.

It was the eleventh of June and inside the palace of Nebuchadrezzar lay the sick and dying conqueror of the world. Just a month away from thirty-three, Alexander had spent a night drinking excessively at a banquet organised by his dear friend Medius of Larissa. By the time the night was over, Alexander was shaking violently from tremors of malarial fever. Alexander's royal cup-bearer, Iollas, knelt by Alexander's side, offering him sips of the medicated water that had been specifically sent by Antipater—Alexander's supreme commander of his European forces—to cure him of the fever. What the divinity did not know was that his medicated water contained hellebore and strychnine—a deadly mixture—that had been transported secretly to Babylon inside a mule's hoof by Antipater's son, not to cure but to kill Alexander, once and for all.

As news of Alexander's sickness began circulating, the troops became anxious. Finally, the generals were left with no alternative but to allow the soldiers to meet Alexander for a final farewell. They were admitted into his bedchamber one at a time. Alexander, who could no longer utter a word, simply gestured mildly with his weak hands as they met him. A day later, the immortal being was dead.

'Alexander has died in Babylon!' shouted the infantry.

'And Phillipos has been killed in Bharat!' yelled the cavalry.

'This is the time to strike!' urged Chandragupta.

'What are we waiting for?' asked Sasigupta.

The combined forces of Chandragupta and Sasigupta thundered out of their temporary camp, as thousands of horses pounded the earth and threw up a huge dust storm. The rumble of the hooves of the beasts was a dreadful, ominous sound, the roll of a machine of death.

Over the next few days they would overrun all the provinces directly administered by the Macedonians. This was relatively easy, given that the structure of command of the Macedonian forces had completely broken down following the assassination of Phillipos. The death of Alexander was an added advantage as it had resulted in a power struggle at the very top of the Macedonian hierarchy with Seleucus' own position compromised.

'The death of a single Alexander is viewed as a tragedy by the Macedonians, but the thousands of deaths caused by his imperial ambitions is considered a mere statistic,' said Chandragupta angrily to Sasigupta. It made his blood boil.

Rakshas seemed to have made himself quite at home in his new surroundings after his exit from Magadha. At his new residence in Takshila, he sat on a gilded chair in the courtyard, his rich cream turban twinkling with diamonds. A pair of gold-handled yaktail flywhisks swished in tandem, held by a pair of utterly gorgeous courtesans. A golden umbrella held by a *chhatradhara*—umbrella-bearer—shaded him from the sun, while another of his attendants held his sapphire-ruby encrusted sword. He sat barefoot, his boar-skin and silver sandals lying to one side. Another courtesan waved a fan woven from palm leaves, *usira* grass and peacock feathers to keep him cool. All his female attendants wore transparent long *antariyas* with loose *kayabandhs* tied in a knot at the centre, the diaphanous material leaving very little to the imagination.

As Chanakya walked in unannounced, Rakshas hastily arose from his chair shooing away the nubile maidens that guarded his elegant person. 'I see you've made your-self quite comfortable, Rakshas,' commented Chanakya, grinning as he saw the opulence that surrounded the inimitable erstwhile prime minister of Magadha. 'I also see that the gifts intended for Alexander by Dhanananda have been put to good use,' said Chanakya, his voice like satin. Rakshas winced. He knew that nothing ever escaped the ugly bastard's eyes.

'A man must eat,' said Rakshas good-naturedly. 'I'm sure you are delighted I am depleting Dhananda's wealth.'

'As also that of the unfortunate citizens of Magadha,' said Chanakya, not allowing Rakshas the luxury of having the last word. 'In any case, my dear friend Rakshas, I'm not here to discuss the penury that surrounds you. I need to chat with you regarding a rather important matter— your contribution to the overthrow of Dhananda!'

'I am with you, acharya. The scoundrel took away from me the only woman I truly loved,' he said as he gestured for his sword-bearing nymph to bring it over. He picked up the heavy sword by its handle and theatrically declared, 'I shall fight to the finish! Only one of us—Dhananda or I—shall live!'

Chanakya snickered. 'Oh no, my dear Rakshas. I do not need you to do something as mundane as fighting with a sword. Your delicate hands and your precious life cannot be compromised.'

'Are you questioning my bravery, acharya?' asked Rakshas indignantly.

'My friend, what is the much-touted bravery that we talk of? Bravery is simply being the only one who knows that you're afraid! Tchah! Your value lies in that scheming brain of yours, not bravery. I need your little grey cells— your *know-how*. Even more importantly—your *know-who*!'

'I'm at your service, acharya. I shall help you in whatever way I can to fight Dhananda,' said Rakshas bombastically. 'No, no, no, Rakshas, I don't need your help in fighting Dhananda. I need your help in winning without a fight. And the solution lies with someone that you know intimately. His name is Bhadrashala.'

⚊⚌

The alehouse at the corner of Yama road and Rangopajivi avenue was one of the best in Magadha. Unlike the other pubs that had a common drinking area, this one had independent rooms that could be booked by serious drinkers. Each room had comfortable mattresses, round cushions to rest one's elbows in Roman fashion, low tables, large windows for ventilation, fresh flowers and perfumed water. Very beautiful female attendants— *ganikas*—served customers from a long list of alcoholic brews fermented from rice, flour, beans, grapes, liquorice, jaggery, mango, honey, wood apple, pepper and other spices.

Adjoining the alehouse was another equally profitable venture—a gambling parlour. This one was famous for dice as well as wagers on every conceivable event. A seasoned gambling master—a towering hulk of a man with the physique of a bouncer—lorded over the house, ensuring that patrons followed his rules and that only undoctored dice were used. He was particular to a fault. His licence from the chief controller of Gambling and Betting was under review and he couldn't afford any cock-ups. Five per cent of the aggregate winnings went to the state exchequer of Magadha as taxes, and additional sums went unofficially to keep the government off his back.

The patron at table six used to be a favourite of the gambling master. He had spent the last few hours throwing dice and losing heavily, as was almost always the case. His debts were becoming unmanageable but the gambling master couldn't pluck up the courage to tell him that further credit would not be extended.

It was getting to be that time of night when the patron in question would lift himself up and walk over to the alehouse where his reserved room, usual drinks and preferred waitress awaited him. He was no ordinary citizen. That much was obvious from his clothes, his jewellery and his demeanour. What was not obvious to the casual visitor was that he was the most powerful man in Magadha after the departure of Rakshas. He was the commander-in-chief of the Magadha army and his name was Bhadrashala.

'Put it on my tab,' said Bhadrashala casually to the gambling master as he headed over through the open courtyard to his watering hole. The gambling master quickly tallied the slips and jotted down the commander's losses in his red-cotton covered *bahikhatha*—his accounts journal. The account was already awash in red ink.

Bhadrashala was very angry to find someone else occupying his usually allotted room. 'Ganika, why is there a stranger sitting in my room?' asked a visibly irritated Bhadrashala of the nervous waitress. 'I tried to stop him, my lord, but he said that he knew you and that he was your guest,' she replied, sending Bhadrashala into an even greater temper as he stormed into the room.

'Better that you share your room with me rather than a prison cell for the officially bankrupt,' said Jeevasiddhi —Chanakya's operative in Magadha—calmly as Bhadra-shala marched in.

'Get out before I have you thrown out,' snarled Bhadrashala, his face red with anger, 'I neither know you nor do I want to.'

'Calm down, Bhadrashalaji,' said Jeevasiddhi, 'your old friend, Rakshas, has asked me to solve your problems. He's worried about you and has asked me to help.'

'But Rakshas is in Takshila. How could he have possibly told you anything?' spluttered Bhadrashala.

'Let's just say that we have an airborne telepathy,' said Jeevasiddhi, referring to the recent pigeon post that had arrived in the morning from Chanakya and Rakshas.

'And why does Rakshas want to help me? I know the rogue too well. He never does anything unless it's in his own interest,' said Bhadrashala cannily.

'He wants you to remain his friend and ally. He may need friends to get him back in favour at Dhananda's court,' explained Jeevasiddhi as Bhadrashala digested the information.

'And who exactly are you?' inquired Bhadrashala suspiciously. Jeevasiddhi put his goblet of wine down on the table, purposefully stretched his legs out on the mattress and said, very casually, 'I'm the solution to your financial problems.'

'How? If you know everything, as you claim that you do, then the extent of my gambling debts would not be hidden from you.'

'Hmm. Yes. Your fiscal situation is a mess. No one in their right mind would extend credit to you on the strength of your personal balance sheet,' said Jeevasiddhi mockingly.

'But obviously you have a solution that will make all my financial worries fade away,' came Bhadrashala's wry response.

'How could you tell?' said Jeevasiddhi, tongue-in-cheek. 'Seriously now, here's the plan. I'm a horse-trader from Kamboja and have a few hundred horses outside the gates of Pataliputra. As you know, having been a cavalryman yourself, the finest horses come from the Ashvakan regions beyond the Indus.'

'Thank you for the corporate pitch,' said Bhadrashala with a sneer but it was evident that Jeevasiddhi now had his attention.

'You're welcome,' said Jeevasiddhi, ignoring the sarcasm. 'The point is that the horses I currently have in my inventory are lower breeds, not the thoroughbreds that my customers in Magadha want.'

'Why the fuck are you wasting my time with this useless trader talk? I am not a fucking horse-breeder!' snapped Bhadrashala.

'I know. If you were, you'd be rich, not bankrupt!' said Jeevasiddhi smoothly. 'The plan that I wish to put before you will make both of us extremely wealthy. Your debts will be wiped clean and you'll still have enough for seven generations!'

'Go on. I'm listening,' said Bhadrashala.

Jeevasiddhi knew that he now had the upper hand. 'You have thousands of thoroughbreds in the cavalry. I propose that we sell them,' said Jeevasiddhi.

'Are you fucking crazy?' shouted Bhadrashala, once again angry at the stupidity of the suggestion. 'I can't simply sell off assets that belong to the state, you crazy sonofabitch. I'm audited by the comptroller every month. The tightasses physically count every horse in the military stables. This is your fucking plan to get fucking rich? Get the fuck out of here, you fucking moron!'

'Take it easy, my good man. Tell me, when they audit the quantity of horses, do they also check the quality of the horses present?' asked Jeevasiddhi innocently.

Bhadrashala smiled for the very first time in the night. 'You want me to switch them?' he asked as the light bulb switched on inside his head.

'I can get you hundreds of ordinary breeds. You can switch them for the cavalry's thoroughbreds. I can sell the thoroughbreds through my network of contacts and you and I can pocket the difference,' explained Jeevasiddhi, driving home his advantage.

'How will the profits be shared between us?' asked Bhadrashala.

'Seventy-thirty. I'm doing most of the work,' said Jeevasiddhi. He had been instructed by Chanakya to negotiate hard, otherwise Bhadrashala would smell a rat.

'Fuck off! Without my thoroughbreds you have no fucking business model. I want fifty per cent, nothing less!' argued Bhadrashala, mentally counting the profits he could earn from the illicit trade.

'Sixty-forty,' bargained Jeevasiddhi. 'Anything more than that would make the transaction unviable for me. Take it or leave it.'

'Taken,' said Bhadrashala meekly.

'How many horses shall I send you to switch?' asked Jeevasiddhi.

'How many do you have available for swapping?' asked Bhadrashala, smiling at his new business partner.

<hr />

'Paurus shall be the force that will help us acquire Magadha. The problem is that he'll be a liability thereafter,' revealed Chanakya to Sinharan, as they sat in their private chamber in the palace of Kaikey. 'He's the medicine that helps stave off an illness but becomes the cause of a new ailment!'

Sinharan spoke. 'Acharya, the messengers have brought good news. The death of Alexander and the assassination of Phillipos have given impetus to Chandragupta and Sasigupta. After having taken over Ashvakans, they stormed the Sindh and were joined by horsemen from Kshudraka and Saindhava. They've overrun Sindh almost completely. In parallel, the armies of Alor, Saindhavavana, Maha Urdha, Brahmasthala and Patala have revolted against the Macedonians and are ready to accept the suzerainty of Chandragupta. As per your instructions, Chandragupta has now been crowned monarch of Simphapura, and has an army of ten thousand Jats—the strongest and fiercest fighters—under his command. That's in addition to Sasigupta's army, my army of Mallayrajya, and our trained mercenaries. Do we really need Paurus?'

'We do, Sinharan. Paurus has cobbled together three hundred elephants, five hundred chariots, ten thousand horses and fifty thousand infantry, besides another seventy-thousand Macedonian, Saka, Kirata, Kamboja, Parasika, Balhika and Ashvakan mercenaries. He can't be ignored. Magadha has the most powerful army in the world, an army that even the mighty Alexander was reluctant to fight. Without Paurus success will be impossible,' said Chanakya contemplatively.

'But what's to prevent Paurus from taking over Magadha after it's been conquered?' asked Sinharan, reflecting Chanakya's own concerns. 'Why would he fight the battle and not take the spoils?'

'There's only one way to handle Paurus. We create another equally strong contender for the post of emperor of Magadha. Chandragupta then emerges as the compromise candidate,' said Chanakya craftily.

'But who would that contender be?' wondered Sinharan.

'Since the past sixty years, the kingdom of Kalinga has been a vassal state of Magadha. They were conquered and subdued by Mahanandin and have since been paying hundreds of thousands of gold panas each year as war repatriation. The king and his people would love an opportunity to teach Magadha a lesson,' suggested Chanakya softly.

'So you'll offer the king of Kalinga the bait that you'd make him emperor of Magadha?' asked Sinharan.

'No. Why tell big lies when small ones can be just as effective? I shall tell him that if Dhanananda is overthrown, Kalinga shall be freed from the unfair war treaty for sixty years. Nothing more, nothing less. I shall then leave greed and ambition to take their majestic course!'

'We have a problem,' said Jeevasiddhi.

'Now what is it?' asked Bhadrashala irritably, draining the tumbler of prasanna and wiping his mouth.

More than two thousand horses had been clandestinely swapped. Jeevasiddhi would send him half-breeds and non-pedigree horses; these would be substituted for the Magadha cavalry's purebreds in the middle of the night. The next day, Jeevasiddhi would arrange to sell the thoroughbreds quietly. The arrangement had made Bhadrashala entirely solvent and he was once again a preferred customer at the gambling dens and watering holes of Magadha.

'It seems that around half the horses that I gave you to switch had small tattoos on their backs. It skipped my attention because the horses would always be draped in saddle-cloth,' revealed Jeevasiddhi.

'What sort of tattoo?' asked Bhadrashala nervously.

'The royal insignia—a very small one, though—of Chandragupta Maurya,' said Jeevasiddhi.

'Cuntfucker! I'll have your balls for this,' hissed Bhadrashala. 'Do you know what would happen to me if they found that horses belonging to Chandragupta Maurya were in the Magadha cavalry?'

'You'd be executed?' asked Jeevasiddhi rhetorically.

'If I go down, I take you down with me!' snapped Bhadrashala.

'I understand your predicament, Bhadrashalaji. I sincerely do. You have my word that this information shall remain secret between us. Nothing shall ever be done to put your position in jeopardy,' assured the smooth Jeevasiddhi, 'provided that a few small requirements of mine can be met from time to time'.

═╕═

It made him sick to the stomach! Rakshas had been allowed to escape and those sons of whores, Chanakya and Chandragupta, had been left free to roam all over Bharat brewing a revolution to uproot him—the indomitable Dhanananda.

The indomitable Dhanananda sat on his throne, shifting uncomfortably. The palace cook had been turning out terrible food, which gave him indigestion and flatulence. He would have to execute the miserable chef for serving crap to him—the mighty Dhanananda. Sitting inside the opulent hall were his council of ministers—a bunch of yesmen. *Let me have men about me that are scared*, thought Dhanananda. It kept revolutions and revolts to a bare minimum. He laughed when he thought back to the days of Shaktar, a prime minister who considered it his duty to correct his king every now and then. And then there was Rakshas—the lovable pimp. Ah! Even though he had run away to Takshila, one couldn't help missing the rogue. He had always ensured that Dhanananda's nights were filled with forbidden pleasures, a more exquisite one each night. Obtaining Suvasini had turned out to be worthless. She was one of those women who appeared desirable as long as they belonged to someone else. *Strange how women instantly depreciate in value the moment one acquires them*, thought Dhanananda. An impudent fly buzzed around his head and was swished away by one of the maidens waving the whisks behind him.

'Is Magadha adequately defended?' asked Dhanananda.

322

The venerable Katyayan arose. 'My lord, the question is not whether we're defended or not. The more relevant question is whether we can make our enemies believe that Magadha is defended.'

Dhanananda sniggered. Why did he have to put up with these bloody intellectuals? 'Katyayanji, I had put the question to Bhadrashala, our commander of the armed forces. I think this question is better answered by him.' Bhadrashala looked around him warily as Katyayan took his seat. He hated these council meetings. He felt as though all the other council members present were scrutinising him. Katyayan, in particular, seemed to stare at him for long stretches, as though he were a biological specimen under observation.

'My lord, our army's on full alert. However, it's my suggestion that the bulk of our men should remain here, within the fortified city of Pataliputra. If and when the enemy attacks, we should lure them into Pataliputra and then massacre them. This should be easy, given our overwhelming strength.'

'And leave Indraprastha and other border towns undefended?' asked Dhanananda incredulously. Bhadrashala gulped apprehensively. Why had he allowed himself to gamble and drink, thus giving that arsewipe Jeevasiddhi leverage to instruct him on what to say at these meetings?

'There is merit in what Bhadrashalaji is recommending,' said Katyayan, jumping in at the very moment when the sweat from Bhadrashala's forehead had started to slowly drip onto the floor beneath him. Katyayan knew that Bhadrashala's words were actually those of Chanakya. Bhadrashala looked on in amazement as Katyayan took over the argument. 'Your Highness, the royal treasury is located inside the fortifications of Pataliputra. Of what use is it to defend Indraprastha and other border towns when the wealth of the kingdom is right here? Moreover, we're likely to be attacked from different directions. Paurus is likely to attack from the west, the king of Kalinga from the south and the king of Nepal from the north. On how many fronts should we divide the army? I think Bhadrashala has come up with a masterful strategy. Lull the enemy into complacency. Let him walk into Magadha. Pulverise him once he reaches Pataliputra!'

Dhanananda looked at Katyayan. He then let his gaze wander over to a relieved Bhadrashala. He then burst out laughing. 'I tolerate fools gladly, but indulge intellectuals even more. Let it never be said that the mighty Dhanananda was too pompous to take the seasoned advice of his counsellors. Have it your way— we wait for the enemy right here!'

'Ambhi knows that Paurus is going after Magadha,' said Mehir, 'and he sees it as an opportunity to attack Paurus's kingdom—Kaikey—while his attention is diverted. How can we prevent that?'

'The answer lies in keeping Ambhi occupied. He should not have the time to look beyond his own borders,' counselled Chanakya.

'How?'

'Stir up internal strife. Keep him busy controlling law and order.'

'Easier said than done. His subjects are happy. What would make them revolt?'

'Make them unhappy. Think, Mehir. Which is the most powerful community in Ambhi's kingdom of Gandhar?'

'The Brahmins.'

'And what's the source of their power?'

'Divine sanction. It's written in the Vedas. They're needed to communicate with the gods on behalf of ordinary human beings.'

'And does everyone accept the supremacy of the Brahmins?'

'No. The Buddhists seem to think that Brahmin rituals and prayers are hogwash.'

'So, what would happen if Ambhi was seen to be promoting and encouraging Buddhism?'

'The Brahmins would be up in arms!'

'Will you still have happy and content people in the kingdom, dear Mehir?'

Mehir smiled, defeated. 'But how do I get Ambhi to encourage Buddhism in his kingdom?'

'The answer lies in Takshila University. It's presently the fiefdom of Brahmins like me. If part of the university were to be converted into a Buddhist centre of higher learning, the Brahmin community would feel extremely threatened.'

'But Ambhi would never spend his own money for a Buddhist cause,' argued Mehir again.

'I agree. The idea would need to be framed in a way that Ambhi gets the credit without having to spend either his time or his money in getting the project off the ground.'

'But acharya, even if we find someone else to finance it, is it wise to use religious differences?'

'My dharma tells me that I need to unify Bharat under Chandragupta. If I need to use religious differences to create unity, so be it. The ends justify the means.'

'But doesn't it go against your conscience?' asked Mehir.

'Mehir, a clear conscience is usually a sign of bad memory. In any case, in the world of politics you can ill afford luxuries such as a clear conscience!'

'Acharya, you're a Brahmin yourself, yet you advise a strategy which may have dire consequences for the community?'

'The only community that I belong to is the community of Bharat. My only loyalty is to the notion of a unified Bharat.'

'So which side are you on?'

'The winning side,' replied Chanakya.

'But why don't we get Chandragupta and Sasigupta to simply attack Ambhi?' persisted the perplexed Mehir.

'Our Chinese neighbours have an execution method that's used for perpetrators of the most heinous crimes. The method is called *death by a thousand cuts*. The condemned person is killed through very slow cuts on different parts of his body. It's a terrible death in which the convicted man is allowed to bleed to death. I plan to bleed Ambhi to death.'

'Why?' asked Mehir.

'Because attacking him openly isn't an option. We must continue to officially maintain that we're friends even though we're not. He must feel comfortable enough to allow us to stay behind him.'

'Why, O acharya?'

'Because you can only stab someone in the back if you're standing behind him, Mehir. That's why!'

<hr>

The monastery nestled within the forests outlying Takshila was quiet except for the chant, *Buddham Saranam Gacchami, Dharmam Saranam Gacchami, Sangham Saranam Gacchami*. The thatched huts were simple and sparse. The grounds surrounding the little dwellings were clean and tidy. The *sangha*—the monastery—was a perfect study in simplicity, cleanliness and quietude. The one hundred *bhikshus*—Buddhist monks—and *bhikshunis*—nuns—walked in single file, their shaved heads glistening with sweat in the hot sun, the bhikshus segregated from the bhikshunis. They wore the usual *antaravasaka* skirt, *uttarasanga* shirt; *samghati* cloak and *kushalaka* waistcloth, stitched together from rags and dyed maroon. Worn-out wooden soles strapped to their feet completed the ensemble. They each owned very little by way of possessions—a begging bowl, razor, toothpick, stitching needle and walking staff. As they walked, they chanted the mantra that meant, *I take refuge in the Buddha, I take refuge in the Dharma, I take refuge in the Sangha.*

Hinduism, with its increasing intolerance of the lower castes, undue privileges for the Brahmins and Kshatriyas, rigidly defined rituals, and emphasis on Sanskrit scriptures, was suffocating those who lay at the very bottom of the caste hierarchy. These were the very first converts to the great new philosophy of Gautam Buddha, a philosophy that preached universal equality.

The man watching them from the treetop wore a short-sleeved tunic, a topknot turban, chin band and earflaps. A sickle hung from the right side of the sash around his waist and an axe was tucked away into the left. A heavy cloak was draped over his left shoulder. He wore no jewellery except for his gold earrings and *bajubandhs*—armbands in copper and semiprecious stones. On his forehead was a large vermillion *tilak*— the proverbial third eye—his good luck charm. He was dressed for battle like a Kshatriya but was actually a Brahmin bandit. He had with him around fifty other dacoits who had surrounded the monastery and were closely observing it. The bandit chief was angry. These mischief-makers—Buddhists—adopted and converted Hindu untouchables, asked ordinary people to shun Brahmanic rituals to worship God, and even had the temerity to write their scriptures in Prakrit instead of sacred Sanskrit. How dare they convert Hindus to some new-fangled faith of hypocritical equality! They were now being extended rights and privileges in the sacred Takshila University too. They needed to be taught a lesson so that they would tuck their tails between their legs and run. Run like dogs! Of course, it helped that the fair-skinned Persian, Mehir, was willing to finance the bandits' expedition and defray other costs.

He silently nodded to his deputy crouched on a branch beneath him. The skies turned dark and birds of prey began to circle the monastery as the carnage began.

≡

Ambhi was incensed. How dare they! If anyone and everyone could take justice into their own hands, what would happen to the rule of law? These Brahmin bandits thought they could murder Buddhist monks and get away with it? They would now see the merciless side of their king!

Upon his orders, the thugs responsible for the monstrous slaughter were rounded up by his *pradeshtra*—magistrate for law and order. This was not about punishment but about retribution. A hundred innocent Buddhists had been killed in order to satisfy the bloodlust of butchers. How could he justify not punishing the perpetrators?

'Line them up stark naked along the street of wisdom, and let everyone see them suffer the worst indignities that can possibly be inflicted on a human being. A red hot iron nail should be hammered into their tongues, their right hands should be dipped in hot frying oil, hot wax should be poured into their left eyes and the toes of their left feet should be hacked off. Thus mutilated, their faces should be blackened and they should be seated on donkeys and paraded through the streets in utter humiliation! They will live, unlike the Buddhist monks who died—but their lives shall be living hell!' ordered a frustrated Ambhi. He did not know that he was sitting on a volcano.

—

'Tell Chandragupta that I need him to pamper the Brahmins of his kingdom. He should be seen as the greatest saviour of the Brahmin community,' instructed Chanakya as he dispatched one of Siddharthaka's pigeons to Chandragupta.

'O wise master, isn't it only just that the Brahmin bandits who murdered innocents should be punished by Ambhi?' asked Siddharthaka naively.

'Every snowflake in an avalanche pleads not guilty, Siddharthaka. Which snowflake should you punish?' asked Chanakya, his eyes narrowing. 'This is the time for Chandragupta to be seen as a protector of the faith.'

The note that had been attached to the pure white pigeon that was already fluttering its wings impatiently, instructed Chandragupta on how he could acquire the halo of a benefactor, defender, rescuer and preserver of the Brahmin way of life. Chandragupta was to ask a thousand Brahmins to perform a great big *yajna*—a Vedic fire sacrifice in which rich oblations including clarified butter, milk, grains, honey and *soma* would be poured into a massive sacred fire. The king was to then hold a great Brahmanic council to discuss the scriptures. Without exception, every participant was to win an entry prize. This was to be followed by a feast for a thousand Brahmins. The programme was to end with each Brahmin receiving further gifts—gold coins, clothes, grain, and a cow.

'Instead of performing rituals, shouldn't Chandragupta attack Ambhi and finish him off once and for all?' asked Siddarthaka.

'No. I shall let Sasigupta do that instead,' replied Chanakya.

'But acharya, isn't it possible that Sasigupta may wish to take over Gandhar? After all, he's just as powerful as Chandragupta. Chandragupta is now monarch of Simphapura and also controls Mallavrajya through Sinharan, Kshudraka, Saindhava, Alor, Brahmasthala, Patala and Maha Urdha—but Sasigupta now controls Ashvakans and Sindh—two extremely large and strategically important kingdoms,' said Siddharthaka.

'He will definitely try to take over Gandhar. And that's what I want him to do. While he's doing that, I want Chandragupta to be busy praying to Brahmins and their gods!' said Chanakya.

'Why?' asked the bewildered Siddharthaka.

'The early bird catches the worm but it's the second mouse that gets the cheese,' said Chanakya cryptically.

<hr>

'Did you know that Ambhi maimed and killed a thousand Brahmins in Gandhar?' asked the local barber. His patron—the goldsmith—looked at him. The barber was busy trimming the goldsmith's moustache. He waited patiently till the trimming was done and then spoke up.

'I heard not only that, I also heard that Sasigupta, the great king of Ashvakans and Sindh, will attack Gandhar to avenge the honour of the Brahmins,' said the goldsmith.

'Hah!' blurted the customer-in-waiting. Neither the barber nor the goldsmith knew him. He seemed to be a stranger in these parts.

'Who are you and what do you wish to contribute to this private conversation, dear sir?' asked the barber. The stranger let out a little burp, an acknowledgement of the sweet and sour apple he had just consumed.

'I am Tunnavaya, a tailor from Sindh, here to sell my wares. I'm familiar with the one you call the great Sasigupta, but do you know that Sasigupta eats beef?'

'He eats meat of the sacred cow?' asked the goldsmith, scandalised. 'How can such a man be a benefactor of Brahmins?'

'Ambhi has donated thousands of gold coins to the Buddhists to set up a university adjacent to Takshila. Did he ever think that he should spend some of his treasury on upgrading the existing Brahmin schools?' asked the local schoolteacher, sipping lassi as he talked to his friend, an ayurvedic doctor.

His greying friend, the physician, took a swig of his own lassi before he spoke. 'I heard not only that, I also heard that Sasigupta, the Ashvakans chief, is planning to overrun Gandhar and restore Brahmin pride,' said the doctor.

'Hah!' blurted the customer seated at the table next to them. Neither the schoolteacher nor the doctor knew him. He seemed to be a stranger in these parts.

'Who are you? Do you have something to say, my friend?' asked the schoolteacher. The stranger let out another little burp, an acknowledgement of the spiced rice platter that had just been consumed.

'I'm Charana, a wandering minstrel from Sindh, here to entertain. I am familiar with the one you call the great Sasigupta, but do you know that Sasigupta's wife is a Shudra?'

'He cohabits with a lower-caste woman?' asked the doctor in a shocked whisper. 'How can such a man be the protector of Brahmins?'

'Ambhi first sold himself to the Macedonians and now to the Buddhists! Does the man have no shame?' asked the astrologer indignantly while reading the palm of his client, an accountant.

His client, a young man hoping for a wonderful prediction of success and riches from the astrologer, indulged the old man's whims and allowed the conversation to stray from his own life.

'I heard not only that Ambhi is encouraging Buddhists to neutralise the power of the Brahmins, but also that Sasigupta has sent him an ultimatum asking him to restore the balance of power,' said the accountant, still gazing at his own palm, which lay in the hands of the whimsical palmist.

'Hah!' blurted the man half-dozing under the pipal tree, which was temporary respite from the noonday sun for all of them. Neither the astrologer nor the accountant knew him. He seemed to be a stranger in these parts.

'Where are you from, my friend? Do you know something that we don't?' asked the accountant, looking over. The comatose onlooker let out a little burp, an acknowledgement of the betel nut that had just helped his digestion.

'I'm Ashvamadhak, a horse-trainer from the Sindh, here to sell my fine steeds. I'm familiar with the one you call the great Sasigupta, but do you know that Sasigupta demolished a Kubera temple to make space for a chariotway?'

'He willingly allows temples to be razed?' asked the appalled astrologer. 'How can such a man be the defender of Brahmins?'

'In statecraft, as in medicine, words are sometimes the most powerful drugs we can use. The power of propaganda should never be discounted,' said Chanakya as he moved the pawn in front of his queen forward by two spaces. To Mehir it seemed like a move that would leave Chanakya's queen in a vulnerable position. He smiled and made his countermove. Effortlessly, Chanakya moved his bishop diagonally three spaces. After Mehir's next move, he zipped his queen diagonally two spaces and let her sit in front of the pawn. The third man in the room watched the game in boredom, dozing off between moves.

Chanakya laughed. It didn't matter what Mehir's next move was. Chanakya would be able to rush his queen straight up to his opponents's pawn, capture it and place the king in checkmate. The king would not be able to capture the queen because Chanakya's bishop would be in the way. He could not move away from the queen, as he would be blocked by his own pieces. Mehir grunted in despair as he realised the futility of his position. It was no fun playing chess with the acharya. He always seemed to get inside Mehir's head and predict his every move.

'Mehir, my dear boy, it's hard to let go of key pieces in this game, but to win you sometimes have to sacrifice strategic pieces. If your opponent is in a tight spot you need to let go of bait simply to get him to move. Just ensure that the sacrifice you make gets you what you want!' advised Chanakya as they wrapped up the game. The observer of the game between Chanakya and Mehir was Sharangrao—ace student and undercover operative of the black Brahmin. He listened to the conversation intently and burped—an acknowledgment of the wisdom that he had just digested.

Mehir sulked as Chanakya rubbed it in. 'There are no points for losing!' chuckled Chanakya.

'So we simply sit here, playing chess, while Sasigupta overruns Gandhar?' asked Mehir, visibly irritated at having lost yet again.

'Mehir, he may succeed in capturing Gandhar, but he'll be bled dry by the Brahmin guerrilla forces which have been substantially financed by us. It shall be death by a thousand cuts. Guerrilla warfare is an economical method of unconventional armed struggle. Our small group of combatants can cause irreparable harm to a much mightier foe by using mobile tactics such as ambushes and raids. Sasigupta's invasion of Gandhar will drain him of his resources, make his rule over Ashvakans and Sindh less stable, and turn him into the sworn enemy of the most powerful segment of Gandhar citizenry— the Brahmins. That's the moment when Chandragupta shall effortlessly run a hot knife through the butter. I don't plan to merely get Gandhar for Chandragupta. I shall also get Ashvakans and Sindh—Sasigupta's own provinces—for him. Let Sasigupta be the first mouse... the trap will kill him. Chandragupta shall be the second mouse. The early bird catches the worm but it is the second mouse that gets the cheese!'

◼▭◼

'Why is it that you're getting laid while I'm getting screwed?' asked Bhadrashala. Jeevasiddhi looked up, tearing himself away from the ganika that lay in his arms. She giggled, and attempted to pull him back for further frolicking but he admonished her. She got up and left

the room, pouting, while Bhadrashala sat down. Jeevasiddhi adjusted his turban and his clothes, then picked
up his goblet and drained the prasanna from it. He wiped
his moustache and said jokingly, 'This prasanna is proof
that God loves us and wants us to be happy! Why are
you so fucking glum?'

Bhadrashala was quiet. Jeevasiddhi probed, 'Did you
get the cabinet to agree to allow our forces to enter
Magadha without resistance until they reach Pataliputra?'

Bhadrashala nodded. 'They shall face no resistance
at all. But you should be prepared for a bloody battle
once you reach Pataliputra.' Bhadrashala took another
swallow and allowed the alcohol to slowly numb his senses.

'What gives you the impression that we'll fight for
Pataliputra?' asked Jeevasiddhi innocently.

'O hear ye, hear ye, and hear ye. The court of the wise
and benevolent Maharaj Chandragupta Maurya, Emperor
of Gandhar, Ashvakans, Sindh, Simphapura and overlord
of Mallavrajya, Kshudraka, Saindhava, Alor, Brahmasthala, Patala and Maha Urdha, is now in session. Come
and be heard!' droned the crier as Chandragupta entered
the council hall. Only Magadha remained to be added
to the list. Chandragupta was reminded of his childhood
when his friends would utter the very same words as
part of the juvenile theatrics of their imaginary world.
He was saddened to realise that his father, the senapati,
would not get to see his son anointed king.

Ambhi was dead, having been killed on the battlefield
by Sasigupta. Sasigupta was dead, having been murdered
by a Brahmin guerrilla set on him by Mehir. Chanakya
had succeeded in killing two birds with one stone.
Chandragupta had simply walked in and taken over
Gandhar. The local population had welcomed him with

open arms. Chandragupta was now more powerful than the king of Kalinga, as powerful as Paurus, but slightly less powerful than Dhanananda. That would soon change.

Before he reached his throne, he took a short detour to the right where Chanakya stood. He bent down and touched his guru's feet reverentially. Chanakya blessed him. 'May you be ever meritorious, victorious and glorious!' he intoned. Chandragupta rose and walked over to an empty seat upon which sat a pair of ordinary sandals. They were his father's. He bowed down before the chair and received blessings from the spirit world before he reached his mother. The simple and frail woman had tears in her eyes as he bent to touch her feet. She placed her hand on his head and said, 'May your world be beautiful, your actions dutiful, your nature merciful and your kingdom bountiful, my son.'

Chandragupta wore royal garments made from fine *cinamsuka*—imported from China through the silk route. His *antariya dhoti* was pale gold, his *uttariya* vermillion-red, and his *kayabandh* girdle was creamy white. Around his neck hung a necklace with a pear-shaped diamond of about seventy-five carats at its centre. Around his upper arms were bajubandhs studded with flawless blue diamonds, six carats each. Each armband was embellished with a forty-carat heart-shaped Burma ruby. On his head he sported a golden turban ornamented with a hundred and fifty carats worth of pure emeralds. He looked every inch the emperor of the world.

Chanakya stepped up to the throne and said to a seated Chandragupta, 'Do you solemnly promise and swear to govern the people of this kingdom of Gandhar, Ashvakans, Sindh, Simphapura, Mallavrajya, Kshudraka, Saindhava, Alor, Brahmasthala, Patala and Maha Urdha and the dominions thereto belonging, according to the laws of kingship as handed down by our ancestors through the Vedas?'

Chandragupta folded his hands in prayer, closed his eyed and said, 'I solemnly promise to do so.'

Chanakya asked, 'Will you ensure that law, justice and mercy shall prevail in all your judgements?'

'I will,' replied Chandragupta.

'Will you, to the utmost of your power, maintain the laws of God, the honour of your Kshatriya blood, the protection of Brahmins, the defence of the downtrodden, and will you preserve unto the ministers and officers committed to their charge, all such rights and privileges as by law do or shall vest to them?' asked Chanakya.

Chandragupta answered solemnly, 'All this I promise to do.' Then laying his right hand upon a stack of the sacred Vedas he said, 'The things which I have promised, I will perform and keep, so help me God,' as the great hall erupted in cheers.

CHAPTER SIXTEEN
Present Day

'I'm unable to understand what's going on here. R&S Aviation is part of the Rungta & Somany empire. Why would they want Chandini out of the way? They're on the same side as us!' said Menon.

'Look beyond the obvious, Menon. Everything is not what it seems,' said Gangasagar as he made a gesture for Menon to allow the next visitor in.

Agrawalji walked in, dressed in a fresh starched dhoti and kurta. He nodded to both men and sat down opposite Gangasagar. 'Is Chandini alright?' he asked.

Gangasagar nodded grimly. 'She's a fighter. She's not frightened. I seem to be more fearful for her life than she is for her own!'

'What can I do to help?' asked Agrawalji.

'The dispute between the R&S partners,' began Gangasagar. 'We need to understand what's happening a little better. I also need to understand Ikram's role in this entire matter—without him knowing it.'

'But it's obvious, sir. Hameed wanted money. When he didn't get it from us, he went to Ikrambhai and told him how we arranged things with the magistrate. Ikram got him to try and have Chandiniji eliminated in revenge,' explained Menon.

'I'm not sure, Menon. Let's not jump to hasty conclusions about Ikram. He adopted Chandini, for God's sake. Something else confuses me, though,' said Gangasagar, scratching his head.

'What?' asked Menon.

'Rungta & Somany came to Uttar Pradesh to set up a global scale steel plant with our political blessings. One partner agreed to pay higher compensation to the farmers while the other disagreed and managed to get me to offer a sales-tax concession.'

'So?' asked Agrawalji.

'The pattern repeated itself when you nominated Rungta to take over the World Bank-funded roadways project. The junior partner—Somany—came along and complained that he had been cheated out of his share by Rungta. In the process he succeeced in getting an armaments contract cleared by us. Now that I think about it, the whole damn episode stinks!' said Gangasagar, cracking his knuckles.

Gangasagar paused. He stared at Agrawalji for a moment and then resumed. 'One partner—Somany— supported the defence minister in his bid for the prime minister's job. The other—Rungta—supported the finance minister. Both knew that irrespective of the outcome, one of their men would hold the top job.'

'I don't understand what it is that you're complaining about, Gangasagar! The rivalry between the two partners brought this present government—along with Chandini and nine other ABNS ministers—into power. Why are you tying yourself up in knots over this?'

'If it looks like shit, smells like shit, and feels like shit, it's probably shit! We've been had—I know it,' said Gangasagar as he got up from his chair.

'You've had business dealings with R&S, right?' asked Gangasagar over lunch. He had calmed down.

'Yes. I transferred my interest in the roadways project that you gifted me to Rungta, remember?' said Agrawalji as he scooped up the remaining rice and lentils on his plate with his hand and slurped approvingly.

'I need you to put one of your finance hounds on their trail,' said Gangasagar, as he passed a bowl of fresh yoghurt to Agrawalji.

'What do you want done?' asked Agrawalji.

'I need each and every share purchased in R&S companies to be analysed. Who bought? Who sold? When? And I want it correlated with their public statements!' growled Gangasagar, wagging his spoon in a disciplinary gesture.

'What do you hope to find, Ganga?' asked Agrawalji.

'I don't hope. I only go out looking when I already know what I shall find.'

'Which is?'

'A pattern that shows these two partners as being in cahoots with each other—using their display of hostility to wangle more business out of the government. Most importantly, timing their public quarrels to coincide with buying of their company stocks, and their cooling off to coincide with selling. They are milking us and the public like we were cows!'

'But why would R&S team up with Ikram to try to bump off Chandini?' asked Agrawalji as he wiped his mouth with his napkin.

'Possibly because R&S are happy with the ABNS *supporting* the government in New Delhi but do not want the ABNS *leading* the government in New Delhi. Chandini is now seen as the only real contender for the top job, and that must hurt Ikram too,' said Gangasagar.

'They also know that Chandini comes as a package deal along with Gangasagar, a terrifying prospect,' joked Agrawalji.

━▆━

'Agrawalji's chartered accountant has done his homework. Share prices of R&S Infrastructure crashed from 1,178 to 900 rupees in a single day when the partners made public statements about going to court over the World Bank project. The very same day, both partners bought huge blocks of shares through known investment companies. A week later, they announced that they had reached an out-of-court settlement and sold the shares at 1,250 rupees!' said Menon, leafing through the reams of analysis provided by Agrawalji's team.

'If they think they can come in the way of Chandini and the ABNS, they'll soon see that Pandit Gangasagar Mishra is not to be messed with. How many employees work in R&S?' asked Gangasagar.

'Around a hundred thousand, as far as I can recall,' replied Menon.

'And how many of those workers are members of ABNS-affiliated labour unions?' asked the Pandit.

'I found out for you, sir. Our Lucknow University Students' Union president—Upendra Kashyap—had gone on to head the ABNKU—our trade union arm. He says that around twenty thousand workers of R&S are card-carrying members of the ABNKU.'

'And the balance eighty thousand workers at R&S?'

'According to Kashyap, they are split equally between two unions. The ABNKU is the smallest chunk—only twenty per cent. The other two unions are around forty per cent each.'

'Which are the other two unions?'

'The CPUK—headed by Vikram Singh Tyagi, and the INWF—headed by Lalji Garg.'

'Menon, I need you to take down two dictations please.'

'Yes sir?'

'Dear Comrade. As you know, the CPUK has been working tirelessly to help the employees of R&S. The problem is that your leader, Lalji Garg, President of INWF, has betrayed you. Garg, who claims to represent your interest, has sold out your interests to Mr Rungta. Increases in emoluments will now be linked to unattainable productivity targets. This allows for higher notional increases in the salary agreement whereas increases in real wages remain insignificant. As a friend and well-wisher of each one of you, I urge you to ditch the INWF and join the CPUK instead. We are the only true voice of the workers of R&S. I look forward to seeing you at our weekly meeting next Friday. With best wishes. Vikram Singh Tyagi, President, CPUK.'

'And the other dictation?' asked Menon, looking up from his shorthand notes.

'Fellow Worker. The INWF has worked diligently to negotiate an increased wage settlement with the management of R&S. The obstacle in this effort has been the president of your union, Vikram Singh Tyagi of CPUK, who has done everything possible to derail the negotiations. His secret pact with Mr Somany entitles him to a large personal payoff for preventing the new salary agreement from being implemented. The time has come for CPUK members to ditch their betraying and corrupt union and join an organisation that speaks up for you first. Join the INWF. I look forward to meeting you at our weekly meeting on Tuesday. Yours sincerely. Lalji Garg, President, INWF.'

'To whom do I have to send these?'

'Tell the president of the ABNKU—Upendra Kashyap—to have letterheads of both the CPUK and INWF printed privately. Send him these two drafts and ask him to have them cyclostyled in huge numbers. The CPUK letter should be sent to INWF members and the INWF letter to CPUK members.'

'But we're letting the two unions meddle in the affairs of the two partners. Is that wise?' asked Menon.

'The partners wanted to put up a façade of battle, where none exists. They used the façade to pull down governments, resurrect new ones, clear contracts, and now they want to use their devious methods to pull down Chandini and the ABNS. If they want a fight, by God, I shall give them one!' thundered Gangasagar.

'But this could lead to inter-union rivalry! It could get violent,' exclaimed Menon.

'When two elephants fight, the grass will suffer, Menon.'

▬□▬

Riot control police, wearing protective helmets and carrying shields and gas masks, cordoned off the thin dividing line between the two warring unions. The line had been declared off-limits to both sides and armoured police vehicles and mobile storage tanks that supplied pressurised water to the cannons had been placed along it. The policemen were equipped for all eventualities— carrying shotguns, tear gas canisters, pepper sprays, lathis and tasers. On either side of the divider demarcated by the police stood thousands of union workers, waving red and black flags and carrying banners in support of their respective organisations. Both sides' vociferous leaders used megaphones to exhort their members to vanquish and destroy the other side, besides destroying the management—the capitalist pigs! The scene was repeated at virtually all locations of the R&S empire— R&S Steel, R&S Agro, R&S Cement, R&S Telecom, R&S Petroleum, R&S Infrastructure, R&S Textiles, R&S Pharma and R&S Aviation.

The former finance minister—he had been forced to resign owing to Gangasagar's machinations—was being interviewed on television. He was saying, 'The situation is fairly serious. I think it's very unfortunate. When you look at the R&S conglomerate, the workers there are the most highly paid! Some elements from outside are creating this problem. I am all for protection of workers' rights. In no way should workers' rights be compromised, but there has to be a fair process by which problems between management and workers are sorted out. My fear is that if it isn't controlled, the situation may get worse.'

'He's taken the bait, the foolish man. It's time to use my straight flush not only to destroy him but also anyone who thinks that they can take me out of the game,' thought Gangasagar as he watched the interview.

<hr/>

'Sir, land for Special Economic Zones—SEZs—was allotted by the commerce ministry without considering the intrinsic value of it. Thousands of acres of land were given away to a single company, R&S Realty,' said the news anchor, 'would you care to comment?'

'No comment,' said the irritated prime minister, 'I was defence minister then, you should ask that of the then minister for commerce.'

'Sir, telecom licences were issued in an arbitrary fashion at fees that were low, even going by ten-year-old benchmarks. Subsequently, the company that obtained the new spectrum allocations sold its stake to outside investors for huge profit. The company that was allocated the licence was R&S Telecom,' said the anchor. 'Can you shed some light on the issue?'

'No comment,' said the angry prime minister, 'I was defence minister at the time, you should ask the then minister for telecommunications.'

'Sir, oil exploration rights were handed out to R&S Petroleum even though oil had already been discovered,' said the news anchor. 'Can you tell us why you did not step in?'

'No comment,' said the flustered prime minister. 'I was only defence minister, you should ask the then minister for petroleum.'

'Sir, large quantities of fodder and fertiliser were procured from R&S Agro for farmers and cattle that did not exist,' said the anchor. 'How could you allow such deals to pass muster?'

'No comment,' said the helpless prime minister. 'I was only defence minister, you should ask the then minister for agriculture.'

<hr>

'The former finance minister ensured that he took the prime minister down with him. The grapevine is abuzz with news that the PM has resigned,' said Agrawalji.

'If he hadn't resigned, the entire government would have come crashing down—we would have had to withdraw the support of our MPs, and all at once, the comfortable majority would have disappeared,' laughed Gangasagar.

'Now what?' asked Menon.

'Well, we knocked out the finance minister so that the minister for external affairs could take his place, thus leaving the external affairs portfolio to Chandini. We've now knocked out the prime minister—in all probability the home minister will take his place. He's the only one who has broad support from all quarters,' said Gangasagar.

'So the home minister's slot will now fall vacant?' asked Agrawalji.

'Absolutely. And you know what, it needs a thug at the helm of affairs to control things,' said Gangasagar.

'Ikram? Are you mad, Ganga? We don't even know whether the plot to sabotage Chandini's chopper had his blessings or not. And you want him as home minister?' said Agrawalji.

'Yes. One should keep one's friends close and enemies even closer,' replied Gangasagar and burst out laughing.

'What's so funny?' asked Agrawalji.

'Ikram's always been responsible for a large chunk of the crime in Kanpur. He now gets to be responsible for nationwide crime!'

'How many people were murdered last year?'
  '32,481.'
  'And, say, fifty years ago?'
  '9,802.'
  'How many people were kidnapped last year?'
  '23,991.'
  'And fifty years ago?'
  '5,261.'
  'How many burglaries last year?'
  '91,666.'
  'And fifty years ago?'
  '147,379.'
  'We need more murders and kidnappings!'

'Why?'

'Don't you see? Your burglars have graduated to bigger crimes such as murder and kidnapping. And as they've moved on, burglaries have actually dropped. Congratulations!' said Ikram in a tone of irony to his home secretary.

'What is the length of the border between India and Bangladesh?'

'4,096 kilometres.'

'India and China?'

'3,488 kilometres.'

'India and Pakistan?'

'3,323 kilometres.'

'India and Nepal?'

'1,751 kilometres.'

'India and Myanmar?'

'1,643 kilometres.'

'Including Bhutan and Afghanistan, a total of over fifteen thousand kilometres, right?'

'That's right.'

'And how do you prevent infiltration of terrorists through these borders?'

'Barbed wire fences and patrolling wherever possible.'

'Bollocks! There's no way you can police fifteen thousand kilometres of border areas. Do you know who knows these borders better than your police?'

'Who?'

'The smugglers. Help them smuggle their stuff. They'll help you catch the terrorists.'

Ikram was visiting the National Crime Records Bureau—the NCRB. He noticed tens of high-speed printers spewing out reams of paper. 'What's that?' he asked.

'Daily reports, crime statistics, national briefings—they are required at various levels of the home ministry. The data is processed here and passed on to hundreds of functionaries within the departments,' replied the home secretary.

'Shut down the reports for a week,' said Ikram.

'What?' asked the worried home secretary. 'It will result in paralysis. How will senior officers manage without the information?'

'Tell the NCRB to make a note of whoever calls up demanding it. The ones who call are the only ones who actually need it. The others merely receive it and file it away. Save time and expense by sending reports to only those who need them!' instructed Ikram.

They were at the offices of the Intelligence Bureau. The director was taking the home minister on a guided tour of the workings of the world's oldest intelligence agency. They had been old friends in their previous avatars as mayor and police commissioner of Kanpur but the new hierarchy made the conversation between the two men a little uncomfortable.

'When was the agency established?' asked Ikram.

'In 1885,' came the reply. 'The Intelligence Department for the British Army was established in Simla to monitor troop movements in Afghanistan.'

'And then?' asked Ikram.

'In 1909, we became the Indian Political Intelligence Office to monitor Indian anarchist activities. The men were trained by Scotland Yard and MI5.'

'And then?'

'With Indian Independence in 1947 we acquired our present form.'

'As a man ages he begins to lose his intelligence. You've become too old,' joked Ikram, as he outlined his plan to overhaul the establishment. 'How do you monitor your success?' he asked.

'Most of our cases are classified, thus we're never able to discuss our successes,' complained the director.

'Neither are you compelled to discuss your failures,' retorted Ikram. 'When citizens are not aware of what you're doing, they can't tell what you're doing wrong! When was the last time you were able to accurately predict a terrorist act or an invasion?'

'There are practical limitations to what we can do,' protested the director.

'With twenty-five thousand employees and agents?' wondered Ikram. He paused for a moment and then looked the director in his face. 'Tell you what, you're familiar with Kanpur, right? Why don't you have a meeting with Ranbir Gill?'

'Who's he?' asked the director.

'He's the president of the Bar Owners' Association of India and the proprietor of a seedy joint in Kanpur that you might remember from your youthful days—it's called the Durbar Club.'

'Why should I meet him?'

'There's nothing that doesn't get discussed when people are drunk. Want to revamp your intelligence-gathering? Speak to sober people who spend their time with others who are pissed!'

══

'He's pissed off,' said the director of the Intelligence Bureau.

'Then cool him off,' said Gangasagar.

'If he starts getting into too many details, we'll have a problem on our hands,' said the director.

'Then maybe you need another solution,' replied Gangasagar.

Ikram and the director of the Intelligence Bureau were walking down the narrow lane of Chandini Chowk—the old city of Delhi. The director had requested the home minister not to come—the area was troubled and he could not guarantee Ikram's safety. The minister, however, had insisted. Hindu-Muslim riots had broken out in the Old City. The lanes of Chandini Chowk were too narrow for the police jeep to pass through and so the men got out of their vehicle and walked. Dirty, congested, and difficult to access, the narrow lane seemed to be filled with dark and dingy corners that were eerily quiet. Chandini Chowk was like the aftermath of a battle zone. Rocks and broken bottles lay strewn all over the street. All the shops were shuttered and there wasn't a soul in sight except for a few stray dogs.

Ikram surveyed the scene and winced. Why was India so easily excited by religion? Indians could tolerate poor sanitation, pathetic hospitals, lack of schools, potholed roads, erratic power, unhygienic water and subsistence living, but say something to offend a man's religion and you had an instant explosion. 'This is the last Hindu-Muslim riot that shall ever happen on my watch as home minister, is that clear?' he told the director as he walked with him through the street. 'There shall be no compromises. Offenders shall see that it isn't a good idea to fuck around with us!'

They had walked a few steps further when there was a crash behind them. They spun around and saw broken glass lying in a puddle of acid. Someone from one of the upper floors of an overlooking building had thrown an acid bomb at the home minister. 'Send your men to search that building. I want all the men, women and children lined up here immediately!' barked Ikram, and his instructions were relayed almost in parallel to the policemen. Within ten minutes around fifty people had been rounded up. 'Anyone else inside the building?' asked Ikram. 'No sir, everyone's here,' came the reply.

'Tell the women and children to return inside,' commanded Ikram. There was a shuffling of feet as the nervous women gathered their children and hurried indoors. Around fifteen men were left standing in a line. 'Stretch out your hands, palms facing upwards,' shouted Ikram and waited for a minute as everyone did what they were asked to. Ikram walked along the length of the human chain observing the palms and occasionally bending down and sniffing their hands. He walked to the end of the line and walked back, repeating the process. He stopped at the seventh man and sniffed again. 'Step forward,' he said softly. The worried man stepped forward, his eyes darting about shiftily.

'Come here, son,' said Ikram to one of the constables, 'lend me your sidearm.' The man who had been asked to step forward went into a panic. 'No wait, you can't do that. Nothing has been proven—'

The shot fired from the gun in Ikram's hand was directly aimed at the culprit's head. He fell to the ground, his brain splattered in a gooey mess. There was pin-drop silence in the street. 'This is a word of advice from your new home minister. Never, ever, fuck with me! Get it? I'll always—always—shoot first and ask questions later. Unless you want to get shot, don't you dare mess with me!' He wiped his prints off the revolver with a handkerchief, returned it to the constable and said to the director, 'Write it up as an encounter. He was hit in crossfire.'

He turned around and spoke to the fourteen remaining men. 'Anyone else in the mood for getting a quick cure for a headache?' Chandini Chowk was back to normal by five pm that evening. Gangasagar had chosen the right home minister.

'He bumped off a civilian without blinking an eyelid,' said the director of the Intelligence Bureau.

'Typically Ikram,' said Gangasagar coolly.

'If he makes this a habit, we'll have a problem,' said the director.

'I made Ikram home minister knowing that you would be around to keep him in check. Do your job,' replied Gangasagar.

The Indian Airlines flight took off from Mumbai en route to Nagpur at three pm in the afternoon with a hundred and seventy-seven passengers and twelve crew on board. Thirty minutes later, as the aircraft passed over the city of Nashik, a ferocious-looking man holding a semi-automatic kicked open the door of the cockpit and ordered the pilot to get up and join the rest of the passengers in the back of the aircraft. He commanded the petrified co-pilot to take control of the aeroplane. Three accomplices—all armed with handguns—brought the passengers and crew under their absolute control. Their leader—a thirty-four-year-old Pakistani—ordered the co-pilot to head towards Muzaffarabad, in Pakistan-Occupied Kashmir. The nervous co-pilot told him that they had just enough fuel to reach the city of Bhopal where they would necessarily need to refuel.

As the information of the hijack was conveyed from the aircraft to the control tower and on to the home ministry, Ikram rushed to the New Delhi control room of the Crisis Management Group—the high-powered officers entrusted with the unenviable task of dealing with such unfortunate situations. 'Shoot at the fucking tyres,' he ordered the commander of the National Security Guards—the NSG—which had already reached Bhopal. The aircraft was standing in the middle of the Bhopal airfield and the tyres were in plain sight of the sharpshooters. It had been awaiting fuel for the past thirty minutes and not a single tanker had approached the aircraft.

The hijacker's animal instincts told him that something was afoot. 'Take off!' he instructed the co-pilot. 'We need permission from Air Traffic Control,' protested the nervous co-pilot but the gun to his head was all the permission he needed. 'Take off now! No fucking permission is needed!' the hijacker growled.

'Why the delay in shooting the tyres? Send in the fuel tanker. It will buy us some time!' said Ikram on the phone from New Delhi to the NSG. 'Sir, if we place the fuel tank in the vicinity of the aircraft, we'll not be in a position to take out the tyres. The slightest spark could ignite the aircraft and the fuel tank into one giant fireball,' argued the NSG commander. 'Then find out how much fuel the damn aeroplane actually has,' barked Ikram. 'Enough to get him to Muzaffarabad,' came the reply. The NSG had tallied the fuel log filed in Mumbai with the theoretical consumption from Mumbai to Bhopal.

'Tell the pilot to take off and jettison fuel midair discreetly—convey it in your pilot gobbledegook!' said Ikram. 'Give him clearance to fly to New Delhi. We'll be lucky if he lands here—we're in a better position to handle things in the Capital,' said Ikram.

'Bhopal ground, IC-617, request radio check,' squawked the co-pilot.

'IC-617, read you five by five,' replied ground control.

'IC-617, gate six, request IFR clearance to Muzaffarabad as filed.'

'IC-617, cleared IFR Delhi not Muzaffarabad as filed, Lambourne four Mike departure runway twenty-six left, initial five thousand feet, squawk four-four-five-five.'

'IC-617, request push and start.'

'IC-617 push and start approved, call for taxi.'

The aircraft taxied and prepared for take-off. The co-pilot was aware that his life depended on the hijacker's finger on the trigger. 'Why did you file a flight plan for New Delhi?' screamed the hijacker to the co-pilot. 'I asked for Muzaffarabad, but they approved New Delhi instead. They know that there isn't enough fuel to reach Muzaffarabad,' replied the co-pilot, sweating profusely. 'I don't care. We're going to Muzaffarabad,' shouted the hijacker.

'Muzzaffarabad airport is a disused facility—it's unlikely to have any night landing,' explained the co-pilot as he manoeuvred the aircraft into takeoff and discreetly jettisoned a thousand gallons of jet fuel as soon as he crossed an altitude of five thousand feet. The special valves, located on the airplane's wings, released fuel into the air, which evaporated into the providentially hot and dry Bhopal atmosphere.

'We're not going to land in New Delhi,' growled the hijacker as he pressed the butt of his pistol into the co-pilot's neck. 'If you have enough fuel for Delhi, you also have enough fuel for Karachi—that's closer than Delhi!'

⊐⊏

'Tell Pakistan to deny the landing request!' said Ikram to Chandini. Both were inside the control room along with the home secretary. Chandini nodded and picked up the hotline to her counterpart in Islamabad.

'Mr Foreign Minister, if you allow IC-617 to land in Karachi we shall use it as an opportunity to tell the world that the Pakistan government actively planned, financed and encouraged this act of terrorism. Thousands of television stations around the world will beam images of the aircraft standing at Karachi airport,' said Chandini over the phone. 'You decide whether Pakistan needs that sort of publicity!'

'Even if we deny permission, it's possible that they may still land,' pleaded the Pakistani minister.

'But you can shut down your Air Traffic Control and landing lights! If you black out communication and navigation, IC-617 will necessarily divert from Karachi,' Chandini said, and slammed down the phone.

'They've shut down all communication,' said the co-pilot to the hijacker. 'I can just about make it into New Delhi from Karachi with the fuel that we now have. What do you want me to do?'

'I can see a fucking stretch of runway down below— land!' screamed the hijacker. The dazed co-pilot, now entirely dependent on his own naked vision, began the descent towards what seemed like a runway. As the plane descended, he realised that what had looked like a runway was just a well-illuminated stretch of road. He was able to climb just in time to avoid what would have otherwise been a massive accident. 'Fine, let's go to fucking New Delhi!' grumbled the assailant, realising the hopelessness of the situation.

As they headed towards Delhi, the pilot of a British Airways plane flying the same route informed them that New Delhi airport had been closed to traffic.

Approaching the city, they saw the runway choked with trucks and fire engines. As they made a low pass over the chaos, the co-pilot radioed New Delhi flight control and informed them they were running out of fuel. 'Give them permission to land. By now they should have run out of reserve fuel,' said Ikram.

The co-pilot was miraculously allotted an automatic landing frequency. Within a minute he observed fire trucks, army jeeps and ambulances being cleared. Landing in New Delhi at ten pm, the aircraft was instantly surrounded by armed troops of the NSG.

'Get me those motherfuckers in the tower!' yelled the hijacker. He made the co-pilot radio the control tower stating that unless the NSG was withdrawn he would start shooting hostages. A standoff ensued with the threatening figure setting a ten-minute deadline and holding his gun to the trembling co-pilot's head.

'Get the NSG out of there,' Ikram commanded the home secretary. 'We can't have innocent blood on our hands.' He then explained what he wanted done. 'Delay the refuelling—buy time!' instructed Ikram as he discussed the alternatives with the home secretary and the NSG chief.

Fed up of Ikram's delaying tactics, the hijacker once again threatened to start shooting passengers and crew if the aircraft was not refuelled immediately. Thirty minutes later, he forced the senior pilot to kneel on the floor near the open door of the aircraft in plain view of hundreds of television cameras and shot him in the head, execution-style, allowing his lifeless body to fall to the tarmac below the aircraft. 'That should teach you motherfuckers not to mess with us!' he shouted into the radio.

Looking at the face of the hijacker on the television screen, Ikram knew that his moment of glory had arrived.

'Tell him the home minister would like to speak to him directly,' Ikram ordered the control tower operator.

A few crackles later, the hijacker picked up the radio.

'I'd like to come aboard,' Ikram told him. 'You have nothing to lose and everything to gain. If we strike a deal, you win. If we don't, you still have a high-profile hostage—the home minister of India.'

'You can come, but no one should accompany you. No airs of arrogant ministers!' replied the hijacker.

'The Prophet has said that as the fingers of two hands are equal, so are human beings equal to one another. Wait for me at the aircraft entrance—you can pat me down. I come in peace—we are Muslim brothers!' said Ikram.

As the hijacker gave his assent, Ikram started walking alone towards the aircraft. He was wearing a earpiece that allowed him to stay in touch with the NSG commander and the control room. The NSG sharpshooters kept the aircraft door within their telescopic vision to prevent the terrorist or his accomplices from taking a shot at the home minister.

<hr />

The NSG commandos approached the aircraft from the rear—a blind spot. Five teams stealthily clambered up black aluminium ladders to access the aeroplane through the escape hatches under the fuselage. The control tower kept the hijacker's attention diverted by discussing in agonising detail the protocol by which Ikram would board the aircraft. Ten minutes later, as Ikram reached the steps leading up to the aircraft, the hijacker stood near the door waiting to pat him down.

In the meantime, NSG commandos blasted open the emergency doors and stormed the aircraft yelling for the passengers and crew to hit the floor. The three accomplices were instantly shot. The fourth—their leader —was awaiting Ikram at the entrance of the aircraft. To his surprise, he saw the home minister pull out a sniper handgun from his pocket and take aim at him from the tarmac.

⚏

The emergency chutes had already been activated and the passengers and crew were evacuated immediately for fear of the aircraft having been boobytrapped. Five minutes later, the commandos radioed 'Grand Slam', the codename for the successful completion of the operation. The crackling information was transmitted to Ikram's earpiece but there was no one at the other end to receive it.

A few moments later a radio signal was sent to the prime minister. Four hijackers down; hostages free; six wounded; one home minister martyred.

⚏

Menon sat in Gangasagar's living room, reading the news aloud to him. 'There was an outpouring of grief across Uttar Pradesh on Friday with much of the state shutting down to mourn the late home minister of India—Ikram Shaikh. His body was flown in an air force plane on Friday afternoon from New Delhi to his hometown Kanpur for burial. Earlier, thousands of people in the capital paid their last respects to the hero who sacrificed his own life to save the hostages of IC-617,' read Menon. He looked up at Gangasagar for a reaction, but there was none.

He continued, 'Ikram Shaikh, who died at the hands of a hijacker's bullet on Wednesday, was laid to rest at Bagmari Muslim Burial Ground in Kanpur, by the side of his parents. The home minister's funeral cortège snaked its way through surging crowds from his home in Kanpur's largest slum to Green Park stadium where thousands, including his griefstricken adopted daughter —Chandini Gupta, minister for external affairs—and hundreds of state and national leaders lined up to pay homage to one of India's finest home ministers. Later, an Indian Army carriage transported the coffin of the deceased to the burial grounds as thousands of supporters paid their last tributes. Police failed to control the surging mourners, who broke barricades at several points to rush towards the coffin. Accompanied by several central ministers, the prime minister laid wreaths on the body placed in the carriage. He also met Chandini Gupta, Ikram's political heir and adopted daughter, and the late leader's political ally and mentor—ABNS chief Gangasagar Mishra. The prime minister issued an appeal asking people not to commit suicide out of grief for the departed soul.'

Gangasagar coughed. Menon stopped reading and looked up. He could see that Gangasagar's eyes were moist. Uncomfortably, Menon rambled on, 'The roads between the stadium and the burial ground were teeming with mourners lined up along the road itself, on rooftops and packed into the stadium to bid adieu to the man who died a sudden, tragic death that they were still coming to terms with. The funeral procession slowly made its way to the stadium where leaders from across the political spectrum paid tribute. Hundreds of vehicles followed the flower-bedecked truck in which the body, draped in the national flag, was kept. Standing by the side of her adoptive father's body was Chandini Gupta, who was appealing to people to allow the vehicle to move. Holding national flags, some ran towards the truck to have a closer look at the casket and console her. In the rest of Uttar Pradesh, a silence fell, with normal life coming to a crippling halt. Schools, colleges, offices, shops and businesses closed as a mark of respect to the leader. The usual morning bustle was missing as the government declared a two-day holiday. The state government declared a seven-day mourning period and cable TV-operators took all entertainment channels off the air.'

Menon reached the end of the article. Gangasagar looked him in the eye and said, 'I must be cruel, only to be kind. Thus bad begins and worse remains behind.' Menon had never studied Shakespeare otherwise he would have realised that his master had quoted from *Hamlet*. 'Call the director of the Intelligence Bureau. I need to speak with him,' said Gangasagar as he walked towards his bedroom.

He was softly muttering, '*Adi Shakti, Namo Namah; Sarab Shakti, Namo Namah; Prithum Bhagvati, Namo Namah; Kundalini Mata Shakti; Mata Shakti, Namo Namah.*'

━━

'I cannot speak, for every word that emerges is one that causes me pain. I cannot sleep, because I have nightmares of losing him again and again. I cannot think, because memories haunt me. I cannot eat, because I feel no hunger. I cannot cry, because I seem to have no more tears left. I cannot see, because my eyes are frozen on one image alone—that of my adoptive father. I cannot mourn, because he lives on in my heart,' said Chandini as she delivered her speech to the gathered mourners.

'I stand before you today and beseech you to remember the sacrifice made by this noble soul—a man whom I am proud to call my father. Even though he's no more with us, his political and social legacy lives on. I dedicate the rest of my life to doing what he did best—

wiping away tears, filling empty bellies, and making people smile.' Chandini omitted to mention that Ikram was also a mafia don with a trigger-happy finger.

'The great religions of our country merged together to create this wonderful unity in the diversity that we call India. I am born Hindu but am the adopted daughter of a Muslim. This was the greatest gift that the Almighty could bestow upon me—it was His way of saying that I belong to no single group—I am the daughter of India and I belong to all of you!' she said, tears running down her artistic face.

'Death is so beautiful—it's a great enhancer,' whispered Gangasagar, seated in the last row with Menon. 'Ikram achieved more for Chandini by dying than he could ever have achieved by living.'

▬▬

Hameeda—previously known as Hameed—stood outside the shop clicking her tongue. 'Don't you want us to bless the shop?' she shouted, swinging her false braid coyly. The shopkeeper avoided looking at her or her companions of Sachla Devi's gang. They looked positively hideous with their garish make-up and muscular bodies encased in saris. Realising that her implied threat had failed to produce the desired result, the remaining eunuchs starting clapping and shouting loudly, creating enough of a ruckus to deter customers from walking in. The shopkeeper quickly reconsidered his position and sought their blessings, for a price of course. Hameeda mentally cursed her fate and thought back to the eventful day when she had—while she was still Hameed—approached Ikram at the mosque. 'Boy! Do you wish to meet me? Out with it!' Ikram had beckoned. A few weeks after that initial meeting, Hameed had met Ikram once again at the mosque.

'I met Rashid, at R&S Aviation, who gave me the job. But he wants me to do something... I'm scared,' began Hameed.

'Why are you scared?' asked Ikram, curiosity piqued.

'He wants me to fill pebbles in the fuel tank of a helicopter. It's to sabotage the machine of your adopted daughter—Chandiniji. Please sir, help!'

'Calm down, son. Do what Rashid tells you to. I'll handle the rest of it.'

'But—but—I don't want to get into any trouble...'

After Hameed left, Ikram picked up the phone and spoke to the director of the Intelligence Bureau.

'He's been asked to sabotage Chandini's chopper,' said Ikram.

'Let's arrest this Rashid immediately,' suggested the director.

'That may not be his real name. Furthermore, he may have accomplices,' said Ikram. 'No. Let Hameed follow Rashid's instructions. Have your men ready to pick him up and make a show of it. I do not want Hameed in police custody, but in yours. Keep an eye on Rashid so that we can get not only him but also his entire network.'

'How the fuck did you allow Hameed to be handed over to Sachla Devi?' yelled Ikram at the director of the Intelligence Bureau.

'What was I supposed to do? Tell Gangasagar that I wouldn't?' asked the director.

'You could have let him get away!' roared Ikram.

'Gangasagar would have come after me and it would have been my balls instead of Hameed's!' explained the exasperated director.

'You could have told Gangasagar the truth—that Hameed was innocent and that we were trying to get Rashid instead.'

'That would have meant also telling him you helped get Rashid as well as Hameed those jobs at R&S Aviation in the first place.'

'There was no need for Ikram to take aim at the hijack leader. Had he left it to the NSG he might be alive,' said the director of the Intelligence Bureau.

'I know, I know,' said Gangasagar. 'But he'd seen the hijacker's face on television. He now knew that the hijacker was Rashid. The fact that Rashid had tried to kill Chandini must have made his blood boil and he must've decided to finish off the man once and for all.'

'The NSG ended up shooting at Rashid in a hopeless effort to protect Ikram,' said the director.

'Ikram was like that—shoot first, ask questions later. Ikram may have been a hotheaded thug, but he had a heart of gold. Yes, he was quick to pull a trigger—but only if he knew that it was meant to deliver justice. And yes, he may have felt cheated when Hameed told him that I had tricked him into renouncing the chief minister's post, but he would never take his revenge on Chandini,' said Gangasagar.

'Since when did you start getting soft, sir?' asked the director.

'Since the time you were unceremoniously booted out as police commissioner, and I felt sorry for you and arranged your posting at the Intelligence Bureau. You used to be Ikram's friend too, you know!'

'Alas, in my line of work there are no permanent friends—only permanent interests.'

The Red Fort—the largest monument in Old Delhi—wasn't merely a site from which the prime minister of

India addressed his countrymen on Independence Day. It was also a labyrinth of cells and tunnels. During Mughal times, more than three thousand people lived inside the fort. Located deep within its bowels were ten specially guarded cells. They were interrogation cells belonging to the Intelligence Bureau of India.

Inside one of these cells, Rashid lay on a hospital bed that had been specially brought here along with sophisticated medical equipment. The only people who knew that Rashid had survived were the director of the Intelligence Bureau and Gangasagar.

'You'll need to release this man into my custody!'

The command was delivered authoritatively. The director swung around in his swivel chair to find out who was impudent enough to interfere. He was shocked to see that it was the chief of RAW.

'You'll need to release him,' said the Secretary (Research) simply.

'Do I get a reason?' asked the director of the Intelligence Bureau.

'He's a RAW agent. Good enough?'

——

'What the fuck are you rascals up to? Rashid was involved in an attempt to sabotage the helicopter of the minister for external affairs. He then hijacked an aircraft with a hundred and seventy-seven passengers on board. Why would a RAW agent be plotting against Indian ministers and hijacking civilian aircraft?' asked the director of the Intelligence Bureau.

'Rashid is an alias. His real name is Makhmud. He's a Pakistani double agent. We had used him in a Chinese operation. Unfortunately, the last part of the operation involved him being arrested by the MSS—the Chinese ministry of state security, and we omitted sharing that part of the plan with him in advance,' explained the RAW veteran.

'But what was the purpose of the plan?'

'Our minister for external affairs was able to negotiate from a position of strength in China due to this successful operation in which Makhmud was used to cause a rift between the Chinese and the Pakistanis.'

'If he was arrested by the MSS, how was he here in India?' asked the director.

'His Uyghur comrades launched an attack on the prison where he was being held in Xinjiang and he was able to flee. He entered India with the help of Nepalese smugglers and reached Lucknow where he sought the assistance of Ikrambhai on humanitarian grounds. Ikrambhai helped him out of his sense of duty towards a Muslim brother but unaware of his background.'

That explains Ikram's anger when he saw that the very Muslim brother he had taken pity on had not only attempted to sabotage Chandini's helicopter but also hijack a civilian aircraft, reasoned the director.

▰

The executive boardroom on the twenty-third floor had a panoramic view of the city. Plush leather swivel chairs surrounded a shining maplewood conference table. Giant portraits of the founders hung on the walls. The room was infused with the heady aroma of Cuban cigars. Mr Rungta and Mr Somany, partners, sat at opposite ends of the table, sipping warm camomile tea.

'The game we played with Gangasagar has boomeranged,' said Rungta as he absentmindedly stirred his tea. 'Your man—the previous defence minister—has been ignominiously booted out from his prime ministerial berth. My man—the finance minister—has to content himself with lecturing at universities!'

'All the deals are falling apart—telecom, oil, fodder, land. The government is too scared to let any of them move forward,' said Somany. 'Even the stock sales and purchases that we timed with our quarrels and reconciliations are under the regulator's scrutiny. The trade union dispute brought all business to a standstill for almost a week!'

The knock on the heavy oak door was soft. 'Come in,' announced Rungta. A smartly dressed secretary walked in. 'Sorry to bother you, sirs, but there's a gentleman outside. He doesn't have an appointment but he says that if I tell you his name, both of you would definitely wish to meet him.'

'Who is it?' asked Somany curiously.

'He says his name is Pandit Gangasagar Mishra.'

<hr>

'Both you gentlemen have seen what I'm capable of. Even though I have the upper hand, I'm willing to declare a truce,' announced Gangasagar. Rungta and Somany looked at each other, wondering where the catch lay.

'There's no catch,' said Gangasagar, reading their minds. 'I'm too much of a pragmatist to ignore the value of friendships with influential businessmen.'

'And what would such a friendship get us?' asked Rungta.

'For starters, I shall avoid getting both of you prosecuted for sheltering a known terrorist—Rashid—in your aviation firm. The very same Rashid tried to sabotage the helicopter of the Honourable minister of external affairs. He then went on to hijack an aircraft in which the honourable home minister tragically lost his life!' thundered Gangasagar.

Both partners were visibly shaken and remained quiet. 'But I'm not here to teach you a lesson,' softened the history teacher. 'I'm here to be friends,' he joked.

'God defend me from my friends, from my enemies I can defend myself,' mumbled Rungta under his breath as Gangasagar began outlining his proposal.

'The ABNS expects to be the ruling party in New Delhi after the next general elections. To achieve that, we're going to need money. Lots of it,' explained Gangasagar.

'You already have Agrawalji,' said Somany. 'He's been a great benefactor of the ABNS.'

'That's my problem,' said Gangasagar. 'Agrawalji is our benefactor, but our benefactor needs benefaction.'

'In what way?' asked Rungta.

'Four of your deals are in jeopardy. The fate of all four proposals lies in the hands of ABNS ministers. If we're friends, I'll tell our ministers to also be friendly,' offered the Pandit.

'How?' wondered Rungta.

'The commerce ministry will find that of the several thousand acres allotted to R&S Realty, a few hundred were undervalued. The balance will still remain with you. The minister of telecommunications will discover that telecom licences were issued at low levels and shall double the fee. R&S Telecom will still make a killing, given that they paid only a tenth of the fair market price. The petroleum ministry will observe that oil exploration rights were handed out to R&S Petroleum because no other private player was willing to take on the huge contingent liability of environmental insurance. And finally, the minister for agriculture shall discover an error in their cattle census and arrive at the conclusion that the orders for fodder and fertiliser placed on R&S Agro are correct, after all. See how much I'm willing to do when we're friends?' said Gangasagar.

'What about the union dispute you caused?' asked Rungta. 'You lit the match. Now how does one put out the fire?'

'Don't worry. Our union—the ABNKU—has used the past few weeks to woo the members of your two main rival unions. The ABNKU now makes up more than fifty per cent of the workers. We're willing to sign a new wage and productivity agreement immediately.'

'And what will this cost us?' asked Somany dryly.

'Agrawalji's firm shall be entitled to ten per cent commissions on all revenues arising from the four deals that are resurrected,' said Gangasagar.

'And why are you being so generous with him?' asked Somany.

'Rice pudding is quite expensive these days,' said Gangasagar cryptically.

CHAPTER SEVENTEEN
About 2300 years ago

The modest and austere hut in the woods adjoining the palace grounds of Takshila was dimly lit. Chanakya, much against the wishes of Chandragupta, had decided that he would not reside in the palace but would continue to live in spartan surroundings. Chanakya sat on the ground at his desk, with two lamps before him—one lit and the other not.

The Greek noble who sat before him also on the ground was short, curly-haired and clean-shaven. He wore an ornately patterned chiton—a tunic of light linen, which left a shoulder bare. Except for his belt, which bore a few semiprecious stones, he wore no jewellery at all. His name was Megasthenes and he was the new Macedonian ambassador sent by Seleucus to Chandragupta's court. 'Please be clear with me,' requested Chanakya. 'Is your meeting with me today personal or official?'

Megasthenes smiled. He had been forewarned of the outspoken Brahmin whose machinations had installed Chandragupta on the throne. 'I'm here in Takshila to officially represent my lord Seleucus in the court of His Highness, Chandragupta, but I'm here today in my personal capacity to meet you, sire. Fame for your abilities, words and deeds has spread far and wide and I needed to see for myself this Brahmin who has acquired the persona of a demigod!'

'Ah! Then you must wait for a moment,' said Chanakya as he efficiently lit the second oil lamp and extinguished the first.

Megasthenes was puzzled. What purpose did it serve to snuff out one lamp while lighting another that was exactly the same? He hesitantly asked, 'Sire, why did you do that? Both lamps shed the same light.'

'They are indeed identical, my friend, but the first one contains oil that has been supplied from the government treasury while the second is supplied with oil bought by me personally. Since your visit is not official, why should I expend state resources?' said Chanakya. The bewildered Megasthenes understood the reason for Chandragupta's success thus far.

'My master, Seleucus, has asked me to informally tell you that while he hopes to have mutually beneficial diplomatic relations with Emperor Chandragupta, he will not compromise on Macedonian control over the territory between Phyrgia and the Indus,' said the ambassador.

'I thought this was a personal visit—you're making me spend from my personal tab quite unnecessarily,' joked Chanakya. 'Let's not talk of war between friends, good sir, let's talk instead about love, marriage and happiness.'

The befuddled ambassador was wondering how to deal with this new tactic, when Chanakya spoke again. 'Our king, Chandragupta, has already married the lovely Lady Cornelia, the noble daughter of your mighty master, Seleucus. Their secret marriage—a Gandharva Vivah—

happened a few months ago. You see, Megasthenes, you and I could well be considered in-laws!'

'Bu—but wh—what is a secret marriage? How did this happen?' spluttered Megasthenes nervously.

Chanakya laughed. 'In an ordinary arranged marriage, the groom gets to screw his wife *after* he gets married, in a Gandharva Vivah he gets to screw her *in order to* get married!' he quipped crudely. Megasthenes shifted uncomfortably—he was overcome by a persistent desire to scratch his crotch but the presence of this powerful thinker prevented him from doing anything so downright physical.

'But Seleucus has not given his permission to the match,' said Megasthenes.

'It seems that Cornelia doesn't need it. Our king seems quite besotted with her. It seems that Lady Cornelia has all the four aspects—mother, sister, daughter and whore—of a perfect woman. Did I tell you that four is a lucky number for us?' said Chanakya.

Megasthenes was struck speechless. Before he could recover, Chanakya said, 'So you see, ambassador, your visit is indeed a personal one. Shall we now discuss the bride's dowry?' Megasthenes' crotch was itching even more fiercely as he stammered, 'D—d—dowry?'

'Yes. After all, the dowry that accompanies the daughter of a monarch such as Seleucus must quite obviously reflect his power and glory. I suggest that Seleucus give Arachosia, Gedrosia, Paropamisadae and Aria to our able monarch. Didn't I tell you that four is a lucky number for us here in Bharat?'

'Would that be all?' asked Megasthenes apprehensively.

'Not quite. Your master, Seleucus, is yet to overthrow the other claimants to Alexander's throne. He still needs to fight Antigonus and Dmetrius, both claimants to Alexander's dominions. Our emperor would like to provide you with five hundred and one elephants to terrorise your enemies and thus contribute to your victory! Five hundred and one is an even luckier number, eh?'

'And would there be any expectations in terms of compensation for these elephants?' asked Megasthenes anxiously.

'Tell your old ally, Paurus, that he can invade Magadha, enjoy her pleasures for the night, but must leave the next morning. His affair with Magadha shall be a one-night stand, not an enduring relationship!' said Chanakya with a devilish gleam in his eye.

It was too frigging late. He had been duped and Paurus was angry. His intelligence chief, Abhaya, had informed Paurus about Chandragupta's coronation in Takshila. Chanakya, that old bastard, had been present to administer the oath of office. There was obviously no rift between teacher and student. But it was too late to do anything about it. His army was already on the move and one simply could not halt a massive war machine in its tracks. Dhanananda already knew that Paurus was on his way to fight him. If Paurus withdrew, what could prevent Dhanananda from attacking him? No, it was clear. He would have to proceed as planned. *But I shall not fucking share the spoils with Chanakya or his puppet, Chandragupta*, thought Paurus. Magadha was his, all his.

His luxurious tent pitched in a field a few yojanas from the border of Magadha was an island of tranquillity surrounded by a tumultuous ocean. The cacophony of sounds produced by a hundred thousand men, forty thousand horses, four thousand charioteers and three thousand war elephants, was deafening. His tent, if it could be called one, was made of wood. It would be assembled each time they camped in a new place. The wooden walls were draped with thick fabric to absorb sound. Within the king's tent stood a four-poster bed and an ornate desk and chair. Silken rugs and fine linen bedspreads conveyed an aura of softness in a room that was otherwise filled with instruments of war—his armour, helmet, swords, daggers and spears.

Abhaya was standing before him. He shifted his weight uncomfortably from one foot to the other. The old king had kept him waiting on his feet for over an hour. The pins and needles in his soles were beginning to bother him. 'Chandragupta has married Cornelia—the daughter of Seleucus. Seleucus has handed over Arachosia, Gedrosia, Paropamisadae and Aria to Chandragupta as dowry. Megasthenes, Seleucus' ambassador in Chandragupta's court, has assured Chanakya that the mighty Paurus shall have no claim to Magadha's throne,' informed Abhaya as Prime Minister Indradutt gazed at the map of Magadha that lay before them.

'Who does Megasthenes think he is?' thundered Paurus. 'He can't make commitments on my behalf. I'm no longer a servant of the Macedonians! Magadha is mine! It's my divine duty to capture it and unite it with Kaikey. No one can stop me—not even God!'

Abhaya shifted a little more. He kept his eyes glued to his toes. He was never comfortable conveying delicate news to Paurus. He flew into tantrums so easily. 'After all is said and done, a lot more is said than done, O King,' suggested Indradutt wisely. 'Megasthenes and his master are fully aware they do not have any bargaining power with us. Let's attack Magadha and use it as a bargaining chip.'

'O wise Prime Minister, there's more bad news. The king of Kalinga, desirous of throwing off the yoke of Magadha's suzerainty, has pledged to attack with fifty thousand troops. He will be attacking from the east as we move in from the west. He may also be a contender for the throne,' said Abhaya quietly.

'That arsewipe who has meekly accepted enslavement by Magadha for the past sixty years now thinks he can sit on the throne of the most powerful kingdom on earth?' asked Paurus with hauteur. Indradutt kept quiet although he would have liked to remind his pompous king that he too had accepted being slave to the Macedonians not too long ago.

'Maharaj, let's not worry about Seleucus or Kalinga. These are not the real obstacles in our path to Pataliputra,' advised Indradutt.

'Then who is?' asked the angry Paurus.

'Chanakya,' replied Indradutt.

⊏⊐

In a dusty old warehouse in Paricharak lane of Pataliputra, no one paid any attention to the several men pounding away at a rather strange mixture. Each man used over-sized stone pestles and mortars to grind the curious concoction into a paste. Surrounding them were various quantities of the ingredients—some of them imported—including costmary, sweet flag, hypericum, gum, sagapenum, acacia juice, illyrian iris, cardamom, anise, nard, gentian root, dried rose-leaves, poppy-tears, parsley, casia, saxifrage, darnel, long pepper, storax, castoreum, frankincense, hypocistis juice, myrrh, opopanax, mala-bathrum leaves, round rush, turpentine-resin, galbanum, carrot seeds, opobalsam, rhubarb root, saffron, ginger, cinnamon, vinegar, and honey. Supervising the men was Jeevasiddhi, continuously referring to the little notes that had been sent by Chanakya using pigeon post.

In an adjoining room sat another group of men wearing thick cotton masks. They were preparing an even deadlier brew. They were roasting *orpiment*, an orange-yellow mineral found along the eastern borders of Magadha. The result was an ayurvedic compound called *phenashmabhasam*—white arsenic. 'Fool!' Jeevasiddhi yelled at one of the men who was using his bare hands to dust off the residue from his mortar. 'Wash your hands immediately! Then apply some of the *mithridatay* solution from the other room!'

Why am I stuck with these idiots who have no fucking clue to what they're dealing with, he thought. He paused to reflect. He then smiled. He realised that they were willing to do the job only because they had no clue. It was always better to operate on a strict need-to-know basis. And these simpletons didn't need to know anything at all.

≡

The creaking bullock cart wound its way through the new chariot road that ran from Indraprastha to Pataliputra. The cart was old and had seen better days, but the bullocks looked surprisingly well-fed and strong. Little bells around their necks tinkled to the swaying motion of the lumbering beasts of burden. Seated on the cart were three men. One of them was old, dark, and had a pockmarked face. He was stark naked—without even a loincloth around his privates. His long hair, beard and moustache were unkempt. Sandalwood paste and cremation ash was smeared across his face and body. His appearance indicated that he was an *Aghorpanthi*—one of a fierce and eccentric sect of yogis who worshipped Shiva, and whose name translated to 'non-terrified' because they did not fear death. Aghorpanthis believed that everything in this world was created from divine matter and thus nothing could be impure. The aggregate of the universe was sacred and flawless as God himself.

Aghorpanthis sat for their meditation and penance in cremation grounds, praying for the souls of the departed and consuming the flesh of the dead. They were necrophagists.

The two other men were quite obviously his disciples. One was sitting in front, directing the bullocks, while the other was seated opposite his guru. Both followers wore scanty loincloths of the same greyish-white colour, stained from ashes of the dead. Aghorpanthis were not to be messed around with. They were human symbols of Shiva himself. They lived in cemeteries precisely because these were the very places that Shiva dwelt. Aghorpanthis roamed around stark naked because their nudity reflected their complete detachment from the illusory world of ordinary mortals. There was a method to their madness. Through their terrible penance they transcended human emotions of attachment, pride, jealousy, and hatred, thus becoming true yogis.

Their cart was not stopped at any of the border checkpoints along the way. The guards were simply too terrified of being cursed by them, or worse, being eaten alive. The three men in the cart chuckled to themselves as they saw the fear in the eyes of all those who passed them. Chanakya, Chandragupta and Sharangrao made the journey to Pataliputra pretty quickly.

Inside the palace grounds, Dhanananda was busy pouring rivers of clarified butter, honey, milk, grain and soma into the grand sacred fire being tended by a hundred and ten Brahmins of the kingdom. It was a fervent plea to the Almighty to grant him victory over the scoundrels who wanted to usurp his throne. After the ceremonies were over, the Brahmins would be led to the royal dining hall where ten senior Brahmins would be fed on crockery of pure gold. The one hundred junior Brahmins who had stood in the background reciting Vedic hymns would also eat, but on a hundred plates of solid silver. Pleasing the Brahmins was the equivalent of pleasing God and Dhanananda had taken out some time from his usual schedule of pleasing himself to attend to the sacred rites.

Prayers over, the Brahmins were led to the dining hall where they were shocked to find three Aghorpanthis sitting before three of the golden plates. 'This is preposterous! How can we sit here with these disgusting men who live among corpses and eat rotten flesh?' asked the chief Brahmin among them. Dhanananda was also livid. Why had his guards allowed these obscene mystics into the premises?

'They said that they would curse me and that my intestines would pour out of my stomach, which they would consume with relish!' said a hysterical guard to Dhanananda. His commanding officer, a handsome young man with an exceedingly well-oiled moustache said in alarm, 'Your Highness, they said that my limbs would fall off and fly spontaneously into your sacred fire. They said that the meat hanging on my bones would be nicely roasted before they took a single bite!'

'O King, we may be Aghorpanthis but we came here to seek divine intervention for your victory. Our powers are far greater than the hundred and ten fat Brahmins who are present in this room. By insulting us you have brought the wrath of Shiva upon you. Shiva's blood shall poison your wells and your citizens shall die of thirst with the enemy baying like wolves at the city gates. Nothing can save you or your kingdom now—not even another a thousand sacrificial fires!' shouted the naked Chanakya as all three men stood up with plates still in their hands. They threw their plates down on the floor in rage and stormed out of the dining hall. None of the guards blocked their exit. Dhanananda too stood motionless, paralysed with fear. It was only a few minutes later that his guards saw the puddle of urine around his feet.

'If a snake isn't poisonous, all the more reason that it should pretend to be so,' muttered Chanakya quietly to Chandragupta and Sharangrao as they left the premises.

'Hurry up! Get the phenashmabhasam poured into all the wells before sunrise. Why must I deal with a bunch of incompetent cretins!' muttered Jeevasiddhi as he supervised the gangs of men who were busy poisoning the wells, cisterns, tanks and reservoirs of Pataliputra.

'Why must we kill innocents to take over Magadha?' Chandragupta had asked Chanakya.

His guru had replied, 'The first ones that drink water in the early hours of the morning are animals. This is the reason that the poisoning must be done at night—human loss shall be extremely limited. Word regarding the curse of the Aghorpanthis has already spread. It's a matter of time before the populace is willing to do anything that we demand.'

'And what happens when the council calls us and pleads with us, requesting that we revoke our curse?' asked Sharangrao.

'Simple. We tell them that Dhanananda must make a supreme sacrifice to rectify the breach. He must leave his palace to live in the forests—in exile. In the meantime, Jeevasiddhi shall get his men to pour the antidote prepared by us—the mithridatay—into the very water sources that were poisoned the previous night. Miracles do happen!' laughed Chanakya.

'But how do we take control of the city?' asked Chandragupta. These complex schemes of his guru always perplexed him. He much preferred a straight-forward battle that he could sink his teeth into.

'Dhanananda's commander—Bhadrashala—has been completely bought over by Jeevasiddhi. The moment Dhanananda exits the gates Bhadrashala will hand over command of the entire Magadha army to you, Chandra-gupta, so long as we pay him the predetermined bribe.'

'But we shall still have Paurus and the king of Kalinga standing at the eastern and western boundary walls itching for battle,' countered Chandragupta.

'They will not have to fight us. We will welcome them as allies with open arms,' said Chanakya.

'So we've gone through this excruciating journey running around naked like crazy cannibals just so that we can open the city gates and hand over the keys to the enemy?' asked Chandragupta, irked at the notion that the conceited Paurus was to be welcomed into Pataliputra.

Chanakya laughed. Turning serious, he said, 'Chandra-gupta, you seem to have forgotten one of the very first things I taught you. Keep your friends close and your enemies even closer.'

Bhadrashala stood to one side watching the procession of chariots, horses and elephants as the mighty Dhana-nanda left his palace and his kingdom to renounce the world along with his unfortunate wives and servants who didn't seem to be in any mood for renunciation. Bhadrashala was relieved—his debts had been cleared and he was now a very wealthy man.

Jeevasiddhi had been told by Chanakya to make sure Suvasini was nowhere near the king while his entourage moved out. She would still be needed for one final negotiation—or so he convinced himself. He was too proud to admit his lifelong infatuation with her.

'I want him killed,' said Chanakya to Sharangrao as he watched Dhanananda ride off in his chariot. The emperor looked as if he had aged ten years in a single day. Gone was the permanent evil smirk that adorned his face. Gone was the arrogant swagger. And gone was the kingdom of Magadha.

'If we have him eliminated, the entire populace shall think that we're behind it—and rightly so,' argued Sharangrao.

'Our bigger problem will be Bhadrashala. He seems to think he's still entitled to his position as army chief. He's been in touch with Rakshas who's been using our carrier pigeons to stay in touch with him,' whispered Jeevasiddhi.

'Has he formally surrendered his sword to us?' asked Chanakya.

'No,' replied Jeevasiddhi.

'Get that done immediately. I need his sword. I have a plan,' said Chanakya as Magadha's populace celebrated Dhanananda's departure. As the entourage left the gates of Pataliputra, Chanakya ordered that a message be sent to Paurus and the Kalinga monarch that they could enter the fortified city and expect a rousing welcome.

'You're allowing them inside against my will,' suggested Chandragupta to Chanakya. His teacher smiled. 'My problem,' said the acharya, 'is that you have a strong will but I have a weak won't!'

The two armies of Kaikey and Kalinga poured into Pataliputra. Chanakya stood at the entrance of the palace to greet the honoured guests. A hundred drummers beat a deafening welcome as their chariots rolled in.

The king of Kalinga was not as tall as Paurus but seemed just as strong. He wore a bronze helmet encrusted with cat's-eyes, a stone that was astrologically auspicious for him. Across his chest was a leather-padded vest armoured with ribs of iron. A long-handled broadsword hung from his belt. He stepped out of his chariot and was greeted by Chanakya. 'Welcome to Pataliputra, O great King,' he said conspicuously and then added softly, 'I sincerely hope that this kingdom shall be blessed by your benevolent rule.'

Paurus had dressed up for the occasion, his pale yellow turban sported a peacock feather fashioned from emeralds and sapphires to match the blue-green hue of the regal bird's plumage. As his towering hulk alighted from the chariot pulled by three white horses, Chanakya greeted him in humility with folded hands. 'Welcome to Pataliputra, O Divine Emperor,' he said, flattering the vain monarch in a loud voice. He then whispered, 'I hope that Magadha shall prosper under your able rule.' Paurus smiled. *I've taught the rogue his true place*, he thought.

When both sovereigns had settled into their luxurious accommodations, the shadowy figure went over to meet them individually. 'I've already told Chandragupta to withdraw from the contest for Magadha,' Chanakya said to each of them. 'The kingdom cannot be left headless. If Chandragupta isn't to rule, then the reins must necessarily be held by either one of you. Rather than getting the armies to clash, it would be better that the two great monarchs have a duel. Let the best man take Magadha,' he suggested. He knew that the suggestion would appeal to the vanities of both men.

＝

Paurus reached over and drew his sword. He held it lovingly, allowing the handle to become one with his

381

hand. He readied his steel, bracing himself for the clash of metal against metal that would follow.

Kalinga gripped his blade in his left hand. Being left-handed was actually an advantage, he thought. Most of his opponents lost their judgement when combating him. They were unused to fighting left-handers whereas he was extremely comfortable duelling right-handers.

The two danced around each other in a classic martial arts routine. As they circled one another they looked into each other's eyes. A single blink would determine who had the upper hand. As both warriors finally enagaged, sparks flew from their clashing swordblades.

There was a sudden pause in the noise as both stood suspended in a deadlock, each with his blade at the other's throat. The frozen stance continued for a few seconds till Kalinga blinked. Paurus thrust his weapon forward but Kalinga recovered smartly, using a three-sixty-degree motion to fend off the attack. Paurus drew blood but not life.

Both antagonists hyper-charged their attacks, putting their entire strength into the fight to the finish. The titans knew that the duel would end with a death but both also knew that they needed a conclusion—and fast.

Kalinga tripped and he knew in that split-second that his life was over. But he sprang up and lunged forward to attack anyway, while Paurus calmly stepped aside and with a single swipe of his sword caused a gaping tear in the side of Kalinga's neck. Blood gushed forth from the wound as Kalinga fell to the ground, his sword clattering noisily. In a profoundly chivalrous moment, Paurus threw his own sword to the ground and knelt before his opponent. As Kalinga's blood flowed and life ebbed, Paurus said, 'Goodbye, O valiant King. Paurus is proud to have fought you.'

One down, one more to go, thought Chanakya.

The unassuming house of dance instruction on Shiva Street, in the eastern district of Pataliputra, run by the former courtesan and funded by the Peacock Trust, was ready to graduate another student. Vishaka was undoubtedly one of their very best products. Her utterly seductive hourglass body, pearl-ivory complexion, twinkling emerald eyes, perfectly full ruby lips, delicate pert nose and cascading auburn hair drew men like they were flies to honey. This particular honey, though, was venomous.

Vedic astrology was based upon the twenty-seven *nakshatras*—or constellations—that occurred in the twelve zodiacs. Each nakshatra had an arc of thirteen degrees and twenty minutes and this, when multiplied by twenty-seven, provided Vedic astrologers with a complete circle of three hundred and sixty degrees. The position of the moon during the birth of a child in any of the twelve zodiacs was known as the *raashi*—the moon sign—of the person, but even more important than the raashi was the position of the moon within the nakshatra of the individual. The ancient seers of Magadha had observed that birth under specific positions of the moon made certain women extremely unlucky for the longevity of their partners. Girls born on Tuesdays during the seventh lunar day of Vishaka possessed unfortunately potent horoscopes that guaranteed that any man they cohabited with would die. They were Vishakanyas— poison maidens.

During graduation week, Vishaka and other girls in the school would have to prove they were truly immune to poison. Each day the graduates would line up while their principal, carrying a large covered basket, would make each girl put her hand inside it. Each basket contained successively more venomous snakes and Vishaka was one of the few who went through the entire week without the slightest reaction to the bites. She was as deadly as the snakes that had bitten her. The principal knew that Vishaka was the one she would offer to Chanakya. The founder of the school could not be offered anything less.

CHAPTER EIGHTEEN
Present Day

Harry Richardson sighed. History was definitely the most boring subject ever. Even the colourful Henry VIII and his fetish for newer and newer wives did not interest him. He adjusted his false collar and white tie as he reread his textbook. His neck was itching. He had never really got used to the school uniform—black tailcoat, waistcoat and pinstriped trousers. Eton was a pain in the arse.

He shifted his bottom uncomfortably on the chair in his private room in Godolphin House. His rump was still sore from five strokes of the cane that he had received from the headmaster the previous day for being late for division. His stomach grumbled. Eating breakfast, lunch and supper in Bekynton—the massive central dining complex—was plain unappetising. The only meals he enjoyed were the mid-morning Chambers snack and the mid-afternoon boys' tea, but today he had missed both because of the work he had to finish. How he longed to be home.

Harry was a handsome boy. His pale skin had a gold sheen to it and his dark hair was thick and lustrous. The seventh grader was already five feet four inches tall and had delicate features. His face was a picture of innocence —delicate lips, chiselled nose and emerald-green eyes.

He had asked his mother, Josephine, many times why he had to be in Eton when he could have lived with her in idyllic Grasmere and attend day school nearby. He was only allowed home for long leave every half, and for short leave, twice, once in the Michaelmas half and once in the Lent half. Mum would say that ever since his dad passed away, she had to look after Harry alone. The only way she could afford a decent life for them— including the outrageous Eton boarding fees—was by working at a furious pace. *How hard could a painter's work be*, thought Harry. Most artists painted because the sale of their work allowed them to eat, drink and copulate. And she never seemed to sell any of her paintings—the house was full of them. Josephine had chosen not to tell Harry that his patron was an old man in India—a man whose generosity allowed Josephine to lead an artist's life—Pandit Gangasagar Mishra. Ever since Josephine and her father had looked after Chandini, Gangasagar had considered it his duty to look after Josephine.

Eton provided for every imaginable sport one could think of—soccer, rugby, hockey, cricket, basketball, rowing, athletics, fencing, martial arts—the list was endless. For the less sporting, every musical instrument— including the didgeridoo—was offered in the state-of-the-art music department, which included an incredible music technology suite and recording studio. There were two theatres in the school and the theatrically inclined could engage in school plays, house plays and even scriptwriting. Beyond this, Eton offered painting, drawing, sculpture, ceramics, printmaking, debating and elocution.

But Harry's only interest was his violin. His had been among the eight music scholarships that had been awarded the previous year and it had been a test of endurance to get it. The Music Scholarship Examination was held at Eton in late January and candidates were required to play two contrasting pieces on their principal instrument and one piece on their second instrument, to sight-read, undergo aural tests and perform scales appropriate to their grades. Harry had passed with flying colours—he had been a Grade Eight on the violin even before he entered Eton. It was almost as though he had been born to the sounds of a string quartet in the background.

Josephine bought a gramophone that she installed in one corner of Chandini's room. She managed to source long-playing records of Chandini's favourite music—violin concertos by Bach, Beethoven, Brahms, Tchaikovsky, and Paganini. Chandini would sit by the window gazing out at the serene Grasmere surrounded by gentle walks and craggy peaks. Josephine would often go to the market while Chandini meditated to the sounds of the violin. Sometimes, when Josephine returned, she would notice that Chandini's eyes were moist and her face stained with dried tears. Sounds of the violin reminded her too much of Geoffrey. Josephine tried to cheer her up by placing a vase of fresh pink chrysanthemums on the windowsill every few days—they were Chandini's favourite flowers.

Eight weeks after moving in, Chandini was ready to deliver. She had not realised that it would be the equivalent of pushing a bowling ball through a nostril. Josephine held her hand while the matron checked her cervix for dilation. Blood and amniotic fluid were seeping out as the nurse urged her to push. Chandini pushed and blacked out as she felt a body covered in slippery gob gush out of her.

When Chandini awoke, she realised that she had been cleaned up and wheeled back into her room with the flower-patterned curtains that framed a picture postcard view of the lake. Josephine was sitting by her side, gently running her fingers through Chandini's hair. Chandini took one look at Josephine and she knew instantly.

'I'm so sorry, honey,' Josephine whispered, 'the doctor says you can have others but this one was stillborn'.

⚊⚊

'Bhabua State Cooperative Bank,' said Gangasagar.

'What is that?' asked Agrawalji.

'I need to ask our appointee, the Reserve Bank of India's governor, to investigate the bank.'

'Why?'

Gangasagar held up a share transfer form. He had a whole bunch of them in front of him. 'See this transaction? Shiva Finance Pvt. Ltd sold this batch of stocks to Vishnu Investments Pvt. Ltd.'

'Since when did selling company stocks become a crime? In any case, what does it have to do with an unobtrusive little cooperative bank in the state of Bihar?'

'Dig a little deeper, my friend. Vishnu Investments Pvt. Ltd sold this same batch of shares to Brahma Securities Pvt. Ltd.'

'I'm still confused, Ganga. The whole point of share-trading is to buy and sell. What exactly have these companies done wrong? And how is Bhabua State Cooperative Bank involved?'

'Don't you get it? The sacred trinity of the Hindus—Brahma-Vishnu-Shiva?'

'Sorry, I just don't see what you're driving at.'

'Brahma—the creator, Vishnu—the preserver, Shiva—the destroyer. Three facets of one single entity. Don't you see that all three entities are owned by the same promoter?'

'Even so, what's the problem?'

'Here's the problem. Shiva sells this batch of stocks to Vishnu on a Monday for 140 rupees per share, the prevailing market price. The next day—Tuesday—Vishnu sells the shares to Brahma for 150 rupees per share, a little higher than the market price. On Wednesday, Brahma sells the shares back to Shiva for 160 rupees each!'

'So?'

'Shiva loses twenty rupees per share and Vishnu and Brahma gain ten rupees each. It's a zero sum game if all the entities belong to the same promoter!'

'But why do it? There's nothing to gain.'

'Because if you do it often enough with the same set of shares and with enough money, you'll end up driving the market price upwards. The share scrip that was traded by these three entities went up fourteen per cent in three days! Three days!'

'And where does the money for these trades come from?'

'Bhabua State Cooperative Bank.'

'But banks have to maintain a cash reserve ratio. There's no way that a small bank in Bihar's rural heartland can possibly advance large amounts for stock speculation without the regulator knowing,' argued Agrawalji.

'Simple solution. Banks only need to report their cash balances to the Reserve Bank of India every fortnight. There are thirteen days in between when no reporting happens. Trades are executed during these thirteen days and the accounts settled on the fourteenth. The regulator never knows.'

'So why not go after the share traders? They're the ones who are speculating.'

'Because Brahma, Vishnu and Shiva are owned by a very important man.'

'Who?'

'The chief minister of Bihar.'

'And what do you hope to achieve by going after Bhabua District Cooperative Bank?'

'What happens each time the music stops in a game of musical chairs?'

'There is always one chair short?'

'Precisely. Freeze the bank's transactions in the middle of their reporting fortnight. They'll be unable to explain the mismatch in funds. That's the reason I wanted my own man in the Reserve Bank of India.'

'And what do you gain?'

'A nervous chief minister of Bihar.'

Chandini reached the village after travelling the last mile on foot. Jitaura Musahar Tola in East Champaran district of Bihar was a village without roads, electricity, drinking water, schools or hospitals. It was almost as though civilisation had decided to entirely bypass Jitaura.

She was spending the night in a Dalit home, if the hut could be called that. Infested with mosquitoes, bandicoots and snakes, the shack provided virtually no shelter from the elements. Spreading a mat on the mud floor outside the hut, she held an impromptu open-house with other Dalits and shared a frugal meal—rotis, onion and salt—with them. These were human beings who were labelled *untouchables* by Brahmins at one time. Even though untouchability had been banned half a century earlier, the stigma remained. She was moved to tears as she heard of poor labourers being forced to sell their children into bonded labour so that they could earn a meal.

Back in New Delhi, two days later, she met Ganga-sagar at her official bungalow at 19, Teen Murti Lane. 'Why did you send me there? The situation is so completely hopeless! Out of two hundred children in the hamlet, only three attend school! The nearest school is six miles away! Forget about hospitals, there isn't even a dispensary to provide basic medication. Sanitation doesn't exist—typhoid and cholera are the villagers' most frequent callers, visiting them every now and again. Doesn't it worry you?' she asked.

'Worry is like a rocking chair; it keeps you in motion, but gets you nowhere,' replied Gangasagar, swaying back and forth on the lounger he was seated on. 'I have asked Agrawalji to set up a privately-funded trust. The money from R&S won't be used entirely for political ends. It shall identify Dalit villages in Bihar—the poorest of the poor—and focus on a few simple issues.'

'What issues?'

'A primary school, clean drinking water, a basic health-care centre and the guarantee of daily nutrition.'

'And which villages are the beneficiaries?'

'Villages in Rohtas and Bhabua districts of Bihar.'

'Does the choice of Rohtas and Bhabua have anything to do with the fact that these districts are the electoral strongholds of Bihar's Dalit chief minister?' asked Chandini shrewdly.

'The chief minister of Bihar wishes to have a meeting with you,' said Menon.

'Ah!' said Gangasagar smiling.

'Why are you so interested in Bihar?' asked Chandini, 'Our stronghold is in Uttar Pradesh.'

'Dear girl, Bihar sends fifty-four MP's to the Lok Sabha. During the last general elections the chief minister of Bihar had a seat-sharing arrangement with the ruling party. His party contested fifty per cent of the seats and the ruling party contested the other fifty. He now wants to contest *all* the seats on his own in the next elections.'

'So why does he need us?'

'Because if he has an alliance with us, we would contest only Uttar Pradesh seats—not Bihar's, and he would contest only Bihar seats—not Uttar Pradesh's. It works for both of us.'

'But you sent me to his stronghold in Bihar!'

'How else could I have got him on the run?'

'Then you used Agrawalji to get his bank in trouble with the regulators.'

'A run on the bank was the perfect method to set the chief minister on the run. Judging by the looks of it, my scheme seems to have worked!'

'But Bihar in itself cannot get us a majority in the house. Even assuming that eighty-five seats of Uttar Pradesh are with the ABNS and fifty-four of Bihar with him, we only make a hundred and thirty-nine. That's still only half of what we need to form a government on our own.'

'The Bihar chief minister will do the rest.'

'How?'

'Didn't you know that he's an intimate friend of the leader of the Opposition?'

'The Americans have decided to supply a couple of billion dollars' worth of military hardware to Pakistan,' stated the RAW chief. 'The news isn't public as yet but will be announced next month by the White House.'

'They're playing a dangerous game,' said Chandini. 'They know that Pakistan's army is busy fighting India rather than concentrating on their real enemy, Islamic militancy.'

'Can't we convince the Americans that it isn't in their own interest to be supplying arms to Pakistan?' enquired the director of the Intelligence Bureau.

'Everything's been tried. There's no diplomatic channel that hasn't been explored. Our lobbyists even met with the American President's latest infatuation. She's rather pretty—a little chubby though,' said Chandini smiling.

'I have an idea,' said the director.

'What?' asked Chandini.

'Gas,' said the director.

'I'm sorry to hear that. Can I get you an anti-flatulent?' asked Chandini.

'Not gas. Gas centrifuges,' said the embarrassed director.

'What are you both going on about?' asked the RAW chief crossly. He was feeling left out of the earth-shattering discussion on wind.

'The designs of the gas centrifuges used by the Pakistanis to produce nuclear material at their atomic reactors were stolen from a company called Uronico in Germany,' explained the director.

'So what? Most of Pakistan's nuclear programme consists of stolen technology,' said Chandini.

'Yes, but Uronico's designs were based on a Russian design. The Russians would willingly share the design with us, if you asked them,' said the director.

'Why should I want to obtain antiquated designs for a technology that we already have?' asked Chandini incredulously.

'Because I have a man in my department who is terrific at creating antiquated designs—he used to work for the Archaeological Survey,' said the director.

'And how would that help us?' snapped the RAW chief.

'We could have the drawings secretly sold to North Korea and Libya,' said the director.

'That's preposterous! We've never engaged in pro-liferation,' said Chandini.

'That's where my chap comes into the picture,' said the director, relishing the attention he was now com-manding. The former police commissioner was now in his element. 'He'll build in a couple of flaws that make the technology useless. But he'll make it authentic enough to ensure provenance.'

'But how does this help in our negotiations with the Americans?' asked Chandini.

'Ah! The designs will indicate that they are Uronico plans redrawn in Pakistan. I'm assuming that with the ruckus that will follow, you'll be able to get the Americans to drop their plans to supply hardware to proliferators.'

━━

'I'm assuming that a large chunk of the money coming in as commissions from R&S is being used as we discussed?' asked Gangasagar.

Agrawalji nodded. 'Besides a small fraction for the work of the trust in Bihar, the balance is all going towards buying the shares of Sentiosys. We now own five per cent of the company.'

'Good,' said Gangasagar.

'But why are we buying Sentiosys?' asked Agrawalji. 'There are better software companies that we could invest in. We'd double the return on our investment!'

'I like the sound of its name,' said Gangasagar, winking at his former boss.

━━

'The leader of the Opposition on a point of order?' asked the Speaker.

394

'Yes, Mr Speaker, sir. My question was regarding this government's handling of the recent hijack—'

'The leader of the Opposition shall resume his seat. The Prime Minister has just begun narrating his version of the events. This house shall hear him—'

'On a point of order, Mr Speaker. The Prime Minister was not even present in the control room. The minister for external affairs was. We'd like to hear from her,' argued the leader of the Opposition.

The Prime Minister sat down, allowing Chandini to get up and speak. 'The hon'ble minister for external affairs may address the house,' said the Speaker.

Sitting in the visitor's gallery, Gangasagar smiled. The leader of the Opposition was turning Chandini into a star.

'*Adi Shakti, Namo Namah; Sarab Shakti, Namo Namah; Prithum Bhagvati, Namo Namah; Kundalini Mata Shakti; Mata Shakti, Namo Namah*,' chanted Gangasagar to himself.

━━

'You should resign. In fact, the entire ABNS contingent in the Cabinet should resign.'

'But we're seen as part of the government,' argued Chandini. 'We can't be seen to be pulling it down!'

'Not unless you have a very good reason,' said Gangasagar. He carefully opened his little silver box—a gift from Agrawalji—took out a paan and thoughtfully placed it in his mouth. He allowed the juices to swirl around inside his mouth as his brain whirred—food for thought. He was sitting along with Chandini in the backseat of her official car as they drove towards the building in South Block that housed the ministry of external affairs.

'And the good reason?' asked Chandini.

'This is the perfect opportunity to bring down this government and bring about fresh elections,' said Gangasagar. 'I had a meeting with our friend, the director of the Intelligence Bureau, this morning. He said Rashid was released from interrogation at the behest of the Prime Minister.'

'Why was that man released? He was plotting to kill me!'

'While that's true,' said Gangasagar, 'it's equally true that Rashid was actually Makhmud, a RAW agent, and you—my dear—were instrumental in having him arrested by the Chinese. Can't blame a man for getting upset.' He grinned when he saw the scowl on Chandini's face.

He quickly resumed. 'But there's no way that the prime minister can reveal that Rashid's a RAW agent. This is our opportunity to glorify Ikram, the ABNS hero who died for his country. It's also our chance to demonise the dastardly prime minister—releasing the kingpin of the plot, Rashid. And finally you, the noble inheritor of Ikram's legacy—resigning in disgust along with all your colleagues of the ABNS!'

'How will we prove it?'

'The IB director is willing to go public. He'll announce that he had Rashid in custody and that he was forced to release him at the behest of the prime minister.'

'If we resign, this government collapses. You do realise that?'

'This government has seen its own finance minister and prime minister resign in the aftermath of numerous scams. Our arrangement with the Bihar chief minister is in place. The leader of the Opposition is waiting for a sign. We should not wait any further.'

'What sign is the Opposition leader waiting for?'

'It looks like the letter "R" dissected by a horizontal line.'

'Huh?'

'The rupee sign.'

'These are difficult times. The Opposition seems to be sharpening their knives. Of course, I am with you. The whole ABNS is with you. You have our assured support,' said Gangasagar to the prime minister.

'Then why am I hearing stories about the imminent resignation of your ministers from the Cabinet, Gangasagarji?' asked the worried premier.

'Rumours travel fast but don't stay put for as long as the truth. You should disregard such stories.'

'I'm happy that we've had this discussion. Now, what is it that you wanted to see me about?'

'Well, given the uncertainties that surround us, I believe that some amount of divine intervention is called for.'

'What do you suggest, Gangasagarji. I didn't know you were one to believe in praying for God's blessings.'

'Sometimes, kneeling keeps us in good standing,' joked Gangasagar. 'In any case, I plan to visit Mumbai later today. As you know, the Ganesha festival is currently being celebrated and I'm paying my respects to Lalbaugcha Raja.'

The prime minister nodded. He'd heard about Lalbaugcha Raja but had never had the opportunity of visiting. Each year during the festival, a massive twelve-foot high idol of Ganesha would be installed in Lalbaug—in the heart of Mumbai's textile mill district—and over a million devotees would throng to him each day over the next eleven days.

'It is claimed that this year over a hundred million rupees will get collected as offerings to the deity,' said the premier.

'Absolutely. I have brought here with me a few thousand rupees, which I would like you to hold in your hands before I take this offering with me to Lalbaugcha Raja on your behalf and pray for our continued success,' said Gangasagar as he handed over a bundle of crisp thousand-rupee notes to the prime minister.

'Thank you, Gangasagarji, for being such a good friend of my government. Man's way leads to a hopeless end but God's way leads to endless hope,' said the prime minister as he handed back the cash to Gangasagar.

The horseshoe-shaped chamber of the Lok Sabha had the Speaker's chair located between the two arms. In the pit of the chamber, just below his chair, was the Table of the House where the secretary-general, secretariat officers and recorders of the proceedings sat. To the Speaker's right were the government benches and to his left sat the members of the Opposition. The prime minister sat at his customary seat in the front row of the government benches. Towards the left was the special box reserved for VIPs inside which sat Gangasagar. Also seated on the first row of the government benches was Chandini. Dressed in a citrus-green saree, her ensemble—together with her green eyes—blended in perfectly with the green leather of the chamber of the world's largest democracy.

Overlooking the chamber opposite the Speaker was a large portrait of Vithalbhai Patel, the first elected president of the Central Legislative Assembly, a man who had stood for high parliamentary traditions. The face in the portrait did not seem to foresee that all parliamentary traditions were about to be broken that day.

'The hon'ble minister for power may address the House,' said the Speaker.

'Hon'ble Speaker, sir, I beg to move for leave to introduce a Bill to provide for the establishment of a Central Electricity Regulatory Commission and for matters connected therewith or incidental thereto,' said the minister for power.

'Motion moved,' said the Speaker mechanically.

'Sir, I have given a notice under Rule 72 to oppose the introduction of this Bill,' said the leader of the Opposition, rising from his seat.

'Yes, yes. The Hon'ble leader of the Opposition may address the House,' said the Speaker.

'Sir, I hold in my hands over a million rupees. This money was given as a bribe by the Prime Minister to one of our honourable members to secure his vote for this Bill in Parliament. I demand an immediate statement—'

The premier's face turned ashen as the proceedings descended into chaos. The uproar was deafening, with the Opposition members shouting 'Shame!' and the occupants of the government benches yelling 'Liar!' The leader of the Opposition, still standing with bundles of cash in his hands, screamed above the din, 'These notes were handed over by the prime minister himself. Let the country's investigating agencies check to see whether his fingerprints are on them or not!'

Trying to be heard above the din, the Speaker shouted, 'I request all the members to please take their seats. There's simply no reason why this House cannot maintain dignity and decorum.'

'It isn't possible to maintain decorum when the prime minister himself indulges in acts of corruption—this government is rotten to the core and this House has lost confidence in it!' The voice was not from the Opposition benches. It was Chandini's. 'At this moment, all eight members of the ABNS have handed in their resignations. This administration has allowed a key operative responsible for the sabotage attempt on my helicopter and the subsequent hijack of IC-617 to walk free! Is this how we should honour the memory of the late Ikram Shaikh, who sacrificed his life for the nation?'

The members of the Opposition rushed into the well of the house and the Speaker was left with little alternative but to adjourn the proceedings. In the visitor's gallery, Gangasagar watched the happenings and snickered. Chandini had been planning to hand in her resignation to the prime minister the previous day. He had advised her against it.

'But you advised us to resign. Why not let us hand in our letters?' she had demanded.

'Because I want live television cameras present when you do,' he had said.

━◼━

'How are we doing with Sentiosys?' asked Gangasagar.

'We now own twenty-five per cent of the company.'

'Good,' said Gangasagar.

'I still don't understand why we're buying Sentiosys,' said Agrawalji. 'The company has shown losses for the past three years. The commissions flowing in from R&S are huge and yet we persist in throwing good money into bad deals. Why?'

'I like the cover design of their annual report,' said Gangasagar cheerily.

━◼━

'Did you get Chandini to agree to procuring the gas centrifuge designs from the Russians?' asked Gangasagar. The IB director nodded.

'And were these redrafted to resemble the Uronico plans, as I asked?'

'Yes—beautifully and aesthetically.'

'Did you get the RAW chief to sell the plans to the North Koreans?' asked the Pandit.

'They fell over themselves to buy it,' said the director. 'They're under the impression they've acquired the plans through the Pakistani black market.'

'And the money?'

'Transferred to the Liechtenstein bank account number that you gave me.'

'Good man. Your debt to me for having you promoted from police commissioner to Director Intelligence Bureau is now repaid.'

The backyard of the sadhvi's cottage in Simla was quiet. The sadhvi—the blessed mother—sat facing a roaring fire. Opposite her, sat three prime ministers. The first was her father—the previous premier who had been forced to resign because of Gangasagar's press leaks about his relationship with the sadhvi. The second was the man who had clambered down a rope ladder from a helicopter following Gangasagar's advice—the former defence minister. He had usurped the prime ministerial chair only to have his government pulled down by the telecom, fodder, SEZ and petroleum scams. The third was the current prime minister—the home minister whose portfolio had been passed on to Ikram—brought down by the recent cash-for-votes scandal and just a caretaker till the next elections.

In front of the three men lay the carcass of a goat covered in black cloth, with a small idol, moulded out of dough, placed on top. Surrounding it were odd items such as lemons, nails, yellow rice and chicken bones. The sadhvi was tending the fire. '*Om lingalingalinalinga, kilikili…*' she chanted as she threw mustard seeds and secret ingredients into the fire, producing strange colours, crackling sounds and odd-smelling vapours.

She nodded at her father. He dipped the old-fashioned quill into a bowl containing the goat's blood and carefully wrote 'Gangasagar' on a chit of paper. He then reached over and handed the chit to her. She dipped the chit into a pot of melted butter and then threw it into the fire. It burst into flames.

She sprinkled water on the dough idol and mopped it with peacock feathers while delicately placing a string around the idol's neck. She gestured for the former defence minister to hold one end of the string while she held the other. As they both pulled, the string tightened around the doughboy's neck like a hangman's noose until the head separated and rolled into the fire.

She then signalled to the cash-for-votes-stung premier. With each chant by the sadhvi of 'Om lingalingalinalinga, kilikili...' the caretaker prime minister would pick up a nail from the pile next to him and thrust it into the torso of the headless dough idol. The sadhvi laughed and the three men smiled in satisfaction. The black magic curse was final. That machinator, Gangasagar, was to learn a lesson.

≡≡

The meeting was held in the seclusion of the sadhvi's cottage. The reporter could not believe he was sitting with the man whose reputation he had helped destroy. The sadhvi-tainted ex-prime minister offered him a cup of tea and then settled into his own armchair. 'I requested you here to tell you that I have nothing against you. You were simply doing your job. The fourth estate must remain independent and fearless if democracy is to flourish in India,' said the seasoned politician. The reporter shrugged his shoulders but kept quiet.

'I'm given to understand that before you were offered the juicy tidbit about the sadhvi—the blessed mother—being my illegitimate daughter, you were out sniffing another story. A story about Chandini,' said the former statesman, smiling at the reporter.

'What if I was?' asked the reporter, trying his best to appear uninterested even though his ears had perked up.

'What if I told you that a trust fund was established by Gangasagar in Guernsey—in the Channel Islands—in order to meet the education and living expenses of a mother and her son in Grasmere in the Lake District?'

'So? The old man's not a brahmacharya after all. Big deal if he banged up a woman—so did you!' said the reporter winking at the previous premier.

'You've not understood the story, my friend. Gangasagar has nothing to do with the mother or child. That child belongs to Chandini—the beloved prime-ministerial candidate of the masses of India!'

'And how did you get this information?' asked the reporter, knowing full well that if someone else were to have asked him that question he would have said he was not at liberty to reveal his sources.

'The former finance minister obtained the information for me from the director of the Guernsey Financial Services Commission. A special favour,' explained the wrinkled and forgotten prime minister.

'My sources have indicated that a child was born to Chandini but that it was stillborn,' said the reporter, carefully choosing his words. 'She had tried to abort it earlier, but had a change of heart.'

'Your sources are wrong,' smiled the politician.

'I shall need to verify the facts for myself.'

'That's why I've arranged a ticket and foreign exchange. How quickly can you get going?'

'There is a eunuch called Hameeda who lives near Tundey's Kebabs in Lucknow. I need to meet her,' said the caretaker prime minister. The bedlam in Parliament had forced another round of general elections on India and the country was under President's Rule. His government was a lame duck.

'I didn't realise the First Lady had given birth, I shall immediately—' started his private secretary.

'It isn't the fucking First Lady,' snapped the premier, realising a tad too late that he had created a title of sorts for his wife. 'I don't need blessings for a newborn. I need this particular eunuch. That's all—get it done!'

<hr>

Hameeda had been asked to dress well for the occasion. She couldn't be taken inside the prime minister's bungalow looking like a eunuch. What would the security guards think? The prime minister's private secretary had arranged for a haircut and a business suit. 'Will I be able to keep the clothes?' asked Hameeda.

The private secretary had nodded. No one would want the clothes after they'd been used by her, anyway. The security detail at the gate issued Hameeda a visitor's pass. It was laminated and suspended from a blue neck cord. The private secretary handed it over to her. 'It works for most of South Block, North Block and Rashtrapati Bhavan for the next sixty minutes. Return it to the guard on your way out,' he said as Hameeda hung the bar-coded pass around her neck.

As they walked into the office, the PM looked at Hameeda and asked slyly, 'What would you do if I told you that there's an opportunity to get back at Gangasagar?'

'I spend each waking moment plotting ways to kill him. I even see myself murdering him in my dreams.

He didn't just have my balls chopped off, he castrated my life!' spat out Hameeda.

'There's a way you can destroy him, honey. Tell Chandini that Gangasagar arranged for Ikram to be bumped off during the hijack encounter.'

'But that isn't true. Ikrambhai was killed by Rashid.'

'But she'll believe you. You lost your family jewels trying to protect her!'

The meeting with Hameeda lasted less than twenty minutes. On her way out Hameeda stumbled and, much to the embarrassment of the hapless private secretary, fell on him with her arms around his neck. 'Seems like we're destined for one another,' she whispered lecherously into his ear. He shuddered.

As Hameeda left, she dropped her visitor's pass into the slot for used passes. She didn't need it anymore. She had the private secretary's instead. Training under Sachla Devi had its advantages.

The former finance minister was seated in a comfortable armchair, flanked by Rungta and Somany. 'You sacrificed me to resurrect your deals. I can understand that. All's fair in business. But why did you agree to let ten per cent of your revenues go to Agrawalji? All you're doing is making them financially stronger,' he urged.

'I agree that we overpaid,' said Rungta, 'but now we're stuck. It's impossible to back out.'

'There is one way,' said the politician softly. 'Drive a wedge between Gangasagar and Chandini. She's the one who now has a national stature. She could quite easily be the next prime minister. Make her hate Gangasagar and she'll happily go along with revoking any arrangements Gangasagar may have made.'

'But how do we drive that wedge between them?' asked Somany.

'If the rumour mills are true, she had an affair with her secretary—a chap called Shankar. Gangasagar was so upset that he had him killed in a hit-and-run.'

'How does one prove it?' asked Somany.

'When it comes to matters of the heart, it won't be your job to prove anything, my friends. It'll be for Gangasagar to disprove it.'

❚❚❚

The caretaker prime minister called in his private secretary. 'This election is going to be different,' he said, sipping his iced tea.

'How so, sir?' asked his respectful private secretary, his confidant of many years.

'Ikram's not around. Who's going to make sure that no dirty tricks are employed in Uttar Pradesh? Ikram's goons would man all the polling stations and would ensure that no ballot-stuffing could happen. Gangasagar has lost a valuable asset.'

'So is that an opportunity?' enquired the private secretary, smiling at his boss.

❚❚❚

'How much of Sentiosys do we now own?' asked Gangasagar.

'Fifty-one per cent,' replied Agrawalji, shaking his head. It had been one of the worst investments that he'd ever made.

'Excellent,' said Gangasagar, 'we can now call the shots in management.'

'I am unable to understand you most times, Ganga. You're so damned obstinate. Are you going to tell me why this company is so important to you?'

'I'm told their CEO is just twenty-four. I like support-ing youngsters,' said Gangasagar, chuckling.

Gangasagar was busy catching up on the previous day's neglected newspapers. He folded the paper he was reading and dropped it on the floor in a pile of other discarded papers. Gangasagar, Chandini, Agrawalji, Menon and Major Bedi were having their session on strategy in Gangasagar's cubby-hole flat in Kanpur.

'Have you considered moving out of this dump?' Chandini had asked him after they had joined the government in New Delhi. 'You're one of the most powerful men in the country and yet you persist with a life of penury.'

'Never forget my lesson about the power of renunci-ation, dear girl,' he had replied.

'Isn't this meant to be a meeting with Major Bedi on election strategy? We still need to finalise candidates for the upcoming Lok Sabha elections and you continue to read your newspapers,' said Chandini irritably.

'There are four of you to decide election strategy. I'd rather keep myself posted on what's going on in the country,' replied Gangasagar.

'But you never used to read the *Economic Times* and *Financial Express*. Why have you started getting interested in financial matters rather than political?' asked Chandini.

'It's all the bloody same! Political power hopes to control the economic resources of the country. Economic power hopes to control the politicians,' he replied jovially. He resumed scanning the company reports, particularly those of Sentiosys.

'So, if I may have your attention for a moment, our candidates for the eighty-five Uttar Pradesh seats will be a mix of incumbents and freshers—' began Major Bedi.

Gangasagar looked up from his crumpled *Financial Express* and asked, 'What was our share of the vote in the last elections?'

'Thirty per cent,' replied Major Bedi.

'And yet we won seventy-six per cent of the seats. What does that tell you?' asked Gangasagar.

'That we won not because we had a high share of the vote but because the remaining votes were adequately divided,' said Bedi, adjusting his turban and attempting to make himself comfortable in Gangasagar's untidy surroundings.

'Don't worry about identifying strong candidates who can increase our vote-share. Vote-share is meaningless. Instead, concentrate on causing divisions and fractures in everyone else's share,' said Gangasagar triumphantly.

'And how do you propose we do that?' asked Chandini.

'I'm working on it,' said Gangasagar, absentmindedly looking at the Sentiosys financials in the newspaper lying before him.

━━

'Ikrambhai's missing this time around. There'll be no one to handle the polling booths if they're captured by the Opposition,' said Menon to Gangasagar once all the others had left.

'You know what makes a humble sandwich taste great?' asked Gangasagar, ignoring the observation regarding Ikram's absence.

'What?' asked Menon.

'Chips on the side,' said Gangasagar.

━━

'EVM!' said Gangasagar loudly.

'Excuse me sir?' said Menon.

'Electronic Voting Machines. They're being used in these elections. No more paper ballots.'

'Ah, yes. They're saying it's more efficient and accurate,' said Menon.

'Do you know what's at the heart of these EVMs, Menon?'

'What?'

'Chips,' said Gangasagar. 'The EVM is like a sand-wich. It's of no use without the chips!'

<hr>

'Did you know that it's a complex algorithm that powers the chips inside these EVMs?' asked Gangasagar.

Agrawalji stopped pouring the tea from his cup into his saucer. 'No, I didn't,' he said. 'Any reason I should know this?'

'Well, the EVMs are made by different companies but they all use the same central chip. It's the one that contains the software to make the machine register a vote and to tally the results.'

'Ah, I see,' said Agrawalji, slurping his tea nosily from the saucer.

'Ever learnt any Latin?' asked Gangasagar suddenly.

'No. I studied English, Hindi and Sanskrit. Never Latin.'

'That explains it.'

'What?'

'Why you didn't realise that the word *vote* in English translates to *sentio* in Latin. You now own the company that makes the chips—Sentiosys.'

<hr>

'But—but—that's cheating, Ganga. We can't rig these machines to give ourselves more votes,' sputtered Agrawalji. There was seemingly no limit to Gangasagar's schemes.

'I agree. If the machines were rigged to give us more votes, it would be cheating. But what if they were rigged to give others more votes?' he asked innocently.

'Are you a raving lunatic?' asked Agrawalji, 'You want to rig the machines so that they give more votes to others?'

'Only to those who need them,' said Gangasagar.

'Just what are you going on about, Ganga?' asked the exasperated Agrawalji.

'Let's take the example of a hypothetical ABNS candidate fighting in a given constituency. Supposing our candidate has fifty-one per cent of the vote share, it's obvious that he's the winner. Right?'

'Right.'

'But what if he has fifty per cent—not fifty-one—instead? What determines whether he wins or loses?'

'How the other fifty per cent is distributed?'

'Correct. If the other fifty per cent is consolidated with one candidate, we have a tie. But if it's divided across two or more candidates, our candidate wins. Now, what happens if our candidate has only forty per cent of the vote-share?'

'Well, his winning or losing depends on how the remaining sixty per cent is distributed.'

'Correct. The remaining sixty per cent could be with one candidate, in which case our man loses. If the sixty per cent is divided across two candidates, our man still loses if the sixty per cent is divided fifty-ten, but if the sixty per cent is divided thirty-thirty our man wins.'

'So what is it that you plan to do?'

'The algorithm will determine dynamically what our candidate's vote-share is. It won't add fictitious votes to our tally but simply reallocate residual votes. I've always maintained that winning isn't only about increasing our strength but also about reducing the enemy's. And let me tell you, we're surrounded by our enemies—people who won't hesitate to use every dirty trick in the book!'

Harry Richardson was excited. The two hundred and fifty seats of the Eton College Concert Hall were packed to capacity. It had been his first ever solo performance and he had been accompanied by the Eton College Symphony Orchestra. The concert had been arranged after the violin virtuoso Itzhak Perlman had heard Harry perform while on a visit to Eton. He then wrote his observations to the school. 'Let's begin with Harry Richardson. He's an extraordinary violinist with a virtuoso technique fused to a musical mind that won't take the slightest detail for granted. Harry seems to find answers where others often don't see questions...'

Tonight's performance had been of *Chaconne in D minor from Partita No. 2 in D minor*, Bach's most famous piece of experimental music. The *Chaconne* was considered the pinnacle of the solo violin repertoire in Bach's time because it covered almost every aspect of violin-playing. Harry had chosen one of the most difficult pieces ever played and executed it flawlessly. He could see his mother—Josephine—in the front row, enthusiastically applauding with the rest of the audience. They were giving him a standing ovation. She was so proud of her precious boy.

The endorsement by Perlman had also ensured that there were members of the press in the audience. Not just from Britain. Flashes lit up the room as photographs were snapped of the child prodigy. In the distance, Harry could even see an Indian reporter clicking away.

'You killed Geoffrey!' she screamed.

'Chandini, listen to me—' began Gangasagar.

'You even had Shankar murdered!' she wailed.

'There were reasons—' he started.

'And what about Ikrambhai. Did you have him killed too?'

'As God's my witness, I loved that rogue. I'm willing to accept all your accusations but not that!' thundered Gangasagar.

'Uncle Ganga. I always knew that you were a ruthless man—that you'd do anything and everything to achieve your ends—but I never thought of you as heartless. Today, my opinion's changed,' she said, dabbing at her tears with the edge of her saree.

'The election results have already come out. It's certain that you're going to be the next prime minister! Chandini, this is not the time to be losing focus. We still have miles to cover.'

'There's no *we*—only *you* and *I*. And I think we both need to go our separate ways. If I ditch you I'll get the support of our caretaker prime minister who hates you anyway. He controls exactly the number of MPs that I need besides those of Bihar and Uttar Pradesh.'

'But he'll prop you up only to pull you down, Chandini. Don't make a pact with the devil,' said Gangasagar.

'Why not?' she shouted. 'I made one with you, didn't I?'

The microphone received the sound waves and vibrated the thin diaphragm, which produced an electrical signal. The electric signals were then beamed out by a transmitter to the receiver several houses away. In an air-conditioned room sat the caretaker prime minister. He laughed as he heard the conversation.

Chandini stormed out of Gangasagar's flat as Gangasagar shouted after her, 'Chandini, come back, I did it for you—' but he was unable to complete the sentence. His words were interrupted by a violent spasm of coughing. He ignored it until he noticed the red specks of blood on his kerchief.

CHAPTER NINETEEN
About 2300 years ago

The dacoits stood on a massive rock ledge and
observed Dhanananda's entourage make its way
across the woods. Their leader, a thug called Bibhatsaka,
was famed to have killed over a thousand people. His
dirty hair was wiry and unkempt. He was clean-shaven
except for his moustache which was curled into circles
on his cheeks. He wore a stained white dhoti, thick
leather sandals and had a dark grey blanket thrown
around him like a cloak. His skin was dark and leathery—
the result of inadequate bathing over many years—and
his teeth were stained with betel nut.

He spat out a thick pellet of phlegm as he watched
his prey. His eyes, bloodshot from excessive drink,
matched the dark red tilak that was prominent on his
forehead. This particular tilak, however, had not been
made using vermillion pigment. It was a blood mark
from his latest victim. In his hand he held a cutlass, his
lucky charm, not so lucky for the thousand throats it
had slit open. In his other hand was a sword that had

been gifted to him the previous night. It was worth it, thought Bibhatsaka. Each victim had not only yielded loot but had also provided sacrifice to the Goddess Kali. He had built a temple for her by the riverbank and always ensured that the blood of a fresh victim was offered to her each day. The spot where his temple stood was avoided by all and sundry. It was called *Kali Ghat*.

'We shall strike when they camp for the night,' said Bibhatsaka. 'There are too many people in the party, including guards. Better to catch them completely unaware. This is going to be fun!' His men—around two dozen in number—laughed. Their chief knew how to take care of his people. They were going to be rich.

Bibhatsaka was already rich. The clandestine midnight meeting with Sharangrao had ensured he would be paid irrespective of the haul. Sharangrao had then handed over to him the sword belonging to Bhadrashala and asked him to ensure that Dhanananda was killed with it, and that it was left at the scene of the crime.

'But acharya, wouldn't it be wise to have the coronation of Maharaj Paurus as emperor of Magadha immediately?' asked Indradutt.

'The Venus-Charybdis conjunction around twenty-three degrees Sagittarius, is tightly wrapped around Maharaj's natal Neptune and, of course, the Saturn-Uranus opposition is present on Maharaj's natal Mercury. Therefore the theme of this coronation must revolve around His Majesty's critical Mercury-Saturn-Neptune-Charybdis pattern,' said the plump rajpurohit as they sat in the massive pleasure chamber of Dhanananda. Chanakya suppressed a grin. Astrology was such a wonderful science. You could get it to say whatever you wanted without ever having to actually say it.

'What does that mean?' asked a bewildered Paurus.

'It means that you shall have to wait for two more days and two more nights for the high noon of your coronation, O mighty King,' interjected Chanakya.

'But what shall I do till then?' asked Paurus.

'I think I have just the solution to keep His Majesty occupied,' suggested Chanakya, as Vishaka gracefully walked in like a tigress.

━━

'Is the tiger ready?' Chanakya asked. Jeevasiddhi nodded. 'Good. Have your secret agents keep him caged in the jungle till Chandragupta reaches there. You shall uncage him once Chandragupta's in sight, is that understood?' instructed Chanakya as he handed over the pouch to Jeevasiddhi. 'Make sure the animal's water is spiked with this. It will make him drowsy and sluggish,' he said.

The largest member of the cat-tribe and the most formidable of all living flesh-eaters was the preferred sport of kings of Magadha. The most common hunting technique was *hanka*—the beat—by which the beast would be driven towards the waiting hunter by baiting it with live buffaloes tethered in the jungle while drummers drove it into more tightly defined territory. Chandra-gupta was stationed in a *machaan*—a treetop platform—hidden away twenty feet above the ground. Smeared on his face was a disgusting, lipid-rich, foul-smelling fluid that had been previously extracted from the urinary tract of a slain tigress. His helpers lay crouched on other machaans in the area waiting for the mighty cat to make its appearance. There was complete silence in the forest, the only sound being that of bated breath.

The hundreds of beaters and baiters accompanying Chandragupta had no clue of the elaborate manoeuvres that were being orchestrated backstage by Jeevasiddhi.

Jeevasiddhi nodded to his aide and the man pulled the rope that opened the gate of the cage and quietly released the magnificent beast into the target area. The drowsy animal walked out of the open cage and sniffed. Tigers were blessed with acute hearing, keen eyesight but not very accurate smell. But this smell was different and any male tiger would be a fool not to pick up on it. It contained pheromones that induced sexual excitement.

As the tiger sauntered into the tightly constricted space that lay below Chandragupta's machaan, the noble king jumped down to the ground and faced the feline squarely, instead of hurling his spear from above. The narcotised animal could barely keep its eyes open—all that it knew was that it needed to find the source of the scent—the pheromones of love.

The animal soon realised that the bouquet was emanating from the cheek of the lovable hunter in front of it. Chandragupta kneeled down, his spear ready to take care of any unfortunate miscalculation, just as the gigantic beast opened its jaws, put out its tongue and lapped up the terrible stinking gob on Chandragupta's cheeks before passing out.

'It's a divine sign!' whispered one of the helpers of the hunt. 'It's a miracle! Chandragupta has heavenly aid. If this isn't a supernatural happening, what is?'

'I agree,' said another. 'This occurrence is one in a million. It's a benediction from God. It's celestial intervention telling the people of Magadha that their true king has arrived and is among them. That king is none other than the great Chandragupta!'

≡

Paurus lay dead with his face nestled in Vishaka's bosom on the silken bedspread of the chamber in Pataliputra's royal pleasure palace, while the peacocks in the royal garden outside continued to dance.

Dhanananda's lifeless body lay in the forest with Bhadrashala's bloodstained sword by its side. Bibhatsaka had taken some of Dhanananda's blood to offer to his diety in Kali Ghat by the riverbank.

The sleeping tiger in the forest snored contentedly.

ᴈ⊏

Chanakya, Chandragupta, Sharangrao and Katyayan were seated in the royal council hall, deliberating their next move. A magistrate of Magadha stood before them, awaiting instructions. 'Arrest Bhadrashala immediately and have him hanged,' Chanakya instructed the magistrate who hurried out to obey and please his new master.

'Bhadrashala helped us, acharya, we should be lenient with him. We know that he wasn't behind Dhanananda's slaying,' said Sharangrao.

'He wasn't helping us but himself, Sharangrao,' said the angry Brahmin, his eyes blazing. 'He'll be a liability for any ruler, be it Dhanananda or Chandragupta! Kingship isn't about mercy, it's about power.'

'Rakshas will be upset. Bhadrashala was his ally,' said Katyayan.

'How does it matter, Katyayanji? Rakshas will come running to Magadha now that he knows Dhanananda is out of the way,' said Chanakya.

'But it seems Rakshas is saying he's very comfortable being in Takshila and that he doesn't wish to return to Magadha,' argued Sharangrao.

'I need that rogue Rakshas back here. His mere presence as deputy prime minister will give legitimacy to Chandragupta's reign,' reasoned Chanakya.

'Deputy prime minister?' asked Chandragupta. 'Wasn't he prime minister under Dhanananda?'

'Yes. But your new prime minister shall be Katyayanji —someone who's not afraid to tell the king what he thinks!'

The old Katyayan smiled and stood up, went before Chandragupta and bowed to his new master. Turning to Chanakya he said, 'But acharya, you can't force Rakshas to return. He's living an extremely luxurious life in Takshila apparently.'

'I trust that Mehir—who I left behind in Takshila specifically for this very reason—has taken care of that problem by now,' said Chanakya cryptically.

'And what were your instructions to Mehir?' asked Chandragupta.

'To tell Rakshas that I'm holding Suvasini hostage and that she will be held until he returns! Leave a little sugar syrup on the floor and see the ants flock to it! Suvasini is my syrup and Rakshas—my ant!' roared Chanakya.

'Acharya! To be frank with you, it seems positively dishonest,' commented Chandragupta.

'Son, one should never be too upright. You've just returned from a hunt in the forest, haven't you? Didn't you notice that it's always the straight trees that are cut down while the crooked ones are left standing?' asked Chanakya.

'So I should sit on a throne that's won by deceit?'

'You're the king, aren't you? You've reached the pinnacle. You have power and wealth—use it wisely, O King!' said Chanakya.

Chandragupta continued to look uncomfortable.

Chanakya spoke once again. 'Birds don't build nests on fruitless trees, whores have no love for poor men, and citizens don't obey a powerless king! Do your duty, O King!' he commanded as he tied his shikha for the first time after having untied it in Dhanananda's court all those years ago.

ⴲⴲ

Suvasini looked around the room. It was windowless but comfortable—clean, airy, and well furnished. She tried opening the door but it was locked from the outside. She frantically banged on the wood, hoping that someone would hear. It was no use. There didn't seem to be anyone outside. Resigned to being held captive, she sat down on the bed and began sobbing quietly. What sort of wretched life was this? To be used by Rakshas, abused by Dhanananda and misused by Chanakya?

As she sat there, pondering over her pathetic life, she heard the shuffling of feet. She then heard the sound of door bolts being lifted. The door creaked open and two guards entered and stood to attention on either side of the entrance. Chanakya strode in purposefully, his hands clasped together behind his back.

Suvasini got up from the bed and rushed over to him, tears streaming down her cheeks and her hair spilling over her face. 'Vishnu! I am so relieved to see you. You've come to set me free, haven't you? I always knew that you would be my ultimate saviour!' she wailed, falling to her knees before him.

'Rise, O Suvasini,' said Chanakya, clasping her shoulders and pulling her to her feet. 'I apologise for having had you locked up in this room, but I knew that if you were visible, you would have had no alternative but to leave the city in exile along with Dhanananda,' he explained.

'I understand, Vishnu,' she said gently. She hugged him, nestling her face to his chest. Her heart was beating wildly as she lifted her gaze towards his eyes, silently begging for his love as she continued to mentally pray for the victory that was already his. *Om tryambhakam yajamahe, sugandhim pushtivardhanam; urvarukamiva bandhanam, mrityor mukshiya maamrital.*

'Can I now leave this confined space? I want to be free again,' she murmured, holding him tightly in her embrace.

'Alas, Suvasini, although I love you, I cannot do what you ask of me. It's in Magadha's interest that I keep you here,' said Chanakya, controlling the emotion in his voice as he conveyed the news.

'What? Dhanananda has died and you still wish to keep me locked up? What has happened to you, my dear Vishnu? Doesn't a normal human heart beat inside you anymore? How can you do this to the only woman that you ever loved?' she asked, angrily withdrawing from the embrace.

'I may have loved you, my sweet Suvasini, but I love Bharat much more. I'm duty-bound to protect it in whatever way that I can. For the moment my concern is Rakshas. Rakshas holds nothing more dear than you, Suvasini. Do you understand my predicament?' asked Chanakya.

'You would hold a woman that you love as prisoner because she's a pawn on your chessboard?' she howled. 'O lord of anger and incarnation of death! I consign you to hell for a few thousand years—to suffer tortures for the murders and villainies committed by you in the name of politics! You shall have no lineage to carry forward your name and the knowledge that you so lust after shall have no useful application for anyone. Both you and your accursed philosophy be damned into oblivion!' she cursed him as she flung herself down on the bed and wept.

'I don't believe in your curse, Suvasini. There are indeed people—sorcerers and physicians—who can kill others by incantations, become invisible or turn themselves into werewolves. There are black magic spells and chants that can cause blindness, consumption, madness or even death. But the curse should be heartfelt, not feigned. You still love me and would never want your curse to come true,' said Chanakya sadly.

'I do love you, Vishnu, but I hate the Chanakya in you!' she said, crying. 'And as for the efficacy of chants and curses, let me tell you the power that you so covet would never have been yours had I not prayed to Shiva for your victory every day!'

'I have no option but to keep you prisoner, Suvasini,' said Chanakya. 'As God's my witness, there's no one that I've ever loved more than you!'

'If my confinement stands, then so does my curse. However, because I love you, I shall offer you a means to redemption. Several thousand years from now, if someone meditates upon a mantra, he shall be able to use Chanakya's knowledge once again, but only if he uses it to advance a woman!' she said, pointing an accusing finger at her captor.

'And the mantra?' asked Chanakya.

'*Adi Shakti, Namo Namah; Sarab Shakti, Namo Namah; Prithum Bhagvati, Namo Namah; Kundalini Mata Shakti; Mata Shakti, Namo Namah,*' said Suvasini. 'If the chant is recited four hundred times a day for over four thousand days, the orator shall have Chanakya's powers to actualise another leader—so long as it's a woman. In the new age, Shakti must trump Shiva!'

Chanakya regarded her gravely. 'As you wish, my only love. Now I have a greater duty to still others, and other ages, and I must leave you one last time. My wisdom and experience must not fade in my lifetime. History, that fickle art, may neglect to record my thoughts for the greater benefit of rulers to come—and the greater wealth of their nations. I must write it all down.'

He backed into the shadows and softly left the room. 'I must write it all,' she strained to hear him whispering to himself as he walked away. 'My *Arthashastra*—my own invention—the science of wealth.'

Chanakya sat down in his austere hut as he recited the mantra to himself. *Primal shakti, I bow to thee; all-encompassing shakti, I bow to thee; that through which God creates, I bow to thee; creative power of the kundalini; mother of all, to thee I bow.*

Chanakya chanted—his eyes closed in prayer— knowing that he had achieved his ambition of uniting Bharat under Chandragupta. But to achieve that he had sacrificed his one chance for love.

Suvasini went on to live till she succumbed, at the overripe age of thirty-eight, to sexual hyperactivity and lovelessness. Even though Chandragupta's deputy prime minister—Rakshas—was ready and willing.

CHAPTER TWENTY
Present Day

The corridors of the All India Institute of Medical Sciences were deserted at this hour. The doctor had requested Gangasagar to meet him just before midnight so that he might run the tests without anyone else being any the wiser. They now sat in his office—Gangasagar and Menon—like accused awaiting the final order of a judge or jury.

'You have lung cancer, Gangasagarji,' said the doctor sympathetically.

'But I don't smoke,' complained Gangasagar, almost hoping his usual powers of persuasion would get the doctor to agree that he didn't have the dreaded disease.

'It isn't only smokers who get it. You live in a highly polluted atmosphere. The black exhaust fumes of auto-rickshaws can be just as deadly. It can be any number of things that could cause it—smoking, passive smoking, air pollution, asbestos—'

'I never had any symptoms till now,' said Gangasagar, defending his life.

'Around twenty-five per cent of patients will not feel anything till it's too late,' explained the doctor gently.

'Will I live?' asked Gangasagar, suddenly aware of his mortality.

The doctor shook his head slowly. 'Miracles do happen, Gangasagarji. Unfortunately, we did not pick up any symptoms until the cancer had metastasised. At this stage, neither surgery nor chemotherapy will be of much help.'

'How much time do I have?' asked the old Pandit.

The doctor shrugged. 'It's difficult to predict these things. My guess would be a month—at most.'

'That's long enough to make her prime minister,' declared Gangasagar, leaving the doctor puzzled. 'You're to keep this information completely confidential, doctor. I'm leaving now. I have too much to do.'

'But Gangasagarji, we must admit you to hospital. We need to monitor your—'

'Listen, doctor. There's nothing glorious about dying—anyone can do it. Menon will bring me in when I'm about to meet my reluctant maker!' he said as he briskly walked out of the doctor's office.

Menon hastily followed and found that his master was murmuring softly under his breath '*Adi Shakti, Namo Namah; Sarab Shakti, Namo Namah; Prithum Bhagvati, Namo Namah; Kundalini Mata Shakti; Mata Shakti, Namo Namah.*'

'She's about to become prime minister and we're about to expose her love child,' said Somany to Gangasagar. 'The newspapers are going to love it.'

'I would think very carefully before doing any such thing,' said Gangasagar speaking softly to prevent another coughing spasm.

'You have no leverage on us, Gangasagar. In any case, why are you bothered? She's ditched you for good,' said Rungta.

'When thousands of people pray to a stone idol, they vest in it their own power. It's irrelevant what the idol thinks. Chandini is the idol and I don't care what she thinks of me. My single-point agenda is to make her prime minister.'

'Your agenda is screwed! A conservative country like India will never allow a woman of loose moral character to become prime minister, Gangasagar,' said Somany.

'Speaking of women with loose moral character,' said Gangasagar, 'I'd like to introduce both of you to a very dear friend. She's been a great pillar of strength to the ABNS,' said Gangasagar.

'Who?' asked Somany curiously.

Anjali, the Bollywood siren, looking positively delicious in a black body-hugging saree walked out. She ignored the men in the room and sat down on the sofa and proceeded to light her cigarette seductively.

'As you know, we were most grateful when you gentlemen requested Anjali to endorse Chandini during the Uttar Pradesh state assembly elections. To express our gratitude our party nominated her as a Rajya Sabha member from our state. Anjali has been updating me quite regularly regarding a special nocturnal friend who visits her almost every night at her elegant sea-facing Mumbai mansion,' said Gangasagar.

Somany's face turned red. Gangasagar continued. 'This special friend is apparently affluent, but it seems that his wife is unable to meet his needs. The question in my mind is this: is a conservative country like India—more particularly Somanyji's charming wife—ready to hear of the bedroom frolics of a tycoon?'

A livid Rungta glared at Somany. 'I'd told you to keep your pants zipped up—that it was essential to play safe,' he shouted.

'I agree. You see, one must always be safety-conscious,' said Gangasagar, nodding his head. 'It seems over eighty per cent of the people in this world are the result of accidents.'

—————

'The deal negotiated by us to give ten per cent of revenues to Agrawalji must be terminated,' said the grumpy Rungta, realising the wind had been taken out of his sails.

'I agree,' said Gangasagar. 'Let's stop the ten-per-cent payment.'

'That—that's wonderfully reasonable of you, Gangasagarji,' said Somany.

'Now, the ten per cent that I've saved you may please be given to the workers. Please ensure that the credit for the whopping increase is attributed to the ABNKU, the union that controls over seventy-five per cent of your workers,' said Gangasagar.

'But that's preposterous! No one shares ten per cent of their revenue with workers!' exclaimed Rungta, loosening his collar to allow his body heat to escape.

'Maybe both of you would prefer that Anjali meet the workers instead. I could invite her to the next ABNKU weekly meeting?'

—————

The former finance minister was running late. A lecture engagement had overrun. His secretary assured Gangasagar that he would be back within ten minutes. 'I'll wait,' said Gangasagar, seating himself on the comfortable armchair in the study.

A few minutes later the former minister walked in. He cautiously greeted Gangasagar. 'To what do I owe the pleasure of this meeting, Gangasagarji?' he asked caustically.

'I just wanted to keep you informed that your friends are now also my friends. I have put aside my differences with Rungta & Somany,' said Gangasagar.

'Just because they have become your friends, doesn't make you one of mine,' said the ex-minister angrily. 'You destroyed my reputation and my career. I shall now ensure that your star student—Chandini Gupta—shall not survive even a day as prime minister—if she gets that far,' said the former Cabinet member.

'I understand completely,' said Gangasagar. 'Shall I call the press conference or will you?' he asked as he slid over a copy of the memo that the CBDT chairman had provided him as an insurance policy.

Hon'ble Finance Minister. Investigations into the activities of R&S have revealed several instances of financial irregularity. Various items on the expense side seem to have been inflated, specifically with the intention of reducing their taxable income. In addition, it seems that private partnerships have been created with a view to parking of profits. Various items on the income side have been deferred, seemingly with a view to deprive the tax authorities of revenue. Certain transactions—particularly sale and purchase of assets—have been carried out at questionable valuations, thus further reducing their tax liability, at least on paper. Given the circumstances, I seek your advice on how the above matter should be handled. Thanking you. Chairman, Central Board of Direct Taxes.

The memo was followed by the finance minister's handwritten reply.

We need to be sympathetic and gentle in our dealings with them. Without their support no government can hope to remain in power. Suggest that adequate flexibility be shown. Regards. Finance Minister.

━☐━

The purohit of the Hindu shelter was happy to receive an honoured guest. Gangasagar sat down on the mattress offered to him and asked, 'How's your son's education getting along? Did the admission to the medical school help?'

The purohit smiled. He was perfectly bald, his face was wrinkled like a prune and his mouth bore no teeth. His toothless smile said it all. 'Yes, Gangasagarji. He shall soon graduate, thanks to your generosity.'

'Do you have the papers? The ones that you *didn't* give to that ghastly reporter who was tracking the story?' asked Gangasagar.

The old man handed over a bundle of yellowed postcards and letters. They were mostly love notes— between a pregnant mother and an absentee father. The evidence was clinching.

'Thank you,' said Gangasagar.

The priest grinned a toothless grin.

━☐━

The former premier and his illegitimate daughter were in Simla. The weather was cold and a wonderful scent of pine was in the air. Gangasagar had made the journey with some difficulty, but he figured that the cold mountain air would do him some good.

The hosts were surprised to receive their guest but were cordial nonetheless. As the servant brought hot apple cider and paneer pakoras, Gangasagar handed over the bundle of papers to them. 'These belong to both of you. No one has any right to be prying into the personal lives of a family,' he said.

The former statesman looked at the papers and a faint smile appeared on his lips. He recalled how much in love he'd been with the sadhvi's mother. She was an incredible woman—intelligent and beautiful—like their daughter.

'Thank you, Gangasagarji, but why are you doing this? You have just lost your leverage on me,' said the former prime minister as the sadhvi appeared to meditate in silence.

'I didn't need all of them. I've just kept a few. I've placed them in a safe-deposit vault and the key has been left as per my will to you. You shall receive it once my will is probated,' said Gangasagar.

'But why?' asked the sadhvi, opening her eyes.

'Getting a will probated in India can take a few years. Even if I die tomorrow, it still gives Chandini enough time to consolidate her position as prime minister.'

■■

The caretaker prime minister's house wore a festive look. Despite having lost the elections, his party had inked an alliance with Chandini. Their MPs would support Chandini's bid for prime minister but would want some Cabinet berths in return. Gangasagar looked depressed. The caretaker prime minister was not fooled by it. He knew that depression was merely anger without the energy.

'I know that you have signed a deal with Chandini,' said Gangasagar, 'and it is my hope that you will not pull down her government prematurely'.

'Why should that concern you?' asked the caretaker PM. 'I'm told you and your protégé are no longer on speaking terms.'

'Ah. Yes. We do fight occasionally, but only to mislead others,' said Gangasagar, 'and it worked. You would never have extended support to her if we had not fought.' Gangasagar continued observing the face of the caretaker PM as it turned red with rage.

<hr/>

'I shall now show both you and your puppet what I am capable of,' thundered the caretaker premier. 'I have enough explosive material to blow you and your protégé sky-high! A trust fund was established by you in the Channel Islands to meet the education and living expenses of the bastard boy. I have enough documentary proof to back it up. I'm going to use it to withdraw support no sooner than she becomes prime minister. She'll go down in history as the shortest-serving prime minister ever!'

'It's unfortunate that you choose to behave like that,' said Gangasagar, almost like a mother admonishing her child.

'I want her to step aside. She cannot take the oath of office. This country does not need a slut at the helm of affairs!' shouted the premier.

'I would suggest that you reconsider your position very carefully, prime minister,' said Gangasagar softly.

'Why should I?' shouted the prime minister.

'Because I have with me the papers of an account in Liechtenstein. It received payments from North Korea and Libya for designs of sensitive nuclear technology— gas centrifuges—I'm told. The odd thing is that the beneficiary of the account is you. So I would be rather careful about withdrawing support for the entire term of this new administration.'

<hr/>

The ambulance wailed as it sped through the dusty streets of Kanpur. In the back, a medic placed an oxygen mask on Gangasagar's face and administered an IV of sodium chloride. The old Pandit had fallen down after getting up from his morning prayers and Menon had phoned for the ambulance in panic. The doctor from the All India Institute of Medical Sciences in New Delhi had suggested that Gangasagarji be flown down to Delhi but the old man was adamant. He was staying firmly put at home—Kanpur.

Menon sat beside the Pandit who was struggling to take in air through the mask and held his hand tenderly. There were tears in his eyes. Gangasagar was everything in Menon's world. Despite his critical state, the old Pandit observed Menon's anguish and began to say something. 'Primal—' he began, but the effort involved in the simple act of breathing prevented him from talking further.

A few hours later, the old man was settled in his room in the hospital and regained a little strength. Menon and Agrawalji sat by his side while Gangasagar continued to recite his prayers.

'Primal shakti, I bow to thee; all-encompassing shakti, I bow to thee; that through which God creates, I bow to thee; creative power of the kundalini; mother of all, to thee I bow.'

The next morning, he lay propped up in bed and asked Menon, 'I hope you didn't tell her?'

'I didn't,' lied Menon. He had phoned Chandini the moment they had arrived in the hospital.

'I need to meet our friend at the Intelligence Bureau,' whispered Gangasagar hoarsely, to Menon. He knew that the doctor had banned visitors to Gangasagar—even the slightest exertion was not recommended in his condition. Agrawalji reminded Gangasagar gently of the doctor's orders.

'He can't kill my ills with pills and instead chooses to kill me with his bills! Screw doctor's orders. Find me the IB director.'

Hameeda walked in to the filthy room and sat down at the man's desk without waiting for an invitation to do so. The room's walls were of exposed brick and concrete. Above the desk, a naked bulb hung eerily. The room had a vaguely musty smell—stale smoke from the man's cheroots. He took one look at her and turned his head away in disgust.

'Why have you come here, *chhakka*?' he asked using the derogatory term for transsexuals.

'Certainly not to make love to you, sweetie,' said Hameeda, falling into the usual eunuch banter effortlessly. 'I've not come to beg. I'm here to buy.'

'What do you wish to buy, chhakka?' he asked.

'A gun,' said Hameeda.

'Sorry, I don't sell guns to guys without dicks. A gun is a very male thing, y'know. No shemales.'

'Listen, ratface, I am willing to pay you fair price for a Stinger .22 Magnum pen gun. If you don't sell it to me I'll get Sachla Devi to come in here and wave her crotch at you everyday. Perhaps you'd prefer that!'

The man grunted. Why did he get all the weirdos of the world as customers? He needed a change of occupation, he thought to himself as he started searching his boxes for the gun the eunuch wanted.

Outside, an agent of the Intelligence Bureau reported what he had observed to the director.

Hameeda's next stop was a little less seedy. It was a contraband dealer's store. The owner sighed as Hameeda walked in. 'You want some money, take it,' he said handing out a fifty-rupee note, 'But please get the hell out of here. My customers will disappear.'

'It's your lucky day,' said Hameeda. 'I'm here to pay *you*. I need a used Asahi Pentax 35mm SLR and am willing to pay a fair price.'

'Why have you come to me, fifty-fifty?' he asked, using the street slang for eunuchs, 'There are other dealers who could get it for you.'

'But no one has a sweeter expression, assface,' said Hameeda caustically.

The owner sighed again. Why did he have to deal with the dregs of humanity? He began wistfully thinking of how good a snort of coke would feel as he sifted through the cartons, searching for the camera that the fifty-fifty wanted.

Outside, an agent of the Intelligence Bureau reported what he had observed to the director.

<hr>

Hameeda was bent over the little wooden table in her room. In front of her lay the used Pentax camera disassembled besides the Stinger .22 Magnum pen gun. She gutted the camera, gently lowering the Stinger in place of the camera's innards. She needed to ensure it was properly cocked via the camera's film-advance lever. It would shoot by pressing the shutter release button—breaking the glass lens elements in front.

Towards one corner of her table lay the pass she had stolen from the prime minister's private secretary. She could only hope that the bar code still worked and would get her into Rashtrapati Bhavan. If visitor's passes were allowed access to North Block, South Block and

Rashtrapati Bhavan, it seemed unlikely that passes belonging to senior functionaries would not.

On one wall was a nail on which was suspended a coat hanger. The suit, shirt and tie provided by the private secretary had been laundered and pressed and was ready for use. *Of what use is your dying to me, Gangasagar?* thought Hameeda. *It has taken away the opportunity for revenge. Alas, it shall now have to be your beloved Chandini.*

The Ashoka Hall of Rashtrapati Bhavan—built to resemble a large jewel box—was actually a simple rectangle, thirty-two metres in length and twenty metres in width. The most striking feature of the hall was that it had a painted ceiling. The central painting—in Persian style—depicted a royal hunting expedition. Originally built as the state ballroom for the British Viceroy, Ashoka Hall also had a wooden dance floor. It was ironic that prime ministers and other ministers took their sacrosanct oath of office and secrecy in this particular hall. After all, prime ministers needed a killer instinct to reach the position first. The rest of their tenure was coloured by the great dance of Indian democracy—defections, rebellions, and general chaos.

The hall was packed to capacity as elected members of the government-in-waiting, as well as the key members of the Opposition, gathered for the historic ceremony symbolising peaceful transfer of power from one civilian government to another. Chandini walked in, dressed in her usual off-white cotton saree, trimmed with a pale gold border, with no jewellery except for a pair of simple solitaire diamond earrings. The assembled crowd instantly gave her a standing ovation. She was the victor arriving to claim the spoils of war. Chandini gratefully acknowledged the ovation and then sat in the front row along with the chief minister of Bihar. The two had proved to be a deadly and unbeatable combination. Together they had swept the Lok Sabha polls in Uttar Pradesh and Bihar, the two largest states of India. The remaining seats required for a working majority had been helpfully provided by the caretaker PM under the assumption Chandini and Gangasagar were foes.

The bugles sounded and the presidential guard marched in, escorting the president of India to the hall. The band started playing the Indian national anthem and the entire Indian political leadership stood in respect, ensuring that their faces were appropriately sombre for television cameras that loved close-ups. Almost a third of the hall had been cordoned off for the press corps. Among them was an effeminate young man with a Pentax camera that never seemed to flash.

$$=$$

Gangasagar watched the scene unfolding at Rashtrapati Bhavan. The President was administering the oath of office to Chandini. She quite obviously had the text of the oath before her on a single sheet of paper but did not seem to need it. It was almost as if she had spent her entire life preparing for the occasion. In her crisp Oxford accent she was saying 'I, Chandini Gupta, do swear in the name of God that I will bear true faith and allegiance to the Constitution of India as by law established, that I will uphold the sovereignty and integrity of India, that I will faithfully and conscientiously discharge my duties as prime minister and that I will do right to all manner of people in accordance with the Constitution and the law without fear or favour, affection or illwill.'

The godfather smiled. Without fear, favour, affection or ill will! Ridiculous! The old man continued mumbling his prayers, a laboured effort to get the words out. It said '*Primal shakti, I bow to thee; all-encompassing shakti, I bow to thee; that through which God creates, I bow to thee; creative power of the kundalini; mother of all, to thee I bow.*'

He saw his protégé—now sworn in as the eighteenth prime minister of India—fold her hands together in a humble gesture of acknowledgement to the television cameras and then stumble backwards. The red stain that spread on her left shoulder—almost in slow motion—had been fired from a Stinger .22 Magnum. The tiny case of the .22 and the subsonic velocities made it well-suited for use with a Ruger 10/22 silencer. It was reliable, deadly, and almost completely silent.

The ornate Ashoka Hall of Rashtrapathi Bhavan exploded into pandemonium as shots were fired and hundreds of India's political leadership ducked for cover. A few minutes later, the director of the Intelligence Bureau had the lifeless body of Hameeda removed as paramedics rushed to the bloody and comatose body of Chandini that lay on the wooden dance floor of Ashoka Hall.

The dance had started.

Pandit Gangasagar Mishra, watching the scene unfold on television, told Agrawalji, 'I need you to ensure that the note that I've written is sent to the lawyer in Guernsey. That's my final instruction to you, my friend.'

Agrawalji and Menon remained standing by his bed. Gangasagar closed his eyes in prayer, and didn't bother opening them again.

Epilogue

She was clad in her trademark off-white saree. A few exceptions to her usual attire had been made, though. She wore silk instead of cotton, because of the autumn chill. She wore a Burberry's coat over her saree and had replaced her usual summer slippers with stockings and Jimmy Choo shoes. Her face bore no trace of age, but her eyes conveyed another story. They were beautiful emerald-green eyes that had seen too much. There were moments when her eyes wished they could stop observing the dark side of human nature and simply enjoy the beauty of life, like this walk in Hyde Park.

By her side, was a young man of twenty-one. He wore a blue Savile Row suit with a green striped Oxford tie. His green eyes matched his attire perfectly. His wavy hair was neatly groomed, save for the strands that hung over his forehead. He walked by her side, holding her hand in his.

The previous night Chandini had attended an event hosted by the British prime minister in honour of her visit. The great sitar maestro, Radhika Shankaran, had teamed up with Britain's hottest violin prodigy from the Royal Academy of Music, Harry Richardson, who was now walking with her. In an interwoven dance between violin and sitar, Radhika and Harry had spun new fabric from the yarn of ancient Indian ragas, each taking the other's notes and rendering them with their own unique perspective. It had been an absolutely breathtaking performance and both musicians had been accorded a standing ovation by Chandini and the British prime minister.

'Why did the Prime Minister hold your hand and help you up?' asked Harry.

'Because his wife wasn't with him?' she joked. Age hadn't diminished her mischievousness. They continued to stroll while a contingent of bodyguards walked in front and behind them, maintaining a discreet distance.

'He could've told me I was your son sooner,' said Harry. 'If not he, then you.'

'Honestly, I didn't know. Uncle Ganga and Josephine were the only ones who did. He built it into the trust deed that your parentage would be revealed only to you— not me—at the age of twenty-one,' she said. 'I'm sorry that I wasn't there for you, Harry. I didn't even know you existed.'

'And are you going to keep me a secret?' asked Harry, hurting from the realisation that he had been viewed by everyone as a liability in her political career.

'It's my third term as prime minister of India, Harry,' she said. 'I've had a long innings—too long, some would say. Uncle Ganga used to say politicians are like diapers, they need to be changed frequently,' she laughed. 'What's important to me is that I have a son!'

'I always felt the absence of a father. Mum—Josephine— always told me my father was of Indian descent and that he died in an air crash,' said Harry.

'I guess she had to explain the dashing good looks you got from your mother,' said Chandini, trying to lighten the conversation.

'In my view, I've now got two mums,' said Harry smiling.

'And both of them adore you,' said Chandini squeezing his hand. 'And so does Radhika Shankaran, by the looks she was giving you while performing last night.' They sat down on one of the benches, allowing the crisp air to hit their faces.

Harry took a sealed envelope out from the inside pocket of his jacket and handed it to Chandini. It had her name written in Gangasagar's bold handwriting. 'This was left with the solicitors. I was instructed to give it to you,' he said. She opened it carefully and pulled out the note and began to read it.

My dear Chandini,

I just wanted to apologise. I couldn't ask the marksman— the director of the Intelligence Bureau—to go for the right shoulder again. It had already been used in Allahbad. The director had assured me that Hameeda's contraption wouldn't work but that they would get rid of him once and for all. He also assured me that your wound would be superficial. Alas, these are the sacrifices one must make for one's political career. In your case it's been both your shoulders and both your lovers.

I pray that when you read this letter you are still Prime Minister—it would prove that my strategy worked. Our country loves sacrifice and renunciation. These are adorable qualities that can cement one's standing among the people. To remain standing one often has to fall. It is a pity that our last conversation—our staged argument—had to be for the benefit of our political adversaries and electronic eavesdroppers.

Otherwise, I would have liked to tell you that I am proud of you.

I'm assuming that Harry is sitting beside you when you read this letter. I had to keep him a secret from you to protect your political career. As for Geoffrey—I had no qualms about doing what I did. He was bad news. Shankar was another matter, though. I think that he truly did love you, but often love can be more ruinous than hate. Elizabeth I ruled England by transforming herself into the Virgin Queen and I needed you to do the same.

Josephine has told dear Harry that she christened him that because his father's nickname had been Harry and she wanted to perpetuate the connection. What she hadn't told him was that 'Hari' also means 'green' in Hindi and that she had chosen the name because of the boy's emerald-green eyes—identical to yours. As you can see, no expense has been spared to nurture him into a young man you can be proud of.

The unity and integrity of India requires strong leaders and often these leaders must play dirty games. Chanakya did that for his protégé—Chandragupta, and I did it for my protégé—Chandini Gupta. Yes, Shakti trumped Shiva—a sign of our times. I have no regrets.

Chandini folded the letter and stood up. 'Are we on for dinner at Le Caprice?' she asked.

'I'd love that, but can we do it tomorrow instead? I have to meet someone,' said Harry.

'Who?'

'Radhika Shankaran,' said Harry, blushing slightly.

'I guess I'll just have to dine on my own,' said Chandini in mock despair.

'I'm told the food's quite bad,' said Harry.

'At Le Caprice?' asked Chandini.

'At Number Ten. His wife's out of town,' said Harry.

Acknowledgements & References

Writers of historical fiction are not historians and they must depend on others for historical information. The narratives about Chanakya and Chandragupta in *Chanakya's Chant* are fictitious although their events and lives depicted may possibly have roots in history or mythology. Several books have been written about Chanakya and his work—the *Arthashastra*. I depended on the following sources to construct my fictional version of Chanakya.

- *Three Men of Destiny*, by A. S. Panchapakesa Ayyar, Published 1939, C. Coomarasawmy Naidu & Sons (Madras)
- *Chanakya*, by B. K. Chaturvedi, Published 2004, Diamond Publications, New Delhi.
- *To Uphold the World—The Message of Ashoka & Kautilya for the 21st Century*, by Bruce Rich, Published 2008, Penguin Books, England.
- *Rule the World—The Way I Did*, by Prof. Shrikant Prasoon, Published 2009, Pustak Mahal, New Delhi
- *Chanakya—His Teachings and Advice*, by Pundit Ashwani Sharma, Published 2009, Jaico Publishing House, Mumbai

- *Chanakya—A Great Visionary*, by P. Khurana, Published 2008, Indiana Publishing House, New Delhi
- *Chanakya Neeti*, by B. K. Chaturvedi, Published 2009, Diamond Pocket Books Pvt. Ltd., New Delhi
- *Building an Empire—Chanakya Revisited*, by Mohan Mishra, Published 2005, Rupa & Co., New Delhi
- *Kautilya—The Arthashastra*, by L. N. Rangarajan, Published 1992, Penguin Books India
- *Canakya On Management*, by Ashok R. Garde, Published 2008, Jaico Publishing House, Mumbai

In the course of writing this book, I used several internet resources for background information. The websites that I used most were:

- http://www.google.com/
- http://www.wikipedia.org/
- http://brainyquote.com/
- http://www.britannica.com
- http://thinkexist.com/quotes/
- http://www.statemaster.com/encyclopedia/
- http://www.anecdotage.com

In addition, I depended upon various online resources to build many of my fictional constructs. Specifically, some of the URL's from which I drew information were:

- http://presidentofindia.nic.in/
- http://pmindia.nic.in/
- http://goidirectory.nic.in/exe.htm
- http://164.100.47.132/LssNew/our%20parliament/par14.htm
- http://www.hinduism.co.za/chanakya.htm
- http://www.livius.org/
- http://www.freeindia.org/biographies/greatpersonalities/chanakya/index.htm

- http://www.sfusd.edu/schwww/sch618/india/Clothing.html
- http://www.whereincity.com/articles/historical/1673.html
- http://www.rationalistinternational.net/article/2008/20080310/en_1.html
- http://www.accesstoinsight.org/lib/authors/thanissaro/bmc2/bmc2.ch01.html
- http://conservapedia.com/English_coronation_oath
- http://factoidz.com/the-aghori-hinduism-cannibalism-and-immortality/
- http://www.prabhatmishra.com/2009/03/street-food-joints-at-kanpur.html
- http://www.tsawebworld.com/story_indianHistory.html
- http://www.theequitydesk.com/forum/forum_posts.asp?TID=488
- http://www.historicflyingclothing.com/archive.php
- http://accuratedemocracy.com/d_stv.htm
- http://www.deaddog.com/?p=624
- http://www.india-seminar.com/2007/575/575_veena_talwar_oldenburg.htm
- http://www.twocircles.net/book/export/html/135411
- http://women.timesonline.co.uk/tol/life_and_style/women/article6336535.ece
- http://www.ukstudentlife.com/Personal/Manners.htm
- http://www.ox.ac.uk/
- http://www.st-hildas.ox.ac.uk/
- http://www.oxford-union.org/
- http://www.ecgi.org/conferences/fese_efmc2005/ou_rules.htm
- http://business.outlookindia.com/article.aspx?262143
- http://www.timesonline.co.uk/tol/news/uk/education/article3257539.ece
- http://www.hrdc.net/sahrdc/inthenews/2004/05-Aug-04.htm
- http://www.desitwist.com/
- http://www.madinpursuit.com/Family/General/abortionist.htm

- http://www.oubc.org.uk/
- http://www.freedict.com/onldict/lat.html
- http://upcmo.up.nic.in/
- http://parliamentofindia.nic.in/lsdeb/lsdeb.htm
- http://www.crikey.com.au/2009/09/17/mr-speaker-on-a-point-of-order-question-time-has-always-been-a-farce/
- http://www.ncbi.nlm.nih.gov/pmc/articles/PMC2721615/
- http://timesofindia.indiatimes.com/
- http://bbc.co.uk
- http://www.cnn.com
- http://www.etoncollege.com
- http://www.gfsc.gg/
- http://www.indianexpress.com/news/rigging-possible-through-evms-exbureaucrat/484802/
- http://www.medicinenet.com/lung_cancer/article.htm

I spent several weeks watching the entire forty-seven episodes of the series, *Chanakya*, directed by Dr Chandraprakash Dwivedi. The series was a starting point for developing the *Chanakya* storyline.

In a section of the book, Chanakya engages in light banter with his students. Some of the ideas expressed therein are adaptations of quotes from the series *Yes Minister* and *Yes Prime Minister* by Jonathyn Lynn & Antony Jay. The specific quotes that have been adapted from the series are:

'People do not want to know how welfare money has actually been spent. Nobody asks the priest what happen to the ritual offering after the ceremony.'

'When anybody says "It's not the money, it's the principle" they mean it's the money.'

'If people don't know what you're doing, they don't know what you're doing wrong.'

'Government is about principles. And the principle is, never act on principle.'

'Politicians must be allowed to panic. They need activity. It is their substitute for achievement.'

'A good political speech is not one in which you can prove that the man is telling the truth; it is one where no one else can prove he is lying.'

'If you do not want Cabinet to spend too long discussing something, make it last on the agenda before lunch.'

'Britain should always be on the side of law and justice, so long as we don't allow it to affect our foreign policy.'

'Ministers are ignorant not because we do not give them the right answers but because they do not ask us the right questions.'

In the story some key quotes attributed to Chanakya, Gangasagar and other characters have been inspired from other sources. These are as follows:

'Any clod can have the facts, having an opinion is an art.' **Charles McCabe**.

'Three may keep a secret if two of them are dead.' **Benjamin Franklin.**

'I am a great believer in luck, and I find the harder I work the more I have of it.' **Thomas Jefferson**.

'It has been well said, that a hungry man is more interested in four sandwiches, than four freedoms.' **Henry Cabot Lodge, Jr.**

'If we desire respect for the law, we must first make the law respectable.' **Louis D. Brandeis**.

'I have come to the conclusion that politics is too serious a matter to be left to the politicians.' **Charles de Gaulle**.

'It can therefore be said that politics is war without bloodshed while war is politics with bloodshed.' **Mao Tse Tung** in his *On Protracted War* (May 1938), Selected Works, Vol. II.

'You can get much farther with a kind word and a gun than you can with a kind word alone.' **Al Capone**.

'Be more concerned with your character than your reputation, because your character is what you really are, while your reputation is merely what others think you are.' **Dale Carnegie.**

'God will forgive me. It's his job.' **Heinrich Heine**.

'The early bird gets the worm but the second mouse gets the cheese.' **Jon Hammond**.

'The only way to get rid of a temptation is to yield to it. Resist it, and your soul grows sick with longing for the things it has forbidden to itself.' **Oscar Wilde**.

'The difference between pornography and erotica is lighting.' **Gloria Leonard**.

'Worrying is like a rocking chair, it gives you something to do, but it gets you nowhere.' **Dorothy Galyean**.

'A free society is a society where it is safe to be unpopular.' **Adlai Stevenson**.

'Sometimes the majority only means that all the fools are on the same side.' **Claude McDonald**.

'Married men live longer than single men. But married men are a lot more willing to die.' **Johnny Carson**.

'The only certainty life contains is death.' **Patricia Briggs**.

'A man on a date wonders if he'll get lucky. The woman already knows' is a quote of Monica Piper.

'The object of war is not to die for your country but to make the other bastard die for his' is a famous view of General George Patton.

'Every battle is won or lost before it is ever fought' is a quote from Sun Tsu's *The Art of War*.

'When you've got 'em by the balls, their hearts and minds will follow.' **Charles Colson**.

'I like long walks, especially when they're taken by people who annoy me.' **Fred Allen**.

'Eagles may soar high, but weasels don't get sucked into jet engines.' **John Benfield**.

'Some cause happiness wherever they go; others whenever they go.' **Oscar Wilde**.

'All the things I really like to do are either illegal, immoral, or fattening.' **Alexander Wolcott**.

'When choosing between two evils, always choose the one you haven't tried yet.' **Mae West**.

'Never interfere with an enemy while he's in the process of destroying himself.' **Napoleon Bonaparte**.

'Don't be humble. You're not that great.' **Golda Meir**.

'A little inaccuracy sometimes saves a ton of explanation.' **H.H. Munro**.

'Politicians are like diapers; they need to be changed often and for the same reason.' **Mark Twain**.

'We have no eternal allies and we have no perpetual enemies. Our interests are eternal and perpetual, and those interests it is our duty to follow.' **Henry John Temple**.

'I am ready to meet my Maker. Whether my Maker is prepared for the great ordeal of meeting me is another matter.' **Sir Winston Churchill**.

'There is no such thing as public opinion. There is only published opinion.' **Sir Winston Churchill**.

'It is often easier to ask for forgiveness than to ask for permission.' **Grace Murray Hopper**.

'Everybody wants to go to heaven, but nobody wants to die.' **Peter Tosh**.

'A single death is a tragedy; a million deaths is a statistic.' **Joseph Stalin**.

What are the critics saying about *Chanakya's Chant?*

'A gripping, fast-paced read, the novel is a true thriller in the tradition set by Dan Brown.'
— *People Magazine*

'Political grooming and conspiracy remain at the core of Ashwin Sanghi's historical thriller. Bloodshed, legal trials, betrayals, murders, assassination attempts and all that make this a page-turner.'
— *Sakaal Times*

'Released in India to wide acclaim, *Chanakya's Chant* is a political page-turner.'
— *Business India*

'Ashwin Sanghi's *Chanakya's Chant* deals with the life and times of Chanakya in a credible yet gripping manner. Sanghi dexterously interweaves a story of modern India with Chanakya's life. This book is a refreshing change from our usual derivative creative writing.'
— **Pavan K. Varma in** *Tehelka*

'Ashwin's rendition of the *Arthashastra* raises the hair at the back of your neck as you see these principles being used even today...'
— *Hi! Blitz*

'With *Chanakya's Chant*, which shuttles between the time periods of Chanakya, to the modern age, Ashwin Sanghi has relived an age and society that are long past.'
— *The Times of India*

'*Chanakya's Chant* is one of those rare books with a storyline that has the potential to be translated into a superbly cinematic and immensely entertaining screenplay. The tale is about the underbelly of national politics, which the book superbly exposes, where strategies developed by Chanakya thousands of years ago are still valid in the modern-day political scenario.'
— *Siddharth Roy Kapur, CEO, UTV Motion Pictures*

What do readers say about Chanakya's Chant?

'I have never read a more engrossing book on history—a novel that delves into the archives of interesting and fascinating tales relating to the life of the brilliant strategist Chanakya.' — **Shail Raghuvanshi**

'The two parallel stories—though different—use different strategies to arrive at the very same conclusion... the father of Indian historical fiction is here!' — **Bhaskar Maji**

'Cunning, action-packed and outrageously twisted, Chanakya's Chant pumps thrill and adrenaline on every page. No one can read it just once...' — **Aman Nathani**

'Chanakya's Chant is a well-paced political thriller that will keep you riveted. It should be in your must-read list...' — **Mitul Kathuria**

'Sanghi's brilliant characterisation of the modern-day Chankaya is a befitting ode to our Machiavellian forefather. Revenge has never been more candidly written about!' — **Manish Agarwal**

'"Gripping political" thriller and "unputdownable" are understatements!' — **Senthilkumar Rajappan**

'A tale well woven: with history and imagination... in a world buffeted by uncertainty and changing power equations, when will the "shikha" get untied again?' — **Roshm: Sinha**

'When I read the first chapter I was breathless and I was hooked! The words "fast-paced" and "thriller" seem woefully inadequate...' — **Baisali Chatterjee Dutt**

'When was the last time you read a book wishing you could start reading it again as soon as you completed it? Chanakya's Chant provides one such instance of that pleasure.' — **Amit Kumar Gupta**

'There are many moments in the book that will chill you to the marrow. Full of drama, like a chess game, it shuttles back and forth between past and present, as though on a time machine...' — **Anjali Garg**

'With his second novel, Chanakya's Chant, Sanghi takes you on an unrelenting underwater tour of the polluted river of Indian politics without ever coming up for air!' — **Uday Gunjikar**

'The sheer magnitude of research that has gone into the book can be lived through as one reads the book. Ashwin Sanghi is India's master storyteller!' — **Sushil Menon**